Venture

Book two

(The Crystal Series)

Nia Markos

Copyright © 2017 by Nia Markos

All rights reserved. This book or any portion thereof

may not be reproduced or used in any manner whatsoever without the express written permission of the publisher except for the use of brief quotations in a book review.

This is a work of fiction. Names, characters, businesses, places, events and incidents are either the products of the author's imagination or used in a fictitious manner. Any resemblance to actual persons, living or dead, or actual events is purely coincidental.

Cover design by: Cynthia Amato

Model: Casther (183875240)/Shutterstock.com

Editor: Jacqueline Snider

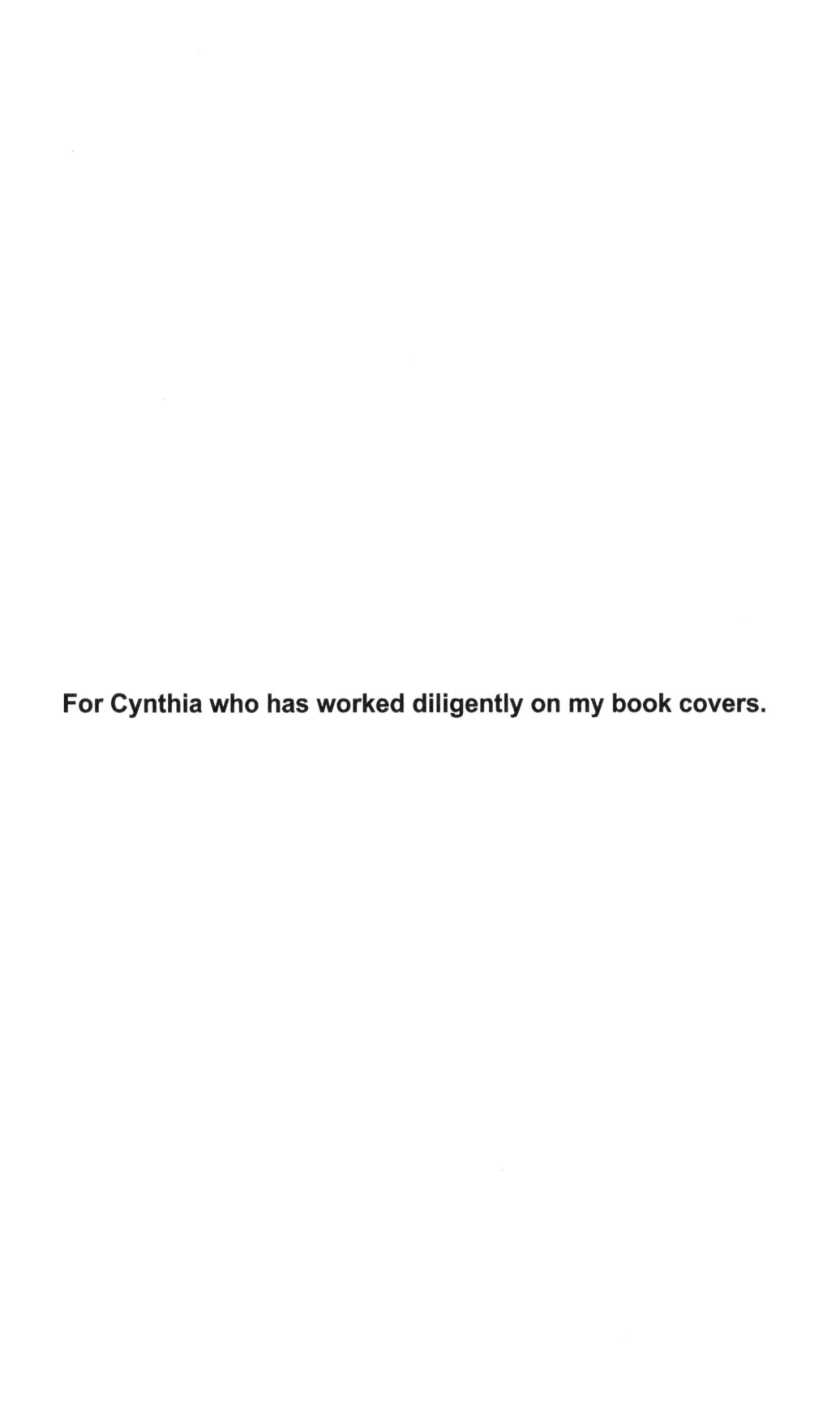

For Cynthia who has worked diligently on my book covers.

Chapter 1

Liam

The mournful hoot of an owl sounded from somewhere in the distance. Inside the darkened bedroom, all was still. Silence permeated the air. The ivory laced curtains, every now and then, fluttered, as a calm breeze wafted in from the half-open window. The curtain's slight movement lengthened and then contracted the crescent moon's attempt to illuminate the room. In the somber bedchamber, the dusty-rose painted walls, light oak furniture and frilly accessories were a stark contrast to the occupant of the room.

Liam would cringe if he found himself surrounded by such unmanly decor. The room was awash in pinks, lavenders and fuchsias. From the nightstand, the soft light given off by the Tiffany lamp barely reached him, as he lay unmoving on the bed. His six-foot frame, with its slack yet sinewy muscles concealed much of the frilliness under him on the double bed, but not all.

The fuchsia pillowcase under his head changed the color of his shoulder-length sandy blond hair making it appear pink under the dim light. Strands of his hair fanned out like a halo around his head. The effect gave his peaceful, relaxed face a somewhat pasty complexion. Pale, with weeks' worth of stubble on his square jaw, his full lips were slightly parted, as he breathed steadily. The serenity of his features belied what was going on inside of him.

For his entire life, spanning centuries, Liam had lived under his brother's shadow. Aidan was to be the savior of their people. His older brother had been raised and trained for that one purpose alone. Liam's needs, his want of love and attention, were an afterthought to their mother, the queen of Eruva.

Belonging to a race known as the Sidhe, their characteristics set them apart from other faerie races. Their height, almost all were at least six-feet tall, along with their vivid emerald eyes and incredible strength were but a few distinguishing features. His whole life he had tried to impress both of his parents. Whereas his father did at times express pride in Liam, he had never received any praise from his mother. Her sole focus was on the prophesy that would have Aidan, along with Alexa, return the long-lost Kaemorra, his people's protective crystal, back to her.

Alexa herself had lived a difficult childhood. Her protective mother allowed her no friends or companionship. Moving often to keep her safe from their enemy, Thalia never explained to her daughter the need for caution. Alexa discovered her origins, the prophesy and the unwanted bonding with Aidan, all at the same time. Liam had to give her credit for how she had handled everything. Never once had she given in to the urge to flee. She might be a petite five-foot-three young woman, but she was stronger than any gave her credit for.

Alexa had readily accepted her role in the prophesy. However, that it involved Aidan as well and that he was supposed to be her soulmate, she had fought at every turn. Her stubbornness had driven Aidan to distraction. Aidan was at a loss to understand why she could not accept they were meant to be together. On her nineteenth birthday, as foretold by the prophesy, Alexa had come into her powers.

As an offspring of a witch and a Sidhe father, it was natural that she would inherit some of her mother's abilities, along with those of her father. The whole range of her powers was still being discovered though. Liam knew there was so much more they still had not seen.

It was incredible how easily she had adapted to her changes. Her outward appearance, as well as her inner strength, was magnified by the source of her newly-formed powers. Her eyes had gone from gray to a steely silver color. A long white streak of hair had appeared, running down the right side of her heart-shaped face. The changes to her body were also profound. Her muscles had become more defined, while her figure grew curvy and fuller.

Alexa had also developed the ability to see visions of the future. She foresaw the attack coming on the night Liam was injured. It was an inopportune time to find out how unpredictable her visions could be. The method of their enemy's assault differed from what she had foretold. They were prepared for warlocks and Sidhe to strike them. The arrival of the shadow people had come as a surprise. With their non-corporeal bodies, Liam and his brother had no weapons to defeat them with. Slithering along the ground, moving silently to box them in, the shadows had given them no chance of victory. Liam's comatose condition was a direct result of that night.

His unconscious state came about when a shadow crossed over his foot. That brief contact was enough to render him senseless. He remembered clearly the night of the attack. The charge by the shadowy beings came swiftly, giving little chance for them to respond. In the garden with Aidan, the slithering forms, as they surrounded them, made it impossible to defend against the threat. With no physical bodies, the shadows were soon upon them. Alexa had arrived too late to save him. He fell, losing consciousness instantly. Since that night, all he had known was darkness.

While his body refused to move, his other senses had been heightened. He was imprisoned in his mind, where he could do nothing but listen to the world around him. Snippets of conversations, the alarmed voices filtered through the gloom he found himself within. He had remained alone for some time now. In the deafening silence, his mind replayed his last contact with Alexa.

She came to him, hoping for any sign he would wake. Her soft voice stirred him, his heart accelerating at having her near. In his mind, he visualized her clearly. It was impossible to forget her heart-shaped, perfectly proportioned, lightly freckled face. Her soft, enticing lips, he was sure were trembling in sorrow.

When she rested her head on his shoulder, her long auburn hair cascaded over him. Her fingers gripped his forearm, begging him to wake. The torment of having her near, but not being able to reach out and gather her to him was pure torture. He endured the scalding tears that fell from her eyes unheeded. They landed on his bare skin, running down onto the bed linens, which were gathered around him.

"Liam, please come back to me. I can't do this without you." Her plea went unanswered. In his dreamlike state, he lay unable to offer her any comfort. His attempts to wake were met with failure. His body refused to answer his commands.

"No. Aidan, you don't understand!" Alexa's next words made him retreat, seeking refuge from the unbearable agony that engulfed him.

The raw pleading in her voice, calling his brother's name was like a stab in his heart. All he had lost, given up, for Aidan, rushed back to him. Liam had gone to great lengths to make sure Alexa turned to Aidan. Her attraction to him was creating tumultuous emotions in his brother. Aidan's well-being had been paramount to Liam. Putting himself out of her reach had nearly destroyed him. Hearing the alarm in her voice was too much for him.

He knew the moment his brother had entered the room. Whatever Aidan saw, whatever he assumed, Liam recognized the heart-stopping anguish his brother had experienced. Aidan was struck, as if by a physical blow. Taller than Liam, more muscular, with cropped ebony black hair, the contrast between the two brothers did not change the fact they were both in love with Alexa.

In his mind, he pictured Aidan's shocked, chiseled face, his narrowed emerald eyes changing from heartsick to loathing. Aidan was actually bonded to Alexa, they somehow had forged the elusive joining their race sometimes experienced when two people belonged together, but Liam had fallen in love with her simply because of her. Alexa had held him enthralled from their first meeting.

Aidan, for his part, was strongly affected by the bond with Alexa. Having her deny him, fight their joining, had him acting out of character. He was volatile, quick to anger and easily mistook her actions or words. His ability to read her thoughts did not make things easier.

Aidan knew all her intimate thoughts about his brother. Finding her with Liam had wounded him deeply. Frozen like a statue by the door, Aidan was in much the same torment Liam was. The silence that followed his arrival became ominous. Liam could sense his brother's despair, and that he would not recover that time.

Alexa left Liam's side, trying to reach Aidan, trying to stop him from what he was about to do. Liam lay powerless to do anything, to reverse Aidan's course of action. Aidan was gone before Alexa could reach his side. He had simply vanished. Any trace of his signature was lost. Liam could not find him anywhere.

How could my brother leave her unprotected? Did he not understand what he was doing to her? Alexa needs Aidan, needs to be safeguarded. Her trembling voice, as she cried out Aidan's name, cried out for him to come back, wounded Liam.

He could do nothing but lie in his bed, listening, as she fell to the floor. Her desolation at Aidan's departure brought renewed tears, her lips repeating his name over and over. Liam cut the memory off. *How many times am I going to subject myself to reliving her desolation? How long ago did these events transpire?* Time was something he could not measure. It held no meaning where he was.

The buzzing silence in his ears was briefly pierced by the repeated hoot of the owl. It seemed to echo his sorrow. Liam was stretched out, on his back, atop a bed covered by a violet-colored duvet. The material was draped across his lean hips, leaving his bare chest and taut abdomen exposed to the room's crisp air. The darkness that held him prisoner would not yield. Getting to Alexa was impossible. That she was still somewhere nearby, he knew with certainty.

What he felt from her errant emotions was filling him with unease. From the start, lost in the depths of the abyss, he was aware of everything going on around him. After Aidan left, Alexa was discovered by her father, distraught on the floor of his room. Carrying her from the room, Rider had firmly closed the door, leaving Liam cut off from the outside world. He felt abandoned, left alone in his endless purgatory.

Even Rina was absent. He recalled the many hours she had spent with him when he was first brought to that room. Either wiping his brow with a cool cloth, or reading to him softly, he at least had some contact. At times, she would climb onto the bed, lie beside him and fill him in on the day's events.

Since Aidan's departure, he had been left alone. *How long has it been since anyone has come to check on me?* He wanted, needed news. Alexa's incessant crying seemed to go on for hours, days. There was no way to know how much time had passed. It was driving him mad. Tortured by not being able to go to her, he could only listen as sobs escaped her. His ears heard every moan, even as she tried to muffle the sounds.

The time dragged on endlessly. *How could Aidan leave her?* He knew his brother had not returned to the estate. Liam was consumed with rage at his brother. Abandoning Alexa in that state was contemptible, leaving her in so much pain inexcusable. He fought with all his might to break free from the hell he found himself in. His need to find out what was going on was compelling him to fight harder. If only someone would come speak to him. He felt as forsaken as Alexa. She was his only reason for not giving up. Even after all that time, after putting himself out of her reach, he still hungered for her.

Keeping away from her did not lessen his yearning for her. Liam was even more in love with Alexa than before. His pretense of being involved with Rina was all for the benefit of Aidan. Rina was a tree nymph living on their estate outside of Verona. Since he had caught sight of her, while she was speaking with Alexa in the estate's garden, she had remained in her full-sized form.

As a tree nymph, anytime a man laid eyes on her, she grew into a beautiful, auburn-haired temptress. Her body, curvy and generously endowed, was made for seduction. Any other time, she shrank to her original size of slightly over four-inches tall, returning to the tree she called home.

Rina understood, knew that there could never be anything between them. They had developed a deep friendship, but it could not compare to what he felt for Alexa. She was everything to him. He let Alexa go, knowing she was bound to his brother. Giving her up was the hardest thing he had ever done. All he wanted was to get to her. He wanted to hold her, dry her eyes, love her like she deserved. Aidan did not deserve her. All bets were off now that he had abandoned her. Liam would do everything in his power to make sure Alexa never shed a tear again.

Her crying stopped as suddenly as it had started. What replaced it was even more distressing to Liam. He could feel her retreating from the world. Dread filled him, sensing what she intended to do. There was no way for him to stop her, as she encased her heart in a block of ice. A steely, icy coldness surrounded her. Behind the walls she had erected, all emotions were driven out. She was unfeeling, so unlike the woman who had captured his heart. He panicked at what she was doing. Her numbness was worse than the crying. Then, he felt nothing. She was gone.

He struggled with all his might to escape the nightmare holding him in its grasp. *Where did she go? Was she safe?* Behind his eyes, a glimmer of light seemed to tease him to grab onto it. Willing it to show him the way, frustration grew at his inability to follow its path to wakefulness. Ready to give up, to rest before renewing his battle, the light flickered, growing in intensity.

Focusing with all his might, he tried to track the path. Sounds of someone in the room had him wrestling even harder to wake. Rina was back. Her soft humming was something else to grasp onto. Even as he fought his way back, the darkness rose to claim him yet again.

Exhausted, Liam gave in to the blackness. Floating in his semi-aware state, he kept the image of Alexa fixed in his mind. His sole purpose was centered on her. *How long has she been gone?* With no understanding of how much time had elapsed since she had left the estate, he felt a deep urgency in escaping his prison. Giving up was not an option.

With renewed strength and purpose, he re-focused his energy on capturing the stream of light he had previously glimpsed. Consumed with the need to find her, to make sure she was safe, he put all his energy into that one task. Just as he feared he might fall back into the chasm again, his eyes opened. The dimness of the room still managed to blind him, as his eyes adjusted to the sights around him.

"You're awake!" Rina came into focus, sitting next to his bed.

"How long?" His throat burned from the effort of uttering his first words.

"Three weeks, two days." Rina rose, pouring water from a

pitcher into a glass. She offered it to him, helping him to sit up.

He greedily drank from the glass she placed in his hand, relishing the water that soothed his parched throat. His hand trembled from the effort of keeping the glass to his lips. Seeing his struggle, the way his hand shook, Rina took the glass from him once he had emptied the contents. Falling back on his pillow, Liam half-closed his eyes before snapping them open again.

Fearing falling back into the abyss, he struggled to rise from the bed. On one elbow, Liam looked out the window, seeing the starlit night outside. From what he could tell, it was well past midnight. His only thought was of Alexa. With no idea where she might be, he needed information on where to start looking. His brother was out of the equation. Any loyalty he owed to him was superseded by Liam wanting to claim Alexa for himself. Liam would keep her safe.

"Where did she go?" He asked Rina.

Rina's face clouded at his question. She knew of who he spoke. Her stricken expression was proof that she understood he was asking about Alexa. Her eyes could not hide how his words pained her. Seeing her trying to hide the effect his words had on her, he flinched from his insensitivity. He knew he had hurt her, but there was little time to waste. Somewhere out there, Alexa was alone. *Who knows what danger she is in?*

Pushing the covers out of his way, he carefully stood on his shaky legs. Naked, except for his briefs, his muscles straining from the effort, he managed to make his way to the bathroom. Each step was an effort after lying unmoving for so long. From the bedroom he heard Rina get up and come to stand in the doorway. His eyes met hers in the vanity mirror in front of him. The pain in her eyes was replaced by acceptance. She knew he would be going after Alexa.

"I'll let you get ready. Meet me downstairs when you are done." She said, leaving him to prepare.

Liam stared at his reflection. He braced his hands on the bathroom counter, seeing how gaunt he looked. He could see he had lost a considerable amount of weight. Hollowed cheeks intensified his haggard appearance. His hair was matted and hung limply on his shoulders. He desperately needed a haircut.

Searching for the scissors, he found them in the medicine cabinet. He placed them on the counter, and then found the electric shaver. By the time he had finished cutting and shearing his hair, his strength had greatly diminished. He ran his hand over his face, feeling the stubble of the weeks' old beard. Drawing on what little energy he possessed, he shaved, exposing pale, waxen skin to his eyes. When he had finished, he leaned against the marble countertop, shaky and spent from those simple tasks.

He would be no use to Alexa in that condition, he needed to regain his strength. Pushing away from the counter, he stepped into the shower. Turning the hot water on, he let it wash away what remained of his lethargy. Revived from the scalding spray, he dried himself, dressed and made his way downstairs.

"I'm out here!" Rina called to him from the garden.

Liam stepped outside to an inky darkness. Gazing up, he saw countless stars speckling the endless cloudless sky. The crescent moon struggled to penetrate the blackness surrounding it. The air was cool with a slight breeze blowing from across the lake. He breathed in the scents from the rose bushes and cedars that adorned the enclosed terrace. The way to the center of the enclosure was lit by torches that lined the cobblestone path.

With each step he took, his strength gradually returned. He found it easier to support his weight. Pleased that his Sidhe physiology was already working to heal him, it would not be long before he regained all his stamina. He would need to be fully restored before going after Alexa.

In the shadowed recesses of the garden, Rina was sitting on the bench nearest to the fountain. Empty, with no water running, the fountain had once housed his father, along with five mermaids who were imprisoned within it as statues. He hesitantly made his way to Rina, stopping, not sure of where to sit. Noticing his predicament, she patted the bench for him to join her.

"I have no idea where she went." Rina told him once he sat down.

Thankful that she was not wasting time, knowing he needed to find Alexa, Liam was grateful she spoke of what was foremost on his mind. His guilt was pushing him though to offer some excuse for his behavior. Rina saw his intent and held up her hand to stop him from speaking. Anything he would say could not lessen the sting. Still he needed to say something.

"Rina, I am sorry. I hope you know that I never meant to hurt you." Liam spoke softly. Only then did he realize the full extent of her feelings for him.

"Liam, I knew how you felt. There really is nothing to be sorry about. We cannot help who we love. I just want you to be careful. She is still bound to your brother." Rina offered him a gentle smile, letting him know there were no hard feelings on her part

"Still he left her. I heard her, Rina. I heard her crying, heard her heart break. Why? Why did he do that?" Liam was beyond angry with his brother. His handsome face showed his fury. Emerald eyes flashed with hatred over Aidan's actions.

Rina shook her head. She understood his anger, but also knew that Aidan and Alexa were separated by a misunderstanding. Liam's heart would be broken over this. Even though she had no choice but to let him go, let him go through whatever he needed to do, she still saw nothing but heartache for him.

"Aidan saw her crying over you, Liam. It broke him. He

misunderstood what she was feeling." Rina tried to explain, to make him understand.

Liam could not fathom why his brother could not read what Alexa had been feeling. She had started to care for his brother. *Why could Aidan read her thoughts, but not her emotions?* It made no sense to him. Being joined should have let Aidan know what was in Alexa's heart. Instead he left her alone, to face things on her own. He placed her in unfathomable danger.

"Rina, I need to do this. I have to find her. Where could she have gone?" Liam had no idea where to start looking for her.

Rina nodded her understanding, her somber eyes half hidden behind her lashes. She stood, holding out her hand to him. Liam took it gratefully, standing, as she pulled him to his feet. Guiding him back to the house, she stopped outside the library door.

Liam wasted no time in entering the room, going directly to the reading table. Rina's soft footsteps followed him to where he stood, scanning the reading material and volumes of books that lay strewn across the desk. On the table, among the weathered yellowed papers, a book lay open. One of its pages had been torn out, leaving no clue as to what it may have held. Picking up the book, he leafed through it, trying to see if he could find a clue.

"Crete." Rina spoke, breaking into his search.

Liam closed the book, letting it drop back on the table. So, she went to the cave where Rhea supposedly hid Zeus. Liam should have guessed she would continue the search. The cave was where they thought the Kaemorra, his race's famed crystal, was hidden. She was alone, in a place where Myrick and Elsam could get to her.

Long ago, the crystal had vanished from their world. Their hidden island, their homeworld named Eruva, lost its invisibility. The Sidhe were forced into hiding their existence from humans. His people spread out across the globe, keeping themselves isolated.

Alexa was pivotal to them reclaiming the Kaemorra and restoring their island's protection. There was a prophesy that together with one of royal blood, this being Aidan, Alexa would put things right. The latest clue to the prophesy led them to believe the Kaemorra was somewhere in Crete, specifically the mythological place where Rhea hid Zeus from his father, Cronus.

"You have a starting point. I will let you know if I hear or find anything else. Keep safe, Liam." Rina interrupted his musing, patting his arm, as she left him.

He would leave at first light. Only when he was with her, would he be able to rest easy. Her safety was the most important thing to him. Liam left the library, taking the stairs back up to his room. On the landing, he leaned on the banister to catch his breath. The climb had weakened him. He took a moment to gather his remaining strength. As a Sidhe, he should be fully restored come morning. Once his breathing was even, he continued on to his room, only stopping as he passed the first open door to his right.

    The door to Alexa's room stood open. He entered it with a heavy heart, feeling her presence as if she were there. Missing her was eating away at him. Her scent still lingered in the air, bringing to mind the soft coconut, citrus smell of orchids. On the bureau next to her bed, a small jeweled box drew his attention. It was the only thing left of her. He wondered how she could have left it behind.

    The box had been gifted to her by her parents on her nineteenth birthday. The magical properties of the box, once opened and peered into, allowed one to see the location of anyone they wished to find. Taking the few steps to it, he picked it up, slowly opening the top. Peering inside, picturing Alexa in his mind, he saw a billowy cloud form. Her image came into focus, showing him exactly where to find her.

Chapter 2

Elron

The island was deserted, the landscape desolate and barren. What was once a peaceful, warm and lush land was nothing but terrain bereft of life. As far as his eyes could see, only scattered brush and deadened grass lay before him. Mountaintops were stripped of vegetation, their sides nothing but the reddish rock that was unique to the island. Winds battered his body, as he stood on the tallest range of his homeland.

At over six-foot-four-inches tall, Elron's size and brawny build were being subjected to the fierce howling winds, which pushed him unmercifully from behind. Loose tendrils from his long blond hair tied at his nape had escaped to lash at his deep-set emerald eyes.

Although the sun shone down, the cold climate had him shivering under the thin layer of clothing he wore. His hands in his pockets for warmth, he gazed down at the once-majestic valleys. All he saw was the destruction Elsam had created. Their home, the island they called Eruva, was reduced to nothing more than an empty, lifeless shell.

Elsam was one of their own. The treacherous Sidhe betrayed his kind, used every opportunity to steal the throne away from their reigning queen, Eliana. Imprisoned for a thousand years within the spaces between time for his actions, upon his release, he resumed his nefarious plans. It was because of him that the Kaemorra was taken in the first place.

The crystal had been spelled to disappear, to protect against Elsam getting his hands on it. Without the Kaemorra's protection, the land, their once beautiful home world, was reduced to the harsh environment in front of him. Elron's purpose for being there was still a mystery even to him.

Was it only three weeks since I left my friends? In the space of minutes, his world was rocked by the whispered words from an unknown source. It seemed like his life ended that day, replaced by an unknown existence. Who he was, he no longer knew. Reclaiming his old life seemed out of reach.

His friends, family, Bet, the woman he loved beyond reason, were but an afterthought to him now. Serving his queen, his best friend Aidan and his people were impossible at the moment. Finding answers to his questions was paramount. He was agitated, nervous and everything in between. He hated feeling out of sorts.

Elron had been in the fields to the left of the estate's gardens when they were attacked. Although they had known of the impending attack, the nature of it differed from what Alexa had foreseen. Instead of Myrick and his warlocks, they faced an enemy known only from legend. The shadows were formidable enemies. Almost nothing could kill them.

Trying to get back to Aidan and Liam, to help them defend the compound, he found himself held by an invisible force. Unable to break free, he stood frozen, fighting the energy field to release him. It was then the voice whispered the words that had brought him there, to the island, looking for answers. To say he was left stunned and unnerved would be an understatement. He feared the truth would bring more upheaval to his life.

When he left the estate on Lake Garda, he knew his journey would bring him there. He only had one other stop to make before he faced whatever he would find on that forsaken land. Leaving Liam, who was still unconscious, and Aidan, his best friend, the guilt at his not being able to help them still plagued him. He should have protected his friends.

Rina's assurance that Liam would be fine did little to alleviate his guilt. Thalia, Alexa's mother, could sense there was something more that was troubling him than his inability to offer assistance. He would have liked to confide in her, but he was told to do this on his own.

Keeping the secret of what occurred that night was difficult. Isolating himself was the only way to hide what troubled him. Alexa had gained enough power and abilities to be able to read him, hear his thoughts. Her mother, Thalia, was also able to see something was eating away at him. Still, when he left, Thalia's last words to him were to take care of what he needed to do and then return to them.

On leaving, his first stop was to return to his family. He needed to make sure Tory, his brother, had arrived safely home after he was asked to leave the estate. His brother had not responded to any of his attempts at communication. His race was able to telepathically call to each other whenever they needed to speak. His younger brother was impetuous and headstrong. Who knew what trouble he had gotten himself into that time.

Elron could only assume what Tory's continued silence meant. Tory was still growing into his Sidhe physiology. He was not yet fully developed. It would be months, maybe a year, before he filled out completely. His strength presently was limited. Elron worried over what he was up to.

When Elron arrived home, his parents pestered him with questions, wanting to know if they had completed their quest. Answering them as much as he could without going into details, he turned the questions on them. They informed him that Tory had arrived home, but left almost immediately afterwards. Where he was going, he did not say. Elron hoped his brother would stay out of trouble. His propensity to find himself in dire predicaments was legendary.

In their youth, Elron constantly extricated Tory from his self-created dangerous, harebrained schemes. Elron stayed the week, asking vague questions about their lives before they had been forced to leave their homeland. His parents were equally vague with their responses. Getting nowhere, he bid them farewell to make his way to the island.

His people abandoned that land, their homeland, more than a thousand years before. Forced to flee after their invisibility fell, the island took on the appearance of the mainland. It had been centuries since he had stepped onto its soil. He used to run, climb the hills with Bet, playing as children, where the trees offered perfect hiding places to surprise each other.

Watching her grow into the woman he loved, he knew with certainty that she was the one. Her delicate face, her infectious smile and womanly curves made it impossible for him to fight what he probably should not feel. She was the queen's daughter after all. That she was above his station was obvious. It was her pursuit of him that eventually made him surrender. She was playful to his reserved nature. Bringing laughter to his life was one of her gifts. *Bet. No, I can't think of her now.*

Her leaving him tore his heart from his chest. That he was still able to function, that his heart miraculously still beat was stunning. Her absence from his side was a constant ache. Anger like he never thought he could feel for her was the only thing that held him together. Their bond was little more than a fragile thread. His hands were clenched at his side, letting the anger grow to stave off the pain. He knew he must let her go. She made her choice in leaving him, taking his child along with her, leaving him to face this revelation alone.

Somewhere out there, hidden long ago, a parcel was waiting for his discovery. It held the answers to his existence. The voice told him to come alone, to search near where his home used to be. *What could still be here after so long?*

As far as his eyes could see, there was nothing to guide him. He was at once eager to get started and fearful of what he would find. Gazing out at the landscape, he pictured how the land used to be, wishing that somehow it was all a dream. Longing he would wake and find himself standing in thick forests, the sun's warmth touching his face was nothing more than wishful thinking.

Night would soon be upon him. He needed to find shelter, somewhere out of the elements. If memory served him right, there was a cave near where their family home used to be that would offer him protection. *The question is can I find it?* So much had changed that it was hard to find any distinguishing markings of where it had been located.

His family lived on the outskirts of the city. He needed to get his bearings, approximate where to start. Looking from his vantage point on the summit of the mountain, he could barely make out any discernible signs. The countryside held no clues. Only the valley below him held any memories. With the sun dipping lower on the horizon, few hours remained to find a place to rest. It was time to get moving.

Climbing down from the mountaintop, it took him less than an hour to reach the base. Once there, he started walking towards the east, making his way to the coastline. He could have easily transported where he needed to go. But taking his time allowed him the chance to think, as well as exhaust himself to the point where he could slip into sleep without thinking of Bet. He had not been sleeping well. Only total fatigue would allow him to rest. Trudging through the dried grass at his feet, he neared his destination just as the sun was ready to set. Dusk's light was fading.

The area he found himself in was familiar. The valley, nestled between the four hills surrounding it was silent except for the crashing sounds of water. Several waterfalls cascaded from the hills, collecting in pools along the base. He allowed himself a small grin at having found what he was looking for. The cave was behind one of the falls. Scanning the land around him, he remembered exactly where it was.

Along the way to the entrance, he gathered strewn wood that littered the ground for a fire. His arms full, he avoided getting wet by stepping gingerly on the small ledge to the side of the cascading water. Inching his way, keeping his back to the mossy wall outside the cave, he slowly made his way behind the waterfall. The entrance barely fit his size. He threw the wood in before he maneuvered his large frame through the opening. His eyesight adjusted instantly, so he could view the cavern before him.

Stepping deeper into the recess, he listened to his echoing steps while making sure he was alone. Seeing that the cave was empty, he relaxed, settling near the center of the space. From his pocket, he withdrew a clear crystal the size of a golf ball. Lightly touching its surface with his index finger, the crystal vibrated briefly. A low white light grew in intensity from within it, infusing the cave with a preternatural glow.

Placing it on the floor, near the back wall of the cave, its light was enough to give him a clearer view of his surroundings. He walked around the space, his hands gliding along the walls. The hard rock at his fingertips was jagged. Its reddish tint from the backlight, bathed the interior of the cave, making the air shimmer in rosy warmth.

Going back to the assorted pieces of wood he had collected, he arranged the tinder and kindling for a campfire. Drawing on his powers, he snapped his fingers above the stack. A flame darted down from his fingertips to the pile, lighting it instantly into a warm fire. With the heat from the blaze radiating around him, he removed his jacket, spreading it out on the stone floor near the back wall. Sitting down on it, he leaned back against the wall, stretching out his legs.

The roaring sound of the water hitting the stone ledge outside thundered in his tiny enclave. It soothed and calmed his nerves. Listening to its steady flow eased his mind. His thoughts again went to what had brought him there. He was given no information on what exactly to look for.

Where to go was another mystery. That it would greatly affect his existence was without doubt. What it would mean to his friends and family made him leery. *Will I be looked upon differently? Will Bet be able to accept me?* He cut off his thoughts of her, unable to bear what the response would be. He was alone. Maybe it was better that way.

With everyone having their own mission to accomplish, Elron allowed the solitude he found himself in to settle over him. The others were off doing what they needed to do. When he finished there, depending on what he found, he would have to decide what direction to take. His thoughts inevitably returned to Bet. He missed her. His desire to share with her was impossible. Feeling the futility of his situation, he cut off his thoughts of her again. Instead, he focused on what he planned to do the next day. It should not take long to find what he was after. A few days at most were all he needed.

Lying down on the cold, hard floor of the cave, he closed his eyes, hoping that sleep would come easily. Stilling his mind was proving to be impossible. He lay awake, well past midnight, going over every possible outcome his search might entail. It was sometime in the early hours of the morning that he managed to drift into a restless sleep.

Chapter 3

Thalia

Huddled over the reading table, Thalia rearranged her shawl, wrapping it around her neck to protect her from the draft of cold air breezing through the vast rows of bookshelves. With her long auburn hair held messily by a clip at her nape, the cold air made her shiver. She was looking at the last recordings of births for the year that Agatha's son was born. The woman was an enigma. Thalia had spent hours trying to find any information on her. All Thalia knew was that she did exist and that she had born a son. Anything else seemed lost to the ages.

Her plain wooden chair was most uncomfortable. The registry building she occupied was of a newer construction, attached to the red-bricked cathedral next door by a vestibule. A vestry secretary had shown her to the stacks, happy to help in any way. On the table, an old banker's lamp gave the only stream of light in the room. It offered scant illumination to make sense of what she was perusing.

Her blue, almond-shaped eyes were tired, dry and itchy from the stale, musty air. Thalia's frustration increasingly grew at not finding any useful information. She closed the volume of registered births that lay on the desk in front of her. The piles of faded writings she had been looking through left her with a slight headache from trying to make sense of the almost illegible scribblings.

She and Rider, her husband, had arrived in the town of Oban the afternoon before. The small town was located ninety-eight miles northwest of Glasgow. Their car ride to their destination had been uneventful. Arriving at a late hour, they had postponed their investigation into finding Agatha's son for the morning. With so many churches in the area that might have some evidence, they decided to start with the closest ones.

Agatha lived just outside of the town, not far from the church Thalia was in. They hoped to find mention of her child within the church registries. So far, she had found nothing on Agatha's son. They would have to fan out to the other churches in town. Hopefully they would find something soon.

Thalia was concerned because she had not received any news from Alexa. Her daughter's insistence they attempt to find the long-lost descendant of their enemy was the only reason she was in that dank, drafty room. Rider's agreeing to the venture was the catalyst to her being dragged to that town. Her skepticism at finding anything was overshadowed by her need to be with her daughter. Alexa's change was more profound than any of them thought it would be.

Her daughter was struggling to control all the power coursing through her. She needed her mother, someone who understood some of what she was going through. Thalia wanted to find anything that would help her. From the beginning, she thought to be on a fool's errand. Her daughter's belief they needed to look for the descendant made it impossible to put off the necessity of coming there. It did not stop her worrying though.

Alexa was sure that finding Agatha's child was crucial to understanding what they needed to do. Thalia was not sure of anything anymore. Everything she knew of the old prophesy was a lie. Her daughter was in peril by forces she found difficult to grasp. Their ancestry, they had discovered, was another puzzle. She and Alexa came from a lineage straight from the goddess herself. *Why was it only Alexa who obtained Meredith's abilities?* Thalia possessed but a small portion of the talents her daughter did.

Eliana had much to answer for as well. Nothing she told them had been true. *Why would she lie to us? What was she after?* Her disappearance worried everyone, but now Thalia wondered if she was intentionally staying away. Asher, Eliana's husband and king to the Sidhe race, had many questions, least of all, why his wife had left him frozen in a statue for centuries. She must have known there was an impostor running around pretending to be him. She also drove a wedge between Bet and Elron. When she returned or was found, she had a lot to answer for. Thalia believed that Eliana would continue to lie and deceive them. Trust was one thing she would not place on that woman.

Thalia recalled her last conversation with Elron. It was normal for him to be aloof, reserved, but what she sensed from him before he had left was disconcerting. He seemed forlorn, lost. It was so unlike him that she wondered what happened to shake him up so profoundly. It was not only Bet's disappearance. Thalia could not help but be suspicious of his actions. On top of everything else that she was dealing with, he presented an added dilemma.

Elron was acting secretive and isolating himself. Thalia knew he was hiding something. She could see the way he avoided eye contact, making sure not to be in the same room as Alexa. It started the night they were attacked. His absence was noticed by everyone. When he was found, he offered no explanation. If she was not sure of his loyalty to Aidan, she would have questioned if he was working against them.

The only thing she knew for certain was that he was pained and scared of whatever he was going through. The cause of his fear was hidden deep inside him. The pain was easy for Thalia to discern. Bet was the underlying cause of it, but there was more to it than that. When he had left, he gave them no indication of where he was going or when he would be back.

She and Rider had stayed on the estate on Lake Garda long enough to make sure Liam was out of danger. When they left, he was still unresponsive, but Thalia could sense a flicker of light reaching his soul. Rina would not leave his side. She sat beside him endlessly, waiting for him to wake. Any indication of when that would happen was hard to see. Liam would have to fight his own battle to wake. Being touched by a shadow was usually fatal. How he had survived, Thalia could not hazard a guess.

And then there was Alexa. Her daughter's anguish at having

caused Aidan to disappear made leaving her nearly impossible. Days of endless tears transformed her into a block of ice. Thalia was scared her daughter was lost to her. She made them leave on their mission, assuring them she was fine. Thalia knew Alexa was anything but fine. Aidan's absence was infuriating. His abandoning Alexa made her question if her daughter really belonged with him. Maybe she would be better off with Liam. He at least would never have left her alone. Alexa needed someone to keep her safe.

Their misgivings on departing, leaving Alexa, were assuaged by Rina. She called on her mother to send reinforcements to guard the estate once Thalia and Rider readied to go. Last she had heard, they were surrounded by an army of her mother's guardians. They could not have been left in better hands. It made their leaving easier to bear.

Once they arrived in Oban, Rider found them rooms at a bed and breakfast near the town center. The owners were two elderly women who knew the area well. They gave them ideas of where to look for records on births in the area. This was the closest church to their room. Thalia was spending the morning looking through all the registries while Rider visited the area where Agatha had lived. He hoped to find someone who knew of her, or at least the lore her death had generated.

Thalia pulled herself back to the task at hand. Pushing away from the table, her chair screeched on the parquet flooring. She shut the lamp off and eased the chair back under the desk. Her hands gathered the registries scattered on the tabletop. Picking up the pile, she returned the books, in their proper order, to the shelves in the back of the room.

It was getting close to lunchtime. She was meeting Rider at the pub across the street at noon. Glancing at her watch, she saw she was running late. It was already fifteen minutes past the hour. She grabbed her purse and left the sanctuary of the church, stepping outside into the frigid weather.

December was brutal that far north in Scotland. The temperature hovered near 42 degrees Fahrenheit. If not for the accompanying frigid northern wind, the day would have been pleasant. Thalia hated the cold. Give her a warm, sunny day by the beach any day. Shivering, she hurried to meet her husband. The wind spun wickedly around her, as she crossed the street and entered the pub. She found Rider sitting at a table near the front window. He had watched her approach.

Rider's legs barely fit under the table. He sat off to the side, so he could stretch them out along the floor. Thalia took the time approaching him, enjoying looking at the striking figure he made. Her husband smiled knowingly, as she studied him. He was beyond a doubt a fine specimen of a man, a Sidhe to be exact. Tall, handsome, with brilliant emerald eyes, the same color as all the Sidhes, Rider exuded masculinity. He quickened her heart whenever he was near. From his expression, she knew he had something to report. While she took a chair, Rider waved at the barkeep to order her a pint.

"I found nothing. Did you have any success?" Thalia asked

Rider.

"Let's wait till we order. Here comes your ale." Rider waited for the man to place the mug on the table.

Thalia took a sip from the chilled glass, the foam covering her lips. Licking off the extra, she scrunched her face at the bitter taste. The local brew was an acquired taste, more potent in alcohol content. Thalia preferred her ales with a smoother, lighter edge.

Seeing her reaction, Rider grinned while ordering their meal. When the waiter departed, Rider sat back, studying his wife quietly. He had missed her. They lost so many years together to keep their daughter safe. She was just as beautiful as ever. Her oval, unlined face currently showed impatience, waiting for him to share what he had learned. He leaned closer to her, took her hands in his from where they rested on the table.

"Have I told you lately how beautiful you are?" Rider smiled at her.

"Not since this morning." Thalia laughed.

"Well, I can't say it enough. You still captivate me." Rider told her seriously.

"Rider, as much as I love you, if you don't start talking about what you found, I will kick you under the table." Thalia grinned at him.

"Fine, but just remember where we left off." He teased her,

before launching into what he had discovered.

"I found no trace of Agatha or any relatives, but she is still remembered, if for nothing but how she died. The tales of her are a mix of reality and fantasy. Agatha was taken in by a farmer in the area. No one knows where she came from originally. Somehow, she arrived in the area with no family or anyone to care for her. She was sixteen when it is said she fell in love with a man passing through the area. This man was a number of years older than her. The farmer who she lived with forbade her to continue seeing him. Like any young girl finding herself in love for the first time, she found ways to meet with him in secret."

"And you would know about young girls in love?!" Thalia interrupted, teasing him back.

"Do you want to go there, or do you want me to continue?" Rider let go a laugh.

"Go ahead." Thalia laughed with him.

"Within a month, Agatha was pregnant. The farmer threw her out of his home. The man she was involved with had left on a business venture, leaving her to seek refuge in the local church. The priest was sympathetic, but got nervous when strange things started happening in his church. Agatha, going through the changes of her pregnancy, was unable to control her powers. She was unable to control what was happening to her. The church was plagued by disturbances. The candles would burn down to the wick within minutes, the walls would be covered by stains of water. The priest, scared that it was the work of the devil, asked her to leave."

Rider paused while the waiter served their meals. Beer-battered fried haddock, along with mashed potatoes and a helping of steamed cauliflower covered the plates. Thalia enthusiastically started on her plate, once the waiter was gone. Rider watched her roll her eyes in pleasure, as she put a forkful of the fish in her mouth. Starting on his own plate, he continued speaking, after swallowing his first bite.

"Anyway, as I was saying, she was out on the streets again, alone. She found shelter in an abandoned barn near the outskirts of town. There is no further mention of the man she was in love with."

"You are speaking of Elsam, aren't you? Why would he have left her?" Thalia asked, while stabbing a cauliflower floret with her fork.

"Yes, from what I can piece together, he was away on business. Agatha was alone to take care of herself and her unborn child. So much destruction was occurring in the area, it was all blamed on her. Severe electric storms, flooding, landslides were all attributed to her. There were already whisperings of witchcraft." He paused to continue eating, and then Rider went on with his story.

"It must have been terrifying for her to lose control of her powers." Thalia remarked.

"You would think she would have left the area. Gone somewhere she was not known. But, she remained. Maybe she was waiting for

Elsam to return for her. At any rate, Agatha gave birth on All Saints' Day." Rider paused to give Thalia a chance to grasp the significance.

"Same day as Alexa's birth." Thalia said.

"Yes, almost at the same time if the story is correct. Elsam was still away when the baby was born. Agatha had only been a mother a day before the magistrate came for her. It is said that when the baby came, more thunderstorms raged over the area. Lightning killed many people. It was all blamed on her. The villagers broke down her door and she was arrested. They immediately charged her with witchcraft." Rider pushed his now empty plate away.

"What of the child?" Thalia wanted to know.

"This is where it becomes tricky. The baby was not there when they arrested her. They found her alone. There was blood on the bed and signs of the birthing, but they never found the child. Agatha was put to death the next day, never telling them where the baby was. There are two differing versions of what happened to her child. One is that she gave it up to the faeries as payment for her powers. The other is that someone appeared to take the baby to safety. That person warned her that the town would be coming for her and that her child would be killed. They offered to protect the baby for her." Rider finished the remainder of his beer, giving Thalia time to think.

Thalia thought about what Rider had said. In Agatha's time, witchcraft was just starting to be blamed for anything unexplainable.

Agatha would have been unable to defend herself against the charges. Once people's minds were made up, their fear would have made them proclaim death as a sentence instantly. Her heart went out to the young girl, caught up in events she most likely did not understand. She wondered if Agatha was aware of what Elsam was, if he had revealed his race to her. Finishing her food, she too pushed the plate away and commented to Rider.

"Forget about faeries, we need to find who she gave that baby to. I don't think we will find any answers in those churches."

"I agree." Rider nodded. "We need to find someone who may know more about her time. There is someone in this area who we both know, who might help us."

"You can't mean…" Thalia started to interrupt, protest in her voice.

"It's the only way, Thalia. We need to see her." Rider insisted.

"I hope you know what you are doing." Was all Thalia said, holding her hands up in surrender.

Chapter 4

Alexa

The stale, humid air held a trace of sulfur. Breathing shallowly through my mouth to avoid the pungent odor, I felt the uneven rocky walls of the cave close in on me. I stood in the center of the dark, damp cavern, listening to the intermittent drops of water that welled and plopped from the ceiling above me. Shivering from the dampness penetrating my thin jacket, I wondered what the hell I was doing there.

My steel silver eyes, their strength magnified by the changes I had gone through, saw nothing but stark emptiness. The inside of the cave was as clear to me as if I were standing out in broad daylight. I saw the deep crevices, the hidden corners, each stalagmite and stalactite that protruded from below and above me. With my enhanced vision, it was easy to forget that it was past midnight. The dark interior of the cave hid nothing from my view. I was alone, aware that what I needed to find was obviously not there. I had run into another dead end.

My journey there had seemed endless. Getting to the island of Crete had taken me three days. Traveling with regular transportation, I was forced to adhere to the available schedules of buses and planes. Not having Aidan with me, it was impossible for me to just materialize wherever I visualized. The ability to transport anywhere I wanted was one I did not possess. Thinking of him was hardly bearable.

Holding onto the walls I erected around my heart, I was numb to everything. Detachment was my salvation. To survive, I tried to keep thoughts of him at bay. It did not erase the fact that there was a hole inside me, that a part of me was gone. Not letting myself feel was the only way to endure being cut off from him.

After leaving the estate on Lake Garda, I took the first available bus to Verona. From there I hopped on a plane, arriving in Athens in the early evening hours the following day. There were no direct flights to Crete at that time. I waited patiently till the next morning to get a connecting flight. Once on the island, I rented a car, driving directly to the small town of Zaros.

Passing through picturesque villages, the hills rising around me along the way, I made it to my destination wasting no time enjoying the scenery. The town I arrived at was almost in the center of the island. The Ideon Cave, where legend said Zeus was supposed to have been hidden by Rhea, was a short drive from the quiet, isolated town. For the privacy I needed in searching the cave, going to the infamous location during tourist hours was out of the question.

Once I found a room to store my limited baggage, the next order of business was to get the lay of the land. The owners of the rooming house I was staying at were helpful in mapping the route for me, advising me of the best roads to take to the cave. Their hospitality extended to a welcoming meal. Sitting with them in their small dining area, we exchanged pleasantries, before they readied for bed.

Bidding them good night, I drove to the base of the mountain around ten at night. No other soul was around. Climbing up the cliff was difficult, and not for the faint of heart. The path held loose stones that turned, twisting my ankles as they came loose from my footfalls. It took me a long while to make it up to the entrance of the cave. From high on the hill, I could see for miles across the landscape. Even in the darkness of the night, I could make out the homes in the nearest towns. Few lights twinkled in the distance. Most of the residents were asleep.

Returning to my task, I faced the opening of the cave. Carefully making my way up to it, I stopped, looking down into the cave's recess. The steps leading down into the cavern were rough and jagged. I climbed down, taking care with my footing, holding onto the wall beside the steps to guide me. Inside the air was clammy with a slight draft seeming to flow through the interior.

Spending less than a quarter hour inside, I knew that my coming there was a waste of time. There was nothing to find. With no idea what to do next or where to go to find answers, I stood unable to come to any decision. Glancing around the cave again, I knew the Kaemorra, the Sidhe race's protective crystal, was not there.

Pondering my next move, I dismissed the option of going back to the estate. I could not go back, could not face the pitying looks I would receive from friends and family. Worried as I was about Liam, I knew Rina would take care of him. I would have to go back to my room and wait till morning to decide on my next course of action.

I was bone tired, unable to think clearly. My lack of sleep since leaving the estate had me drained of energy. I needed to rest, if possible. What few hours of sleep I managed, were not enough to fully restore me. Adrenaline could only take me so far. I was starting to feel the effects of constantly being on the move, driving myself to exhaustion. My eyes burned, my body struggled to follow my commands. Closing my eyes, I rolled and stretched my neck. There was nothing to do but go back to my room. With a long climb down and a drive in front of me, I could not waste anymore time there.

Taking the steps back up, out of the cave, I stopped to gaze up at the night sky. Millions of stars shone in the blackened sky above me. Down the slope, in the distance, fewer lights danced from inside the homes I could see. The temperature outside had dipped further while I had been inside the cave. Pulling my jacket closed, I drew the zipper up, and then put my hands in my pockets.

My car was barely visible down below the hill. The descent would take some time. Knowing of nothing else I could do at that moment, I walked down slowly, letting the silence of the night wrap itself around me. I kept to the edge of the path, where the terrain was more even and held less stones for me to slip on.

Thankful to have reached the bottom without killing myself, I looked up to where I had been. The cave opening was nothing but a blackened spot in the mountainside. I would get no further answers from remaining there. Pulling the key to the car from my pocket, I opened the door and slid behind the wheel. Buckling in, I turned the key in the ignition, hearing the engine roar to life. I backed up, spinning the car around to face the direction I needed to take. Clouds of dust rose behind me, as I drove off on the dirt road.

Thoughts of my friends intruded into the silence around me. I worried about Elron. He was not himself. What he held back from me, what he hid, troubled me. I wanted to help him, but he had made it clear there was nothing I could do. Bet on the other hand would find out we had lost all patience with her. She caused so much upheaval by taking off, I was not sure if I could forgive her. The pain she put everyone through was inexcusable. Asher had not been able to find her anywhere. The poor man was beside himself with worry over her, and over Eliana, his wife. His wife's continued disappearance was puzzling. Where could she be?

My parents were the only ones I knew who were not in any danger. They had informed me when they arrived safely in Scotland, just before they left Glasgow to drive to Oban. It was the last contact I had had with them. I let my thoughts drift to Liam. Rina was taking care of him, thankfully. Protected by guardians, they were both safe on the estate. Aidan. His name brought a sudden lurch to my heart. Pain tore through me. I closed my mind off, refusing to think of him. There was only so much I could bear.

It took me over a half hour to reach Zaros. I managed to clear my mind while maintaining the detachment I needed over any thoughts of Aidan. The ice wall around my heart was difficult to hold. His absence was distracting, constant. The heaviness I felt was becoming harder to ignore. Concentrating on the present, I drove into town, finding a place to park across the street from the boarding house. Where I was staying was nothing more than a simple home really. The owners had converted it to take in boarders for added income.

The town was silent at that late hour. Only a single light over the doorway illuminated the way, as I approached the entrance to the house. It was unlocked for my return. I entered the tight hallway seeing no one around. The owners had retired to bed long before. When I had left, they had informed me they went to bed early, so I was to come and go as I pleased. Quietly, not wanting to wake them, I made my way to the stairs, where I paused as I felt a presence.

I stopped, listening at the bottom step, trying to identify what caused the feeling. Losing the essence of whatever I sensed, I thought I must have imagined it. The steps in front of me were lit by a single bulb that had no globe or lampshade covering it. I climbed the stairs, reaching the second floor landing, where two doors faced me in the dim corridor. Going to the one on the left, I turned the doorknob and entered the small, sparsely furnished bedroom. Closing the door behind me, I flicked on the light, taking a step back at what I saw.

"What are you doing here?" I gasped at my surprise guest.

Liam, who from what I could see was waking, startled at my entrance, sat up in my bed. His expression mirrored mine, as we stared at each other in matched surprise. Quickly getting to his feet, he took a step towards me. I backed up, bumping hard into the door I had closed. Cornered, I held my hand up as if to ward him off. Halting his advance at my reaction, his eyes raked over me.

His dislike at what he saw showed in the way his eyes narrowed, the way the muscles in his jaw clenched. Flashing, angry emerald eyes bored into mine. Striding over to me, forcing me to press further into the closed door behind me, the look in his eyes scared me. Seeing my fear, he stopped a foot away from me. Putting out his hand, he opened his palm to let me see what it held. The jeweled little box lay there, calling to me, as it glittered from the light that fell from the overhead bulb.

"You forgot this." Liam spoke into the silence.

"I didn't. I left it on purpose." I replied.

Brushing past him, avoiding his touch, I removed my jacket and hung it over the back of the chair by the bureau. My answer left him puzzled, trying to understand what I meant. That I had confused him was obvious in the way he was staring at me. My parents had given me the box so I could find them and my friends when I needed them. How could I explain that having the box was a temptation to look for Aidan? He did not want to be found. Holding myself together was becoming challenging with Liam's arrival. I was not ready for what he would force me to face.

"Alexa." Liam started.

"No, Liam. You need to go. I can handle this on my own." I stepped away when he tried to come to me. His presence was reminding me of all I had lost. The icy coldness surrounding me was cracking. I needed to keep it in place, stop him from thawing my protection.

"No. You need me."

Liam came to stand in front of me, forcefully turning me to face him. His hands held onto my shoulders, not giving me a chance to escape. He looked deeply into my eyes, seeing everything I was holding inside.

"Where is Rina? Shouldn't you be with her?" I managed to pull away from him.

My anger at his intrusion into things that did not involve him grew. In the small space in which we stood, there was nowhere to go to hide. I turned my back on him, walking to the window to look out. Letting the anger fester, I kept my back rigid as I stared outside. The ice around me thawed further. I fought to hold onto it.

"I have to be with you. Rina understands." Liam said to my back.

What was he talking about? How could Rina understand that? I refused to look at him. Letting him see my face, letting him in, would crumble my defenses. I was losing the fight even as I tried to hold onto the last icicle over my heart. A lone tear broke free, traveling down my cheek. I struggled to hold myself together. It was no use. A sob broke from me. The gaping hole in me, the space Aidan occupied, grew, making me gasp from the searing pain that ripped through me. In an instant, I felt Liam's arms around me. He spun me around so I faced him. I buried my face in his chest, letting the tears fall uncontrollably.

My body shook from the sobs. In my heart, I could feel Aidan's blood beat to the rhythm of mine. The drop of his blood he had gifted me with on my birthday was a reminder of all that had gone wrong. It meandered endlessly, mingling with mine, as it wound its way through my veins. Empty, I felt so empty without him. Our bond seemed splintered, leaving a vacant hole where he should be. Liam held me, not saying anything, until I cried myself out.

"I lied. Everything I said to you was a lie." He murmured in my ear with his cheek pressed up against mine. Pulling away, he looked at me. His hands came up to gently cup my face, my lips inches from his. He wiped the tears away with his fingers. Those eyes, so similar to Aidan's, were begging me to understand what he was saying. It was the thought of Aidan that made me back away from him. Liam dropped his hands when he realized I was thinking of his brother. Hurt and anger were plainly etched on his face.

"Liam, it would be better if you go."

I was unable to handle anymore. He would always remind me of Aidan. Liam's presence was forcing me to face what I had denied for so long. Aidan was a part of me, whether I wanted him to be or not. We were joined and I feared that there was no way to escape what his leaving me did to me or to him. We could not survive without the other.

"I kept away because of my brother. I felt I owed him my loyalty. I lied to you, hurt you. He's a bastard for doing this to you." Liam spoke harshly.

"No. It's my fault. I didn't let him in. Didn't explain what I was feeling." I defended Aidan, believing that I was the cause of his abandoning me.

"I am not leaving you. I care too much about you." Liam took my hands in his.

I was clueless on what to do. Liam had gone out of his way to make me believe he did not care. Now it was too late. Wasn't it? Could I allow myself to feel again? When I closed my eyes, Aidan's face was ever-present. He was so much a part of me. There was a void in me when he was not near.

"Let me stay, Alexa. Let me be here for you. You need me." Liam begged.

I had no more fight in me. Exhaustion made me unable to think clearly. I needed sleep. Liam was still waiting for me to decide, but the decision was out of my hands. He would stay whether I wanted him to or not.

"I'll sleep on the floor." Liam could see I had given up.

Chapter 5

Asher

Asher opened the door guardedly, not knowing who or what he would find inside. Turning the doorknob, the click of the latch pulling back sounded magnified to his ears. He paused, listening before using his fingers to push the door open slowly. Luckily there was no creaking, as it swung on its hinges. He took one step through the doorway and stopped.

This was his last hope of finding either his wife or Bet. His last stop had given him no clues on their whereabouts. Alexa had seen Bet, in her little box, near Meredith's home three weeks before. The anguish she felt from Bet had Alexa begging Asher to go find her.

When he had arrived at the location, Bet was nowhere to be found. Finding himself alone, by the coast of Scotland where Meredith had lived, mere miles from their abandoned island, Asher was disheartened at arriving too late. Signs of someone having been there were everywhere. In the wet soil around the tiny home, multiple footsteps were visible. Inside, the fireplace was still warm. The grate held the ashes of dying embers. He shuddered at the visible destruction he saw when he entered the small living space.

The first evidence of a struggle showed in the overturned table near the door. Around the room, chairs lay on their backs, broken, strewn across the floor. He feared for both Bet and his wife. *Had Elsam been able to capture them?* Their continued absence was worrisome. There was still no word from either of them. Righting the furniture gave him something to do while he thought of where to go next. He cleaned up the mess as best he could. Some of the furnishings were beyond salvage. These he discarded outside.

Leaving the area, Asher continued his search for them in numerous places. He tried all their known favorite hangouts. It was as if they had dropped off the face of the earth. With that thought, he came to the realization he should try the one place not on earth. Going there should have occurred to him sooner, but lately he had not been thinking clearly.

Bet was not herself. Concern for her and what could possibly have happened to Eliana, his wife, was increasing with each place he found no trace of them. Mixed in with the concern for his wife was a healthy amount of anger. Asher understood why Elron would not go looking for Bet, even though she was pregnant with his child. The anger his son-in-law felt was not unlike the burning rage Asher felt for his own wife.

He was in the one place that held sanctuary for them. None but the Sidhe, and those loyal to them, could enter that land. Walking further into the hallway, he closed the door softly behind him. Total silence greeted him. He looked up the winding stairway to the landing upstairs, his instincts telling him he would find no one. He was alone. It was too much to hope that someone would be there to greet him.

Turning towards the main living room, he entered, walking to the large windows facing the garden. There was no one in Deis-dé. Only the sounds of nature could be heard through the partially open pane. Asher sighed in frustration, dragging his hand through his hair. He wiped at his face, feeling the stubble on his unshaven chin. His anger and worry fighting for dominance, he focused his eyes instead on the scene before him. There was nothing to be gained by giving in to either of his emotions.

Outside, the never-ending daylight lit up the garden. The brilliance of the auras of the multi-colored flowers, touched by the ever-present sun, nearly blinded him. He had no ideas left. Having tried everything and everywhere he could think of, he was close to giving up. His body and mind were exhausted, fatigued by the constant worry.

Deciding to try to get some rest, he pulled on the curtains to close them, dimming the light in the room. He went to the other windows and pulled the rest of the drapes closed. In the now-darkened room, he stepped to one of the sofas, lying his weary body down. Stretching out his almost six-foot body, its mass still not fully recovered from his ordeal, he pulled a pillow under his head.

His muscles were slowly regaining their shape and strength, while his features worked to reclaim their youthful appearance. His hair had returned to its normal chocolate brown color. It was a feature that made him stand out among his race. Why he had been bestowed the shade was a curiosity. Rarely did any Sidhe possess any other color than different shades of blond.

How much longer before he felt like himself, he did not know. Being frozen in a statue for centuries, having lost so much time, he still felt uncomfortable drifting off to sleep. Rolling onto his side, facing the back of the sofa, he closed his eyes. Sleep eluded him. His mind was racing. He forcefully blanked his thoughts, concentrating on his breathing. Finally, tiredness overtook him and he drifted off into a restless slumber.

Sometime later, Asher was roused by what sounded like a scraping sound. He wondered if he had imagined the faint noise, or maybe he had dreamed it. Fully awake, he sat up, listening for the sound to come again. Whatever had woken him, he was more or less certain the sound came from somewhere inside the house. He must have been sleeping soundly for someone to enter without him noticing. Just as he thought he must have dreamed the sound, the scraping noise came again. Asher glanced at the doorway to the foyer, while slowly rising to his feet. He took silent steps towards the sound, standing against the wall, waiting.

He did not have long to wait. A shadow extended from the doorway across the floor of the main room where he was hiding. He waited for whoever it was to enter. Ready to defend himself, he held his breath as seconds ticked by, while the unknown arrival paused. Finally sensing who it was, he pushed away from the wall, moving to face the person.

"Dad?!" Bet was clearly surprised to find him there. She stumbled backward at his appearance.

Asher studied her carefully. She had lost weight. It was clear she was not taking care of herself. Asher saw hollowed out cheeks on her previously round face. Her eyes showed deep shadows beneath them. Her rounded belly was sticking out from her emaciated form. Seeing the disapproval on his face, Bet shook her head, walking by him into the living room to sit down. He had so many questions, he did not know where to start. *What has she been doing all this time? Why has she not responded to my calls? Has she seen her mother?*

"I don't want to talk about it." Bet informed him, stubbornness overtaking her features.

"Well, isn't that too bad. Do you know what we have all been going through? Any ideas on what has been happening? Do you even care?" Asher lost his temper.

Bet winced at his accusation. Her own temper had her rising to her feet to flee. Before she could move, Asher blocked her exit.

"Sit down! You are through running when things don't go your way." Asher pushed her into a sitting position. "Do you know where Elron is? Do you care about the father of your child?" Asher continued, incensed now that she was in front of him.

"Elron is where he always is, with Aidan." Bet snidely responded.

"Well, you're wrong. We have no idea where Elron is. As for you, I don't think you can fix things this time. I have never seen him so angry." Asher let her know.

Bet closed her eyes, leaning her head against the back of the sofa. Whatever she was feeling, she kept carefully hidden. *Does she care about her husband, about any of us?* Asher was losing patience with his daughter. He needed to know where she had been, what she had been doing all that time. Bet loved Elron. *What was keeping her from him, especially with the baby growing inside her?*

"Bet, what is going on with you? Why do I feel this is more than just about your mother? What have you been up to?" Asher pushed her for answers.

"Dad, please, let me rest. I will tell you later. I haven't slept in days." Bet told him, her eyes tearing up.

Asher could see she was exhausted. His instincts warned him not to press her yet. He would give her the time she needed to rest. He held his hand out to her. Once she took it, Asher helped her to stand. Pulling her into his arms, he held his precious daughter. Whatever she was going through, he would have to put aside his anger. Bet let out a sigh, her own arms holding onto him. He let her draw strength from him, hoping that she knew there was nothing he would not do for her. Stepping away, he walked her to the doorway. Still holding her arm, he spoke gently to her.

"Go upstairs and rest. I will want those answers later. Make sure you don't leave here without telling me what you've been up to." Asher's voice held a pleading note. Bet nodded wearily, leaving his side, while he stood watching her climb the stairs to her room.

Returning to the sofa, he slumped down onto it. Too upset to sleep, he knew he would be unable to get any rest. His daughter needed him. Somehow he needed to get the truth out of her. *What could possibly be driving her?* His mind turned to his wife. *Where is she?* It was unlike the woman he knew to stay away from her family when things were so out of control. The point was he did not know the woman. She was not the wife he loved so long ago. It looked like a stranger had replaced her. *Could it be that she was an impostor as well?*

Asher ran his hand through his hair, frustrated, stressed and totally at a loss to explain what was happening around him. Having no sense of his wife, no connection to grab onto, he had nothing to go on. *Was she hiding on purpose?* She must know he had been awakened. He needed something to do until Bet returned or his thoughts would drive him crazy.

Standing up, he walked to the patio doors, pushing aside the drapes he had closed. He pulled the latch to the door, swinging it open. Outside, the weather was the same never-ending warm and clear summer day. The path from the house led down towards a forested area.

The tall trees there would provide shade from the sun beating down on him. Asher walked the path, past the flowered gardens, towards the canopy of trees.

 Once in the shade, he found a bench to sit on. He had a clear view of the house. The reflective stones of its walls were lit up and colored by the glowing flora around them. Somewhere upstairs Bet was sleeping. He looked up to the second level of the structure, trying to remember which room was hers. His eyes were drawn to a shadow at one of the windows. Focusing on the spot, he saw the curtain flutter back as someone stepped away out of view.

Chapter 6

Elron

Forced from sleep by the thunderous pounding of water, Elron started awake, cramped and sore from a night spent on the cold, hard stone of the cavern. Bleary eyed, he lay on his side, facing the mouth of the cave. A translucent curtain, formed by the torrential rush from the cascading water, distorted his view of the world outside. Light from the morning sun had rainbows forming along the base from where the water flowed down towards the pool basin. The continuous flow was mesmerizing with its rhythm. It would be impossible to try to drift off and get some more sleep. Fully awake, he could not procrastinate.

His makeshift bed, consisting only of his jacket, offered little in comfort. Flipping onto his back, he watched the roof of the cave that was fluorescing from formed calcites. Any other time, he would have eagerly explored the formations. Sensing time running out on finding answers, he stood up slowly. He stretched the muscles in his body as he rose.

The fire he had started before going to sleep had extinguished sometime during the night. Numbing cold replaced any heat the fire had generated. Reaching for his jacket, he quickly put it on. His rumbling stomach, echoing in the confines of the cavern, reminded him that he had not eaten since early the previous day. Elron's first priority was to find something to eat. All of a sudden he missed Alexa. She would have had a ready table, set with numerous choices to choose from.

Knowing he could not count on any help from anyone, Elron gingerly stepped out of the cave, making sure not to get wet from the cascading water. Standing out of reach of the water, on the elevation of the ledge, he looked out across the valley. The landscape was just as dreary as he remembered.

In the daylight, it appeared even more forlorn. There was nothing to be offered in easing his hunger. With his options of food limited, he would have to make do with whatever he could find. No animals were living anywhere on the island, except maybe a bird or two. There was nothing that could satisfy his immense appetite. Maybe he could find berries or vegetation that he could eat.

Scanning the horizon, Elron tried to visualize where his family home had been. Seeing nothing from inside the valley he found himself in, he climbed the nearest outcrop to get a better view. From that vantage point, he could just barely see the seaside harbor close to where they used to reside. He had a vague idea of where he should start his search.

Right then, his needs were more basic. He climbed back down, walking towards the pools of steaming water. Stopping near the edge of the biggest one, he knelt down, letting his fingers touch the pool. The hot spring that replenished it changed his first order of business. Ignoring the hollowness in his belly, he gave in to the call of the hot water.

Needing a bath, as well as warmth, Elron slipped off his clothes, submerging himself in the welcoming heat of the pool. Warmed by the hot water, his bones seemed to sigh in contentment. *This is heaven*, he thought, as he floated on his back. Arms out to his sides, he closed his eyes letting the steam wrap around him. How long he stayed there he did not know. At some point, he felt the sun high above him, reminding him there were more pressing things to do. His stomach rumbled loudly in protest, reminding him again that it needed to be fed.

Reluctantly, he lifted himself out of the pool, dressing quickly before the cold air could penetrate his softened skin. He climbed the tallest of the hills that encircled the valley to get his bearings again. In the distance, near the shoreline, something glittered, reflecting the sun's rays. *What could that be?* Eyeing it suspiciously, he tried to identify what it was. From where he stood, it was impossible to make anything out. He would have to investigate later.

Returning his attention to his need for nourishment, he scanned the horizon further. Not too far from where he was, there was a small meadow that looked like it might have wild berries. Elron vanished from his spot, reappearing in the middle of the field. What he found surprised him to no end.

Above an open fire hung a pot, holding some kind of stew that beckoned his nose. Skeptically, he approached the pot slowly. Beside it, he found a wooden plate and utensils. A thermos was also propped against a rock, which looked like it would seat him comfortably. He opened the thermos lid, sniffing the liquid inside. The strong smell of ale hit his nostrils.

How did all this materialize between the time I jumped from where I was to here? It had not been there while he stood near the pools. *Who put this here for me?* Too hungry to care how it had presented itself, Elron sat on the rock, spooning the stew onto the plate. He brought the plate near his nose to smell it. The aroma was too enticing for him to refuse. He gulped down the food, his hunger overtaking any need to use caution. Before he knew it, the whole pot was gone. He drank down the ale, feeling the strong brew awaken his throat. Thanking whoever had put it there, he rose to continue his quest.

As he took some steps away from his little campsite, the setting faded away until everything disappeared. There was no sign that anything had ever been present. The area looked undisturbed. Shaking his head, Elron continued marching towards the glint of light he had seen earlier. He visualized the place in his mind and was suddenly standing at the spot. There was nothing there. Pacing a circle around the area, he found nothing that could have shined in the sun. As it was, the sun was already setting. He had lost another day.

While trying to decide what to do, whether he should return to his cave, Elron watched as the air shimmered nearby. A few steps away, the area faded in and out. From within the shimmering, he saw a small tent start to materialize. It faded into view, gradually becoming whole.

Carefully, he walked up to it, not sure if he would find someone inside. Pushing aside the rawhide that covered the entrance, he walked inside while drawing his sword. Ready for any danger, he saw no one within the tent. He was alone.

In the center, on the floor, a small hearth held a fire. Furs covered a makeshift bed. He drove his sword into the ground, impaling it into the dried earth beneath his feet. Removing his jacket, he flung it onto the bed. Whoever was helping him, they obviously wanted him to stay. He would give it one more day. Tomorrow night, if he found nothing, he would move on. At least, for tonight, he would get a comfortable night's sleep.

The following morning, Elron sat cross-legged on the ground in front of the tent. After eating a breakfast supplied by whoever was aiding him, he decided to wait for a sign on what to do next. He had a suspicion that his wait, to see if anyone appeared, was going to be a long one. The day stretched before him, as the sun came up. He had risen just as daylight started to break through the clouds overhead. Waiting was all he could do at that moment. If nothing happened soon, he would return to Aidan. His patience was at an end.

With his sword lying across his lap, glinting in the early morning light, Elron passed the time by gliding a rock he had found across the blade, sharpening its edge. A small fire burned nearby, magically appearing when he felt the wind pick up. Warmed, peaceful in his surroundings, the sun rose high, as it had the previous day. It was around the same time that he had seen the glitter. Still nothing, and no one had appeared.

Frustrated, giving up, he stood, preparing to jump to Aidan's last known location. As soon as he found his feet, the area around him distorted. From behind him, the tent disappeared, leaving no trace it had ever been there. Without the structure, the winds it had blocked behind him were now hitting him full force. Unprotected, they whipped around him, growing in intensity. The steadily increasing turbulence blew the dusty earth up, blinding him, scratching his eyes.

In front of him, through the maelstrom, the air was replaced by glittering multicolored prisms of color. They rose from the ground, swirling and gradually coalescing into the face of a woman. Elron knew that face. He had seen it before in Scotland, rising from the bottom of a well. *What is Meredith doing appearing to me?*

Meredith was the witch who had cast the spell on the Kaemorra, so that it disappeared from the Sidhe's island. It was Meredith who set the prophesy in motion. Recently, they had discovered she was not a witch, but an immortal. Her lineage was traced back to Rhea, who was herself daughter to the earth goddess, Gaia.

Elron held his hands in front of his eyes against the wind, peering through his fingers as Meredith coalesced steps from him. As suddenly as the winds had grown, they ceased. Silence encompassed the area around him. Elron waited for her to speak.

He studied her face, seeing the striking resemblance to Alexa. They both had the same cheekbone structure, same eyes and nose. Meredith remained mute, her face gazing off into the distance. Elron was becoming anxious at her inactivity. He was summoned to this cold forsaken land, with no real reason given to him.

"What do you want of me?" Elron bellowed at the image.

Meredith's image seemed to gain awareness of him. She turned her head, so that she faced him. Her eyes focused on his face, a sad look in them. Elron needed answers. On the night the shadows attacked, he was caught in an energy field. Unable to escape, he heard a voice telling him to come there, to get his answers.

Being told he was not who he thought he was had been a great shock. Asking questions had been met by silence. The same voice warned him not to tell anyone what he had to do, at least not yet. He needed to understand before he rejoined the others. There he was, standing facing an image who promised to give him answers. Yet, the image before him was staring at him mutely. Growling in frustration, Elron made to leave.

"Elron, hear me now." Meredith finally spoke. "A long time past, a child was born between Elsam and Agatha. This child was protected, it had a purpose to its birth. Agatha died to protect her child. She could not be allowed to continue her association with Elsam. I was heartbroken at her loss, but the gods were angered at what she had already let happen. Listen to me Elron, you must find what Agatha hid on this isle. Elsam sneaked her on the island before he was incarcerated. She hid a package for her child. This needs to be found and hidden from Elsam. You must do as I say."

"Why me? What do I have to do with this?" Elron was bewildered as to why he was important in finding the package. *How am I involved? What does any of this have to do with me?*

"Elron, you are Agatha's child. It is your destiny to right her wrongs." Meredith answered him.

"What? You're insane. How can that be? I am Sidhe. My family has always been Sidhe." Elron was furious with her pronouncement.

She is wrong. She has to be. I have always lived with my family on Eruva. He had no memories other than being Sidhe. His childhood was spent on that island, far from the mainland. *Why is she saying this to me? Is this the work of Elsam?* He would not put anything past the man. Grasping at straws, wanting to refute her statement, Elron refused to believe her.

"Your family hid you well. They have been my greatest allies. Now the time has come for you to embrace all that you are." She spoke her words with pride.

"What do you mean all that I am?" Elron was afraid of what the answer would be. He still was not convinced of what she was saying.

"My sister Agatha was an immortal like me. You are as well. She has bestowed on you all her powers." Meredith explained.

"What powers? I have no powers." Elron insisted, laughing at the absurdity of what she was telling him. *The woman must be mad.*

"The hut, the food was not of my making, but of yours. You have started to come into your powers now that you have set foot on this land again. They will increase as the time for you to aid your friends draws nearer."

Meredith's image started to fade. Stepping closer to her, Elron watched as she nearly vanished. He had too many questions to let her leave. Reaching out to touch her, his hand went right through her. There was no way for him to force her to remain. She was rapidly losing form.

"Wait, where will I find this package?" Elron asked, hoping she would at least give him directions.

"There are friends coming to help you. Wait for them. They will have the location you need." Meredith's last words were nothing more than a whisper.

Elron sank to the ground, completely floored at what he had been told. His mind could not comprehend it. Behind him, the tent rematerialized. A hollow laugh escaped him, at what the fates divined for him. He was their enemy's descendant. Elsam was his father. *How am I to explain this to my friends, and what of Bet? Why would she want to be with me now?*

Chapter 7

Rider

The stepping stone walkway was lined on both sides by blackthorn shrubs devoid of their white spring blossoms. Running along the right side of the house, the path traced its way along the driveway. The shrubs were trimmed to a height of three feet so that the rock garden, which was centered on the lawn in front of the small cottage, could be viewed from the street.

Walking on the flagstones leading to the house, Rider caught a glimpse of his mother, as she disappeared behind the neat row. Stepping over the shrubs, he cut a path through the grass, reaching her with Thalia in tow. His wife would have given anything to be anywhere but there.

"Mother." His calling to her drew no reaction.

Towering over her, Rider watched the woman that was bent down, on her knees, tending to her roses. Giving no indication that she had heard him, she continued to trim branches, keeping her back to him. Impatiently, he waited for her to finish, knowing she was aware of his presence. It was just like her to take her time before responding.

"I see you brought her with you." His mother finally responded, without stopping what she was doing.

Thalia rolled her eyes, already exasperated with having to put up with the woman's disdain. She kept her eyes trained on the woman, just in case she tried anything. It was not beyond the realm of possibility she would send something flying her way.

Rider's mother had never liked Thalia. She disapproved openly, showing in the smallest ways how Thalia was not good enough for her son. Even the birth of Alexa had not softened the woman's contempt. Although she showered Alexa with love, there was no softening in her attitude towards Thalia.

"It's nice to see you as well." Thalia responded, putting as much sarcasm as she could into her words.

Rider gave Thalia a silent, pleading look to not further aggravate the situation. His mother rose from her position, turning slightly to look towards Thalia. Her face showed her scorn, as her eyes traveled up and down her daughter-in-law's frame. Thalia raised an eyebrow, folding her arms across her chest and giving the woman her most innocent look.

Smiling brightly, Thalia watched the other woman's eyes narrow. She would not give her mother-in-law any satisfaction by cowering before her. Rider's mother, choosing to ignore Thalia, turned her attention to her son. He waited for her to finish looking him over.

"I see you still look the same. The years have been kind to you, even with the company you keep." She started walking back to her house, not waiting to see if they followed.

"Do we really need to do this?" Thalia asked Rider, watching the woman enter the cottage. His only response was to push Thalia towards the open door. Muttering under her breath, Thalia allowed him to pull her into the house.

Inside, the room they entered was beautifully decorated. Thalia could not fault her mother-in-law's taste. The space was a sea of greens. Obviously the woman loved the color. A comfortable looking forest green sofa was covered with sea foam colored pillows. The two armchairs were of similar design, but in a delicate moss green. The walls were papered with a leafy green and yellow motif. In the center of the room, a glass table was held up by a weathered base made of green treated wood.

Bypassing the room, they found Rider's mother in the kitchen, putting on a kettle to boil. The kitchen itself was furnished with all the modern appliances. An oak table with four chairs was already set up for tea. She had placed several plates of sweets and cheeses on it. *Anything for her son*, Thalia thought. The woman had gone to great lengths to assemble everything that Thalia did not find appetizing. She assessed the food on the table suspiciously. Poisoning her would be just what the woman would try if it would get her away from her son.

Rider pointed to a chair, his eyes begging Thalia not to start anything. Thalia reluctantly perched herself on one of the chairs, hoping Rider would get to the point of their visit quickly. She held her tongue, knowing there was no point in further aggravating the woman. They needed her to answer their questions.

"To what do I owe the pleasure of your company?" His mother was by the stove, reaching for a tin holding tea from the overhead shelf.

Thalia examined the woman. It was impossible to know her age. Her height was average for a Sidhe. She stood a few inches shorter than her son, who was slightly over six-feet tall. Her features were youthful. Thalia would have given her thirty-five years, if she were human. She knew that Rhona, Rider's mother, was well over a thousand years old.

Eyes as green as her son's, they held no lines around them to mark her age. The round contour of her face was lovely. With high cheekbones, a delicate nose and rosy lips, she was youthful in appearance. Her strawberry blond hair was piled in a bun on her head. Slim and fit, she was wearing a pair of old black trousers and a form-fitting pink camisole. She obviously did not feel the cold. It was a wonder how anyone who looked so pleasant could hold such a cantankerous soul.

With the water boiling, Rhona poured some in a teapot to let the leaves steep. She brought it to the table, placing it in the center. Sitting down, facing Rider, who seated himself next to Thalia, she ignored her daughter-in-law completely. Rhona placed her elbows on the table, wrapped her hands together and waited for him to speak. He in turn was debating how to approach the subject they came to see her about.

"Out with it. Spill it out. What do you need?" Rhona demanded.

"It's to do with the prophesy, Mother. We need information on Agatha." Rider, having no other idea how to broach the subject, just came out with it like she asked.

Rhona seemed surprised by the reason for their visit. She quickly hid her expression from them. *Was she thinking we'd come for something else?* Deep in thought, her hand tapping on the table, Rider reached for his mother's hand. It was a known nervous habit of hers. Thalia wondered what could be making her jittery. Stilling the movement, Rider held onto his mother's hand.

"Is there something wrong?" Thalia asked.

Rider continued to regard his mother carefully. There was definitely something bothering the woman. Thalia's senses were screaming out that something was not right. Knowing Rhona hated to be read by Thalia, she hesitated before reaching out to grasp what was affecting Rhona so deeply. Thalia gasped at what she saw.

"What is it?" Hearing the catch in his wife's breath, Rider was curious to know what had caused it.

"It's Alexa. She's worried about our daughter." Thalia said. Rhona gave her a dirty look for intruding on her thoughts.

Rhona rose from her chair, leaving the room without a word. Rider was ready to go after her, but Thalia stopped him. His mother was only going to fetch something. Thalia was just as curious as her husband about Rhona's reaction. *Was Alexa in danger? Why does she think we came about our daughter?* Thalia's thoughts were interrupted when Rhona walked back into the kitchen.

In her hands, she held a small wooden box. Placing it on the table, Rhona sat down again. She expelled a heavy breath before pulling the lid off. Inside, papers were stuffed haphazardly. While she searched for what she was looking for, they waited in silence.

"Here it is." She finally said. From within the box, she pulled out a scrap of paper no bigger than a business card.

"What is that?" Rider wanted to know. *How does this have anything to do with Alexa?*

Rhona held onto the paper, shaking it in front of them. Thalia was losing her patience with the woman. Her worry over Alexa was growing with each second Rhona gave no response. *Will the woman ever answer a simple question?*

"Rhona, if you don't tell us what is wrong with Alexa, I will make sure you feel my entire wrath." Thalia warned her.

"Oh, keep your cool, Thalia. There is nothing you can do to me. Alexa will be fine now. I was worried about her being alone, but she has company now." Rhona let them know.

"Is Aidan back?" Rider was curious how she knew that.

"No, it's the other one. I must say I was disappointed in how our prince treated my grand-daughter. He will be back, but he may find he will have his work cut out for him. Liam is with her. The boy has deep feelings for her." Rhona let them know.

Thalia had no idea how Rhona knew that. She herself had no contact with Alexa. If anyone should have knowledge, it should be her mother. *How is Rhona getting her information?* Rider was at a loss as well. His face showed how concerned he was to hear Liam was with Alexa. His daughter was bound to one brother, and now the other one was with her. The fact that Alexa was part witch, that the bond with Aidan was not fully formed, gave her a choice. *Would she go against what the prophesy had said to be with Liam instead? How would that affect the outcome?*

"Stop being guided by these foolish prophesies. Alexa will come through for us. I have no doubt about it. That girl has a good head on her shoulders. She is smart and sensible." Rhona shook her head at them.

"How do you know all this?" Thalia wanted to understand.

"I have my ways. Ones I care not to discuss." She haughtily replied.

Thalia was at the end of her rope with Rider's mother. She would have gladly given her a few boils to mar that pretty face of hers. Rider saw his wife's growing irritation and tried to deflect her from what she was thinking of doing.

"What is that paper in your hand?" Rider pushed the conversation back to the reason they were there.

Rhona glanced at the paper, as if she had forgotten she still held it. It was crumpled in her fingers, clenched around it with the tension Thalia had caused. She straightened it out, handing it over to Rider. Only one word was written on the plain white cutting.

Elron.

That is all it said. Rider's eyes widened at what it meant. *How is this possible?* He handed the paper to his wife, who read it and wore the same look as Rider did. Rhona smirked at them both. She was enjoying having gotten one over on them. Rider had no idea how his mother had that information. *How long has she known?*

"Mother, why do you have this? How long have you known?" Rider was incensed she had waited till now. Knowing of this would have helped months ago.

Rhona poured the tea, taking a sip from her cup before answering. She pointed to their cups, expecting them to drink as well. Thalia had had enough. Her chair screeched as she stood up, bending over the table, towering over her mother-in-law. She was ready to do her bodily harm. Rhona gazed up at her, one eyebrow raised, with no fear of what Thalia could do to her.

"Mother!" Rider brusquely called out. "Answer now!"

"From the beginning." Rhona kept her eyes glued to Thalia, as if daring her to try something.

"How?" Thalia did not back down. She looked down at Rhona, waiting for her answer. Her hands gripped the sides of the table, furious at the woman.

"Meredith told me." Rhona's answer had Thalia sitting down heavily in her chair. *Confound the woman, how could she keep that secret? Why would she hide it?*

"Listen, I had no choice. Meredith told us to keep him hidden. Only when he was needed could he find out who he was. The time for that is now. Elron is on our island. He is searching for something his mother left for him. Whatever that is, I have no idea. I only know where it is. Agatha told Meredith. No one knows of Elron's real ancestry. Not even his real father. Elsam has no idea that Meredith placed him with a Sidhe family." Rhona finally explained.

Rider and Thalia exchanged a look. Both were finding it difficult to comprehend. *If Elron is who they are looking for, how is it he holds no powers?* Agatha's son would be a powerful warlock. It was impossible that he would not have inherited her strengths. On the other hand, he was a gifted warrior, stronger and more accomplished in the way he handled combat. That, he must have gained from his father.

"Why does he have no powers?" Thalia asked.

"He is being protected by a spell. I can tell you that it is fading. He has already begun to feel their effects. He needs guidance. I hate what I am about to say, but only you can help him. After all, it is your side that he needs training with now. We have done an exceptional job on our side. See if you can match what we have given him." She laughed at Thalia's look.

"Where is what he is looking for?" Rider touched Thalia's arm to stave off any retaliation. He needed to get the answer, and take his wife away. If they stayed any longer, he would not be able to stop the fight threatening to break out.

"It is here." Rhona entered Rider's mind, showing him the location.

Chapter 8

Asher

Using his Sidhe speed, Asher bolted to the residence. He was worried about Bet being in the house alone. Deis-dé was protected, but that did not mean someone could not find a way in. Anything was possible.

Asher increased his speed. His sudden acceleration created a streak of hues behind him, as he raced to the house. Anyone looking would see a blur flashing across the sectioned gardens. Fear that whoever he had seen may pose a threat, he quickened his pace. He entered through the same patio door he had left out of. The main room was empty.

Dashing into the hallway, Asher did not hesitate. He flew up the stairs, straight into the room where he had seen the curtain flutter. What he saw made him stop in his tracks. Dumbfounded, he stared at his wife, who sat on the bed, as if waiting for him.

Dressed impeccably in a chartreuse empire robe, her ethereal face gazed at him guardedly. Many thoughts assailed him at once. *How long has she been here? Why can I still not feel her presence? Where has she been all this time? Why did she leave me as a bloody statue all those years?* That last thought had him seeing red.

Seeing his anger, Eliana rose from the bed, approaching him

hesitantly, wary of his reaction. Carefully, she placed her hand on his cheek. Letting the wall guarding her essence fall, her presence filled the room. It surrounded him with its warmth. Her love for him was ever-present. She was pained, guilt ridden over what she had done.

Not ready or willing to make things easier for her, he gripped her hand, pulling it away from his face. She had much to answer for before he could think of forgiving her. He dropped her hand and stepped back.

"You must forgive me, Asher. For the longest time I had no idea." She finally spoke.

Asher was at a loss how to respond. He was not ready to let go of his fury. He needed answers, an explanation, before he could think of what to do. Conscious that he was still infuriated with her, Eliana turned her back to him, going towards the bed. Sinking into the soft mattress, she eyed him nervously.

One of her hands gripped the duvet, while the other went to the pendant hanging at the hollow of her throat. He had given her the beautifully crafted golden representation of his undying love when they wed. The magical properties of the red ruby, set in the center of the seven-pointed star, were to strengthen them, make them rise above petty hurts and grow stronger together. *Obviously it was not working*, Asher thought.

Turning away from her, Asher strode to the window, pulling the drapes aside. He gazed out, for what seemed like an eternity to Eliana, before he turned back towards her. His expression held no emotion. Eliana would have preferred he vented his anger with her instead.

"How long were you going to leave me like that?" Asher wanted to know.

Eliana lowered her eyes, not answering his question. Unable, or unwilling, her lack of response gave him the answer anyway. She would have left him there, indefinitely, for as long as it was in her plans. His eyes flashed in outrage. He wanted to hit something.

That woman had been his partner for centuries. He thought he had known her. *Why was she willing to let me suffer like that? How could she leave me there while bedding an impostor? Was she comparing us?* Jealousy was an ugly emotion, one he thought never to feel. Stamping down the vile feelings rising within him, he turned away from her, unable to keep looking at her.

"Asher, I will explain, but I need to see Alexa first. There are things that I have to put right. We need everyone involved, together, to understand what I had to do." Eliana begged him to accept the delay in answering his questions.

A noise from the doorway drew his attention. His daughter was standing rigid, hands clenched in outrage at her sides. Her eyes were fastened on her mother, who blinked back tears at the way Bet was glaring at her. Eliana rose from the bed to go to her. She took two steps before Bet's words stilled her.

"Oh, no! Stay where you are. You do not want to come near me!" Bet told her.

Seeing the futility in going to her daughter, Eliana stayed where she was. She waited nervously for Bet to say something more. Bet continued to stare daggers at her. Finally, without another word, she pivoted on her heel, springing from the room. Eliana could only stare at the spot where Bet had stood.

"I'll go see to her." Asher said, leaving the room.

In the hallway, Asher could hear Bet running down the stairs. He needed to make sure she did not take off again. Whatever was causing her to act irrationally, running away was not going to help. He wanted to keep her close. His questions about her whereabouts the last few weeks were still unanswered.

As quickly as he could, he tried to catch up to her. Relieved, he saw Bet enter the living room instead of running out the door or vanishing. When he entered the room, he saw her pacing back and forth.

"How can I bring my child into this family?" Her words were laced with revulsion.

Asher could come up with no easy answer to Bet's question. He only knew he loved his daughter. Her hurts were his own. Taking the few steps that separated them, he wrapped her in his arms. Bet brought her head down onto his shoulder, shaking from the emotions she was experiencing. Her whole body trembled, as she broke down. It was breaking his heart to see her in so much pain. He let her cry, holding her while she let go of all the anguish she had been holding in.

"Your child will know love, Bet. You, Elron, me and your brothers will shower it with affection." Asher rubbed the back of her head, while she made hiccupping noises. He made sure not to mention her mother.

Bet sniffed back her tears, raising her head to look at her father. Asher wiped the wetness from her face. Her red, tear-stained eyes were searching his, looking for reassurance. Seeing that he was speaking the truth, she nodded at him to let him know she was all right. Sighing, she stepped away from him. She walked past him to sit on one of the sofas. Asher followed her, taking the seat beside her.

"Dad, why are we so messed up? We have got to be the most dysfunctional family around." Bet remarked.

Asher laughed at her description. In more ways than one, she was right. Their family was messed up, but there was also a lot of love there. His sons were the world to him. Bet was his most treasured creation. There was nothing he would not do for them. His grandchild would have another piece of his heart.

"We are unique, but we do love you, Bet." Asher put his arm around her shoulders, drawing her closer to him.

They sat in peaceful quiet, drawing strength from each other. He waited for her to speak, to let him know why she stayed away from her family. She always was an emotional child. Every slight seemed magnified to her.

"I don't know how he can love me." She finally said.

"Who, Elron?" Asher was stunned at her statement.

How could someone not love you? Of course Elron loves you. He would not be so hurt and irate if he did not love you completely. Asher moved to face Bet. She sat back on the couch, her head resting on the cushions behind her. Defeated, she avoided looking at him. Asher could see that she was truly confused and heartsick over what she was going through.

"Is this why you ran, why you stayed away?" He asked her.

"He shouldn't want me. Dad, I have a mother who will do anything for her own gain. I have a half-brother somewhere out there, who is fathered by Elsam of all people. Why would he want to get mixed up with all this?" Fresh tears sprung to her eyes.

"You listen to me. That boy loves you with all his heart. You are the world to him. You have no idea what you have put him through. The last time I saw him, he was but a shadow of his usual self. You need to make this right, Bet. Go to him now." Asher said, exasperated.

"Not right this moment." Eliana stood in the doorway.

How long has she been here, and how much has she heard? Was she aware of all the misery she has put everyone through? Bet tensed beside him. His hand went to her arm, making sure she stayed put. The last thing he needed was for her to disappear again. Eliana should have left them alone. Her presence was intrusive at that moment. He watched his wife enter the room, gliding towards them. She knew to keep her distance. Her feet stopped somewhere midway from the door and where they sat.

"We need to get everyone together. I have much to answer for. Please, give me a chance to make things right." Eliana pleaded with them.

Asher was curious how she could explain her actions. *What could she say that would make sense of what she has done?* Bet rose from the sofa, standing up to face her mother. Eliana seemed to brace herself for what was to come.

"I have to find Elron." Bet stressed.

"Yes, we need him as well. There are things about him you need to know." Eliana answered her.

Asher saw the resentment take hold of Bet. He needed to diffuse the situation, and quickly. Rising to his feet, he placed himself between the two of them. Eliana blanched, as she realized how her words could be misinterpreted. Her eyes sought Asher's showing their regret and panic.

"Eliana try not to make things worse." Asher touched Bet lightly on her arm.

"I am not trying to keep them apart. I only meant that he has a role to play, one that you need to be made aware of." Eliana tried to explain her words.

Bet shook her head, looking disgustedly at her mother. She marched off angrily towards the door. Eliana's next words caused her to halt in mid-step.

"Aidan is missing."

Both Asher and Bet stared at her. Eliana's face showed deep concern for her son. From what Asher knew, Aidan was with Alexa. *Could something have happened to them?* He opened his mind to try to reach his son, but found no sign of him. *How long has he been missing?*

"I haven't sensed him in weeks. Alexa is with Liam in Crete. We need to gather everyone back at our estate." Eliana let them know.

"I need to find Elron." Bet insisted.

Eliana placed herself in front of her daughter. Bet was unaware of the love and respect her mother had for her. *How could I have let things go this far?* She was so focused on regaining their homeland, that she had neglected her children. Aidan most of all. She still knew he was lost to her, but she could not deny how much she loved him. A piece of her would die when things ended.

"Bet, Elron will join us once he has finished what he needs to do. Of that you can be sure. He has a destiny to fulfill. Be patient a little bit longer. It will only be a few days more." Eliana gently touched her daughter's cheek.

Bet pulled away, breaking the contact. There really was no choice. With Aidan missing, they needed to pull together to save him. They must do what her mother asked. For now, Bet would put aside her animosity. Once Aidan was found, she would have nothing more to do with the woman who had given her life.

Chapter 9

Alexa

A beam of light crossed my eyelids, awakening me from a restless sleep. Sounds of birds chirping, a rooster crowing marked the beginning of a new day. Squinting against the sun entering the room, I woke with the images from my dreams still fresh in my mind. Elron was on an island, searching for something. I had a clear sense that he was shaken, fearful of what he would find. Asher had found Bet. They were finally together.

Flitting scenes of where they were, what they were all doing had permeated my dreams. Whether they were actual dreams or visions was not clear. I was pulled away from trying to understand them by an uncomfortable pressure deep within my chest.

Aidan's drop of blood, the one he gifted to me on my birthday, meandered its way through my veins. He had placed it on my palm where it had been absorbed into my skin, joining with my own blood. My every nerve ending felt his absence. I was but a shell of my former self. It was no use hiding behind walls. There was no escape from the never-ending ache I felt.

Was it less than three months ago my existence had altered? So much had happened, I was struggling to accept what my life had become. Living in fear of shadows, the constant, never-ending upheavals, made me long for my previous ignorance of what I was. Could I leave all that behind and return to my uneventful life? I felt the impossibility of it all. There was no going back. All I knew was that the way forward had no clear outcome. Danger was all around me.

A rustling sound of movement in the room, reminded me of the arrival of Liam yesterday. He was still sleeping on the floor where he had made his bed. He must have turned over. From my angle on the bed, I could see him lying with his back to me. His heavy, even breathing marked his deep sleep. True to his word, he had not pressured me on his confession.

The fact that he had lied to me, when I wanted nothing more than for him to be with me, made me apprehensive. Whatever I felt for him had lessened after weeks of seeing him with Rina. I was not prepared to face how he made me feel now. The only thing I knew for certain was that Aidan had somehow managed to make his way into my heart. To repay his patience and steadfastness, I had hurt him immeasurably.

Liam stirred in his sleep, mumbling incoherently. Should I wake him? Maybe it would be better if I told him to go. Even as I thought it, I knew he would not leave me. His anger with his brother was misguided. It was entirely my fault. I had pushed Aidan to the breaking point. His leaving was because of how I had treated him. I longed for him to come back to me. Was it only the bond that was making me miss him? I was not sure of anything anymore. I needed to keep busy. It was the only way to function with the gaping hole that had been ripped in me.

"Alexa, are you awake?" Liam whispered softly.

"Yes." Was all I said.

Afraid to say anything that would bring the conversation back to why he was there, I lay staring at the ceiling. I had no idea what to say to him. What could I say that would not hurt him? I wished he had stayed with Rina. At least then I would be ignorant of his true feelings.

Fear of getting close to him, only to be pushed away again when Aidan returned, was a good reason to keep my distance. Liam would eventually see that Aidan only left because of me. The fact that we were bonded would still be a factor. I was holding out hope that Aidan would come back, that we would figure things out together.

"We should go back to the estate." Liam finally broke the silence.

Remembering the place I last saw Aidan, brought back the memory of his stricken face. The place where I had caused him such torture, had broken his heart, was the last place I wanted be. How had I let it get that far? Could I have done things differently? Aidan gave me no chance to explain. His anguish was the last thing he let me feel before he vanished before my eyes.

Since then I had had no sense of him. Our bond always allowed me to find him, no matter where he was. Was he deliberately keeping himself shielded, away from me? I wished my mother was there to help me. Would she know how I could survive without him?

The bond that joined us together was stronger than ever. There was no way that I knew of to cut the cords that linked us. I felt them expanding, growing in strength and resolve with each moment that passed. Would I really have a choice on who to be with?

"There might still be something to find in the library." Liam explained, when I did not answer him.

I rolled onto my side, so I could see him. He was bare-chested, covered from the waist down by a thin sheet. He looked up at me, waiting for me to say something. He could be right. We may have overlooked or missed some piece of information. Going back was the only path open to us.

"You're right. I know you're right. It's just painful. You should have seen him, Liam. What I did to him." I felt tears spring to my eyes. I pushed the emotions away that threatened to have me crying my eyes out again. I had to be stronger than that.

Liam sat up. The sheet covering him fell away, exposing him completely. Nearly naked, unashamed to show his body to me, I saw how perfectly he was put together. He could still cause my insides to quiver. His flat stomach rippled as he turned, so he could brace his back against the wall to face me. I averted my eyes from the tantalizing picture he presented. Lowering my eyes, staring at the floor instead, I was uncomfortable with my reaction to him.

Seeing the way I avoided looking at his state of undress, he grabbed the sheet, draping it across his lower body. When he was partially covered, I returned my gaze to him. His eyes held mine. My reaction had pleased him. I could see it plainly on his face. A sultry grin rested on his perfect lips, his eyes were sparkling seductively.

"Liam, your brother is not at fault." I tried to make him understand. My words only made him shrug.

"Maybe, but he still left you. He would have come back by now if he cared about you." He stared at me, his face showing anger.

There was no way to change his mind. He felt sure that Aidan was to blame. I rolled over, so I was lying on my back again. Seeing that I did not want to continue that line of discussion, Liam got up to go to the bathroom. I could not help my eyes appreciatively following his backside as he strode across the floor.

At the door, he turned, catching me at my indulgence. Soft laughter escaped him, as he entered the bathroom. Closing the door behind him, the sound of the bath curtain being pulled aside was followed by the running water from the shower. With him out of the room, I too got up. I dressed quickly not knowing how long it would be before he came back.

Waiting for him to finish so that I could freshen up as well, I started gathering my things together. On the bureau, my jeweled box drew me to it. I stepped up to it, reaching with my hand to take it.

Holding onto it, I let my fingers play along the edges of the gems that surrounded it.

I was tempted to open it. My need to find Aidan was pushing me to see if I could get a glimpse of where he was. Only the fear of what I would find held me back. His being gone meant that he had stopped believing in us. Looking for him would only show me what I knew. He hated me.

I dropped the box into my backpack just as the door to the bathroom opened and Liam stepped out. He eyed me suspiciously. Before he could ask me anything, I walked hastily into the bathroom, shutting the door softly. The mirror reflected my despondency back at me. I needed to take better care of myself. Running the water in the sink, I splashed cold water on my face. As I dried off with a towel, I stared at my reflection.

The face that stared back at me was pale, splotchy. My freckles stood out against my blanched complexion. Deep hollows emphasized my steel silver eyes, which were red-lined from tiredness. Gathering what remained of my courage, I straightened my back and pushed my shoulders back. I would need all my reserves to face Liam and whatever else lay ahead of us.

Leaving the bathroom, I found Liam waiting for me. Dressed in his signature black leather pants and white shirt, he looked gorgeous. Damp hair from his shower was darker than its normal shade. His blond hair was cut short now, causing me to miss the wavy tresses that used to flow to his shoulders. The three top buttons of his shirt were open, exposing his neck and sternum. Under the shirt, his chest muscles strained the fabric. Emerald eyes studied me back. His virility put mine to shame. It must be a Sidhe thing, I thought. He showed no sign he had been incapacitated for over three weeks.

"Let's get going." He smiled at me, as he reached my side.

He took my hand, and with no warning, he transported us instantly to the estate. The beauty of the place was just as I had remembered it. He had placed us in the garden where the empty fountain lay barren of sculptures and running water. The mermaids who were imprisoned there were long gone. Asher had been freed along with them.

I marveled that even in the winter, the estate was resplendent with blooms of every color. The plants, native to the area around Verona, were still flowering and releasing their perfumes into the air. I took a deep breath in, closing my eyes, as I inhaled the fragrant air. It was midday, and no one was around.

Opening my eyes, I found Liam's eyes twinkling at my enjoyment. Still holding my hand, he lifted it to his lips and placed a kiss, while his eyes held mine prisoner. Breaking free from the moment, I took my hand back, not knowing what to do with myself. A heavy sigh broke from me. I could not let this happen. I took a step back when Liam reached for me again. Shaking my head, tears blinding me, I wandered over to the path that allowed me to see the shore.

That was where Aidan had taken refuge most times when he was avoiding me. I could almost picture him standing there, his back rigid, staring out to the opposite shore. Was it really only weeks since I had seen him? It felt like a lifetime ago. A single tear trickled down my cheek. Brushing it away, wiping my eyes, I steeled myself to fight what I was feeling. Liam was not for me. I had to make him see that it was impossible for us to be together. Why then did it hurt so much?

"You're back." Rina cut into my reveries.

Pushing away the unwanted thoughts, I turned to face her, to gage her reaction. Did she hate me because Liam came to me? From her expression, I saw no indication that she held any ill will towards me. Strolling to Liam, she embraced him, placing a soft kiss on his cheek. When she came to me, she smiled, putting me at ease. She gave me a quick hug, hooking her arm through mine once she let me go.

"You must be hungry. Alexa, you've lost weight. We can't have that." She started to guide me into the house.

Once inside, the enormous main room quickly transformed into a dining hall. The magical properties of the room let it change into whatever setting the person in it required. Sensing my hunger, it gave me exactly what I needed. The enticing aromas of the different offerings that lay on the table beckoned me. I was suddenly ravenous.

For the next half hour, I did nothing but eat. The sugar I consumed entered my bloodstream, replenishing my waning energy.

Anything sweet, sugar-laced was my elixir. It was what I craved when my energy reserves were low. I lost track of Liam and Rina. They left me alone while I ate everything in sight.

Eventually, unable to eat another bite, the room remodeled itself into a sitting room. In the hallway, Rina and Liam were deep in conversation. I could not hear any of what they were discussing. I let them be. Maybe there was still hope for the two of them. Giving them space, I meandered around the room, emptying my mind of the upsets and negativity. I needed to focus on only one thing.

In order to end the upheaval in my life, I needed Aidan back. Noticing the change in the room, Liam left Rina to come to me. Her eyes met mine, beseeching me not to hurt him. It was the last thing I wanted to do. Not only for Liam, but for myself. I could not put my heart in play again. He had hurt me once. I saw no outcome where he would not do it again.

"I'll start looking in the library. Come join me." Liam held his hand out to me.

"In a bit. Start without me, Liam. I need to check on something first."

He looked intrigued on what I could possibly need to do. Still, he left my side when I did not elaborate. What I needed was to speak to Rina without him being privy to our conversation. My fear that Liam would turn away from me when Aidan returned needed to be addressed. His loyalty to his brother would eventually resurface.

Where would that leave me if I opened up myself to him again? What would I feel if Aidan came back? The bond between us was growing even as I stood watching Liam walk towards the library. I was conflicted in a way that I hated. Aidan was supposedly my mate. Did I have true feelings for him or was I just being influenced by our joining? Exiting the house, I found Rina outside where she usually sat by the fountain.

"Rina?" I called out to her.

"Alexa, come sit with me." She moved over to give me room.

"How are you doing?" I asked her. It was obvious how she felt about Liam. She must be hurting.

"This isn't your doing, Alexa. It is mine. I caused all this trouble all on my own. It was my suggestion to pretend we were together. If I had left well enough alone, I wouldn't find myself in this position." She admitted.

"We have all made our share of mistakes. That doesn't stop the hurt though." I could see how much his coming to me affected her.

Before she could say anything more, a shimmering caught my eye. Beside the fountain, three figures started to materialize. In a matter of seconds, Bet, Asher and Eliana stood before us.

Chapter 10

Elron

On the ridge, high above the seashore, Elron waited, his eyes fastened on a small craft as it bobbed its way towards land. Breaking waves marked its advance, as it rapidly sped towards him. Every now and then it dropped out of sight when a surge concealed it beneath its swell.

The blustery wind blew with such force that it jostled him, making it extremely challenging to maintain his balance. With his legs spread, anyone seeing him would mistake him for an old world pirate. His long leather jacket billowed behind him. Dressed all in black, his face covered by a week's worth of whiskers, he looked dangerous and surly. He had spent another dismal night alone.

When dawn broke on his third day on the island, his churlish mood woke with him. He was tired of waiting, fed up with the changes he was being forced to confront. From the moment he had stepped on that soil, the things he had experienced kept him unbalanced. He hated the state of uncertainty he found himself in.

From the creation of objects he needed, food he required, there were other more pronounced differences in how he saw and sensed things around him. He needed to find what he was told to retrieve, so he could understand what was happening to him. His mother, a woman he knew nothing about, had left him something that would help him understand. Meredith told him friends would be coming to help. These must be the friends.

Rising above the sound of the wind and crashing waves, the motorboat's engine whined as it neared his position. The two people who occupied the craft were still unidentifiable. Although he could make out the number of passengers, he still could not make out who they were. He left his spot, transporting instantly onto an outcrop closer to the beach.

Standing on the ridge, the ledge was low enough to the sandy beach that the waves crashed around him. The spray from the water washed over him, drenching him with its foam. It left him shivering from the cold that seeped into his bones. Licking his dry lips, the taste of the salty water did nothing to alleviate his thirst. As the boat rode the waves, he prepared to jump closer to the water's edge.

Vanishing from the ridge, he reappeared on the beach, waiting impatiently for the boat to make it to the shore. His hand came up to shield his eyes from the sun that sat on the horizon. The boat seemed to disappear within the light being cast. Striding to the water, his feet sinking into the rough-textured sand with each step he took, the noise from the speedboat rose above the sound of the waves pounding the shore.

As it neared, he got a clearer view of who was inside it. The driver skillfully avoided the scattered rocks that rose from the water, as they closed in on Elron's position. He could finally see who was coming to his aid. Thalia was eagerly waving to him, while Rider maneuvered the boat.

As they floated to him, Elron waded into the waves, grabbing onto the hull to help them beach the craft. His breath caught, as the frigid water lapped up to his thighs. Rider cut the engine, quickly hopping off the side to help Elron. Together they dragged the boat further onto the sand, making sure it was out of the water. Thalia climbed out on her side when the boat was secured.

She reached Elron within a few steps, hugging him exuberantly. Elron, not used to shows of emotion, stood still while she squeezed him. Rider laughed out loud at how uncomfortable Elron looked. She finally let him go, grinning at his still dazed, speechless condition.

"It's good to see you. We should find shelter." She said, looking up at the fading sun.

Elron glanced up, then back at her. Still recovering from the shock of being held by her, he found it difficult to find his voice. She left his side, going to Rider who was close to breaking out in laughter again. Elron looked up at the sky again, noticing the change in weather fast approaching.

Seeing the threat of rain from the ominous darkening clouds overhead, Elron wished for protection from the weather. Behind him, a safe distance from the water, two tents appeared. He could smell the wood burning from a campfire that had flamed into life. Thalia looked impressed, and maybe a little bit suspicious at the appearance of the campsite.

"It's been a crazy few days." Elron finally spoke in his serious tone.

"So I see." Was all she said, continuing to stare at the scene before her.

Rider, still grinning at Elron's expense, took Thalia's arm, guiding her to the tents. Elron followed cautiously behind them. He worried what their reaction would be once he told them who he was. Reaching the campfire, they sat down on the pillows and blankets that materialized around it. None of them knew where to begin the discussion of why they were all there. Elron was unsure how to begin to explain what he had discovered.

Will they be fearful of me now? Thalia, sensing his apprehension, spoke first. She filled him in on what they had found out. She saw him relax once he realized they already knew of his lineage. He listened as Rider finished by telling him they knew where to look for the package his mother had left for him.

"Any ideas on what it is?" He asked, once Rider had finished.

"We only know where it is." Thalia admitted.

It was fully dark. The wind had died down to a comfortable

breeze. With the moon hidden behind dark, menacing clouds, only the flames of the fire lit the night. Dancing, flowing embers spiraled upward into the air. The sound of the crackling fire, joined with the lapping of the waves, gave a semblance of tranquility. Having Rider and Thalia there, and them knowing who he was, gave him added courage for what lay ahead.

Another day had passed. Tomorrow he would have answers. Whatever he found, he was sure it would change his life forever. He was eager to get it over with. Knowing would at least end all the questions consuming him. He was still the same man. Nothing would change who he was at his core.

Agreeing that tomorrow they would need to start early, Thalia and Rider bid him good night, leaving him alone with his thoughts. Together, they entered one of the tents, leaving Elron alone to ponder what had become of his life. He stared up at the threatening sky. Rain was a certainty that night. Standing up, he entered his own tent, feeling the first drops starting to fall, knowing sleep would be elusive that night.

Thalia called out to him the next morning, waking him from dreams he wished he could forget. Bet was the main character in the nightmares that filled him with dread. The few hours of rest he had managed, left him wishing to be left alone.

Most of the night he had spent preoccupied with what he would find. His curiosity increased with each passing moment he lay awake.

Bet was never far from his thoughts as well. He presumed it was the reason why she invaded his sleep-deprived mind. His anger at her had diminished, bringing to the fore the pain he tried unsuccessfully to keep at bay. Plagued by not knowing where she was or how she and his child were was eating away at him. He was second-guessing his decision not to go after her.

Thalia's voice, calling his name again, brought him back to the present. Pushing Bet out of his thoughts, the reason for his being there rushed back. The only way forward was for him to get it over with. He rose from his fur-lined bed still dressed in the same clothes he had arrived on the island in. Dirt covered, stained, they afforded little to him in warmth.

He would have exited his tent, if not for the shimmer that grew next to his bed. On the extra pillows that lay strewn on the floor, a fresh change of clothes had appeared. Shaking his head, rolling his eyes, he quickly changed into the warmer outfit. When he was fully clothed again, he pulled the flap that acted as his door out of the way.

Outside, Rider and Thalia were ready to get going. Before he could even think about it, his hunger conjured up the makings of a breakfast. Over the burning fire, a pot of coffee brewed on the open flames. Beside it, a pan holding eggs and bacon appeared. Warm bread occupied a separate place next to it.

"We'll eat before we go, shall we?" Thalia giggled. She sat on the blanket on the ground, patting the spot next to her for Rider to take a seat.

They ate in silence, each preoccupied with what they would find. Elron wanted to ask after everyone, especially if Bet had been found, but at the same time he was dreading the response. Focusing on the here and now was all he could do. He knew that eventually he would have to decide what to do about her, but he was not ready yet to examine what that should be.

Finishing his plate, he placed it next to Rider's, who had already polished off his own. Elron was suddenly uncertain of continuing on their quest. Thalia could sense his unease. Rising to her feet, she held out her hand for him to take it.

"It will be okay. We're with you, Elron. Whatever we find, we will make sense of it together." She assured him.

Taking her proffered hand, he rose to his feet. Her calming energy flowed into him through her touch. She was right. Not knowing was only making things worse. The tents, fire and blanket vanished into thin air. He shook his head at how unpredictable his new power was. He really had no control over it. It acted on its own volition, guided by his basic needs. *Is that how Alexa felt when she started manifesting her powers?* He had a growing respect for the way she had handled it.

"We need to go to our old city's port. It's not far from here." Rider broke into the silence.

Elron vaguely recalled the location. The small inlet was off to their right. It would take less than twenty minutes to reach it on foot. Rider put his hand on Thalia's forearm and they both disappeared. So walking was not their first choice. Elron followed their signature, reappearing beside them. He was facing in the direction of the shore. There was no beach there, only a cliff, dropping into the crashing waves below.

"Under the water, there is a small cave. Here." Rider pointed to the location. "You will find what she left for you there." He continued.

Of course he would have to get wet. Sighing, he started to remove his clothing. The sting from the frigid air made goosebumps rise on his exposed skin. Down to his briefs, his skin was chilled by the air, as he marched quickly to the edge of the cliff before he lost his nerve. Casting a glance behind him, nodding at his friends, he took a deep breath of air.

He dove straight in, not giving himself the chance to change his mind. The coldness of the water made him gasp. He needed to be quick about it. It would not be long before his muscles numbed. He dove deeper, searching for the cave that Rider had mentioned. The water was murky, making it difficult for him to see.

With no clear idea of where he needed to go, he was surprised when a light suddenly appeared in front of him. It seemed to hang in the water, offering him enough illumination to see the area in front of him. The rock face of the cliff ran down to the deepest levels of the sea. He treaded water, trying to find the entrance to the cave. From his position, he could make out an opening in the rocks near the shore.

He quickly swam towards it. His strength was fading from the numbing effects of the frigid water, his muscles protesting what they were being subjected to. The closer he got to the cave, the more he struggled to keep moving.

Out of breath, he just barely managed to enter it, rising up to find that an air pocket existed within it. Gulping in air, he spun around within the confines to locate what he had been sent to find. The space was only large enough for his head to rise out of the water. He had to hurry or he would not have the strength to get back out.

On the beach, Rider held his head tilted to the side. The voice that spoke to him was urgently telling him they needed them back. Thalia could see that someone was communicating with her husband. She waited for him to relate to her what he was being told. Her eyes returned to the water, waiting for Elron to reappear. He had been down there too long. *What was taking him so long?* She scanned the area, her concern increasing each second he did not emerge.

"He'll be back." Rider was finished with his conversation.

"It's been too long!" Thalia kept her eyes glued to the water.

How long can a body withstand the temperature of these waters? Hypothermia was a great risk to anyone swimming there. Thalia held her hand across her breast, willing Elron to come back soon. She took a step towards the edge of the cliff, peering down, seeing nothing. Rider came to join her, rubbing her back, as her eyes remained fixed on the water below. A bubble of air broke the surface, then another. Elron's head broke free.

He swam towards them, jumping up once he could get a foothold. Running to his clothes, shivering dangerously, he made it to the pile in front of him just as a large bonfire appeared before him. Elron fell to his knees in front of it. The heat wrapped his body within its warmth. Thalia ran to him, placing a heavy blanket that had materialized around his still-dripping body. They gave him time to catch his breath, waiting to see if he had found anything.

"I have it." He managed to get out between his chattering teeth.

"We will have to wait to see what it is. We have to go." Rider told them.

Chapter 11

Liam

In the windowless library, the aisles of bookcases were overshadowed by the intermittent fluorescent lighting. One of the bulbs flickered annoyingly. The turning of pages was the only sound. Liam leafed through the book he held, his mind not focusing on the words written within it. He was standing in one of the numerous rows of bookcases numbering in the hundreds. Books surrounded him on all sides. There were so many of them to go through, he wished his father were there to help.

They urgently needed guidance. Thoughts of Alexa were intruding, keeping him away from the purpose of his coming there. He required distance to formulate a plan. Alexa must see that Aidan was not coming back. His brother would have returned by now, if he cared anything for Alexa, or at least for their people. Aidan had a destiny to fulfill. Liam assumed that he did not care about it any longer.

Returning the book to the shelf, Liam listened for her arrival. He picked up another volume, turning the cover to read what it was about. It was no use. The words were nothing but a blur to him. *What could be keeping her? Should I go find her? No, it would only make things worse. She needs time. Her guilt at Aidan leaving is ridiculous. My brother is a grown man, making his own choices. I'm a better match for Alexa.*

Fury erupted in him at his brother, startling him with its intensity. The suddenness of it stilled his hand from turning another page. Dark thoughts clouded his mind. Images of killing Aidan, keeping Alexa for himself, made him close his eyes, fighting to clamp down the scenes that ran through his mind. It was as if something had taken possession of him. He could never kill his brother. The idea was abhorrent to him. Getting his self-control back, he sank to the floor, fearing what he had been thinking of doing. *Do I really hate my brother that much?*

Liam tried to still his racing heart. He closed his eyes, but the images could not be driven out. Sickened by the thoughts of harming his brother, Liam groaned loudly. Deep inside him, a voice was encouraging, driving him to exact revenge against his brother. Aidan had to pay for hurting Alexa. What he was putting her through was inexcusable. It took all his strength to stop the murderous thoughts he was having.

He glanced guiltily at the library door, which stood open, afraid that his thoughts would be easily broadcasted to others. He had to gain control of himself. Rising to his feet, he picked up the book that had fallen out of his hands. He placed it back on the shelf, then leaned up against the bookshelf, his thoughts inevitably returning to Alexa.

She was keeping her distance from him. *Why is she not here with me? What could be more important?* Liam knew Alexa had been attracted to him first. Those feelings had to still be in her. He just needed to remind her of them. Alexa would realize she belonged with him. Spending time with her, keeping her close was a start. Wondering again where she was, what she had to take care of made him anxious for her to join him. *Is she trying to find Aidan?* His mood quickly boiled over into hatred again.

The animosity towards his brother was like a hot blade, ready to strike. Liam was tired of always being second best to his older brother. This time he would not lose. There was no way he was giving her up again. She would be his or she would die.

His breath caught at the thought. *What is happening to me? How could I even think of harming her?* Knowing it was only a matter of time before she appeared, he had to get a hold of himself. He forced thoughts of her and Aidan away.

Liam pushed away from the bookcase and returned to his task. Scanning the shelves, he saw the books were placed in no particular order. The spines had titles that offered no clue as to their use. *How could anyone find anything in this mess? I will have to go through each volume one at a time. It will take time, but what other choice do I have?*

Starting at the back of the aisle, he read each title, as he made his way through the books. So far, nothing stood out. He made his way around to the next aisle, his fingers gliding over the books. In reality, he had no idea what he was looking for.

He was just starting to go through the third row, when he felt the arrival of his parents and sister. Their presence was unwelcome. They would try to influence Alexa against him. Instantly on guard, he rushed out to find her. Whatever brought them back, he knew how badly his mother had treated Alexa. He needed to make sure that Alexa had his support when dealing with her. Whatever they said, he would make sure that Alexa turned to him. He would protect her. No one would stand in his way.

Charging outdoors, he found Alexa with Rina, his family a short distance away. He moved to stand next to Alexa, keeping her close to his side. When he tried to take her hand, she moved a step away from him. His narrowing eyes bitterly fell on her face. She was focused only on the people in front of her.

Liam was torn away from assessing Alexa by Bet, who broke away from the group and ran over to her. He would have to wait to ascertain why Alexa pulled away from him. Alexa was his. She just did not know it yet. Shaking his head from the possessiveness his thoughts had bred, he took in his sister's appearance.

Bet looked tired, thinner than when she had left. Wherever she had been, she had not taken care of herself. Aidan would pay for that as well. He was to blame for everything that had gone wrong. The voice inside him gleefully filled Liam's mind with its dark, hateful words again.

He watched as Alexa wrapped Bet in her arms, cradling her as his sister started to cry. Liam forced his attention back to the situation at hand, blocking the murmurings in his head, as they tried to gain strength. He stared at his mother. There was something different about her. Her eyes met his, hers surprisingly showing regret.

"Has anyone heard from Aidan?" His father asked.

Alexa froze, her eyes darting to Asher. The guilt, written on her face, disturbed Liam. She had nothing to feel remorseful about. Aidan was to blame for being gone. Reminding Alexa of him was cruel. Liam was not worried about Aidan. His brother could take care of himself.

Still, he could see Alexa was hoping for some news. The voice inside his head fanned the flames of his displeasure. His parents would pay as well. *How dare they try to take her away from me? They always preferred my brother over me. I will show them all.*

"Asher, we need everyone before we speak." Eliana reminded her husband, giving something sane for Liam to focus on. "The others will be back tomorrow. We need to wait for them. Elron has something to share with us also."

Bet, cried out and dry eyed, stared at her mother. Liam saw the fear that ran through Bet at the reality of having to face Elron. Liam had no idea how Elron would react to seeing her again. He had been so angry with her. *If he hurts my sister further, I will make him pay. Everyone will pay*, he heard in his head. That voice was getting harder to ignore, to push the thoughts away.

"It will be all right." Alexa soothed Bet. "You'll see. He loves you. Never forget that."

Eliana left them to enter the house. On reaching the door, her steps faltered. Turning around, her sharp gaze landed on her son. *Can she sense my inner conflict?* Seconds ticked by, as he was caught in her sight. Nervous, Liam broke their lock, turning his back to her. Eliana visibly shook herself, fearful of what she had sensed. Not knowing what to do with the information, she entered the house, resolving to think on it.

His father, having seen the short exchange, followed after her. Liam breathed a sigh of relief once they were both gone. He wondered if anything would go back to normal again. As if sensing the internal battle raging within him, Rina observed him. He caught her openly staring at him, her forehead creased in worry.

"We need to get some food in you, Bet." Alexa's voice managed to deflect Rina from asking questions for the moment.

While Alexa guided Bet indoors, Liam stayed outside with Rina. He had to make sure she had no notion of what he was feeling. Keeping himself relaxed, the voices stilled, he let her study him. It was obvious that she had concerns.

"Be careful, Liam." She said, before sitting on the bench.

His heart accelerated at her words. *Could she know what thoughts I am having? Or was this something else? Did Alexa say something to her? No, this is Rina being worried about me. That is all it is.* Liam refused to believe Alexa cared nothing for him. *I need to go to her, stand by her faithfully, show her that I am the one she should rely on.*

"She is conflicted, Liam. The bond with Aidan is growing." She said to him.

If he could not have her, there was nothing left for him. His worry must have shown on his face. Rina reached and pulled him down next to her. She held his hand, as he stared at nothing. Liam would fight for Alexa. Doing anything less was unimaginable to him. He loved her more than he thought possible. *My brother will have to step aside. If she does not choose me, if she chooses Aidan, then they both will have to die.*

Chapter 12

Alexa

The back part of the main room had reverted into a luncheon setting. A long, massive sideboard appeared once we entered the spacious room. Scents from the bowls and platters resting on it, holding a variety of prepared dishes, drifted over to where I sat.

I lounged on one of the cushioned sofas while Bet wasted no time in going to the fare. Pleased that the house included all her favorites on the menu, she had, without a word, begun feasting. Not bothering with a plate, she dug in with a fork, devouring anything she could reach. She said nothing of where she had been or what drove her away.

I rested my chin on the back of the red velvet sofa so I could study her unobtrusively. My questions would have to wait. She needed nourishment more than I needed answers. I gave her time to finish eating before broaching the subject of where she had been.

Preoccupied as she was with satisfying her hunger, I focused instead on her appearance. She had lost so much weight. Gnawing at my bottom lip, I was not sure how alarmed I should be that she was not taking care of herself. Was she going through morning sickness? Was that why she looked undernourished?

"Bet?" I finally tried to get her attention.

"I'm fine, Alexa." She reassured me. She did not stop reaching for another bite as she spoke.

She came over to the sofa, carrying a bowl of potato salad along with her. Sitting down next to me, she folded her legs under her, not losing a beat in forking food into her mouth. While she continued eating ravenously, she started speaking softly of what she had been going through.

Hearing her fears that Elron might stop loving her, I shook my head at the foolish notion. The man lived for her. There was nothing he would not do for her. Her faith in him was shaken by her mother's actions. Bet needed to see that it had no bearing on Elron's love for her.

"You do realize how silly you are?!" I admonished her.

Bet shrugged her shoulders, saying nothing to contradict my assessment. That she was uncertain of how Elron would react to seeing her again was obvious. Leaving as she did with no explanation, made her fear she had killed any chances for them. Would he be able to forgive her? Was I the only one that was sure their love would survive? They had too much to lose from both of them being stubborn.

Bet needed to think before she acted. It was not the first time she had taken off without a word. I thought Elron was beyond patient to put up with her impulsive nature. Discussion of how her actions were affecting everyone, risked her fleeing again. I needed to handle it delicately. The last thing I wanted was to drive her away. Would she listen to my opinions? Would I anger her? Their child needed both its parents. Convincing Bet to take responsibility for her volatility was going to take time.

"What happened with Aidan?" Her question made me cringe.

Changing the subject was a blatant tactic on her part. She did not want to discuss her situation further. Bringing up Aidan was her way of avoiding what I had to say. It was a good ploy. Forcing me to think about my own problems gave her a break in dealing with her own. How could I explain, though? Even now, I was at a loss to make sense of what had occurred.

We were finally at a place where we could work together. Aidan had stopped avoiding me. We had gotten closer. He had even started to find a place in my heart. How could he misinterpret my words to Liam so readily, so easily? My only wish was that Liam would recover quickly. He was a friend. Aidan had read so much more into my words, into what he walked in on.

I explained to Bet what had taken place on the day Aidan left, how he walked into the room to find me crying over Liam. The look of hurt on his face would forever remain with me. Aidan had been devastated by what he assumed was going on. He gave me no chance to explain, simply vanishing before I could speak. My guilt at causing him so much pain was unbearable. Reliving the memories did nothing to ease my conscience. I was to blame for everything.

"Are you sure that Aidan was wrong?" Bet asked me, showing concern for what had taken place.

Startled by her question, I thought back to the events leading to Aidan's disappearance. My reasons for going to see Liam that day were innocent. I went to wish for his recovery, to say good-bye. I had no ulterior motive. As far as I knew, he and Rina were happily together. Any romantic feelings I had for him were gone. There was no other reason for my tears. I was looking forward to going with Aidan on our mission. We were packed and ready to go. My motives were purely concern for Liam's well-being.

"I know you cared for Liam. Are those feelings really gone? Could Aidan have sensed your true intentions?" Bet interrupted my thoughts.

"I only know that we were in a good place, Bet. Aidan and I were closer than ever. Liam was with Rina." I was not sure of anything any longer. Liam admitting to me that he had lied about his feelings was confusing me.

"And now, Liam is here. Aidan is gone. What are your feelings now?" Bet pressed me for an answer.

I could not be sure of how I felt. Liam had gone out of his way to keep me at a distance. He lied to me, sending me off to his brother, not caring how it would hurt me. If he did it once, what was to stop him from doing it again? Aidan would return. I was sure of it. Would

Liam step aside again once Aidan was back? I could not risk opening myself up to that pain again. I remembered clearly how devastated I was the last time Liam pushed me away.

"I don't know. Honestly, Bet, I have no clue. All I know is that I can't trust that Liam will stay with me once Aidan returns. He pushed me away once. Will he do it again?" I told her.

Bet did not answer or offer her thoughts on the subject. Instead, she dipped her head to hide her misgivings. The gesture was a tad too late for me not to see her doubts. She too had the same reservations. Liam would realize that Aidan left because of a misunderstanding. He came to a wrong conclusion, one he would realize eventually. When he rejoined us, would Liam step aside, once again, for his brother? Whatever I was feeling for Liam, I had to stop developing it further. I had already caused enough problems with my wavering between the two brothers.

"I'll help as much as I can. Liam is stubborn. I think what my mother has to tell us may change his mind about Aidan." Bet let me know.

Apprehension returned at her mentioning Eliana and what she had to tell us. Something was wrong, and it involved Aidan. Asher asking if we had heard from Aidan made me realize that he had been out of contact for way too long. Someone should have heard from him by now. If not me, he would have reached out to someone else.

Trying to find him was impossible. I had not felt his presence since the day he left. Any link to him was non-existent. How far had he gone for me not to have a sense of him? Where could he be? Bet's hand grabbed my own, sensing my agitation. She squeezed it tightly, her eyes showing the same fear as mine.

"Are you finished with the girl talk?" Liam interrupted us.

He stood leaning against the wall next to the doorway. From his expression, he had been listening in on our conversation. How much had he heard? However much it was, I could tell our discussion had not pleased him. He was looking for any reason to maintain his anger with Aidan.

With his arms folded across his chest, he was glaring at both of us. The animosity I saw in him was unnatural. He looked flushed. The redness on his neck crept up to stain his cheeks. There was something feral in his eyes. I glanced over at Bet, seeing she was regarding him tensely.

"What mother has to say will not change how I feel!" He pushed away from the wall, coming towards us.

Reaching us, he towered over the two of us, waiting for a reaction from me. His stare unnerved me. Liam was angrier than I had ever seen him. He continued to stand over me, his unflinching stare making me uneasy. I was saved from the uncomfortable situation by the arrival of Eliana. She calmly walked into the room, taking in the tension that surrounded us. Pointing to Liam, she motioned for him to follow her.

The setting behind us changed instantly. The sideboard and dishes disappeared, as she neared the back of the room. An extensive conference table took up the space instead. Without a word, she took a seat, waiting for Liam to join her. Asher entered next. He also went directly to the table, taking a seat opposite his wife. Liam finally moved off, but not before giving me a final direct glare. Leaving us, he went to sit next to his father. I let go of the breath I had been holding.

From the doorway, motion drew my eyes. Entering the room, my mom and dad were followed by Elron. At seeing Bet, Elron's steps faltered. His guarded look was focused entirely on Bet. Not sure what to do or say, Bet had risen from her seat. Wary in finding themselves in the same room, they remained frozen, staring at each other wordlessly.

Ignoring their awkwardness, I rushed by both of them, running straight to my parents. Glad to see them safe, I hugged them both, eager to hear what they had found out. My mom silenced my questions with a shake of her head. I would have to wait to hear their news.

Elron brushed by us, going directly to the table, making sure to keep his distance from Bet. He sat next to Liam, who looked put out at the way Elron was avoiding his sister. My parents and I made our way to the table, grabbing Bet as we neared her, making sure she came along with us. Sitting her down next to Elron, I took the seat next to hers. The only one missing was Rina. Before I could ask where she was, she came in to join us.

"I have much to say, to explain." Eliana started.

Chapter 13

Alexa

Everyone waited for Eliana to continue. She sat proudly in her chair, regal and every ounce the essence of a queen about to speak to her subjects. Around the table, I saw differing reactions to her presence. Her husband was staring at a spot on the table in front of him. His jaw was clenched, his eyes hooded.

Bet had her hands folded on the table. From the whiteness of her knuckles, the stress she was experiencing was evident. Whether it was because of her mother or the fact that Elron was sitting rigidly, unresponsively next to her, I could not tell. My parents, on the other hand, were patiently waiting for Eliana to continue. Rina, next to Liam, was watching him, troubled by what she was seeing.

Liam sat facing me. When our eyes met, what I saw in them alarmed me. Dread spread through me, as I saw his contempt directed at me. His slight grin, the way his eyes bored into mine had me frozen. So much hate emanated from him. I watched as Rina gently placed her hand on his arm, drawing his attention away from me. I tried to calm my racing heart, closing my eyes to what I had seen. I risked a glance back at him, relieved to see he was now concentrating on his mother.

Returning my attention to Eliana, I saw she was now tense,

unsure if we would give her a chance to explain. The silence that hung in the air chilled me. A shiver ran through me, as I faced the possibility of receiving unwelcome news. I feared for Aidan. Eliana must know what happened to him.

Whatever she had to say, I hoped she would offer a clue as to Aidan's whereabouts. His being gone, not contacting anyone, was increasingly raising alarms in me. Trying to find the thread that bound us together was impossible. Wherever he was, he was carefully keeping his signature hidden. It was as if he had dropped off the face of the earth. Finally, Eliana started to speak again.

"On the day that Elsam was caught and sentenced, I met with Sara and Meredith. Elsam had kept Meredith prisoner for months. No, that's not accurate, she allowed herself to be kept his prisoner. Seeing what his actions would allow to happen, she had set a plan in motion to thwart him. When we found her, she was in a bad way. Months of being tortured by Elsam had left her weak. Before she revealed her identity to me, I had already sensed she was no ordinary witch. Sara and I were surprised to find that Meredith had been waiting for us. She could have escaped her prison at any time. Still, she waited for us so she could tell us what she had done. It was astonishing to watch as she healed before our eyes. In no time, she was fully restored. She let me into her mind, allowing me to see how she had tampered with the timeline. What she had done still had a potential for failure. We worked together to make sure her plan succeeded. In the process, I knew that I would have to give up someone I held dear." Her eyes downcast, she stared at her hands clenched on the table.

I wondered if it was Asher she had to give up. He had been left as a statue for centuries. A sudden feeling of dread warned me that I was wrong. My heart sped up as my certainty grew. It was not Asher. She meant Aidan. It was Aidan she was speaking of. No way! No, I would not let that happen.

There had to be a way for me to save him. Whatever they had done, whatever they set in motion, I would find a way around it. I was not letting anyone die. How could she sacrifice him so easily? Was it worth losing her child just to return back to their land? She noticed the effect her words had had on me. Her eyes met mine, grieving already for his loss. She continued speaking, not giving me a chance to grill her on what she meant.

"Meredith knew that Elsam would continue with his plans once he had served his sentence. She warned me that, at his bidding, she had placed a spell on our crystal, giving him sole access to it once he was released. I would lose any control over it. But she had bested him. Intertwined with the spell he had asked for, she interlaced her own. The Kaemorra would disappear before he was released. It was the only way to keep it out of his hands. Knowing that our people would have to abandon their home, we worked together to find places where we could hide our nature. In order for our plan to work, we had to stay out of the human's natural course of history. Meredith was adamant that we not influence their development." She explained further. I was still waiting to hear about Aidan.

Everyone around the table was fixated on her story. She held them captive, finally revealing what took place so long ago. Across the table from me, Liam was staring at me again, knowing I was getting increasingly frightened for his brother. I ignored the look of bitterness that he gave me. I had to concentrate on the rest of her tale. Finding out how Aidan was involved in the spell was more important than dealing with Liam at the moment.

"I did not know at the time that Elsam was incarcerated that I was pregnant. We had been involved a number of years. Our liaison was nothing but a distraction. I knew we were not meant to be. My future was with Asher, but it was still years until we would meet. Finding myself with child, the father a traitor, I decided to give it up. I spent months in seclusion, waiting for its arrival. Vanya was kind enough to accept the child as her own. She raised him away from court, no one knowing of his connection to me. When I finally met Asher, I had no link to the child. In my mind, he was Vanya's." She was looking for understanding from her husband.

Asher was not moved by her explanation. He still had not heard why he was left trapped in the fountain for centuries. How could she have left him there? Was she so unfeeling that it was nothing to her? Bet on the other hand was livid, looking at her mother as if she were an alien. I glanced at my parents, seeing that they too were upset at what Eliana was telling us. Eliana, disregarding the animosity she faced, and went on with her story.

"Meredith exacted a price for saving our people. I was to lose one of my children in order for us to have our home back." Her voice caught, showing for the first time her emotions. My blood ran cold at her words. Aidan. No.

She saw my stricken face, aware that I knew of who she spoke. Liam had partially risen from his seat, ready to come to me. Asher held him back. I was grateful for his action. Liam was too volatile, too out of control. What I saw in him earlier terrified me. I had no time to ponder how he was doing. I wanted details on how she was to lose Aidan, how I was to lose Aidan. My blood ran cold at what she was willing to allow.

"Meredith made sure that Aidan and Alexa would join. She knew that if they were to be separated, Aidan would not survive. By returning the Kaemorra, Aidan would be forced to return to our world. She made it so that he couldn't remain on this one. On his return, his aging process would accelerate. His life would be over in a matter of months. If he stayed here, he would die instantly. Either way, Aidan would die." She continued with a pained look on her face.

No, I would not let that happen. I would make sure that Aidan survived. Somehow I would find a way to change what they had done. Why had Meredith been so cruel? What was the reasoning behind her doing this? Why would she let me suffer this? I felt my mom's hand on my arm, but my eyes were still glued to Eliana, who refused to acknowledge my growing agitation.

"I am sorry for the way I have treated you, Alexa." She spoke directly to me. "But, you are a constant reminder of all I will lose. I know it is not your fault. I only wish that I had another way for this to end."

Meeting my incredulous stare, Eliana winced upon seeing my reaction. She tilted her head, staring at me curiously. Before I knew what was happening, the room around me seemed to tremble. The table rattled on its legs. A dizzying buzzing sound filled my ears. It grew in intensity, the noise blocking my mother's voice, as she tried to calm me. All I could think of was Aidan.

Anger at the fates, at what Meredith and Eliana had set in motion, was building inside me. Grief threatened to overpower me. In my distress, my fingertips glowed with an unreleased bluish electric current. Crackling, spreading, I struggled to hold it back. Losing control, the charge traveled down the length of the table towards Eliana.

Only her removing her hands from the tabletop saved her from receiving the shock. She showed none of her usual haughtiness towards me. Understanding met my eyes. With my mom's hand firmly on my arm, I felt her using her ability to ground me. Some of the threatening energy washed away. The rest I managed to keep an unstable control over. It would not take much to set me off again.

"How could you keep this from me?" Asher wanted to know. He was completely incensed with her.

"We had to keep it secret. Anyone finding out may have changed the course we had set in motion." Eliana answered.

Asher rose from the table, pacing the room in frustration. I tried to dampen my own distress. The emotions running through me made it impossible to handle the power fighting to break free. Breathing evenly, I pushed down the pulse of energy that was renewing itself. Frying her was not going to give me answers. I still had no idea where Aidan was, what danger he might be in. When was she going to tell us why I had no contact with him? I clamped down the energy threatening to explode.

"I am starting to believe that Meredith did not tell me everything. For the first time, I believe that there is a way to save everyone. Elron, please tell us what you have found." Eliana addressed Elron, causing him to jump at hearing his name.

We all turned our eyes on him, wondering what he could possibly have to add. I knew that there was something troubling him. He had avoided me since the night of our attack by the shadows. Even then, he never once glanced my way. Nervous, he sat in silence, keeping himself isolated from everyone near him. Aidan kept me from confronting Elron back then.

Now I wondered if it was something I should have insisted on. I saw him visibly jerk into movement. From his inside jacket pocket, he removed a cloth-wrapped parcel. Placing it on the table in front of him, he frowned at what he held in his hands. The object he deposited on the table was about ten-inches long and six-inches wide. Whatever it held, it lay hidden under a worn cloth. Elron was clearly leery of its contents.

"What is it?" Bet gently asked him, her hand moving towards him. He avoided her touch, pulling his hand out of her reach. Taking a calming breath, he started to carefully pull the material away from what was hidden inside it.

"The night we were attacked, I was visited by someone. An energy field surrounded me, making it impossible for me to move. Unable to break free, I could not get back to Liam and Aidan. All I was told was to go to our island, to find something that had been left there for me. I had no idea who was speaking to me or what I would find. I was told to tell no one." Elron related the details to us.

I let his words sink in. Elron's tone gave away his guilty feelings for being kept away while we were under attack. He was also blaming himself for Liam's injury. I would have liked to tell him that there was nothing he could have done, but it would have fallen on deaf ears.

Bet's reaction to what more he had to say was also eating away at him. I could tell that there was much more to share, and that he was hesitant to continue. I studied the wrapped package, wondering what could have him so thrown. His fingers had stilled in opening it, choosing to relate his story before we saw what was hidden.

"When I arrived on the island, strange things started occurring. I assumed that someone was helping me. Whenever I was hungry, food would appear. When I needed shelter, a tent with bedding would materialize. I was wrong. There was no one helping me. On the second day, just as I was about to return here, Meredith visited me." He stopped to draw a deep breath.

Arriving at the pivotal point of his story, his demeanor changed to one of uncertainty. What had Meredith told him to cause him to be so apprehensive? I saw Bet take his hand, giving him the courage he needed to continue. Letting her hand remain in his, his eyes sought me out. He spoke as if his words were directed at me.

"Meredith told me that Agatha, Elsam's lover, was her sister. She was an immortal. Elsam brought Agatha to our island while she was pregnant, to prove to her that he was of our race. While there, she hid this parcel for her son. She had already started to distrust Elsam. Her sister warned her of what Elsam would become, how he would betray his people. Agatha wanted her son to have a weapon that could stop him." His eyes remained fastened on me.

Understanding, that somehow this was related to our quest, spread through me. Elron had a purpose in what we were to do. Still, I was curious why he was sent to retrieve the object. How was he involved? Slowly, realization dawned on me. It could not be, could it?

Chapter 14

Alexa

"We joined Elron on the island." My father spoke into the silence, as I grasped the enormity of what it meant.

Shock was on everyone's face, as they digested what Elron was saying. The only one who showed no reaction was Eliana. She had known all along. Elron was the descendant I had tasked my parents with finding. How did they know to go find him? That they went to meet up with him must mean they also discovered more on Agatha. The importance of what was being said was not lost on me, but my mind kept going to the one thing I still had no answer for.

Everything I had heard so far brought me no closer to finding Aidan. I had to get to him, had to make sure he was safe. With every second that passed, the urgency, the danger I felt him in, grew exponentially. My mother touched my hand and with a look, stopped me from the questions I would have asked. She motioned with her head for me to listen to what my father had to say.

"My mother, your grandmother, Alexa, had the location of where the package was. The details are not important. We can go into it later. With only us knowing where Elron needed to go to find the package, we went to meet him." Rider added.

Elron was still preoccupied with the contents of the package. He paid no attention to Bet, who gave his arm a squeeze to get him to continue. Rider cleared his throat to get his attention. Noticing everyone waiting for him, Elron finally brought his eyes to Bet's, who gave him a nod, encouraging him to finish his tale. From his other pocket, he withdrew a weathered piece of paper. It looked ready to disintegrate from age. The ink was faded, barely visible. Elron drew a steadying breath, as he started to read the contents.

"My son, it is with much sorrow that I write these final words to you. You are barely formed within me and yet I love you more than my own life. I cannot express how much you were wanted, how I would have liked to see you grow. I was young, foolish to give my heart to one so dark. Your father must never know what has become of you. I must keep you safe. Everything I do going forward will be to make sure of this. I place no value on my own existence. My dear sister has warned me of what Elsam will put in motion. That I alone have the power to put things right, to atone for my actions, has been made clear to me. It has killed any hope in me that the man I loved could be swayed from his actions. Your father will try to destroy our worlds. Whether or not I had come into his life, he was destined to this end. Already he has used warlocks to begin his rise to power. It has never been about me. Know that he only seeks power. His aim is to take the reins and subjugate all peoples. His queen does not see the evil within him. He hides his dark soul beneath his looks and outward smiles. He is cunning, my son. I am on this island because he cannot help himself in his arrogance. Thinking

I would be impressed by his power, I am now more than ever certain of what I must do. I pretend to fall deeper under his spell. His vanity makes it easy to fool him. He has no idea who I really am, and I must keep it that way. The queen called for his presence earlier. He was not pleased to be summoned like a commoner. Angered, he left not too long ago. His absence has given me the freedom to write these words to you and to hide what is inside the parcel. When the time comes you will know what needs to be done. Your friends will guide you. I go in peace, knowing that you will be placed with a family who will love you. Upon my death, all my powers will transfer to you. I have already woven the spell that will keep them under control, hidden, until you are ready. Meredith has promised me you will be watched. She will make sure that no one knows of your heritage. Only when you are to retrieve this parcel, will you begin to come into your own. I hope your life will be joyous and filled with love. Know that I, your mother, love you beyond measure. Good-bye, my son." Elron's voice choked with emotion, moved enormously by his mother's words.

He refolded the letter, making sure not to tear it in his hands. Stealing a glance at Bet, he took his other hand from hers. The tears that formed in her eyes threatened to spill over. My own vision was blurred from the same emotions. I was awed at the love and sacrifice his mother had given for his safety.

Elron brought his hands to the package, unwrapping it carefully. Bringing the last of the cloth out of the way, I stared at the object. A dagger, its hilt made of some type of metal, gleamed under the light given off by the chandelier above us. Its blade was a clear, dazzling, enormous diamond. The edges were sharp, its tip a dangerous point. It would easily cut through anything.

Staring at it, my sight shifted, the buzzing in my ears returning. The room faded, rippling, as I found myself somewhere else. A vision replaced the room I was in. In the place I found myself, Aidan held the Kaemorra in his hands. My own were wrapped around his as we held it, watching rays of ruby-colored light escaping from it. The colors danced around the room we were standing in. We were in a place I had never been before. The room was lit with torches. I was not able to discern any other features.

Facing each other, Aidan and I were mesmerized by the energy the Kaemorra was giving off. Elron was by our side, just inches away. He held the blade, the diamond edge glowing brightly in his hands. Bringing it down, striking it into the Kaemorra, the blade cut and entered it, merging the two together. The crystal absorbed the diamond within it. The usual red of the Kaemorra mutated into a blinding icy blue.

I gathered the elemental currents around me, feeling power unlike anything I had felt before coalesce within me. Letting go of the electricity, I drove all its force into what we held, melding the two items together further. The room we were in started to tremble.

Thrown apart by the force of the blast that I had created, I was separated from Aidan. Clear across the room from where I landed, a rip in time and space was opening. I watched helplessly as it expanded, the center of it twisting and swirling, reaching where Aidan and Elron lay unable to move. I was in much the same state.

I was held by an invincible force, unable to go to Aidan. The vortex reached out, moving over the two men. I could only watch as Elron and Aidan were dragged into its core. Their bodies were whipped about, as they entered the anomaly.

Aidan was drawn further away from me, deeper into the middle of the maelstrom. His hand tried to reach for me, his eyes panicked at not being able to. Then I too was dragged towards the energy. Everything around me was being pulled into whatever we had created.

A feeling of peace enveloped me. I let go of resisting its pull. Closing my eyes, I let it grab me, let it take me into its light. The men were nowhere to be seen. Then, I too was no more. Everything around me erased into nothingness.

I came back to the present, seeing that no one had noticed me having a vision except one. Shaken over what I had glimpsed, I let my eyes move over the faces around the table. They were not aware of what I had seen, only Eliana was watching me carefully. It was clear from her expression that she had seen it all. I knew what we needed to do. It was our only chance. I knew how to fix everything. Agatha gave us the means to fulfill the prophesy, but in my own way.

"She doesn't say what I am to do with this." Elron was saying.

I knew, but I was not going to tell them, yet. They would never agree to it. Elron would have to learn of it eventually. For the moment, I had to keep it to myself. Eliana nodded slightly at me, agreeing with my assessment. It would be our secret. Knowing what I had to do, I had to make sure Elron was kept in the dark. As my distant cousin, coming from immortals, he would possess the same powers I did.

I could already see the changes he was going through. His very essence was transforming before my eyes. Soon he would be reaching my level of ability. He may very well exceed mine. It would be my turn to help him discover his potential. Together we would build our powers to succeed in our venture. Eliana's voice broke into my thoughts.

"After Elsam was imprisoned, his cohorts did not stop preparing for his return. Myrick was his most loyal follower. Elsam promised him much to get him to agree to his replacing me. Centuries went by. I kept my eyes on them all. I was too late to save Asher from falling into their clutches. His replacement was obvious. It was easy to see he was an impostor. I could have saved you, Asher, but it was easier to keep track of them with your replacement running around." Eliana admitted.

Asher could only stare at his wife. Her admitting to him that she knowingly kept him imprisoned as a statue left him dumbstruck. He found it reprehensible that she had so little faith in him. They should have handled the threat together. Did she think him incapable of offering any help? He was struck mute. How long before he blew, I wondered. Bet was also upset at her mother.

"We confided in that man. We were wounded by his lack of affection. You stood by and let us all go through misery. How could you let us think of that impostor as our father?" Liam finally spoke, his voice showing how disgusted he was with his mother.

Sneering, he turned his full contempt on me. Eyes flashing in disgust, he bitterly saw my worry for his brother as an affront to him. I was stunned by his anger. There was more than what his mother let happen driving his fury. He was also affected by my need to find Aidan.

More and more, I was realizing that my future belonged with Aidan. Liam did not understand the forces that were driving us together. It was more than worry I was facing. A part of me was missing. I would not be whole again until I was reunited with Aidan. Thankfully, Rina pulled him back into his seat when he looked ready to come at me.

"I have lost Aidan's signature. I can't locate him anywhere." Eliana's words tore through me.

Liam laughed at her pronouncement. He still thought his brother was avoiding me. I was beginning to seriously have doubts about Liam's sanity. He was so volatile, he scared me. Did anyone else see how out of control he was? What I sensed in him was petrifying. His mother was right to be concerned. I also found my connection to Aidan severed. Eliana and I were the only ones to grasp what it meant. Aidan was in danger. Someone was shielding him from us. We had to find him.

"He's probably off sulking somewhere." Liam said harshly.

I had had enough. His attitude was blatantly unfair. Aidan had done nothing to warrant Liam's derision. Not caring if I hurt him, I cast a seething look his way, before addressing Eliana.

"We have to find him. Tracing his steps might help. Do you know where he went when he left here?" I asked her.

She thought for a moment. I could see she was trying to envision his route. Her face concentrating on finding his signature, I saw she was not able to pinpoint a place. I let her sit in quiet, not interrupting her while she searched.

"I need time. I'm sure I will see it." She got up from her seat, stepping away from the table. Asher left the room before she could get near him. Bet dragged Liam with her, going after their father. Liam had not glanced my way since I asked to go find Aidan. From the way he left the room, I knew I would be confronted by him later. I needed to speak with him anyway. Make him understand. We had to get Aidan back.

My parents remained at the table, speaking softly with each other. Eliana resumed her seat when her family deserted her. I felt for her. It must not have been easy to make the choices she had. I could see she was still trying to locate Aidan.

On the other side of the table, Elron sat dejectedly, lost in his thoughts. He was thrown by all that had been revealed to him. I was glad that we had found Agatha's son. I knew I could count on him. I wound my way around the table, to take the seat next to his. Placing my hand on his shoulder, I grinned at him.

"So cousin, what should I teach you first?" I teased him, trying to lighten his mood.

"I will let you know if I find anything you are better at." He laughed softly, finally meeting my eyes.

"Maybe you should go make up with your wife first." My answering remark had him frowning.

Chapter 15

Bet

Bet fled to her room, needing time alone. Her father made it clear he needed his own space to think. Liam had huffed off somewhere. Avoiding Elron, she took the stairs, seeking solitude. Her misery lay like a cloud over her. Elron wanted nothing to do with her, and she could not blame him. She felt further away from him than ever.

The peaceful silence blanketing her bedroom did not lessen the clamorous thoughts that invaded her mind. Standing at her window, her mind replayed every word and gesture Elron had shared. He could not even stand to be touched by her. The tranquil view outside her room did nothing to calm her. Holding the curtain aside, she stared vacantly out the window.

Her emotions were conflicted. All she had heard from her mother had her questioning her life. She had escaped to her room, requiring time to get perspective on what her mother had divulged. Her father had escaped out to the gardens. That he needed time to come to grips with what her mother had done to him was something she could not deny. Bet thought that there was no chance for her parents to resolve their issues.

Her mother's actions, her lack of remorse, made it hard to

forgive. She had the same doubts about herself and Elron. With all she had done lately, she was not one to point fingers at others. She had discarded her husband with no explanation. *How can I expect him to forgive me?* He had not said a word to her. His silence was worse than having him yell at her. *It means he does not care. Elron has every right to write me off.*

"What are you doing?" His voice reached her from where he stood in the doorway.

Staring out the window, she was startled out of her musings. With her back to him, she did not see how he grimaced at his choice of words. *What will I find if I turn to face him?* Afraid to see his disappointment, she stayed where she was. His footfalls came nearer until he was standing next to her. Still, she could not look up at him. Only when he drew her fingers away from the curtain, did she dare hazard a glance.

"I have to go." He said, his comment driving a stake through her heart.

She knew it. He was leaving her. She had killed any chance they had. Biting her lip to control the tears that were threatening to break free, she walked away from him. She made it to the bed where she dropped, sinking into the mattress. Her whole body was trembling from trying to keep it together. Bet had no one to blame but herself. This was all her fault. She deserved to pay for what she had done. If leaving her was what he wanted, she would not stop him. Elron sighed loudly, following her to sit beside her.

"I need to find Tory. He is missing." He explained.

Is that the only reason? Will he come back? Bet raised her head to look at him. *Is there any hope for us?* She was terrified to ask, to hear him say they were finished. As further tears gathered, Elron wrapped a finger around a lock of her hair. Unsmiling, he continued to stare at her, absentmindedly twirling the strand. Whatever he was feeling, he gave nothing away.

"How long will you be gone?" The tremor in her voice had him frowning.

Noticing her red-rimmed eyes, Elron let go of her hair, draping his arm across her shoulder. He pulled her towards him, placing a kiss on her forehead. The gentleness of his action had tears running down her cheeks. She berated herself internally for being so insensitive to his needs, for being so impulsive.

She would give anything if he would just continue to hold her, telling her that they would be all right. Surviving without him would be impossible. He had every right to be mad at her. She had done nothing but hurt him. As sobs broke from her uncontrollably, he wrapped her in his arms.

"I will only be gone at most a day. Bet, please stop crying. You're killing me." Elron rubbed her back.

All her pent up emotions were difficult to control. She hiccupped while trying to rein in her tears. Holding onto him, needing to have him close, she closed her eyes, breathing in his familiar scent. Her hands gripped his arms, refusing to let go.

Elron gently pried her fingers away. Grasping her shoulders, he pulled her slightly away, so he could look at her. Her face was blotched, her cheeks flushed. Bet gazed at him, understanding what he had said. *A day, he will only be gone a day*, she repeated to herself. *He is coming back*. Elron was coming back. Hope built that they could work it out. She got herself under control, drying her tear-stained cheeks on his shirt.

"Wow, really? Can I get you a tissue?" He pushed her away, eyeing his drenched shirt. His joking elicited a small giggle from her.

Could things go back to normal, or as normal as their relationship had ever been? She had always been volatile. It was something she would have to work on. *He did not deserve what I had put him through.* Why he chose her was always a question she had no answer to. She drove him nuts.

Drawing away, putting distance between them, Elron leaned back supporting himself on his elbows. Back to being serious, he guardedly eyed her. Bet knew she had a lot to make up for. Her instinct was to go with him, but she knew better than to fight him in going after his brother alone.

"What's happened to Tory? How can I help?" She asked him.

As much as she thought working together would bring them closer, she could tell he was not ready for her to tag along. Bet needed to be patient with him. From the way he regarded her, it was obvious she had a long way to go before she was back in his arms. His response to her offering to help was to rise to his feet. He looked down at her with a brief grin on his lips.

"I really have to go. Tory has been gone without a word for weeks. My parents, as usual, are worried about him. I'm sure he is only off making mischief. There is another reason I need to see my parents. They have to answer for keeping me in the dark. You should stay here, rest, take care of our child." He turned away from her, making it to the door, where he stopped with his back to her.

Bet got up and went to him. His stiffening back was all it took for her to stop a foot away. Afraid he would rebuff her, she hesitated touching him. On its own volition, her hand came to rest on his back. The muscles tightened at the contact, but he made no move to pull away. Bet bit her lip, not knowing what to say to him.

"I can't, Bet. It's too soon. Too much has happened." Elron's pained voice was too much for Bet.

She had caused him nothing but grief since coming into his life. Her volatility, her avoidance, taking off at the slightest affront, she knew the fault lay with her. Taking her hand away, she took a step back, giving him space.

"I am still mad at you. If I stay I might say something I'll regret later." Elron turned to face her.

Bet studied his face. His jaw muscles were clenched. His eyes flashed at her in anger. Taking a breath, she took another step back, knowing she had to let him go. Loving him the way she did, she had to give him space.

"Stay here and take care of our child. Try to think of someone besides yourself for once." His words were hurtful. Bet knew she deserved them. She watched him leave, not knowing if she had lost him forever.

Chapter 16

Alexa

I sat, alone, braced against one of the chestnut trees on the estate's property line. In front of me, the dazzling petals of the flora I had trampled on were magically being restored. The field was awash with its year-long multi-colored blooms. I took no pleasure from the amazing world around me. All I hungered for was a moment's peace. I had sought a place where I could empty my mind, where I could shut the world out.

Achieving that goal was proving to be impossible. I wanted to hide, escape the dread consuming me. Regret had me reliving every one of the wrong decisions I had made so far. On the top of the list of things I was berating myself for was how I had handled being joined with Aidan. I let my resentment over being bonded with him fester to the point where I had driven him away. Guilt ate at me. The danger he was in was the result of my insensitivity. My stomach was in knots over causing him to flee.

Breathing out unsteadily, I tried to refocus on the view before me. I cleared my mind and attempted to replace the upsetting thoughts with something more soothing. The overgrown blades of grass around me rustled in the scented breeze. I inhaled the sweet essence of the perfumed air. The distinct aroma of the sweet clover was intoxicating.

Inevitably, it triggered a memory of Aidan guiding me to the middle of these grasslands. His eyes had sparkled at my reaction to the enchanted field.

Bringing me here had been his way of bringing some joy to an otherwise bleak situation. Where he was, what he was doing, were still questions for which I had no answers. I closed my eyes against the memory and leaned my head against the trunk behind me. There was no escaping the images playing out like an endless movie in my mind.

I saw Aidan hurt, beaten, in danger. I was not the only one willing to do anything to find him. Everyone but Liam understood that Aidan had been captured. It was the only explanation for his not contacting one of us. I did not expect him to reach out to me. Rather, I was sure he would have found a way to communicate with his father or Bet. Thinking of the others, who were wisely keeping their distance from me, brought a fresh set of worries.

Bet was still locked up in her room. Since Elron's departure, she had not ventured out. What she was doing with her time, what she was feeling were impossible to know. I had barely seen her. The one time I stopped by her room, she politely asked me to give her time.

Giving her till the end of the day to wallow in self-pity, I decided that come the evening, I was going to drag her out of her room to join us for dinner. She had to snap out of it. Elron would be back. Isolating herself was not going to bring him back any quicker. I needed my friend. I wanted someone to tell me what to do.

The waiting for Eliana to pinpoint Aidan's location was unbearable. Eliana was not able to find any trace of him. She had stayed barricaded in her room, in the dark, since leaving our discussion. The longer I remained with no idea of where Aidan was, the more petrified I became. I needed guidance, but no one could offer me any solutions. My parents, as well, left me alone, seeing that nothing they could do, or say, would ease my distress.

"Has my mother found anything?" Liam dropped to the ground beside me.

His steps had been muted by the tall grass. Surprised by him, I silently cursed at his finding me. He was the one I most wanted to avoid. I was not ready to deal with him yet. Shielding my eyes from the sun, I opened them to find he was sitting cross-legged next to me, playing with a blade of grass.

Uneasy and unsettled by the changes I had noticed in him, I had been avoiding him, not wanting to deal with his open hostility. Suspicious as to his motives for asking about his brother, I avoided his glance while trying to think of a response. Was he really worried about his brother, or was he hoping his mother had found nothing? His lack of caring about Aidan was starting to annoy me. I shut my eyes at the mounting anger I could see on his face.

"He can't have you!" He said harshly.

Had I heard him correctly? I gasped, my mouth falling open at the tone of his statement. My body stiffened in response. Jolted by his words, my eyes snapped open, staring incredulously at him. Seeing the sneer on his lips, I was rendered speechless. Liam seemed not to realize that he had overstepped his bounds. I bristled at his assumption that he had a say in what I did.

My anger at his insensitivity quickly rose to meet his. What was going on with him? I hardly recognized the man next to me. There was something seriously wrong with him. I could not believe what he had said. As my fury grew, the energy around me gathered, making my fingers twitch from the current of electricity that searched for a release. A small bolt of crackling energy escaped me, scorching the grass beneath my fingers.

"He can't have me?!" I repeated, sounding out each syllable as I spoke. My indignation had my voice rising in outrage with each word.

A vein in his temple pulsed threateningly, as if readying to burst. His eyes flashed at me in displeasure for not agreeing with his remark. I refused to back down. Staring at him steadily, my eyes glued to his, I was rapidly losing control.

When he tried to grab me, I found my feet, rising to stand over him. His eyes never leaving mine, he followed me up, his height towering over me. It was too much. How dare he? Here we were, all beside ourselves with worry over Aidan's disappearance, and all he could think of was who I belonged to. Losing control, I felt the wind gather its force around me. It lashed at us, forcing Liam back, away from me.

"I am not a possession to be passed around, Liam! I go where I want. I will be with who I want!" My fury made the wind relentless in its assault. I tried to control it, to pull it back, but it was too late. The only way to stop it was to put distance between us.

"That's not what I meant. I know you get to choose. Only, he can't expect you to want him after all he has put you through." Liam blocked my way when I went to leave.

I could not believe what he was saying. What had Aidan put me through? He had been patient with me. Okay, once he had lost control. The blame for that was mine as well. It happened when Liam had rebuffed me. Aidan had lost control when he saw my desolation over his brother's hurtful words. Liam had been cruel.

Telling me that I was embarrassingly throwing myself at him, saying that for him it was a playful flirtation, Liam's words had replayed in my mind with Aidan hearing every thought. If I could have blocked Aidan's access to my mind, I would have. I had no control over Aidan's ability to hear everything I thought. Seeing me in the state I was, hurt and in pain over Liam, Aidan had lost it.

It was then that he had pulled me to him, forcefully kissing me to drive Liam out of my heart. Liam was as much to blame as I was for Aidan's response. Now Liam was presuming he had a say in what I did. I took a step away from him, only to have him bridge the distance I had put between us. Only the look in my eyes stopped him from touching me. I was incensed. He gave me space while I tried to stop the pounding in my ears. It took all my strength to not cause him physical harm.

The tightness in my chest slowly eased as I took in even, measured breaths. Control was slowly coming back to me. The lashing winds I had created died down, but remained a rough breeze. Liam was glaring at my reaction to him. Not caring if I hurt him, I spoke in a tight voice.

"Liam, Aidan only left after we hurt him. He misunderstood what he saw. If he is in trouble now, it is our fault. Yours and mine. We drove him into danger. I can't waste time over anything else. You have to let this go. We have to find him, save him from whatever he has walked into. He's your brother. How can you not want to help him?" I brushed past him towards the garden and avoided his hand reaching to stop me. It was useless trying to get him to change his mind.

I made it to the terraced section of the garden with him close at my heels. He did not leave my side, as I entered the estate, going directly into the main room. There was no escaping him. He was not going to let it go. Inside the immense room, I saw it had been set up with a sweets table for me.

With no appetite, I ignored what was laid out. I had not been overly using my powers and needed no refueling. I paced the room, upset over Liam's attitude. Aidan needed us. We needed to pull together to save him. Each moment that went by, my gut screamed that Aidan was losing his way back. I was certain he thought I was with Liam. What would that do to him? Our bond had, from the start, affected him more profoundly. Would he even want to be saved?

"I do care, Alexa. He's my brother. Of course I want to help find him, but it won't stop me from wanting you. I gave you up once. I won't do it again." Liam followed my path, as I paced.

"You may have no choice. I may end up without either of you." I said before I could stop myself.

He stilled at my words. Suspicion had him narrowing his eyes at me. I could tell that he was trying to figure out what I meant. I had spoken without thinking. This was something I had to keep hidden. Lost as to how to distract him, I needed something to draw him away from formulating any questions. Luckily, my mother walked into the room.

"Alexa, there you are." She raised an eyebrow at seeing Liam.

She could tell that something alarming was going on. Shrugging my shoulders, I turned away from both of them. Going into it would only raise more questions. Bypassing Liam, she came over to me. Her touch on my shoulder was meant to sooth. She was using her abilities to settle me.

Somewhat calmed, I glanced back at Liam. He knew that he had lost the opportunity to question me. He excused himself, leaving without a backward glance. He was not happy. I knew that the first chance he got, he would corner me again on the subject. My resolve to keep him at a bay would have to be strong enough. The future I had seen held no promises of either of them being with me.

"Sweetheart, what is going on?" My mother wanted to know. She worriedly watched my face, as I avoided her eyes.

I waved my hand, dismissing the subject. My love life needed no discussion. Only one person needed my focus. Aidan. Without thinking, I went to the table and reached for a donut. Stuffing it into my mouth, the sugar entered my system, instantly increasing my reserves.

The influx of extra energy had an overloading effect. A burst of electric current escaped me. The white linen tablecloth caught fire from the flames that shot out of my hands. Just as suddenly, I saw a stream of water appear to douse the flames. I frowned at what had happened.

"How long has it been since you practiced or used your powers?" My mother's hands were still outstretched from putting out the fire. Water cascaded down from the table.

Not since Aidan left, I thought. With him missing, there had been no opportunity to practice. I was preoccupied, giving no thought or time to spare on training. Elron was the only one who could work with me now, anyway. I was not going to let Liam help. Keeping my distance from him was imperative.

Liam's attitude was something I wanted to avoid at all costs. I could not deal with him and look for Aidan at the same time. Elron and

I had more than one thing in common. Both of us were new to the forces inside us. We both also had the same commitment to finding Aidan. From my lack of response to her question, my mother knew what the answer was.

"You need to expel some of that energy. Find an outlet, even if it's on Liam." She tried to sound serious, but her smile gave her away.

Her teasing elicited a slight grin from my lips at the image of my zapping Liam. Maybe he deserved it for the way he was acting. Mom always had a knack for making me feel better. Her eyes dimmed as she turned all serious, her expression alerting me that she had something important to say. I was instantly on guard.

"Eliana has traced Aidan's movements to his disappearance. He had gone to Greenwich. All trace of him from there is gone. He must be somewhere near there. Your father and I are leaving to see if we can find him." She let me know.

Greenwich was where we thought Elsam had his base. Could he have captured Aidan? Was he being held there? We had to go find him. Aidan needed me. I had to explain to him about Liam. My mother saw my intention and quickly dashed my hopes of going with them.

"You have to stay here. We can't risk you too. We will bring him back, Alexa. Please don't do anything foolish."

How could I stay there, knowing the danger he was in? Only I could make him fight to come back. Deep within me, I knew he had given up. I had to go with them. If they did not take me with them, I would go alone.

"Alexa, you will remain here, even if I have to spell you." My mother warned.

"Listen to your mother. We will find him and bring him to you." Rider entered the room.

Fine, I thought. I got it. Little Alexa was too fragile to face what was out there. I would give them a week. If I heard nothing I would go after them.

"Fine, I'll stay." I told them, adding, "For now."

"Promise me you won't do anything foolish!" Mom eyed me suspiciously.

"I promise." I answered her.

Seeing she had gotten through to me, she embraced me before leaving. Rider hauled me into his arms, squeezing me gently. Letting go, he winked at me. His smirk let me know he knew what I was thinking. If they did not get back with Aidan soon, I would not stay idle for long. Leaving me, he followed after my mother.

Knowing where Aidan was, unable to go after him, I had no idea what to do with myself. Maybe I could practice on my own outside. I had to let go of some of the unspent energy in me.

I just made it to the front door, when I saw Asher coming down the stairs. Exasperation etched on his face. What now, I thought.

"Bet left with them."

Great, Elron will be royally pissed, again.

Chapter 17

Alexa

The scorched ground was evidence of how out of control I was. Blackened by the escaping electric currents leaving my fingers, the stone paving around the fountain was permanently discolored. I could do nothing to ease the panic that had overtaken me. My parents were missing. We had received no communication from them since they had left to find Aidan.

"Where are they? It's been over a week." I was outside, having come out to the garden for everyone's sake.

A bluish glow surrounded me, as I tried unsuccessfully to rein in the bolts of electricity escaping me. Discharges of snapping, sizzling energy were threatening to scorch everything in sight. Inside the main room of the residence, singed carpets and furniture were being replaced by the house's enchantments. I could sense the impatience from the magic covering the estate. It was not pleased with all the damage I had caused. At least outside, there were fewer objects to destroy.

I was stomping around the cobblestoned walkways, a whirlwind steadily following my steps. The undertow from the wind was kicking up the dirt from the ground. A dust cloud whipped relentlessly against my ankles, as I continued to pace. Any chance at restraining the forces seeping out of me was lost in the turbulent emotions I was experiencing.

I was past being petrified at my parents' disappearance. Panic had taken hold. The effect made my skin translucent, my bluish veins standing out like cracked glass. Red-veined lines had formed in my eyes, frightening Asher who was trying to calm me. Watching me wearily from a distance, he was trying his best to disarm me.

"Alexa, control yourself! Try to relax." His words had no effect on me.

My parents should have been back by now, or they would have contacted us if they were delayed. Something had gone wrong. I never should have let them go on their own. Keeping me there had been a mistake.

Frustrated at not knowing if they were safe, a spark escaped my hand, sending the current blazing towards Asher. His eyes grew round, as he trailed the electricity racing towards him. Barely managing to step out of its way, he walked over to me, grabbing me by my shoulders.

"Sit down!" He pulled me to the bench, forcibly sitting me down.

Remorseful over almost frying him, I let him sit me on the bench. The power in me ebbed slightly, as I grasped what I had almost done. That I almost electrocuted the king, gave me enough sense to pull back the rest of the violent energies still present. Most times, I forgot who he really was. Asher gave no airs of his title. No one would know, to look at him, that he was the ruler of the whole Sidhe race. He was just Asher, Liam and Aidan's dad, to me.

I took shallow breaths to calm down, dropping my head down towards my knees. Asher kept his hand on my back. As I relaxed, I tried to still my mind, to think more clearly and to come up with a plan. Going after them, with no idea where they were would be foolhardy. Asher must have some idea where they had gone. I knew it was somewhere in Greenwich, but I had not been told exactly where.

"Where are they, Asher?" I pleaded with him to give me any information.

Standing up, leaving my side, he walked back and forth. He made a track from where I sat to the length of the fountain. My insensitivity to what he must be experiencing left me waiting impatiently for him to answer my question. I knew he was just as distressed as I was about his son. Fear of having me fly off the handle, do something dangerous was also clear in the way he took his time.

He stopped next to the fountain, sitting down on its ledge. From the way he held his head, tilted to one side, I knew he was trying to communicate, hopefully with my father. While he was occupied with his attempt, I tried to find my mother. Reaching out with my mind, her essence was impossible to detect. Wherever she was, I was unable to establish a connection. From the growing frustration showing on his face, Asher was not having any luck either.

"Has Eliana said anything?" I asked him.

Eliana had spent her days in her room. I had not seen her since before my parents had left. Her husband and Liam were both still unwilling to forgive her. Understanding what she had done was not easy for either of them. I could see the toll it was taking on Asher. Disappointed and injured, a cloud of despair hung around him. Her son, on the other hand, held so much anger in him, I feared he would explode.

Liam was a stranger to me. His usual carefree, boyish self was replaced by an uncaring, cruel individual. From his growing resentment of Aidan, to the cutting remarks he made, Liam was nothing like the man I had grown fond of. Deriding his brother had become a pastime. Making me feel idiotic, foolish for believing in Aidan had become tiresome.

Fed up, scared to face what was happening to Liam, I avoided spending time with him. Only Rina seemed able to put up with his moods. She spent as much time as possible with him. She followed him around, making sure to keep him occupied and away from me. I was thankful for all she was doing.

"I can't find them either." Eliana appeared beside me.

Her sudden appearance startled me. Rising to my feet, I was stunned speechless at her appearance. To say she looked awful would not do justice to her state. Her hair, usually tidy and held back by a clip, was greasy and unkempt. Her skin was pasty, her eyes lack-luster. Deep wrinkles covered her hollowed out cheeks.

In the same clothes that I had last seen her in, her dress seemed to hang on her frame. She gave me no chance to address her. Avoiding glancing towards Asher, she walked by us, going to the path leading down to the beach. There, she stopped, her back to us, lost in her thoughts. Asher was gaping at his wife, trying to come to grips with her dishevelment. A flash of alarm crossed his features.

"Eliana, please sit with me." I called out to her.

She gave no indication that she had heard me. I walked over to her, saw that she was gazing blankly to the opposite shore. Had she slept at all? Eaten anything? Seeing no response to my standing beside her, I took her elbow and guided her to the bench.

When she was comfortably seated, I conjured a plate of fruit, placing it on the bench next to her. Finally, I saw recognition, as her eyes landed on the fruit. Picking up a pear, she gingerly took a small bite. Her attention was diverted as Asher came and stood over us.

"There is no trace of them." Asher continued to stare at his wife.

Eliana's head came up, meeting Asher's eyes. The forlorn look she gave him made him back away. Would the two ever resolve their problems? I hoped they would. They must have loved each other once. I did not believe that they had lost those feelings. Eliana finished the pear, without responding to her husband. She got up from the bench, ready to return to her room.

"Let me help you to your room." I rose with her.

Dizziness swept over me as I stood up. A vision was slowly warping the space around me. It built slowly, changing the landscape around me. Eliana grabbed onto my arm, as she too felt the stirring take hold. Finding myself in a strange, tight corridor, seeing through someone else's eyes was unnerving.

Whoever I was seeing through, they strode purposefully towards a door at the end of a hall. Yanking it open, they stepped into a dimly lit room resembling an office. Inside, behind an ornate desk, Elsam sat perusing mountains of papers. He threw aside the scroll he had been reading, clearly annoyed that he was being interrupted.

"What is it now?" He bellowed.

Advancing into the room, the unidentified person braced their hands on the desk, leaning in towards Elsam. I saw Elsam's green eyes flash in arrogant disinterest. Belligerent and unafraid, the Sidhe slammed his fists on the desk, standing to face whoever had entered his office. Elsam towered over the desk. His face inches from whoever's eyes I was seeing through. Being that close to the man, I trembled, not knowing if it was my reaction or that of the other person. Elsam's eyes snapped with uncontrolled hatred.

"You promised me I would have her! How long must I wait?" The voice of Myrick made itself heard.

Realizing who I was seeing through, I was instantly on my guard. I must be careful not to let him notice I was seeing through his eyes. Eliana squeezed my arm to warn me to pay attention. Elsam, in one swift move, stepped around the desk, grabbing Myrick around the throat. Lifting him off the ground, Myrick struggled to break free. He hung in midair, his legs flaying for a foothold. Elsam sneered at the man. I could feel that loss of consciousness was seconds away.

Whatever Myrick was suffering, I was equally afflicted by it. My head swam from the loss of oxygen. Elsam let go at the last second, dropping Myrick onto the floor. Both of us were gasping for air. Only Eliana's firm grip on my arm kept me upright. From Myrick's position on his knees, I was seeing the towering Sidhe, looking down contemptuously. Elsam's lips curled, as he laughed at Myrick.

"Don't be fooled into thinking you have any control over me." He continued his maniacal laughter. The man was truly mad and terrifying.

Elsam returned behind his desk, sitting down calmly. Myrick got back to his feet, his use of magic useless to him. He would have gladly used his powers to harm the other. Unfortunately for him, there was some kind of enchantment over the place. I glimpsed the spell that shielded the room. It made the room resistant to any magic. Elsam must have other witches and warlocks working for him. Myrick was without his powers.

"Your last attempt was useless. She managed to defeat the

shadows you sent. You have her bonded, it should be easy to get her to come save him. I will have her!" Myrick's words made a shiver run through me.

They had sent the shadows to attack in order to get to me. Why was I so important to him? Why did Myrick want me so badly? They had Aidan. It was the only information I clung to. Aidan had been captured because of me. Eliana pulled my focus back to the discussion by squeezing my hand.

I saw Elsam was ignoring Myrick while he read a scroll he had picked up. His fascination over what he was reading had him preoccupied. His eyes gleamed at something he saw. I saw a menacing smile form on his lips. Pure evil emanated from him.

"It was but a test, to see her strength." Elsam finally, coldly replied to Myrick. "I have found what I need." He gleefully waved the scroll in his hand.

Myrick came closer to the desk, curious about what Elsam had found. Focusing all my strength, I tried to see what it was. It was no use. I was stuck seeing only Myrick's perspective. Elsam got up from his chair, placing the scroll back with the others.

"With the shadows on our side, we only need to convince the Daimon to join our cause." Elsam pronounced.

Daimon? I wondered. Eliana trembled at hearing the word. Her eyes had grown twice their size at what Elsam had said. Myrick backed away from Elsam. I could feel his fear, as it took hold. Whoever these Daimon were, they were enough to make even Myrick fearful.

"I will let loose the shadows and wait for the Daimon to take possession of this earth. Nothing will stop me from ruling both worlds. The Kaemorra will be mine. I will reopen the way to Eruva. The land belongs to me. I will claim the throne that was denied me. You either stand with me or against me." Elsam threatened, clearly insane.

Myrick, with no abilities to aid him, quivered in fear while standing before the man. Where were they? I had to get to Aidan. There was no mention of where they were. Unable to sense the location, hopelessness made me reach further into Myrick's mind. He had to tell me where they were.

"Oh, Alexa, come to me." I heard him say.

Fear gripped me, as I realized he knew I was listening in. I tried to regain access to his mind. Any force I applied to get control of him was met with resistance. I was suddenly thrust back to the garden. The images of the room I had been in faded away. Eliana held onto me, righting me as I came close to losing consciousness. We looked at each other, worried for everyone that was missing.

"You cannot go on your own. I will call Elron for help. If they capture you as well, all will be lost." She tried to make me see reason.

Knowing she was right did nothing to make waiting more bearable. I was panic-stricken that my parents were also being held.

Asher, seeing the state I was in, was beside me in an instant. We answered a bevy of questions from him. He wanted to know every detail of what we had seen. At his suggestion, we reconvened in the living room, where he called Liam and Rina to join us. Filling them in on what we had seen, we were all shocked at Liam's response.

After telling me I was a fool for continuing to believe that Aidan was in trouble, he stormed out of the room. Eliana paled, as she told us he had vanished, his trace no longer within the boundaries of the estate. Now we had another person to worry about. Liam was not himself. I did not know how much more I could take. I was being pulled in so many directions.

First Aidan went missing, and now my parents along with Bet could be in trouble. Adding Liam to the mix was one more thing to the growing issues I was facing. That something was wrong with him was obvious. He was being controlled somehow. It was the only explanation for his changing.

Chapter 18

Elron

Elron had arrived in the western Scottish highlands expecting to find his parents at home. The grasslands covering the shore on the opposite side of Fort William were coated in an early morning fog. Rain had dampened the ground sometime overnight. Under the illusion that guarded and made the house invisible, he could sense no movement. His family had not strayed far from their homeland. The island was but a short distance away. Elron was alone.

From what he could sense, there was no other living soul around. Sounds of nature, birds, flowing waters were all that he could hear. A nudging in his mind alerted him to an incoming communication. Listening to the message, he was aghast at what was being transmitted. Responding that he had understood, and that he would return promptly, he listened further, as Eliana pressed the urgency of the matter.

Disconnecting the link with his queen, Elron shuddered at what he had been told. Shadows were bad enough, but Daimons were unpredictable and cunning. They followed no one's course but their own. *Elsam is insane if he thinks he can trust them. The Daimons will turn on him before he knows what hit him.*

Being told that Thalia and Rider were now missing as well, Elron wanted to rush off to find them. He brushed away the nagging suspicion that Eliana had not told him everything. Needing to finish the errand he came back home to do, overrode, for the moment, his being called back by Eliana. A few hours were all he needed. He hoped that the delay would not endanger his friends further.

Turning his attention back to his family home, he approached it slowly. The area appeared undisturbed. Anyone passing through would not be able to see the vast gardens or the modest house that lay in front of him. The spell guarding the location influenced humans to step around the property. No one ever made it past the illusion. All they saw was a continuation of the open fields, the sweeping valleys and the rising hilltops.

Elron was able to see past the charms. What he saw alarmed him. His mother's flower beds were quickly being overtaken by weeds. The usual pristine lawn was overgrown with violet-blue flowers of ground ivy tracking across it. The vegetable garden was yellowed, and most of the crops had been eaten by the sheep scattered across the lawn. His father would never have let that happen.

Hurrying, he passed through the invisible cloak, making his way to the front door. Without knocking, he turned the handle, opening the door and stepping inside. The silence that greeted him confirmed his earlier suspicion. His parents were away. The house was empty, silent and abandoned. He had no idea how long they would be gone. *Were they out looking for their idiot son, Tory?* His brother was still not answering his calls. He closed the door, the sound of it echoing throughout the hallway.

Infuriated at having no one to give him the answers he came for, he bypassed the living room, going directly to where his father kept the important documents. Elron entered his father's den, marching directly to the antique desk covered with papers.

In the darkened room, the blinds shut to keep the daylight out, he flicked on the desk lamp. The light streamed across the top of the desk, affording him a look at what lay there. Sitting down on the swivel chair, Elron's hands grabbed some of the papers, reading the words written on them. Finding they only held court business, he tossed them away.

Where would they keep anything pertaining to me? Why have my parents never told me where I came from? Where are they? Elron blew a breath out in frustration. His need to have answers was for more reasons than just curiosity. His future was at stake. He had no idea where he fit in any longer, where to go from there.

Bet was at the center of his uncertainty. *How does she fit in my life, now that they have learned who I really am?* Leaving her tortured him. Seeing her hurt was not something he wanted. The truth of his ancestry formed a barrier between them, one he was unsure of how to breach. Until he knew everything, he was hesitant to make any decisions.

Forcing his attention back to what he came for, he pushed away from the desk, looking around the room for a hiding place. He knew his father had a safe, but he had no idea where it was. Walking around the room, he looked behind the paintings on the walls. Finding nothing, he returned to the desk, looking in and under all the drawers. He was about to check under the desktop when the sound of feet approaching made him stand up straight. The state of his brother, as he calmly entered the room, had him outraged. *What had he gotten himself into now?*

"Where have you been?" Elron bellowed at him.

Tory came in and made it over to the leather sofa in the room. His limp was pronounced. Pain marked his face with each step he took. Holding his side, he grimaced, as he leaned to sit. Falling down on the couch without a word, Tory eyed his brother apprehensively.

He was disheveled, dirty and bruised. Elron went to him, dragging a chair along so he could sit facing him. Up close, the bruises on his face were more pronounced. He had a purplish-blue hew under his right eye. His left cheek was scratched, with deep gashes running from under his eye down to his top lip. *What the hell was he up to? Who did this to him?*

"What the hell happened to you?" Elron wanted to know.

Tory reclined back, taking his time offering an explanation. His usual energetic personality was subdued by what he must have endured.

Elron was relieved to see the bruises were healing themselves. His brother's Sidhe physiology would quickly heal him. The injuries were not life-threatening.

"Are our parents here?" Tory asked.

Letting him know that they were alone, Elron still had no answer to his original question. Tory seemed upset upon hearing their parents were absent. Distrust showed on his features at the mention of their mother and father. Elron was at the end of his rope with him. He wanted answers.

"They have lied to us." His brother's comment had Elron leaning forward on his chair.

Does he already know who I am? Is this what he means? Disturbed by the way Tory was looking at him, Elron wondered if they would still be brothers after Tory found out the truth. *Will he see me differently?*

"Tory, what have they lied about?" Elron needed to know how much Tory knew.

"Everything! They have lied about everything." Tory would have risen from his seat, if Elron was not blocking him. Agitated, he gripped a cushion, bringing it to his chest. Elron watched him, perplexed at what he meant.

"Mom and dad are not who they say they are. They are not

Sidhe. We are not Sidhe." Tory finally explained.

Elron sat back in his chair. Knowing already that he was not Sidhe, he was stunned at his brother's statement. *What does Tory mean about their parents? What is he saying that he is not a Sidhe?* Tory needed to be told about Elron's parentage. Their sharing information now was crucial.

Starting from the beginning, Elron filled in Tory on everything that he had discovered. He left nothing out, including what he was there to find. Any documents that would shed more light on how he came to be with that family could only bring more clarity to the situation. Tory listened, his eyes widening as Elron told his tale. When he was finished, Elron watched his brother absorb what he had heard. Only the small tick in his left eye let Elron know Tory was incensed.

"The safe is in the floor, under father's chair." Tory informed his brother.

Elron sprang from his seat and raced to the desk. He shoved the chair out of the way, trying to see any outline on the floor indicating where the safe was. He saw no indication that there was anything beneath the floor. Getting down on his knees, his hands felt around the floor for any hidden latch.

Ready to give up, believing his brother to be wrong, Tory pushed Elron aside. His left foot slammed down hard on the floor. On the spot in front of Elron's right knee, the floorboard gave way. One side of it sprang loose to reveal an opening. Tory sat down next to his brother, smirking at Elron's surprised look.

"Told you! Let's see what's in there." Tory was leaning over the floorboard.

Elron grabbed his wrist, stopping him from reaching into the opening. He extended his own hand to pull the board out of the way. Beneath the opened space, there was a safe that required a key for it to be unlocked. He grabbed the small handle on the vault, trying to force it open with brute strength.

It would not give. Tory, who had left his side, returned and dangled a key in front of him. His grin at having gotten another one over on his brother had Elron rolling his eyes. Grabbing the key out of Tory's hand, he pushed it into the keyhole. Turning it, the door clicked open.

"Let's see what's in there." Tory repeated after sitting next to Elron on the floor.

Elron drew the door open completely. Inside he saw numerous documents, as well as some of his mother's jewels. Pulling out the papers, he handed half of them to Tory. His brother eagerly took them, looking through them quickly.

Elron started to read the ones he held in his hands. Some were property documents, documenting the purchase of the house. Bought soon after they had to leave their island, the house had originally belonged to a known sorceress. That woman was now dead.

Looking further, the next paper was his father's appointment to the queen's council. The wax seal was still affixed to the letter. Ripping it open, not caring if it angered his father, Elron read the queen's handwriting.

His father had been put in charge of monitoring Deis-dé, the land in-between that was their safe haven. Eliana wanted to make sure that Elsam could not enter the space. Protection spells had been cast to make it impossible for Elsam to gain access.

Tory pulled Elron's attention away from that document by handing him a sealed envelope. Elron took it, seeing that it was addressed to him. His father's handwriting was easily identifiable. Tearing it open, he began to read.

Son, in the event that something happens to us, there are things you need to know. You and Tory have been a blessing to us. Each has their own purpose. Keep each other safe. Meredith placed you with us at a time we thought never to have a child of our own. We took you in, knowing that one day we would have to tell you the truth. Your finding out had to happen at the right time. Our placement, our assimilation with the Sidhe was done for your protection. They have been kind to us. Our own race is almost extinct. Meredith reached out to us, through her mother, when we were at a crossroad. Our life had spanned thousands of years and we were ready for it to end. She gave us a reason to go on. Raising you gave us a purpose again. If you are reading this, it is now time for you to know the truth. As ancients we have watched the world unfold, keeping a record of all that has transpired. We will continue to monitor and write the histories as they happen. It is after all what we have been created to do. Our time has come to join our remaining people. We leave you with a heavy heart, knowing that you will have to face many perils before the end. Our hope is to see you again, if not in this life, then in the one that is to come. Meredith foresaw how Elsam would destroy all the worlds. Yes, there are more than just the two you are aware of. There are more beings and lives involved than you can possibly imagine. We are all counting on you to save us. Your real mother, Agatha, has left you a dagger that will help in what has to been done. You must use it when the time comes. Alexa will know what to do. Time is running out. On the summer solstice you must help Alexa and Aidan. Alexa must find the Kaemorra before June twenty-first of this year. Beware of Elsam and his cohorts. They are powerful. I am sorry that I cannot be more helpful. What you need to do has been kept from us. Meredith has promised that Alexa will know when the time comes. Tell Tory that he must remain with you. His purpose in coming to us has been kept secret. All we were told was that he holds the key. Take care, my son. Know that we have loved you both as our own. You brought us back to life. Your father, Jeremy.

    Elron handed the letter to Tory so that he could read it as well. Both were not Sidhe. Where Tory came from Elron had no clue. He could just imagine how his brother would feel, remembering his own uneasy discovery. He quickly scanned the rest of the documents hoping to find an envelope addressed to Tory.

Seeing none, he put the rest of the papers back in the safe, closing the door, making sure it was locked. He repositioned the floorboard, pushing it down to close it. Tory, who had finished reading the letter, sat lost in thought. Elron could see how it had affected him.

"What happened to you?" Elron brought Tory back to the present.

"I met up with some Daimons. They have taken over the town of Caol. They had me in their clutches before I realized the danger. I was lucky to escape with minor injuries." Tory explained.

"Come. We have to get back to the estate." Elron prodded his brother to stand.

He needed to report to the queen. If Daimon were already active, they had no time to spare. They had to find Thalia and Rider, who were missing. Elron was also concerned for Aidan who they had not heard a word from. Finding them all was imperative now. They had a deadline for what they had to do. With Tory by his side, they envisioned their destination, disappearing from the room. Elron's last thought was of seeing Bet again.

Chapter 19

Bet

Under the blinking stars in the night sky, the shadows grew and diminished around the gently swaying trees. Bet was crouched down behind a large oak, hidden in the shadows of the forest around her. Thalia was off to her right somewhere, having found her own place to hide. They had arrived in Greenwich, getting their bearings before venturing out to scout the area.

Their exploring had identified a section of land near the town of Welling, which lay just east of Greenwich. Thalia had noticed a vast spell shielding the area. Near Oxleas Wood, an ancient castle was closed to visitors. Its gray stone turrets gave Rider a perfect view over the region, however. He had returned to them after scouting the area with a plan on how to approach their destination. They had entered the wood, advancing stealthily to the center where Rider had seen a deforested meadow.

Elsam had hidden his base well. If not for her Sidhe sight, Bet would have been unable to see the structure that rose into the night sky. The tower was immense. In the dark, she could not make out the actual height of it. Somewhere close by, Aidan had to be under its barrier.

Peering out from behind the oak tree, the area surrounding the enormous tower was deathly quiet. The stillness in the air was unnatural. They split up to get a better sense of what they might be facing. Bet had seen no one since they had arrived. Rider was exploring the area on the other side of the tower, which rose high into the night sky. They were waiting for his return.

A shuffle of feet drew Bet's eyes to her right. Relief filled her upon seeing Thalia slowly making her way to her. Joining Bet behind the tree, Thalia warned her by bringing her finger to her lips. Listening for what Thalia heard or sensed, Bet stayed still and quiet. Sounds of running feet broke the silence around them. Keeping motionless, they both held their breaths. Discovery would be disastrous. Whoever was closing in on them was within feet of their location.

"Did you see anyone?" The voice of a woman spoke.

The static of a walkie-talkie hissed through the air. While waiting for a response, the unidentified woman walked casually by the tree where they sat. Thalia and Bet's eyes met, uneasy with what the person on the other end would answer. *Had they found Rider?* Listening closely, they waited for what they would hear.

"No. Nothing." Came the reply.

Thalia almost let out a breath, catching herself before giving away their position. Bet gripped her forearm, making Thalia wince from the pain. Seeing she was hurting Thalia, Bet eased off the pressure. They heard the woman start walking again and then stop, as someone else arrived.

"They should have come by now. We need their help." The voice of a man said.

"We have to get back. He will notice our absence." A tremor of fear could be heard in the woman's voice.

Their footsteps came again, the sound drifting away, as they ran back towards the tower. Bet knew the voice of the woman. Vanya was there. She could only guess at the identity of the man. *Could that have been my half-brother? Why are they out here looking for someone? Who are they waiting for? Is it possible they know we're here?* She looked at Thalia to see if she understood anything. Thalia shook her head.

The crunching of leaves had them backing up further behind the tree. Hearing the hoot of an owl, Thalia relaxed. She peered out to see Rider coming to them. He made his way carefully, keeping to the shadows.

Once he was next to them, he inclined his head for them to follow him. Together, they made their way back to the main road, where they had hidden their car. When they were all in the vehicle, Rider started the engine, driving back towards their hotel. Leaving him to concentrate on maneuvering the dark roads, Thalia and Bet remained quiet.

Bet tried again to reach Elron. Every time she was disheartened to have no response. He was blocking her. *Will he ever forgive me?* She wanted him to know where she was. This time she had left for a reason. It was not an unplanned impulse that drove her to take off. *He needs to know I'm coming back for him.*

The drive back to town was uneventful. Their car was the only one on the roads. At that late hour, the residents of the town of Welling were asleep. Rider pulled into the parking lot at the back of their hotel. He chose an available spot closest to the street and cut the engine. They all piled out, without a word. They encountered no one as they entered the lobby. Only one employee was behind the desk. Greeting them, he wished them a good night, as they made their way to the elevators.

Rider pushed the button, the door opening for them without delay. They rode up to their floor, exiting into a well-lit hallway. The brown carpet had seen better days. Stains covered it in places. On the walls, the paint was faded and chipped. Walking to the first door on the left, Rider passed the electronic key in the door's slot and opened it. He held the door, allowing the women to enter first. Only when it was closed behind them, did he speak.

"The place is impenetrable. I found no way inside." He told them.

Bet was aware of the gravity of the situation. The spell over the area was a good indication of the steps Elsam had taken to protect his fortress. Rider spelling it out only made things worse. They had to find a way in. Aidan was depending on them to save him.

"There must be a way. Every guarded place has a weakness. We just have to find it." Thalia paced back and forth in the room.

Rider had not seen a way in. Giving up though was not an option. They would have to look more closely. As dangerous as that was, they needed Aidan back. Tomorrow night they would go back. He would reassess the security, see if he could find a point of access. Thalia could try to see past their shield, see if she could locate Aidan. They would sleep tonight and get back out there tomorrow. Preparing for bed, Thalia used the washroom first. When she exited, giving Rider his turn, Bet was already asleep, fully clothed in her bed.

The next night went no better. Under an overcast sky, the moon cast no light to help them. Rider found it impossible to find an entry point. Thalia was not strong enough to penetrate the shield. Bet was getting more careless in her reconnaissance of the area. They were all frustrated. Meeting up with Thalia, Rider explained his lack of success. Bet had gone off alone. Thalia had no idea where she was.

Expressing her doubts of finding a way in, Thalia tensed suddenly. Rider felt the presence of a threat, but could not identify where it was coming from. He saw his wife's hands coming up to ward off an attack. Her attempt was ineffectual, as a bolt of energy flashed their way.

Jumping out of the way, they found themselves surrounded by five men. Thalia could sense the magic in them. All were warlocks. They did not stand a chance against them. Thalia's powers did not include combat. She could heal and calm others, but had no talents in fighting off that kind of attack.

Rider pushed his wife behind him, putting himself in front of her. The power coming from their opponents was unlike anything Thalia had felt before. Doing all she could, she tried to put a force field around her and her husband. It was not enough. Chains materialized, binding their arms behind their backs.

"Well, well, what do we have here?" Myrick pushed past his men, smiling menacingly at Rider and Thalia.

Thalia would have liked to smack the arrogant smile off his face, but her powers were being drained. Feeling the blanket of an energy shield surround her, she found she had no strength. All her magic deserted her. They were at the mercy of their captors.

All of them combined were too many for Thalia to take on. Rider fell to his knees beside her, appearing to pale as he was enveloped by the field. The iron chains binding his wrists were burning his skin and making him weak. She hoped Bet had gotten away.

"Elsam will be so happy to greet you." Myrick waved to his men. They came at them, grabbing Thalia and Rider, forcing them to walk towards the tower.

Thalia knew it was useless to struggle. Her feet continued on their march to the doorway, she realized they had in fact found a way in. She gave a wink to Rider, who returned a lop-sided grin. Entering from a side door, they were met by Vanya. Not acknowledging them in any way, she glanced at Myrick who was behind them. Thalia was certain she glimpsed unbridled contempt on the woman's face. Pushed from behind by one of the guards, Thalia bumped into Vanya, hearing her pass on a whispered message.

"He has Bet inside. Be careful." Thalia was chilled at her words.

Vanya stepped aside to let them through. She followed them into a vast chamber. Elsam had created his very own throne room. Resembling Eliana's, the space had been transformed with Roman columns reaching up to the ten-foot ceiling. Thalia was pushed again to advance to where Elsam waited for them. Passing by the columns that were on either side of her, the length of the room was impressive. She counted two-hundred steps to reach the front.

On reaching the end of the long aisle, the man behind her grabbed her and pushed her to the ground. On her knees, she caught Rider, who fell beside her from being forced into the same position. Elsam laughed at their treatment. He stood in front of a gilded throne, watching them with a sneer.

Dressed all in black, his emerald eyes stood out like beacons. At his feet, Bet lay crumpled on the floor. She was unmoving, her complexion ashen. Thalia made to get up and run to her side, but was stopped by Rider. He warned her with a look. Elsam looked upon them scornfully.

"Did you think it would be so easy?" His hard eyes met Thalia's.

Not responding, she sat back on her heels, waiting to see what he would do with them. Rider's shoulder brushed against hers. He inclined his head subtly for her to follow his eyes to see what held his attention. She found him staring at Vanya, who was kneeling beside Bet. Bet moaned at her touch. Relief flooded through Thalia at Bet showing signs of life. Vanya got up, meeting Rider's eyes. What they saw had them puzzled. Vanya was distressed at Bet's harm.

"Take them to the dungeon, Myrick. Do as you wish with them." Elsam interrupted their study of Vanya.

Grabbed from behind, hauled to their feet, they were both propelled towards the stairs at the far end of the room. Thalia kept her eyes on Bet, who was roughly picked up by another guard. Not caring how he handled her, he half-dragged her body along. With no escape, they allowed themselves to be manhandled down the stairs. Going down one level, they were ushered down a stone-walled corridor. Myrick stopped in front of a heavy wooden door. One of the guards pushed through to use a key to unlock the cell.

Wasting no time on niceties, Myrick called to his men to lock them in. Without a backward glance, he left them to the mercy of the guards. Rider was thrown in, landing near the back wall of the bathroom-sized room. Thalia gave them no chance to touch her again.

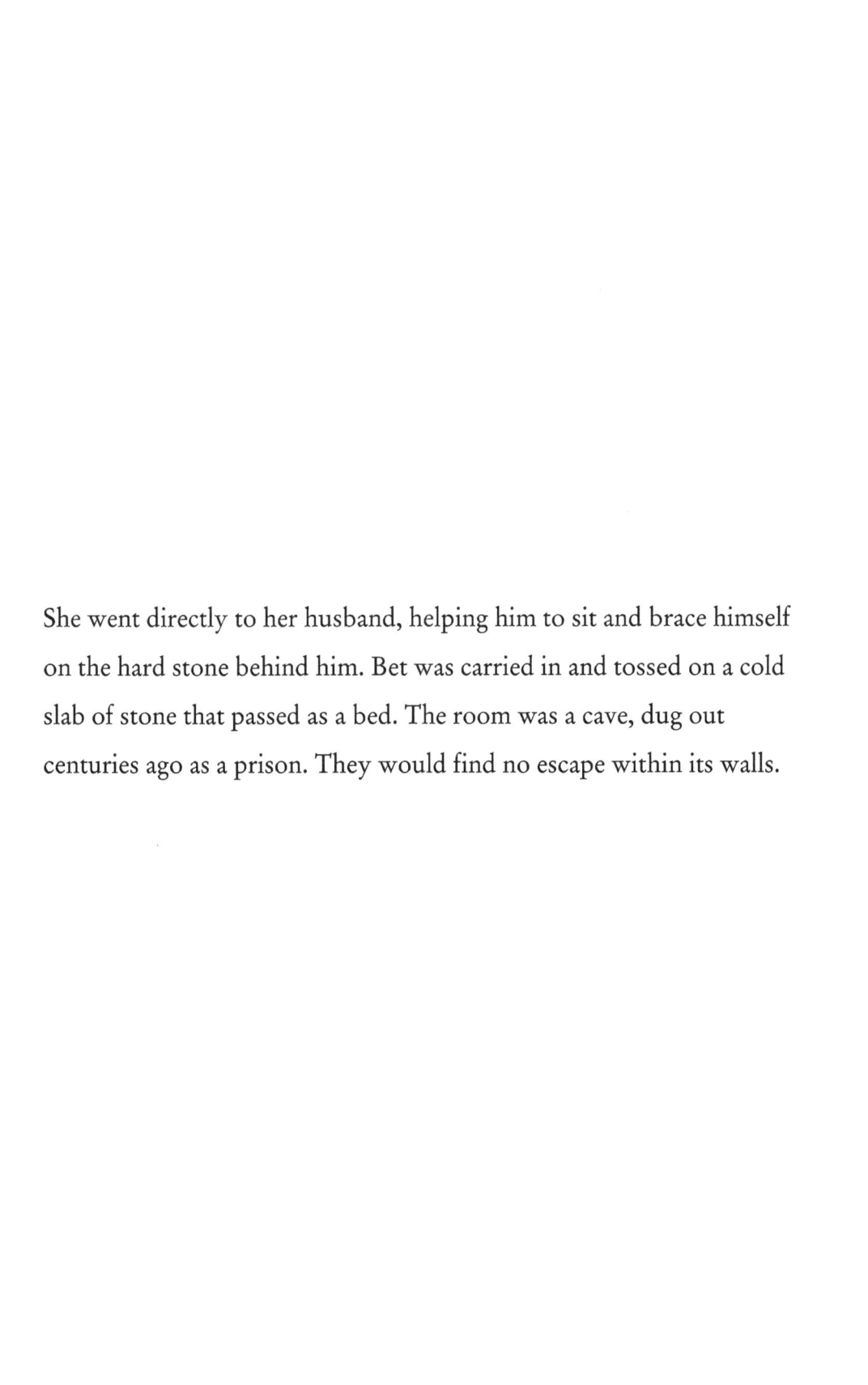

She went directly to her husband, helping him to sit and brace himself on the hard stone behind him. Bet was carried in and tossed on a cold slab of stone that passed as a bed. The room was a cave, dug out centuries ago as a prison. They would find no escape within its walls.

Chapter 20

Alexa

February was upon us. Christmas and the New Year passed without notice. I was not sure if the Sidhe even celebrated these holidays. Did they have the same beliefs as humans, or witches, or did they follow some other deity? Most certainly, everyone had forgotten whatever faith they believed. Four months ago my life had been uneventful. Since then, time had simply flown by. So much had happened that I was only just realizing the extent of my altered reality. Life as I knew it had ended.

Alone, in my room, I took stock of my life. Aside from the poor handling of my being joined with Aidan, I stubbornly dragged Liam into my indecision. I should never have encouraged my attraction to him. That I was feeling the pressure of what I had to do was obvious in the way I was losing the battle over controlling my powers. My emotions were all over the place. One moment scared, the next angered, I was discharging energy whenever my mood changed. Everyone stayed clear of me. I could not blame them.

Liam was still gone. Days went by with no word from him. Whatever was going on with him, the change in him was alarming. His personality had gone through a transformation. He was not Liam. What it meant, what caused it, was anybody's guess. Without him there, it was impossible for Eliana to get a sense of what possessed him. I was anxiously waiting for him to return.

His parents were frantic over both of their sons. With both Aidan and Liam missing, we had no idea what to do. My parents' disappearance, along with Bet's, added to our frayed nerves. The only bright light was Elron's return. I hoped he would know how to find them. We desperately needed his help.

Arriving with Tory, he let me read the letter his father had left for him. The time frame of when to act was spelled out for us. I had another four months to find the Kaemorra and use it. The summer solstice was our deadline. After reading it, I was left with more questions. If his parents were truly ancients, why did they leave? Why did they not stay to help us? How was Tory involved in this?

The brothers had no answers for us. They were as much in the dark as we were. Finding out he had no family, that Elron was not his real brother, had left Tory morose. I longed to see his sweet smile again. The marks on his body from being attacked by Daimons had healed completely. What the beings were was still a mystery to me. I needed to ask Eliana about them.

Elron did not need to be told that Bet had taken off again. He knew immediately after re-appearing on the grounds that she was not there. His stoic, reserved nature gave away nothing of what he was feeling. I tried to make excuses for her, but he would not discuss it further. Instead, he focused on our need to find everyone. Filling him in on where they went and why, he left us to plan our next steps. He had since been cloistered with Tory in the library for hours.

I glanced down at the object I held in my hand. Sitting on my bed, I stared into the opened jeweled box, hoping to catch sight of any one of those who were missing. Inside, the space lay empty, no trace of them could be found. Closing the lid, I got up to place it on my bedside table. I walked over to the window, looking down at the empty garden. The cobblestones were wet from a late afternoon rain. Clouds were dispersing, allowing the sun's rays to lighten the day. Below me, no one was about.

The remnants of the damage I had caused to the area were still visible. There was nothing that could wash away the grayish streaks I had blasted into the pavement. Everyone was indoors somewhere. A wind kicked up dirt in the spot near the fountain. Where one moment it had been vacant, the next moment Liam stood where my eyes rested. Instantly, I raced down the stairs, leaving the house and running up to him. Pleased to see him, I put my arms around him, resting my cheek against his chest. Stiff and unyielding, his arms stayed at his sides.

"Have you come to your senses yet?" His cold voice reached my ears.

I stiffened at his words. Stepping away from him, my arms fell listlessly to my sides. I frowned at the malice he projected. I took another step back, as his arm reached out for me. Where was my Liam? Who was this man in front of me? His emerald eyes turned a murky green. The way he regarded me left me cold. There was no warmth to him.

"Aidan is not coming back. Deal with it. You are mine." The words passed his lips, showing no emotion.

A cold shiver ran down my spine. His arms tried to grab me, as I made to get away from him. Escaping, I ran back into the house, away from the stranger who occupied Liam's body. I had to find Eliana. Hopefully she would know what was wrong with him. The person I ran into was Rina. She was coming down the stairs. One look at me and she could see my distress. She met me at the bottom of the stairs, asking me what was wrong. Filling her in on Liam's arrival, she went past me to see him. I continued on my search for Eliana.

Finding her in her room, seated by the window, I entered without knocking. Her window faced the opposite side of the garden and from what I could tell she was unaware of her son's arrival. I saw she was tilted to the side, her brow creased, concentrating on what a vision was showing her.

The sound of my entering focused her eyes on me. Seeing me standing in the doorway, upset, she came to me and in a startling move, wrapped her arms around me. It was the first time she had ever shown me any kindness. She turned her head back to the window, her eyes narrowing on sensing Liam.

"We will figure it out." She tried to reassure me.

Close to tears, I tried to rein in my emotions and simply nodded my head at her. Eliana pulled me to the settee by the window. Sitting us both on its plush pillows, she took my hands in hers. Whatever she was going to say was put off by Rina running into the room. Rushing to us, her face full of fear, she dropped to the floor, on her knees, in front of us.

"He is not Liam. There is something controlling him." Rina exclaimed, her panic palpable.

Hearing the catch in her voice, I felt my own anxiety increase at what she said. Eliana was staring off, her eyes clouded, trying to see if she could discern what had Liam in its possession. Rina was focusing her own energy to find an answer. My own visions, powers were dormant. I only had one way to see, to know, what had Liam in its clutches. I needed to see him for myself again.

Without warning, I took off, running back to the garden. I could hear Eliana calling me to come back. Ignoring her, I ran out to see Liam again. I found him leaning on one of the trees, on the path to the forest, as if waiting for me.

"I knew you couldn't stay away." His voice mocked me.

Words left me at the hateful look on his face. I was struck mute as he advanced on me. The look in his eyes frightened me. Nearing me, he laughed at my terror-stricken expression. His hand grabbed my forearm before I could get away. He hauled me up against him, his lips crushing down on mine, painfully bruising them. I struggled to break his hold.

It was no use, he was much stronger than I was. Beating at him with my hands, pushing at his chest, did nothing to stop his manhandling me. Going limp in his arms, he finally realized he was getting no reaction from me. He angrily pushed me away like a rag doll. I fell, landing on my behind on the ground. Towering over me, he sneered down at me.

"Poor Alexa, you chose the wrong brother." He taunted me.

I crawled backward away from him. He followed me, as I tried to put distance between us. I did not want to hurt him, but my fingers itched to throw a bolt of lightning at him. Control was slipping away. Jumping to my feet, Rina's approach drew his attention. He regarded her with no emotion. She, on the other hand, her face hard with fury, was striding towards us. I placed myself between them, frightened of what he would do to her.

My back to Liam, I saw Rina gasp, her eyes widening in terror. Before I knew it, I felt an excruciating pain in my upper back. I fell to my knees, my vision blurring from the agonizing sensation. A burning traveled down by back, my knees gave out at the tightness in my chest. Prone on the ground, I lay face down almost losing consciousness. My vision faded in and out. The pain retreated to a dull throbbing. Elron's face came into view, creased with worry.

"Stay down. Eliana is coming. She will heal you." His words made no sense to me.

He gently held me down when I tried to rise. Eliana appeared next to me, replacing Elron. My eyes were losing focus on the world around me. I was going numb. Coldness seeped into my bones. Shivering, my breath was raspy and my lungs hurt from the effort of dragging in air. My limbs refused to respond to my will. With my cheek on the cobblestones, I tried to make sense of what was happening to me.

I felt Eliana's hand come to rest on my back. Her touch seemed to lessen the pain. Focusing her energy, she closed her eyes, her hand now hovering over my shoulder. I had no idea what had caused me to fall. Where had the pain come from? Eliana opened her eyes, grabbing for my hand to help me up. On my feet, I swayed unsteadily.

"Where is your blade? The healing stone in it should always be with you." Elron's words were laced with exasperation. He looked past me, his scornful stare drawing my eyes to what he was focused on.

Behind me, Liam lay on the ground, held down by a force field. It sparked as he fought against it. In his hand, a blade, covered in my blood, was still pushing to find me. His stare was menacing. Eliana walked closer to where he lay, bringing her palm to rest on the energy surrounding him. Whatever she did, Liam crumpled to the ground, all fight leaving him. Unmoving, he lay as if asleep, the blade falling out of his grip.

"What happened?" Did Liam really try to harm me?

Rina explained how Liam came at me with the knife. Caught by surprise, she had been unable to stop him. She barely had time to raise a shield when it looked like he would stab me again. Elron came upon us by chance. He had been out walking the grounds. Calling Eliana, he had put pressure on my wound, staving the flow of blood.

I watched, uneasy, where Liam lay unconscious from what Eliana had done. Was he hurt? I went to join her, standing over him, both of us troubled. He looked so peaceful, it was hard to imagine he had purposely tried to harm me. I knelt down next to him. Placing my hand on his chest, I felt the rise and fall of his breath.

"We need your mother, Alexa. I can't see what has taken hold of him." Eliana told me.

"It is the darkness in him. It's been there since he was touched by the shadow." Rina was studying Liam from a distance.

All this time, and we had not made the connection. I attributed his change to how I kept him at bay. Thinking that I was the cause, for not choosing him over Aidan, I believed that Liam was angry because of me. How were we to save him? I stood up, waiting for someone to offer a solution.

"Let the field go, Rina. He won't be waking anytime soon. I will take him up to one of the bedrooms." Elron spoke to Rina.

Upon dropping the energy, Elron heaved Liam onto his shoulder, carrying him inside. I followed him up the stairs, watching as he deposited Liam on his bed. I drew up a chair, sitting down next to him, taking his unresponsive hand in mine. I could suddenly sense the surge of darkness rising to reclaim him. Even in that state, he was fighting the attack from within. I felt his self-condemnation at having hurt me. The wound in my back no longer gave me any pain. Whatever Eliana had done, it seemed as if it were completely healed.

"Liam, I will fix this." I whispered, lowering my head to his ear.

Not knowing how, but willing to try anything, I placed my hand on his chest, over his heart. Elron stood ready to pull me away on the other side of the bed. Aware of Eliana's presence in the doorway, I kept my focus on Liam.

Black-veined tendrils were wrapped around his heart. They almost completely covered it in their mass. I reached in, my senses humming in response. Feeling my way into Liam's essence, I pulled at the strands. Sensing what I was attempting, they fought back, wrapping themselves more firmly around his core.

How was I to remove them? I studied their makeup, the way they responded to my nearness. They moved away from where my hand rested on Liam's chest. I focused on the dark mass, realizing what I needed to do. It would be dangerous. I did not know if they would consume me, as they had Liam.

With my hand still on his chest, I found a tendril and pulled. It unwound, entering my forefinger. I pulled harder, drawing the darkness, one strand at a time, into myself. I watched as they snaked their way out of Liam. The veins in my hand were coal colored, as they wound their way through me.

Finally, the last coil left him, entering me with a vicious snap. Irrational rage consumed me, my body trembled from the outright hatred I felt. How did Liam manage to function with this inside him? I was being bombarded by images of those closest to me, betraying me, laughing at my ineptness. Their voices were condemning, blaming me for all that had taken place. They rose in volume, filling me with their censure. My hands grabbed at my head. I must have screamed in agony and fallen to the floor from the sights and sounds that overtook me.

Writhing on the floor, Elron was holding me down, as I fought to escape him. Eliana had made it to the bed, where Liam was now sitting up. She was trying to hold him back. Her attempt was unsuccessful. Liam dropped to the floor beside me, his body covering the length of mine. I pushed and struggled to get him away from me. Growling, I shoved at him. Straddling me, he held my arms to my sides so I could not use my hands. The tips of my fingers had bluish streaks of electricity forming.

"Alexa, honey, please stay with me. You can do this." Liam yelled above the snarling sounds I was making.

How could I fight this? Liam grabbed my face, forcing me to

stare into his eyes. I was mesmerized by the deepening emerald color. His pupils dilated, making me still under his gaze.

Somewhat calmer, the voices faded slightly. It would not take much to make them rise again. Liam held my attention. His essence was surrounding him, creating a piercing white aura around him.

I focused all my senses on the light emanating from him. His goodness, kindness drew me like a moth to a flame. The darkness in me shrieked at the rays of light that were infusing my being. The bright white glow spread, wrapping itself around me and Liam. Once it encompassed us, the light created a burst of energy that exploded out of me.

Electricity traveled its way through my body. As the force blew out, waves of black threads left my body. They floated above me, searching for a way to re-enter me. As they descended towards me, a bolt surged out of me, catching them in its power. As I collapsed from exhaustion, I saw the dark cloud disperse, its existence destroyed.

Liam's weight on me grew heavy. Noticing I had trouble breathing, he balanced himself on his arms. We silently stared at each other. He repositioned himself beside me, his hand caressing my cheek. His smile was easy, his eyes softened, as they continued to look into mine. Liam was back. I had managed to extricate the evil that had taken possession of him. He rose to help me up. The floor underneath me was stained crimson from my bloodied shirt.

"Don't. It's not your fault." I told him, seeing his eyes cloud with guilt.

Dragging his eyes away from the evidence of what he had done, he extended his hand out to me. I took it without hesitation. As I stood up, I gave him a trusting smile. Tiredness made me wobbly on my feet. Lifting me into his arms, he deposited me on the bed, stretching out beside me. Elron and Eliana were gone. The door to the room was shut.

"I'll get you something to eat. You need sugar." Liam, supporting himself on his elbow, was leaning over me.

"Later." I managed to get out, before my eyes drifted closed and I lost myself to sleep.

Chapter 21

Thalia

With no natural light, it was impossible to see the extent of the damage. A single bulb overhead, centered in their cell, was the only one she had to work with. The shadow she cast bending over Bet did not help matters. A deep gash on Bet's arm was bleeding out. Her body showed multiple contusions. Thalia could not make out the difference between bruises and dirt on the young woman's face. Her left eye was swollen shut. Running her hands down Bet's body, Thalia was thankful no bones were broken. The child inside her lay motionless.

Continuing to bleed, the gash on her arm was the worst of her injuries. Thalia had torn off a strip of her shirt as a tourniquet. The wound was not healing itself, however. There was not much else Thalia could do. Putting pressure on it only caused Bet more pain. The young woman moaned hoarsely whenever Thalia tried to staunch the blood. Writhing on the cold slab she lay on, Bet's body shivered dangerously.

Thalia touched her palm to Bet's forehead, growing increasingly concerned by her rising fever. Myrick had taken great pleasure in torturing the young woman. Thalia had no idea what he had done to Bet. Every couple of hours, guards appeared to drag Bet out. They returned her, each time in worse shape. *How much more can she endure?* Thalia shuddered to think.

Rider was pacing their cell deep in thought. He spanned the space in two strides in either direction. The tight area gave him no room to release his tension. He had been trying to reach their friends since they had been thrown into the cell. Unable to reach anyone, Rider was furtively watching the door. He expected the guards to appear any moment to take Bet again. Without any weapons, he felt useless. Every now and then, he would tensely look at his wife, worried she would be taken next.

Deep beneath the tower, the cold, stone-faced cell offered no solutions to their situation. Spelled with magic, whenever they tried to break through the door, the walls drew closer around them. They had already lost several inches of space. In the cramped area, they could not afford to lose anymore.

Bet's squirming drew Thalia's attention again. Her eyes were half-open, unfocused. Mumbling incoherently, she was covered in sweat. Thalia reached out to touch her cheek, trying to heal her again. Any powers she possessed were drained by the force field that covered the area. The walls moved another inch closer at her attempt.

She felt pathetically ineffectual. She could do nothing but watch the blood seep out of Bet and drip down the slab onto the floor. Bet's body trembled. On the hard surface of her resting place, Thalia watched the young woman begin to shiver uncontrollably. With no blanket to cover her, Thalia lay next to her, offering Bet her own body heat. Wrapping her in her arms, she pulled Bet closer, trying to still her shivers.

"Thalia, tell Elron I'm sorry." Bet breathlessly spoke through chattering teeth.

"You will tell him yourself. Don't you dare give up!" Thalia gripped her tighter.

Bet gave no response. She fell unconscious. Thalia took her pulse, making sure Bet was still alive. Her hand went to Bet's belly, feeling no movement from the child. She had no idea how it was doing. Bet's baby had to be under great strain from what its mother was enduring. Thalia's distress quickly changed to anger.

If there was one thing she would do, above all else, when a chance presented itself, was make Myrick pay. The traitor to his people would suffer greatly once she got her abilities back.

Giving up was not an option. Thalia would prevail. All of them would. *Rider and Bet will be fine*, she thought. She would make sure of it. Her musings were interrupted by the sounds of footsteps nearing them from outside. Rider went over to his wife, holding her back when she stood up. Keeping her within his arms, they waited apprehensively.

The door opened, squeaking on its hinges. Two guards entered and took positions on either side of the door. A third guard blocked the exit. He stood to the side allowing Myrick to step into the room. The warlock took in their demeanor with a sneer on his lips. His eyes traveled to Bet. Seeing she was passed out, he called the guards to take

Rider instead.

Thalia cried out, kicking the first guard who took hold of Rider. Rider yelled at her to stop. The guard she attacked slapped her hard across the face, making Thalia's ears ring, as she fell to the floor. Rider continued to yell at her to stop, to stay back. Myrick laughed at the commotion.

Rider was propelled out of the room by the other two guards. The one Thalia had hit, gave her a final kick in the ribs before following the others out. Thalia landed hard on the floor, gasping for breath. She could only watch, as Rider was forced out. The door slamming shut echoed through the cell.

Alone, her face throbbing from the hit, she sat huddled in the corner of the cell. She cried tears of defeat. *Will we ever make it out of here?* Time passed slowly. How long Rider was taken for, she had no idea. Only the need to take care of Bet made her get control of herself. She went to Bet, lying down beside her again. Weariness overtook her.

Bone tired, she fell asleep. The sound of the hinges moving again brought her back to awareness. A shape was thrown into the cell. Fully awakened by the slamming of the door, Thalia saw Rider land on the floor. Eyes closed, breathing shallowly, he lay unmoving in a heap. Thalia jumped from the bed, dropping down next to her husband.

A deep wound on his cheek was still bleeding. His right eye was swollen, blackened from repeated punches. Thalia examined him further, looking to see what other injuries he had sustained. Her hands ran down his body, feeling a cracked rib, more bruising on his legs, a welt on his chest.

Her powers were useless to heal him. Elsam had effectively barred their use of magic. She screamed her frustration. Swearing loudly, she dragged Rider over to the wall. Once he was braced there, she tore off her sleeve to wipe away the blood on his face. If this continued, she would have no clothing left.

"I'll be good as new before you know it." Rider was smiling up at her.

Confound the man! It was not the time to tease her. She needed her anger to keep her going. Sensing his wife's irritation, Rider straightened himself up. With his arm, he pulled her to him, holding her close. He knew she was terrified for him and Bet.

We will find a way out. When he felt her relax against him, he closed his eyes, grateful that so far they had not taken her to be tortured. Thalia stayed by his side, needing his strength. She knew the exact moment sleep claimed him. The only sound in the room was Rider and Bet's heavy breathing. Bet had still not woken. Rest was the best thing for both of them. *Who knows how long before they come back for Bet or Rider. Or will they take me next?*

Inching away from Rider, making sure he did not wake up, she went over to check on Bet. Her fever was still high, but the shivering had stopped. She was peacefully sleeping. The bleeding on her arm had stopped as well. Unable to do more for her, Thalia returned to Rider. She sat next to him as he found oblivion in sleep. She tried to use her magic, testing the strength of the field that blocked her.

Surprised and suspicious at what she sensed, she retried by focusing her energy on Rider. *Can it be possible? There it was.* Why she suddenly had access to her healing gift, she did not stop to ask. She turned her hands to Rider, letting the energy flow into him. Drawing back from her full power, she healed him just enough to take the pain away. His being fully cured would give her away. However it was possible, she needed to keep the secret for now. Thalia went to Bet next. She let her energy revive Bet just enough to keep her and the baby safe.

With them still sleeping, all Thalia could do was wait. She needed to discuss it with Rider. Maybe he had access to his powers as well. She glanced at Bet, wondering if that was why her arm had stopped bleeding. *Is she healing herself?*

Something must have happened or someone was helping them. It was the only logical explanation. *Has something happened to Elsam's protection?* She would have to test it again, but for now she would rest. Lying back down, she nestled into the curve of Rider's body, taking comfort from his nearness. Her thoughts briefly drifted to Alexa before sleep took her. *Alexa has to be kept away from here.*

Chapter 22

Alexa

A bee hovered over the oleander shrub, which was resplendent with cherry-colored blossoms. The bee's rapid wing beat could be heard, as air was dispersed by the bee's flight. For the last fifteen minutes, I had been following its trajectory, as the bee flitted to and fro above the overgrown bush. I had nothing else to do. Nature had a way of calming me, keeping me grounded from the premonitions I was having.

I knew we were in trouble and that we needed help. Rina was presently in the center of the field, where she had been concentrating for hours. She was motionless, staring up at the sky. The mangled, pressed flowers that had shown her footfalls stood magically restored to their former shapes. I sat under a tree near the clearing, my mind on our missing family. We had not had any word from my parents and Bet.

Rina was trying to contact her mother again. So far, there had been no response. Watching her frustration grow as time passed, I could do little to offer support. It was something only she could do. From behind me, the sound of someone approaching interrupted my thoughts. I did not have to turn to recognize who it was. Liam was back to his easygoing self.

Trying to make up for how he had acted, he went out of his way to be accommodating. No matter how many times I told him I did not blame him for attacking me, he still could not forgive his actions. When I looked at Liam, I saw Aidan's face staring back at me accusingly. Liam would always remind me of the mess I had made of everything. I could not look at him without wishing that his brother was beside me. I wanted Aidan back.

Whether it was our being joined, or that I honestly longed for him, was immaterial. He was essential to my life. I could not go forward, continue on our quest, without him. Where he was, if he was hurt were questions driving me to distraction. It was just one of the reasons I was anxious about the mission Elron had undertaken.

He had left earlier in the morning accompanied by his brother, Tory. After hours of arguing my case for going with them, I was forcefully held back by Rina. My outrage at Eliana ordering Rina to enclose me in an inescapable field of energy had dwindled down to annoyance. I understood their reasoning, but I still felt affronted by their behavior. Elron's solemn promise that he would bring everyone back gave me hope.

Seeing his fierce determination, I could not doubt he would do everything in his power to make it true. When he left, I saw him off alone. There was something I needed to give him, something I felt Aidan needed as proof of my commitment. I had pierced my thumb with my blade, letting drops of my blood collect in a small vial. Sealing it, I then placed the glass tube in Elron's hand, closing his fingers around it.

"Give this to Aidan when you find him. Tell him I am waiting." I squeezed his hand.

Elron understood what I needed of him. He nodded and, without a word, inserted the vial in his pocket. His hands came up to lightly rest on my shoulders, but whatever he was going to say, Tory interrupted. Dropping his hands and taking a step back, Elron waited for his brother to reach us. Tory stepped closer, smiling with his usual lopsided grin.

Now that I knew they were not related, I was not surprised they had nothing physically in common. They were opposites in fact. Elron was tall, over six-feet, four-inches tall actually. His body was well-muscled and imposing. His long blond hair fell past his shoulders, tracing his square jaw.

Tory on the other hand was less than six feet. I would say he barely passed five-feet, eight-inches in height. His muscles were less pronounced. He was slight in build. His hair was a deep chocolate brown, cut short, and he was baby-faced. The only thing they shared was the deep emerald eyes I had come to associate with the Sidhe. Why they both had that feature was a mystery. We had no idea what or who Tory was.

Elron waited patiently for his brother to make his way over to us. Once he had reached us, they wasted no time in departing. Elron simply bowed his head, gave me a small salute and they both vanished. I prayed they would be successful.

Shaking myself out of my remembrances, I got to my feet as Liam neared. I could see Rina was still at it. How much longer was she going to attempt to get her mother's attention? Maybe, with Liam's help, I could get her to take a break. I waited for him to reach me, so we could speak with her together.

When he was standing in front me, his arms went around me, pulling me against his firm chest. He rested his chin on the top of my head. His steady heartbeat, his comforting embrace, steadied me. I could not help but think if things were different, he would be everything I would ever need. If only we had met under different circumstances. He held me in a comfortable silence, as we both stared off into the distance, not saying a word. Only when I felt his mother's presence did I gently pull out of his arms.

"Liam, your father needs you in the library." Her voice held no condemnation at how she had found us.

Liam left me, giving me a final pensive look before going to his father. He had not mentioned how he felt about me since his recovery. Putting no pressure on me, he simply stayed close in case I needed him. I was torn again. Seeing him back to his old self, I was reminded of all that had attracted me to him.

The only thing that kept me from acting on it was the constant reminder of Aidan. The hollowness in my chest could not be ignored. With each passing hour, the emptiness I felt was spreading more and more through my being. How I really felt about them both was impossible to tell. Until Aidan was back, I could not make any decisions.

"How long has she been at it?" Eliana stared at the spot Rina occupied.

"Since early this morning." I glanced up at the sky, seeing that the sun was already past its peak.

She motioned for me to sit. We sat down together, using the large trunk of the tree for support. Conversation between us was still difficult. Although she had been supportive lately, I still held back from confiding in her. Sitting in silence, we watched Rina, her eyes closed and face turned towards the sun.

We had no word on whether Meredith would agree to see us. Since the last appearance of Rina's mother, we had no news from her. The guards she posted on the estate when I left for Crete were nowhere to be found. They had returned to wherever they came from. Rina was desperate to hear from her mother, to find out if Meredith had been located. We needed help. I had no idea what to do, where to go from there. With the Kaemorra still hidden from me, the summer solstice was looming closer.

"It will all work out." Eliana's words cut into my thoughts.

"Do you see something I don't? My visions have stopped. Since helping Liam, my powers have diminished. Every attempt to use my magic seems to weaken them further." Even now I could feel my power waning.

"The longer Aidan is away, the more you will feel the effects. You are tied together. He is probably experiencing the same thing. I only meant that things have a way of working out. I have to believe we will prevail. Anything else would be disastrous." Her explanation did not put me at ease.

If I knew anything, it was that things had a way of going wrong where I was involved. A niggling sensation crawled up my spine. My back stiffened when the sensation reached the back of my neck. Something was seriously wrong. The loss of my powers was not just because of Aidan. Something else was causing it. Brushing aside my negative thoughts, I took no comfort from Eliana's words. I continued to watch Rina. From the corner of my eye, I caught Eliana turn towards me, her expression serious.

"Both my sons are exceptional men. Where Liam is blessed with an easy, joyous outlook on life, Aidan is more reserved, serious. I love them both equally. For the longest time, knowing that Aidan would be taken from me, I tried to feel nothing for him. I blame myself for the way he carries himself. It was not easy for him, growing up with me as a mother. I put so much pressure on him, to be better, to be stronger. He has been burdened with this prophesy since his birth. I certainly did not make things easier for him. Aidan has gone through life not feeling love, not from me or the women who latched onto him due to his title. What he feels for you, he does not know how to handle. In the beginning, he probably thought it was just the bond, like you assumed. Alexa, the bond does not happen between two people who cannot love one another. It is there to strengthen the love that already exists. Not accepting Aidan into your heart is a losing battle. Don't wait too long to let him in." Her warning washed over me.

Could it be so simple? Why then did I want to fight against being forced to accept the inevitable? Was it stubbornness that made me want to turn to Liam? I could go crazy trying to figure out my motives. Having said her peace, Eliana got to her feet. She brushed her dress to wipe off any grass that was clinging. She left me with more to ponder than I had already been weighing. In the field, Rina gave no indication that she had noticed anyone's comings or goings.

I turned my thoughts away from the two men who were constantly keeping me unsettled. Trying to clear my head was nearly impossible. Worry over my parents, Bet and Aidan could not be easily brushed aside. No word had come from Elron on whether he had found them. As long as they were missing, I could not rest. A sudden movement from the field drew my attention.

From up above, I saw a twinkle of light brighten the clear blue sky. Descending, it wound its way towards Rina. Finally, I thought.

Jumping to my feet, I raced across the field just as it hovered in front of Rina. Eliana, who was nearly at the terraced garden, halted her steps, returning to the edge of the tree line just as a figure started coalescing in front of me. Rina's mother stood before us, finally. Anxious to hear news of Meredith, I took a step towards her.

"Daughter. Alexa." She acknowledged us. "Why have you called me?"

Rina pulled me out of her way, taking my place to address her mother. Whatever she was going to say was cut off by the arrival of another being. Facing what could only be another god, the man towered over all of us. He must have been well over eight-feet tall, he was bare-chested with only a tunic covering his lower body. His well-defined chest swelled with each breath he took. Long muscular legs peeked out from beneath the tunic. On his feet, sandals were tied up to his calves. His arms were massive, his biceps bulging even in repose.

"Father." Rina addressed him.

"Daughter, I could not let your mother have the pleasure of seeing you again without me." His enormous arms surrounded Rina, almost completely hiding her from view.

I waited patiently for the family reunion to be over. Rina was released from his embrace, staggering back from suddenly being freed. He put his hand on her head, steadying her, as if she were a doll. Slapping his hand away, Rina ignored him and spoke to her mother.

"Have you managed to communicate with Meredith? Is she willing to see us?"

Her father smiled at me, while reaching out to touch my head. The size of the man's hand had me backing away. He could grab me and hide me in his palm. Showing irritation at my retreat, he lost his smile, and took a step towards me. Rina, seeing my predicament, placed herself between us.

"Father, please don't hurt Alexa." She admonished him.

Surprised at her words, he stopped, noticing my look of fear. Contriteness entered his eyes. In a sulk, he sat down sharply, causing the earth to tremble beneath us. Rina went back to her mother once he had left me alone.

"Meredith has been called home by Rhea. The goddess has forbidden anyone from contacting her. I have no way to pass along a message. I am sorry to report that you are alone." Her mother informed us.

Sighing heavily, I spun around to return to the house. We would get no help from anyone. Heaviness settled around me as hopelessness grew. Stomping across the field, I fell on my behind by the sudden appearance of Rina's mother cutting my escape.

"Time is running out. You must find the Kaemorra soon." Her words made me grimace. She should be telling me something I did not know.

"Any ideas on where I should look? I have none." I looked up at her from the ground.

"You know where. Open your mind, Alexa. The memory is there." She laughed, as she started to fade.

I was not given a chance to ask her what she meant. She was gone. Rina's father rose to his feet, giving us a slight bow and directing a smile to his daughter. Looking up at the sky, he faded, leaving me with another thing to try to figure out.

Chapter 23

Thalia

How long they were held in their prison, was impossible to know. Thalia lost all track of time. There were no windows to let her know if it was day or night. Bet lay unconscious. Another round of torture had completely rendered her senseless. Rider was in a similar state. When one of them was in no condition to be abused, they took the other.

Thalia had not been taken. She had no idea why. Each time Bet or Rider were brought back, Thalia used a portion of her power to heal them, just enough for it not to be noticeable. Rider told her they asked no questions, only took pleasure torturing them.

Bet's fever was raging again. Her fetus was struggling. Sitting beside her, Thalia placed her hand on Bet's belly, healing the child as much as she could. So much anger was brewing in her that her hands were trembling. They would all pay.

Thalia would find a way to punish each and every one of those responsible. She would start with Myrick, the warlock who had betrayed his kind. The many ways she was imagining hurting him were broken off by Rider awakening. She moved to his side. Her hand stroked his face, his weak smile bringing tears to her eyes.

"How is she?" He wanted to know.

"I don't know how much more she can take." Thalia whispered.

Rider tried to sit up. The effort caused him enormous pain. He gritted his teeth, as the laceration on his chest started bleeding again. Thalia helped him by grabbing him under his arms. Once he had settled back, braced against the wall, she saw to the wound. At her touch, the bleeding stopped, a scab forming over the cut. Rider grabbed her hand, bringing it to his lips. His soft kiss caused Thalia to let go of the tears she had been holding back. She sat next to him, cuddling into his side, as he held her.

"Why haven't they taken me? Why only you and Bet?" Thalia cried on his shoulder.

"I'm just thankful you have been spared."

Brushing the tears from her face, Thalia drew back so she could look at her husband. She would switch places with them in a second if it would help them. Although Rider was able to withstand more than Bet, he would not last much longer.

Bet was the more worrisome of the two. The young woman had not woken in over an hour. *Can I risk healing her some more? Will they notice?* Leaving Rider's side, she went back to Bet, using her senses to see the injuries she had sustained. Finding ones that she could heal without detection, she went about her work.

Finishing up, the sound of someone coming to the door made her stand to face whoever it was. She would not allow them to take Bet or Rider again. She would fight them. She ran to Rider's side when she saw him attempting to get to his feet. Holding him back, she blocked him from seeing who was coming. As she faced the door, the key turning in the lock had her eyeing it furiously. They would not take either one that time. Thalia would offer herself instead.

The door creaked open, allowing light from outside to filter through the room. In the doorway, Vanya hesitated to enter. Seeing Rider, bloodied and bruised, Thalia could see the woman was uncomfortable with what she saw. Without saying a word, she went directly to Bet. Thalia was kept back by Rider. Suspicious of what Vanya would do, Thalia struggled to free herself from Rider's hold.

Her narrowed eyes watched Vanya's hand touch Bet's forehead. The other woman sat down beside Bet. Vanya was doing her best to push aside her bitterness at what she was sensing. The woman was agitated at seeing Bet in that condition. Thalia saw a whitish glow form where she was touching Bet.

Whatever Vanya was doing, Bet was slowly recovering. The bruises covering her body were slowly fading. Vanya removed her hand and inserted it into her jacket pocket. From within it, she drew out a flat white-colored stone. She then put it into Bet's pant pocket. The healing stone would finish reviving Bet.

Next, Vanya came hesitantly towards Rider. Thalia was too

stunned at seeing her helping them to think about protecting her husband. Vanya took Rider's hand, opening his palm. She placed another healing stone on it, closing his fingers around it. Rider was staring incomprehensibly at her. Finally, Thalia shook herself out of her shock, attacking Vanya with her fists. She punched Vanya in the face, and then placed continuous punches on her chest. Vanya did not fight back.

"Fight you bitch!" Thalia screamed at her.

Rider pulled Thalia away from Vanya, restricting her in his arms. Vanya just stared at them. Breaking eye contact, she returned to Bet. Thalia watched her, as she checked to make sure Bet was healing. Relief showed on her face. Thalia was bewildered at her actions.

"What is this? Are you trying to give us a false sense of hope?" Thalia accused her.

Vanya said nothing. Her focus was on Bet. Thalia saw Bet visibly recovering from her wounds. Rider, beside her, was also showing a marked improvement. The gash on his chest was a thin line. His bruised face was repairing itself. Thalia had no idea why Vanya was helping them.

"I have to get you out before they come back." Vanya finally said.

Rider was guarded, suspicion showing on his face. Thalia was not ready to trust Vanya either. Getting up from where she was crouched next to Bet, Vanya faced them. She could see their distrust. Thalia's eyes were drawn to Bet, who seemed to be waking.

"She'll have to be carried. Rider, I think you should be able to carry her. Thalia, I know you don't trust me, but I will get you out." Vanya insisted.

Rider went to Bet, carefully gathering her in his arms. Vanya stepped to the door, peering outside to make sure the coast was clear. Waving her hand for them to follow, she exited the cell. Thalia raised an eyebrow at Rider, who tilted his head for her to go. They had no choice but to follow Vanya. If they wanted to escape that hell, they would have to believe she meant to help.

Winding their way through dimly lit corridors, Vanya would stop at times to make sure they were not being followed. Endless stairs lay between them and the outside world. Making it up to the main floor, Vanya went through the throne room, to the back wall. The tower was empty. *Where could everyone be?*

Thalia had no time to get an answer. Vanya held her hand up to stop them. Pulling a lever, the wall opened up to a secret passage. Guiding them through, she entered last, pushing the wall back in place. In the dark, Thalia drew on her powers to create light for them to see with. A long passageway lay before them.

Vanya brushed by them, rushing down the hall. They followed her. Bet moaned softly from the way Rider was gripping her. At the end of the passage, Vanya flung a door open. The sounds of the night reached their ears. Pulling them through, Vanya took a path down towards the water. Waves could be heard splashing the shore. When their feet touched the sand, Vanya stopped and pointed to their left, down to the beach.

"Elron is there searching for you. You should be able to reach him in less than ten minutes. Take care of her. Take her to him." Vanya turned to go back.

"Come with us. You can't stay here." Rider halted her steps.

Vanya looked at them, obviously resigned to her fate. Her place was there. There was no going back for her.

"I have to stay. My son needs me. Elsam already suspects us, but he won't harm us. He needs my son and for that he can't hurt me. Tell Eliana that Elsam has Aidan. I don't know where he is keeping him. I will try to get information and pass it on if I can. Take care." She vanished into the foliage, leaving the three alone on the darkened beach.

Rider quickly took charge, repositioning Bet in his arms. He silently motioned Thalia to go ahead of them. Trudging through the sand, his feet sinking with each step, Rider was losing any strength he possessed. His muscles strained to carry Bet and support his battered body.

Ten minutes later, he sank to his knees completely spent. Bet landed on the sand in a heap. Winded, he fought to catch his breath.

Sweat poured down his body. Thalia was beside him, trying to help any way she could.

Running feet approached them. *Have we gotten this far only to be captured again?* Rider was in no condition to defend himself, let alone Bet and his wife. Defeat settled over him. It was too late, they were caught.

"Bet." Elron's hoarse cry reached him.

Closing his eyes, Rider felt relief flood through him, it was a friend who had found them. Elron fell to his knees beside Bet, pulling her torso up and cradling her in his arms. His hand moved over her face, feeling each cut and abrasion. Fury at finding her like that emanated from him. Her lack of response only made him swear more loudly.

Tory appeared behind him suddenly. He went to Rider, trying to help him, while Elron took care of Bet. Only time would heal the marks he saw on Rider. Elron continued to use words few thought he even knew. His face was dark and vengeful.

"We have to get her back to the estate." Thalia stopped him.

Elron looked over at Rider, who rested on his knees, close to losing consciousness on the sand. Thalia was trying to revive him by using some of her energy. They needed to get them home, cleaned up and tended to. Elron placed Bet gently on the sand. He held onto her hand, while placing his other on Thalia. Rider put his hand on Elron's shoulder. Tory was at the other end of the circle they formed. Thalia saw Elron focus on the path between places. The beach around her faded, replaced by the main room of the estate.

Chapter 24

Liam

Liam found Alexa outside, in the exact spot she had been for the last couple of days. Staring down at the beach, as if his brother would miraculously appear, she had been keeping her emotions bottled up. He thought about leaving her alone, but somehow his legs moved of their own accord towards her. When he reached her, she turned and buried her face in his chest.

Her sobs tore at his heart. Wrapping her gently in his arms, he felt each heave as it left her body. Her tears were not for herself, but for what everyone else had been through. She did not, or could not, see her strength. Liam let her cry, knowing that she needed to let it out.

The cool breeze rolling in from across the lake had Alexa shivering in his arms. Pulling her closer, Liam used his body to shield her from the wind. His own emotions were close to the surface. What he had attempted to do to her was still eating away at him inside. He had almost killed her. He remembered the act of driving the blade into her clearly. It was a memory that he would have to come to terms with.

Right then, all he could do was be there for her. The ugly voices that drove him to do her harm were gone. She had so much to deal with, he wished he could take some of the burden from her. The fact they needed to find the Kaemorra by the summer solstice was still pressing. Deterred for the moment from going after it, Liam thought back on how he had found his sister and Rider bloodied and bruised. Thalia thankfully showed no injuries from their ordeal.

It was by chance that he was in the living room when they appeared. He had sought solace in there, away from everyone. Finding a place where he could be alone was easier said than done. His parents were avoiding each other. That meant if one was in the library, the other was in the living room. For once, when he had entered the main room, he had found it empty. That had been a relief.

He had only just sunk into the couch when he saw the air shimmer, announcing the arrival of Elron and the others. Seeing the state of the injured, he called out for his mother. Bet was lying unconscious on the floor with her head on Elron's lap. Rider was curled up in agony from the numerous cuts that Liam could see all over his body.

Liam immediately went to his sister's side, trying to ascertain how hurt she was. He was pushed away by Elron, who would not let anyone touch her. Eliana tried to pry him away so she could help her daughter. It took both their efforts for Elron to let them see to Bet. Needing something to do, Liam went to Thalia, who was doing her best to aid Rider. Alexa's father was conscious, but in extreme pain and discomfort.

In that mayhem, Alexa had raced into the room, stopping short at the scene before her. Her stricken face was burned in Liam's mind. Standing like a statue, she did not know who to go to first. Liam left Thalia's side to go to Alexa. Putting his arm around her, he guided her to the couch. Her eyes were two round orbs, as she watched helplessly.

Shock rendered her immobile, not knowing what to do. Liam stayed with her, knowing he could do nothing to help the others. Alexa's eyes were glued to her father, who Thalia was attempting to heal. Having done all she could, her mother came to Alexa. She knelt in front of her, wrapping Alexa in her arms while murmuring words of comfort.

Eliana was still looking after Bet. His sister had not moved since appearing. It was decided that they would move her upstairs to her room. Elron lifted her gently, carrying her out. Liam was torn over what to do. Concern for his sister overrode his need to stay with Alexa. He climbed the stairs after them.

In her room, they carefully placed Bet on the bed. Elron would not leave her alone for a second. His mother was able to heal the superficial wounds, but the internal ones were more difficult. Hours were spent focusing on those. Bet finally woke hours later, confused over where she was. Seeing Elron beside her did wonders for her rejuvenating powers. She was recovering well.

The state of her baby was still a cause for concern though. Eliana could hear the heartbeat, but it was faint. Bet needed to gain her strength, so that the child could draw on hers. Sometime in between the hours spent with Bet, Liam also helped take Rider to his own room. The man was still in bad shape. Thalia lay next to him, exhausted and spent from using her magic to heal him.

All that had occurred three days ago. Since then, Alexa had not spoken a word. His eyes would follow her anxiously, as she came and went. What she was thinking or feeling was hidden behind her vacant stare. He could not leave her alone any longer. He needed to do something, anything, to bring her out of her despair.

She stirred in his arms, bringing him back to the present. Over her head, he could see the lake and the mountain range rising from the opposite shore. He caressed her hair, holding her head gently against his chest. Hesitant to let her go, to lose the brief contact, his arms refused to relinquish her.

Closing his eyes, he breathed in her flowery scent. Everything he had done while he was under the shadow's influence had made him keep his distance from her till then. Denying what was in his heart was a losing battle. He would gladly give his life for hers. *If I look into her eyes, what will I see there? If I kiss her, will she respond?*

Sensing Liam's heart beginning to race, Alexa pulled herself out of his arms, turning around to face the lake again. Her soft sigh was the only indication that she was aware of where his thoughts had gone. His hands itched to pull her back. Forcing himself to stand still, he waited as she gazed endlessly across the water. *What is she thinking?* He would give anything to know what she was feeling.

"I can't." She turned to face him. Her hand came up to gently cup his cheek.

She looked panicked. Liam did not want to cause her anymore suffering. She already had so much to deal with. Wanting to ease her distress, he smiled at her, taking her hand from his face. Holding it in his own, his thumb brushed her palm. Her forehead was creased with doubt. His hand lifted her chin, so that she could look into his eyes. What she saw had fresh tears threatening to fall. Bringing his lips to hers, Liam placed a chaste kiss on them. He pulled back, turning her to face the shore. Wrapping his arms around her waist, he simply held her.

"He will be back. When all this is finished, you will know, Alexa." Liam's heart lurched in his chest, already preparing to be broken. It was inevitable who she would choose. Liam believed she was Aidan's. His feelings would have to be pushed back.

Alexa relaxed against him, leaning back so that he supported her weight. They stood like that, at ease with the silence around them, for many hours. Finally, with the sun setting, the air becoming cooler, they returned to the house. In the living room they found his father, sitting alone at the table with a heavy volume opened in front of him.

Asher was back to being a recluse, avoiding his wife and all those around him. He had checked on Bet once, only to assure himself that she was on the mend. The majority of his time he spent in the library again. In there he found the peace that eluded him when forced to face his wife.

"Father." Liam addressed him.

Asher looked up from what he was reading. His eyes were dazed, unfocused, as he took in their arrival. Without a word he went back to reading, not responding to his son. Liam and Alexa exchanged a concerned look. Asher was exhibiting all the signs of someone who had lost the will to participate in life. His isolation was unnerving. Liam would give anything to have his father back. Watching him drift further away from his family was excruciating. He walked over to where his father sat, taking the chair next to him.

Asher gave no indication that he was aware of his son's presence. He continued reading from the book. Alexa, curious over what he was studying, came over to join them. Sitting down on one of the chairs, her hunger had her wishing for something to eat. Instantly half the table transformed, creating heaping plates of differing dishes and sweets. Alexa grabbed a plate, cut a piece of chocolate cake and dug into it.

"Read this." Asher suddenly said, pushing the book towards Liam. Once the book was facing Liam, Asher left the room without a backward glance.

Liam shook his head at his father's retreating back. He frowned, wondering what he could do to help him. The only thing was to try and speak with him later. He turned his attention to the book his father had placed in front of him. He glanced over at Alexa. She was licking her spoon, cleaning the chocolate icing from it. Her eyes were fastened on the open volume. Liam grabbed it, pulling it towards him so he could read. He read aloud so she could hear what it said.

There is a legend of a great crystal holding incredible powers. The book that speaks of it was last seen in the Loch Ness region in the year 1306. All traces of the book have since vanished. Whether it was destroyed to keep it from the hands of the invading English, or hidden elsewhere, I have not been able to discern. In the book, the location of this crystal is in a language no one has been able to decipher. Where most of it was in ancient Gaelic, the passage describing the exact location is a mystery.

"It was written in Sidhe. It must have been." Alexa was excited at what Liam read.

Liam reread the words, coming to the same conclusion as Alexa. If the book were missing, how were they to find it? An expedition was in order. They had to go to Loch Ness to see if they could discover it. Alexa was already on her feet, the cake she had been feasting on forgotten. She was expectantly looking at him to get going.

Liam shook his head at her, pointing for her to take her seat. Begrudgingly, she perched on the chair, resuming taking small bites of her cake. They had to plan. He was not going to go anywhere without a plan. Liam reached out telepathically to call his mother, father, Thalia and Elron. He needed them there, now.

Eliana entered the room first, already aware that they had found a clue. She was followed by Thalia and Elron, who were curious about being summoned. His father stayed away. Intrigued as to why Liam had called them, they each sat down, waiting for an explanation. Liam read them the passage, their reaction confirming his suspicions. It had to be about their Kaemorra.

"We can't go until Bet is well. I am not leaving her behind again." Elron insisted.

"And Rider. We have to wait for him to gain his strength." Thalia added.

Liam agreed with them. He too did not want to leave anyone behind. This time, they had to stay together.

Chapter 25

Elron

The bed shifted under his weight. Carefully, he stretched out on the mattress, bunching the pillow so that his head was elevated. He could not take his eyes off the woman who made his breath catch every time he looked at her. There was no denying that without her he was nothing. Elron lay on his side, his fingers tracing a line down Bet's cheek. Facing towards him, her eyes shut, breathing evenly, she was finally sleeping peacefully.

She lay curled on her side, with a slight smile on her lips. Her hand automatically reached out for him, as if sensing his nearness. Her fingers were gripping his shirt tightly, as if fearing he would leave her side. The bruises on her face were mostly faded. Cracked bones were healed. His child was showing no distress. A week of seeing her tortured by nightmares, thrashing in their bed, had undone him. He wished to take it all on himself. Bet did not deserve to be put through that hell.

He heard the steps coming up outside their door seconds before Thalia opened it slowly. She quietly entered the room, stopping just inside the doorway. Her hand motioned for him to come over. Elron tenderly removed Bet's hand and placed it on the mattress. She moaned at the loss of contact, reaching out for him even in her unconscious state. Rising from the bed, keeping his eyes on her, he stepped to where Thalia waited. He led her out into the hall, closing the door slightly so they would not disturb Bet.

"How is she?" Thalia asked him.

With dark shadows under her eyes, Thalia looked pale and worn out. She had been taking care of Rider, giving all her strength to him. Elron could see the toll it had taken on her. She needed to rest, to recuperate. He knew she would do no such thing, as long as her husband was not healed.

"Much better. How is Rider?" Elron whispered.

"He still has not woken up. I don't know what more I can do for him." Pained, she looked down the corridor towards the closed door where Rider was resting.

Elron followed her eyes, not knowing how he could help. Rider's injuries were slow to heal. Alexa had tried to mend his broken bones and treat his internal bleeding, but her powers were waning. She was slowly becoming human. His own abilities seemed to be non-existent. Eliana tried her own hand for hours, but as far as she could see, Rider was improving, albeit slowly.

"Alexa asked me to tell you that Liam is ready with a plan. We will wait until everyone is able to travel. However long that takes. We will not be separated again." Thalia stressed.

Hopefully it would be soon. Elron knew they were running out of time. Months, that is all they had. Thalia left him to return to her husband's side. He entered his room, lying down beside Bet again. Her hand, instinctively reached for him, touching his stomach to make sure he was there. Elron placed his own hand over hers, closing his eyes, thankful she was still with him.

"What time is it?" Her mellow voice drew his attention.

Beautiful green jeweled eyes were staring at him. A slight smile played on her lips. Elron's eyes softened at seeing her delicate face shine with her loving look. His arm wrapped around her expanding waist, dragging her closer to him. Their bodies touching, Elron kissed her forehead, feeling blessed to have her whole, near him again.

"It's a little after three in the afternoon. Are you thirsty, hungry?" Elron pulled back to look at her.

Bet stretched. Her lithe form rubbing up against him elicited a different reaction from Elron. He growled softly, pushing gently away from her. Getting to his feet, he saw her smile enticingly at him. The woman was still recovering. Bet patted the mattress next to her. Elron shook his head.

"I will get you something to eat. Do not dare move." He quickly left the room, hearing her soft laugh at his escape.

Downstairs, he found the room occupied by Liam and Alexa. The table held the makings of an afternoon snack. Without a word, he went directly to it, piling the first thing his hand could grab onto a plate. Next, he lifted the pitcher holding some type of juice and sniffed it to see what it was. The citrus smell of oranges invaded his nose. Grabbing a glass, he filled it to the rim. Putting everything onto a tray, he started towards the door.

"Hungry?" Liam laughed at him.

"It's for Bet. She's awake." Elron told him, rushing out and back up the stairs.

He found Bet sitting up in bed, waiting for him. She had placed the extra pillow behind her. The sheet covering her was draped just below her waist. Wrinkled and disheveled, she was the most magnificent sight he had ever beheld. His feet took him to her side, where he placed the tray across her legs.

She eyed the food, raising an eyebrow. Elron looked down to see he had mostly brought her scrambled eggs. A single piece of bread lay beside the plate. Wincing, he started to go back for more, when Bet stopped him.

"It's fine. I need the protein." She laughed.

Elron dragged a chair next to the bed and sat. He watched her devour the food, gulping down the juice. When she finished, he took the tray away, placing it on the bureau next to the door. Bet patted the bed again, waiting for Elron to return. He took the chair instead. She needed rest. But Bet had other ideas, pouting at him. Seeing his serious expression, she gave up.

"I'm sorry. I promise not to ever leave your side again." She swore to him.

She had avoided any discussion on what she had gone through. Every time he tried to bring up the subject, she feigned tiredness. Elron needed to know what they had done to her, and why they had subjected her to so much torture. Seeing his intention, Bet stubbornly refused to let him ask the questions that he was prepared to.

"I don't want to talk about. There was no purpose to what they did." Bet stared Elron down.

He would get no answers from her. Maybe it was better she did not relive the experience. Bet fell quiet, biting her bottom lip. Pushing her was the last thing he wanted. She only needed his support, nothing else.

"How are you feeling?" He asked her instead.

Bet smiled at him for letting it go. Relief visibly showed on her face. Elron walked to the other side of the bed, climbing in beside her so that he lay on his back. Bet flipped to her side, draping her arm across his expansive chest. She lay her head on his shoulder, sighing with contentment. *Yes, this is where she belongs.*

"I need a shower. Will you wash my back?" She stroked his arm lazily.

Elron laughed, pulling her closer. The woman was maddening. Still waiting for his answer, she grabbed his behind, giving it a squeeze. There was no way they were doing that now. Elron took her hands in his, stopping her from any further exploration. He yanked her out of bed, depositing her feet on the floor in front of him. Turning her to face the bathroom, he pushed her towards the door. Inside, he ran the bath, letting the warm water fill it. Bet took the opportunity to start stripping off her clothes.

His eyes took in the changes her body had gone through. Her belly was swelling, her breasts were fuller. She took great pleasure in slowly exposing herself to him. Elron's heart started to race. His body instantly reacted to seeing her naked. Bet took a step towards him, her hand reaching for him. Using all the strength he possessed, he removed himself from the bathroom. He closed the door sharply, breathing in deeply.

Her giggle followed him, as he paced the room. He heard water splash, as she sat in the bath. Picturing her naked and wet did little to control the need to go to her. Her humming softly as she cleaned herself was enough to drive him mad. He forced his mind to the plan that Liam had come up with. They would need to discuss it soon. Bet should be well enough to travel. Rider was another story. Hopefully, he too would be well enough soon.

His attention was drawn back to the now-open door of the bathroom. He had not heard her finish her bath, or get out of the tub.

She stood there, wrapped only in a short towel, with her long legs exposed to his eyes. She approached him slowly, a teasing smile on her lips.

Elron backed up, forced to stop by the frame of the bed. She let the towel drop, came up to him and wrapped her arms around him. Her breasts brushed his chest, forcing a low groan from him. With no escape, Elron fell, landing on the mattress. Bet straddled him.

"Wait. Wait." He stopped her hands from caressing him.

Bet did not want to wait. She fought to liberate her hands. This only made Elron hold on tighter. They were not ready yet to finish what she wanted. Things still needed to be said. Elron was, in spite of having her safe, still peeved that she had placed herself in danger again. Bet saw the look that crossed his face and removed her body from his. She lay back on the bed beside him, staring at the ceiling.

"I know you are still mad at me." She said.

No, he was not mad. He did not know what he was. Anger would have been easy to identify. He felt she did not trust him, that she had no faith in what they had. It had been easy for her to push him aside. He was tired of having to prove his love for her. *When will she realize she is my world? Without her I am nothing.*

Reading his thoughts, Bet sat up and gazed down at him. Her slightly protruding belly touched his hip. Her words were silenced by a flutter of movement where their bodies touched. Elron pulled himself up on his elbows, curious at what the sensation was. Bet was looking at him excitedly. She grabbed his hand, placing it on her belly. A rolling wave went through their joined hands.

"Your son is awake." Bet said in awe, tears in her eyes.

"Son." Elron mouthed the word, his voice choked with emotion.

The movement stopped as suddenly as it had started. Elron worriedly looked at Bet. Smiling, she lay down.

"He's resting now." She assured him.

"Does this happen often?" *How much have I missed?*

Bet studied him, her face turned towards him. She breathed out, working through what she needed to tell him.

"It's the first time." She wanted him to know he had not missed out on anything. "Elron, I love you beyond reason. I do trust you. I trust that you believe in us. Only, why would you? Why am I worthy of your love?"

He could only stare at her. *Is she serious? Does she really think she is unworthy?* He knew he had to find the right words. Somehow he needed to make her realize what she meant to him.

"Bet, do you remember the first time we met? We were but five years old. I looked at you and saw the most beautiful girl in the entire universe. It wasn't your external looks that drew me, though they certainly helped. It was your inner light, the way you went out of your way to help those around you. I remember coming across you one day, crying over an injured baby bird. You were racked with guilt because you had tried to lure it to you. Only, it had fallen out of its nest, its wing broke from the impact. No matter how I tried to console you, you were heartbroken. I watched as you used whatever power you had at the time to try to heal it. It wasn't enough. You ran to your mother, asking her to fix it. Do you remember what she told you? It is only a bird, Bet. I saw your shock at her words. It was at that moment I fell in love with you. Your ability to love was not about how insignificant the existence of another was, but that it deserved to be loved nonetheless. No matter what you do, what is thrown at us, you deserve my love. You are the strongest, most caring person I know. Your fierce protectiveness of those you love, may take you into danger, may make me crazy, but it is who you are. I wouldn't change anything about you." Elron spoke from his heart.

Bet fought back tears at Elron's declaration. She marveled at the man beside her. He was her rock, the one who held her heart in his hands. Accepting her, faults and all, he had no idea how his words had touched her. Leaning over him, she kissed him, letting her tongue trace his lips. Elron hauled her over him so that she lay atop him. No more words needed to be said. They lost themselves to the desperate passion they felt for each other.

Chapter 26

Alexa

The bed and breakfast we were staying at was right on Loch Ness Lake. Liam and I had left the others to revisit the ruins of the castle that were not far from where we had settled. Outer walls were all that remained of the structure. Blocks of stone lay strewn haphazardly on the ground from walls that had completely collapsed centuries before.

Years of neglect left a shell of what was once a thirteenth century fortification. Coming back was a wasted effort. Only our having nothing else to do made me agree to accompany Liam. Our first foray into the site yielded no clue to the whereabouts of what we were searching for. If the book that spoke of the Kaemorra's location had ever been there, it was not there now.

We reached the site and separated to cover more ground. Liam went to the southern section where no structures remained. I climbed the steps of the almost-intact tower in the northern part. The square configuration of the tower had three of its walls standing. The other had disintegrated long ago. Its wooden steps were newly constructed for visitors.

Within it, there was a platform built that overlooked the lake.

From there tourists could gaze out and imagine what the past had looked like. At one time, it was a royal castle. Attacks by rival clans were frequent due to its strategic location. Abandoned completely sometime in the seventeenth century, it had only been recently that some upkeep had been done to the place.

Standing on the platform of what remained of the tower, I could see far into the distance. The lake lay tranquil, glistening in the afternoon sun. Down below, Liam was winding his way around the stones that lay on the ground. I could see his frustration mounting at the futility of our being there. Only a breathtaking view was to be found in the place.

I squinted against the sun, looking out at the water below. The legendary monster of the lake had not made an appearance. It might seem whimsical, but knowing about witches, Sidhes and gods, it was not too much of a stretch to believe in its existence. People all along the coast swore to having seen it at one time or another.

Liam's voice reached me from below. I saw him striding towards me, his hand waving for me to come down. I gave it one more attempt before leaving. I stretched out my senses, trying to see if I could get a trace of anything. My limited powers were still enough to perceive if something were there. Since leaving the estate, I was increasingly losing my abilities. It was aggravating to look for them and find growing emptiness.

"Alexa. We should return to the inn. There's nothing here." Liam called out again.

Getting nothing from my senses, I climbed down to meet him. He was waiting for me near the road back to the inn. We walked back together in silence, both of us disheartened at our lack of progress. The inn came into view as we made a left on the fork in the road. Built on a slope, facing the water, the gray stone exterior of the building stood out like a beacon. It rose above the green foliage and lilac trees that surrounded it.

As we neared, we saw Bet and Elron seated on the veranda that ran the length of the front of the house. On a swing chair, they waited for us to reach them. It was good to see them relaxed, at ease with each other again. Elron had his arm casually draped across her shoulders. Bet was leaning into him, her legs folded under her. They both wore huge smiles on their faces upon seeing us.

"Anything to report?" Elron asked, once we climbed the porch steps to join them.

Taking the available seat next to Bet, I shook my head at his question. Liam opted to remain standing. He leaned against the house, filling them in on our lack of findings. Elron was skeptical of the book being there. Too much time had passed. Whether it ever was within the castle was anyone's guess.

We needed information on the fortress's history. My parents left early in the morning to see my grandmother again. They hoped she knew more that she would share with us. My mom's displeasure at having to see her mother-in-law again was clear for all to see. She originally declined to go along, but Rider insisted. I did not blame her being exasperated. My grandmother was not an easy person to get along with.

Dad would need my mom's help. His recovery was still ongoing. Rider woke not long after Bet. Weakened, he still struggled to get around. He tired easily. Mom did everything in her power to help him. She still showed signs of the excessive use of her healing powers. Looking as if she had aged ten years, I could not help but worry about her.

I had no strength in me to help her. Weakened myself, all the sugar I consumed did little to stave off my declining powers caused by what I presumed was Aidan's continued absence. I was rapidly losing my magic. Needing him back was about more than the foreboding I felt. What he was going through, I had no idea. All I knew was that it could not be good.

I was faced with the possibility that I would not be able to reverse the loss of my abilities. On top of that, I was finding that I was still unable to rid myself of my lingering feelings for Liam. Having him near was making it impossible to forget what I once felt for him.

Torn, a part of me welcomed his nearness, while the rest of me was hungering for the return of Aidan. His absence was bringing the inevitability of our being joined in stark realization. The longer he was missing, the more I knew I required our connection to fully function. I had to find him, soon. The urgency of the situation was not lost on everyone. They could see how it was affecting me.

My thoughts strayed to Eliana, who had become my support system. She was quick to offer advice, to console and to help guide me. I stayed near her, if only to lend my own support. Asher did not come with us. He remained at the estate with his books. His excuse was that there might be more hidden within the library. It was obvious to all what his real reasoning was.

Eliana did not argue with him, instead she accepted his unwillingness to be near her. He did not even come out to see us off. The hurt she was experiencing was carefully buried under a mask of indifference. Rina thankfully came along to keep Eliana company. They were somewhere inside the house, probably gossiping with the couple who ran the inn.

"Alexa." I heard my name spoken.

I met Liam's eyes, his expression troubled. How long had I been absent from the conversation? It must have been a while from the way they were all looking at me.

"Sorry, what?" I asked him.

"We are going into town. Come with us." Bet tried to persuade me.

"No thanks. I think I'll stay here." My answer was met with silence.

Liam sank down on his knees in front of me. I could see he was going to plead with me. Wanting to take my mind off our problems, his eyes begged me to go along. Would it hurt to go have some fun? Aidan's face crossed my mind, his look of anguish at our last parting, making me wince.

"Feeling guilty, depriving yourself, will not bring him back sooner." Liam frowned at me.

"Please, Liam, I'm not up to it. Go with them. I'll wait for my parents." I could see my words had hurt him. He backed out of my way as I stood. Leaving them, I entered the house, hoping he would go with Bet and Elron. I needed to be alone with my thoughts.

Inside, I was intercepted by Eliana who met me at the bottom of the stairs. She dragged me into the living room, forcing me to sit beside her on the plaid sofa. I could hear Rina talking with the owners in the kitchen. Their words were no more than murmurs to my ears.

Eliana did not speak right away. She seemed to be trying to read me. I attempted to block her from any further exploration into my mind. It was too late, she had already latched onto what I was trying to hide.

"You must go with them. You must not stop living, Alexa. Aidan would not want that for you." She scolded me.

Did she know what she was asking? Giving hope to Liam seemed cruel. Aidan was not there to offer his opinion on the matter. How could I enjoy myself, knowing he was being held, being subjected to who knew what? I could see she would not be swayed. Her intent was confirmed when Liam walked into the room. She had called him.

"Go. It will do you good." Eliana insisted.

"It's only a walk, Alexa. Think of it as exercise." Liam piped in.

Angry at being forced into going, I huffily gave in. Walking past Liam, I glared at him. I stomped out to see Bet and Elron waiting on the path for us. Seeing my mood, they took off, leading the way. I marched behind them, keeping away from Liam. He rightly kept his distance from me. I was ready to throttle him. Stomping to catch up with Bet, I hooked my arm through hers, dragging her forward. Elron and Liam fell behind. Bet laughed at my indignation.

"What is the purpose of this? How will this help?" I huffed at her.

Still snickering at my expense, she kept up with my pace. Her infectious grin blew away my anger, drawing a small chuckle from me. Soon we were laughing hysterically, tears running down our cheeks. Unable to go further, we stopped, bent over at the waist. When the men arrived next to us, they had no idea how to handle the situation.

"Are you two okay?" Elron asked us, unsure of what to make of our shenanigans. Liam was doing his best not to laugh along with us.

Ignoring them, I pulled on Bet's arm to continue towards the town. I saw Liam shrug at Elron, who raised an eyebrow, wondering what to make of our laughter. Seeing them at a loss made me smile. It had been too long since I found anything amusing. Bet bumped her head against mine, giggling.

Together we reached the edge of the town, taking the main street towards the center. The road held gift shops, outside artisan stalls and refreshment stands. Winding our way around them, stopping once in a while at different stalls to peruse the wares, we eventually strolled over to a park that was nestled between a grocery and hardware store.

The park was small, rectangular in shape and matching the size of the buildings on either side. It was lined with hydrangea shrubs that were in full bloom. The violet flowers were the only color that invigorated the space. On the ground, what little grass remained seemed to be fighting for life. A walkway made from gravel wound its way around a large boulder that lay in the center. Several benches were placed along the path.

Behind a chain-link fence, a large stone was on display with a sign that offered information on its importance. Going by it, what captured my attention was the inscription engraved around the base of the rock. The information sign on a plaque in front of it said the stone had been discovered near the castle during a recent excavation. It explained that the language engraved on it was still being studied, as it was not known. I stopped Bet, leaning down to read the words.

Excitement raced through me at what I saw. I shook her arm in glee, as she recognized what we were looking at. I had no idea what it said. The language it was written in was what was important. Liam wandered over to us to see why we were elated. His jaw dropped open, as he took in the engraving.

"What does it say?" I grabbed his arm, shaking it.

He continued to read without answering, following the writing around the base of the stone. Elron was also examining the words. I followed behind Liam, anxiously waiting for him to translate for me.

"Well, it's a legend, sort of." Elron spoke first.

"What does it say?" I repeated, punching Liam's chest.

Chapter 27

Alexa

Liam ignored my question. He was concentrating on reading the words instead. As he made another turn around the stone, with Elron on his heels, I could not do anything but wait for them to finish. All of them, including Bet, were equally absorbed in examining the line of words encircling the boulder.

Growing impatient, I grabbed Liam's arm when he made his way back to me, stopping him from continuing around again. Elron, who had been tracing Liam's steps, stopped short of colliding with him. It was hard to read their expressions. Whatever was written on it, finding it there had surprised us all.

About to ask again what it said, I saw Bet step over the chain and lean down to trace her fingers over the writing. At her touch, the letters emitted a brief indigo glow. The words suddenly were clearer to see, but still impossible to understand. I had little energy left in me to translate what was written.

Devoid of my powers, I had to wait for them to fill me in. My hand was still gripping Liam's arm, stilling him from moving from my side. From the look on his face, the pressure I was exerting must have been hurting him. I relaxed my fingers, but did not let him go.

"It speaks of the book we are looking for." Bet finally said. She climbed out from the enclosure to where we waited.

"What does it say?" Could it help us, I wondered.

Elron shook his head, motioning to bring my attention to people approaching nearby. He silenced me with a look. We could not continue our conversation with so many bystanders. People had stopped along the path and were watching us curiously. Bet was the first to react at our being scrutinized. Waving and giving them a bright smile, she went over to the crowd, asking questions about the stone.

Their attention was momentarily distracted from us. Still, we could not linger for much longer. Raising suspicion in the town would not help us. Trying to blend in was our only chance of finding the book we were searching for. Bet came back to us, waving a final farewell to the onlookers.

On reaching us, she shook her head slightly for us to put off any discussion. Liam suggested we head back to our inn. We retraced our steps back to the main road without a word. While some of the people behind us started going about their business again, others were whispering, staring openly at our retreat.

Trying to act normal, we wound our way around the stalls, making it to the edge of town within minutes. We strolled as if time was not pressing on us, saying hello to people we passed. The residents of the town were pleasant, wishing us a good day as we passed, their attention mostly on their own affairs. Once we reached the outskirts, we picked up our pace, making it to the inn in no time. Eliana was sitting on one of the rattan chairs on the porch waiting for us.

"What's happened?" She asked immediately upon seeing us.

She could sense something brought us back, but was unable to see what it was. It was further confirmation that she was also being affected by whatever was draining my own powers. Lately, she seemed as lost as we all were. Before I could question her, her eyes met mine, her look telling me to leave it alone. I let it go for the moment.

"We found an inscription in town. It was in Sidhe." Elron said, as we all took seats.

"The book we are looking for was part of a legend, a story of faeries." Bet interjected.

Eliana sat up, leaning forward in her chair at Bet's statement. Did this mean the people of that time knew of their existence? Her brow furrowed, she nodded for Elron to continue.

"The stone mentioned that the one who understands the language would be able to find the faeries. It continued to say that someone would come to retrieve the book, travel a great distance and return it to the faerie queen. In presenting the book to the queen that individual would obtain great powers and riches. The inscription on the rock was done in the year 1327. It says the book was within the walls of the castle guarded by the local clansmen. They were waiting for the one who would come for it." Elron explained.

What had happened to it since then? Where could the book be now? If it were protected, would they have moved it somewhere else? We were no closer to finding it. I felt an overriding need to go back to the ruins, to see if I could sense anything. Rising from my chair, I made it to the porch steps just as Elron blocked my path, forcing me to stop. I tried to go around him, only to have Liam grab my arm.

"Alexa, where are you going?" He turned me to face him.

"I need to go back to the castle. I may sense something I missed earlier. Please Liam, I have to try." I begged him to let me go.

Liam released me, seeing that I was adamant about going. He agreed to it after insisting he would accompany me. I was to wait for him. Leaving my side, he and Elron stepped away to have a private conversation. What they discussed I could not hear. I paced back and forth, waiting for them to finish. Rina appeared behind the screen door of the house. She pushed it open, joining me and wanting to know what was going on. Bet explained to her what we had found, telling her that I wanted to go back to the ruins. Rina studied me for a moment. Coming to a decision, she spoke.

"I will come as well." She told me.

If only the guys would stop talking and get a move on. I stepped off the porch, walking off towards the castle without them. Rina caught up with me, both of us ignoring the others calling to us to wait. Liam and Elron ran after us, matching our stride. They took positions on either side of us, guarding us as we neared the path to the castle. I made it to the crumbled outer walls, stepping over the stones, going directly to what would have been the main building. What remained of it was nothing but an outline of disintegrated rocks.

I walked around the space, trying unsuccessfully to feel the book. Frustrated, I called on my powers to guide me. It was no use. I was empty. Circling what would have been the audience room, I could not get a glimpse of anything. I had completely lost use of my powers. Liam's sudden cry startled me out of my attempts. When I turned to see what caused his shout, I saw Rina on the ground, her body convulsing. I ran to her, sliding down on my knees beside Liam, who was already trying to help her.

Her eyes closed, her breathing ragged, she did not respond to our touch. Liam pulled her head into his lap, trying to keep her still. I held her arms, which were thrashing around. Suddenly, she went still. Her eyeballs behind her closed eyes were moving rapidly in all directions.

Elron was scanning the area for any danger. He stood guard over us, as we focused on Rina. I let go of her arms. Deathly still, the only sign that she was still living was the movement from behind her eyes. Sensing that she was reliving something, but with no idea what, I looked to Liam to see if he had a clue.

"She's in the past." Liam said without taking his eyes off of her.

We waited for what seemed like hours for her to return to us. Rina remained motionless, mumbling at times. Uncomfortable, I rose and stretched, leaving Liam's side. Along with Elron, I sat on the stones that lay around us. As quickly as she fell, Rina woke, sitting up, her face stricken by what she had seen.

"We have to see Eliana. She'll know what must be done." She attempted to get to her feet.

"Come on. Get a move on!" Rina spoke. Liam helped her up, supporting her weight when she swayed on her feet.

Recovering quickly, she took off, almost running back to find Eliana. Rushing after her, I left Liam with Elron to follow us. I saw her disappear into the house, her voice calling for Eliana. Stepping into the house, I found them in the main room. The owners were nowhere in sight. Bet appeared behind me, just as Liam and Elron made it to the front door.

In the cramped living room, we all waited for Rina to tell us what she had seen. I was relieved to find my mother had returned. She sat near the window, in one of the high-backed chairs that furnished the room. My mother was looking at me, her expression questioning. I wished I could enlighten her, but I was just as much in the dark as her.

"Eliana, the book was destroyed in a raid not long after the stone in town was engraved. English troops set fire to the main building during the attack. The villagers tried to save it, but the fire grew rapidly.

The book does not exist in this time. You know what must be done. Is it possible? Do you still have enough strength to manage it?" Rina was looking at Eliana fearfully.

So Rina had also noticed Eliana's weakening state. I wondered what she was asking Eliana to do. My mom was shaking her head, refusing to agree to what Rina was suggesting. If the book no longer existed, how were we to find it? I backed up into Liam, who was behind me, as the realization of what Rina was suggesting hit me. His hands came to rest on my shoulders, steadying me. I suddenly understood. Was Eliana capable of this?

"Wait, are you saying we could go back in time? Is this possible?" I was staring at Eliana for a response.

"No, I advise against it." My mother interjected.

Eliana seemed to ponder the feasibility of that course of action. Her weakened state would have an impact on whether she could do it. Liam, understanding the meaning of what Rina was proposing, left my side to go to his mother. Falling on one knee in front of her, his eyes sought hers, realizing that his mother was not herself.

Was she going through the same thing I was, losing her powers? I was pulled from my reverie by my mother. She took me out into the hallway to try to dissuade me from going. All I knew was that we needed that book. I knew that with it, I would find Aidan and that we would save him. I gave her no chance to speak. My look said it all. I re-entered the room with my mother on my heels.

"I will need Thalia to attempt it. I could manage to open a gateway, but I'm not sure for how long." Eliana looked to my mother.

"Mom, please, we have to try." I implored her.

"Alexa, you do not know the time period you will enter. It was vicious and cruel. If you are caught, we won't be able to help you." My mother tried to reason with me.

"I will go with her." Liam stepped over to us.

"And that is supposed to make me feel better about this?" Mom was starting to lose it.

"Thalia, we can do this. They only need to find the book and return. I will place them as close to it as possible." Eliana tried to assuage my mother's fears.

I knew the moment she gave in. Grabbing me, she shook me, before pulling me into her arms. I could feel her trembling. Her fear gave me pause, but I brushed it aside. We had to do this. There was no other way that I could see.

Chapter 28

Alexa

Two days later, we had tentatively agreed we had little choice but to attempt going after the book. I should say most of us had. My mom was still skeptical of what she called our harebrained scheme. Rider did his best to convince her that it was our best option. Her apprehension did not lessen as we discussed the logistics of the how and when.

Eliana was trying to determine the best way to enter the castle, and when to enter it. After much discussion, chaos erupted when I interjected what I thought was the most advantageous opening. We had to arrive during the storming of the castle. The castle would be in chaos. Everyone would be distracted trying to fight off the English invasion.

"Have you gone insane?" My mother snapped in protest.

Her voice was not the only one objecting. They all had points of contention. It would be dangerous, but I saw no other solution. Trying to explain my reasoning to them took time. If we arrived any time before that, our risk of discovery increased. We would not be able to blend in as easily. Our mannerisms, our speech would give us away. It was only during the attack that we could blend in with the chaos.

Hours of discord led to them finally seeing I was right. Our conversation then focused on when to go. It was imperative to do it as quickly as possible. Eliana was weakening rapidly. Rina ran off a list of what we would need. Clothes were but one of the items she specified. Argument broke out again at my insistence that we leave immediately.

"I have acquired the clothes you will need." Bet's voice rose above the raucous exchange.

She had come into the room while we were caught up in our disagreement. In her hands, she held a plain white tunic, along with a shawl and clothes for Liam. She deposited the items on a chair and went over to join Elron. She had no idea what we were arguing about.

While he explained it to her, I approached the chair to see what she had brought. The plain worsted-wool tunic was rough to the touch. Liam's clothes would be just as bland as mine. Commoners of the time period did not possess finery. With the clothes available, I saw no reason to delay further.

"When will Eliana be ready? We can't postpone our departure any longer." I had felt her weaken further as each day passed.

It was the main reason for my edginess. We had to go before we lost further use of our abilities. My mother was showing signs of weakening as well. Whatever was going on, we were all losing strength. I had not seen Eliana for over a day. She was preparing for our departure, preserving her energy while the rest of us planned our steps. How we would go back in time, I had no idea.

Eliana had asked Rina to procure a floor-length mirror for her. It had been placed in Eliana's room the day before. Keeping the owners of the bed-and-breakfast out of our way became an impossible task. Rina luckily was able to implant a thought in their minds to visit their son. They had left the day before, leaving us the run of the place.

"She will be ready this afternoon." Rina entered the room, answering my question.

"So we will have the book soon. When we get back, we can go after Aidan." His whereabouts was still unknown to me, but something told me I would be able to find him when we returned.

I left the room not waiting for confirmation. Agreeing to undertake time travel did not mean I had no reservations about it. A lot could go wrong. I needed some time alone to gather my courage. Stepping outside, the afternoon sun gave little warmth. I sat on the steps, feeling the cool wind as it wrapped itself around me. The smell of the lake reached me. I was so lost in thought, I did not hear Liam as he sat down next to me. Taking my hand, he wrapped our fingers together, pulling me towards him. I rested my head on his shoulder, staring off into the distance.

"Take a walk with me." He said, pulling me up.

Together, we strolled down towards the lake. The heavenly scent of fresh lilacs permeated the air. All along the walkway, the grove of mauve-colored blooms covered us in shade. At the end of the lane, a patch of grass was all that lay between it and the sandy beach.

Stepping out from under the trees, we traversed the lawn. Water lapped the shore gently. The lake was still, barely moving. Strolling closer to the water, Liam sat down on the sand. He beckoned me to sit in front of him, facing the lake. He wrapped his arms around me, positioning me so that I rested my back on him for support.

"You must stick close to me. Do not put yourself at risk." He warned me, his voice sounding strained.

I tried to turn to look at him, but he stilled my movement. I heard him sigh softly, as he dropped his chin to rest on my shoulder. He placed a soft kiss on the hollow of my neck. Shivers ran up and down my spine at the sensation. Sensing he needed me to stay silent, I simply let him hold me. I relaxed against him, both of us staring out across the lake.

"It's time." I heard Bet call out to us.

Liam's arms tightened around me. His fear was about more than something happening to me in the past. It might be the last time we had alone together. What the future held for us was causing him great suffering. I could see he was preparing himself for Aidan's return. He held little faith that I would wish to remain with him once his brother came back. I wished I could reassure him, but I had no idea what effect Aidan's return would have on me either.

"It will all work out. Come, let's get this over with!" Liam helped me to my feet.

With his arm draped across my shoulders, we walked back to the house. Bet was waiting for us at the bottom of the stairs. Together we climbed up to the landing leading to our rooms. She distributed the clothing, coming to my room with me to help me dress. Liam left us at my door, going into his own room to prepare. Bet closed the door behind us once we entered mine. She placed the dress I was to change into on the bed.

I stripped off my clothes, gathered the tunic in my hands and slipped it over my head. It lay like a bag over my frame. My body was smothered in the loose material. Bet stifled a giggle at my expression. She came to me with a leather belt, wrapping it around my waist. Gathering the material that was bunched around me, she arranged it into pleats. I went to the mirror on my bureau and studied my reflection. I looked ridiculous. Seeing my hesitation on wearing the outfit, Bet sat me down on the chair facing the mirror.

"It's not that bad." She said.

Bet left my side, went to the bed and returned with some ribbons. She went on to part my hair down the middle, plaiting two braids out of the sections. These she joined together, fastening them with the ribbons. My hair had grown out to the point where the braids lay between my shoulder blades.

Once she was satisfied, she stood me up, draping the dark green shawl over me. She pulled it up to cover my hair and hide my features. The ends, she arranged over my shoulders so that the shawl stayed in place. The final touch to the outfit was the shoes. Plain, moccasin looking, they were the most uncomfortable shoes I had ever worn.

A soft knock on the door had Bet responding to whoever it was to enter. Still studying myself in the mirror, I did not see Liam come in. He stood in the doorway, his eyes traveling over my ensemble. He grinned at how idiotic I looked. Rolling my eyes, I mirrored his grin, looking him over.

Dressed in a similar tunic, he made a contrasting image to mine. Where my tunic draped down to my ankles, his went to his hips. His legs were covered by trousers that hugged his hips and thighs. The material of the pants flowed down to his feet where he wore identical shoes to the ones that were pinching my feet. A dark leather belt kept the pants resting lightly on his waist.

Where I looked like I was dressed for Halloween, his outfit belonged on him. He leaned against the doorframe, his eyes smiling at my examination. I saw he had pushed his sword through his belt, letting it hang on the side of his hip. I could picture him in the time we would be visiting.

"Wonderful, you're both ready!" Rina was behind Liam in the hallway. "Come with me."

Taking a last look at my reflection, I followed the others out. Rina led the way to Eliana's room. We found her, with my mother, in front of a massive mirror. It was over six-feet tall and four-feet wide.

Held up by a stand, it stood close to the window. Eliana did not acknowledge our arrival. She was concentrating all her power towards the mirror.

Hands held out, she let her remaining energy flow into it. A streak of amber light was streaming from her fingertips, creating a distortion in the glass. My mother was helping her by adding her own source of power. Holding onto Eliana's arm, I could see she was concentrating just as hard on her task.

"You will have only three hours to find the book and get back. I will place you in what I hope is a safe place. My strength is weakening. You must hurry. Liam, you go first." Eliana whispered to us.

Liam approached the mirror, which had gone a murky white. A swirling cloud was flowing in a circular motion within it. Putting his hand into the distortion, I saw it disappear. Glancing back at me, he nodded for me to come closer. He did not wait to see me respond.

Stepping through the mirror, he disappeared from our time. Approaching it slowly, I turned to look at my mom. Her eyes held mine. Fear for my safety was plain on her face. Smiling to reassure her, I took a deep breath, and followed after Liam.

Chapter 29

Eliana

Eliana sat slumped in a chair a few feet in front of the mirror. The old world charm of her bedroom with its textured walls and wooden ceiling beams was largely ignored. A wrought-iron chandelier above her head hung unlit from the rafters. Her bed was unmade, the bedding wrinkled from its last use. She could not remember when she had last slept.

As the afternoon sun bathed the room, she wished she could escape under the covers and give in to her need for rest. For the moment she was alone. With her eyes closed, she concentrated all her energy on maintaining the portal that lay active in the mirror.

Liam and Alexa had been gone less than an hour. She struggled to keep what little strength she possessed trained on the object. Her waning powers were draining, as she fought to keep the passage open.

Thalia had left her a few minutes before to confer with Rider. He was keeping the owners of the bed and breakfast, who had returned unexpectedly, occupied. Eliana opened her eyes, staring at the swirling cloud within the mirror. It was slowly closing and she could do little to stop it.

She wondered how much longer she would be able to sustain the field before she collapsed from exhaustion. Fidgeting in her seat, she tried to sit up straighter. There was only one person who would be able to help her. She was awaiting the arrival of Asher, who had finally acknowledged her summons.

The air in the room stirred, drawing her attention away from her efforts. The brief interruption of concentration made the portal blaze in response. Its interior changed to a fiery reddish tone. Eliana raised her hands, fighting to regain control of it. Once she managed to contain the field, she afforded a glance at her husband. Asher stood near the open door, his stance casual but distant.

He made no move to come closer. They eyed each other warily, neither sure what to say to the other. Breaking eye contact, Asher went over to the window seat. Above it, the window lay open, giving him a clear view of the land below. A cool breeze fluttered the curtains. Eliana's bedroom faced the opposite side of the lake, giving him a panoramic picture of the meadow that stretched for miles.

"Almost as beautiful as I remember it." He finally said, taking a seat on the bench.

Eliana spared some of her focus to watch him cautiously. She did not want to do anything to antagonize him. Now, more than ever, she needed him, needed his strength. What was happening to her was unimaginable. Losing her gift was like losing a limb. She was unable to make sense of it.

"Asher." She began, only to be cut off by her husband.

"Where are our children?" Asher asked her.

Conversing with him was taxing her, but she made an effort to give him her attention. Eliana filled him in on recent events. She kept nothing a secret. Bet was safe downstairs with Elron. Her explaining about where Liam and Alexa were caused Asher to rise in his seat from exasperation. When he would have interrupted with questions, she forestalled him by going into the details herself. It did little to calm him.

She felt his blame falling squarely on her. She accepted it, not excusing her part in the turn of events. If she had handled things differently, they would not have found themselves in this predicament. Two of her children were accounted for, even if one was in dire danger. The one that was the most on her mind was nowhere to be found.

Aidan was still missing. They had no idea where to start looking for him. She had more to ponder on than his disappearance. Thalia, Rider and Bet had been saved by Vanya of all people. Eliana had no idea why she had helped them.

"I can see you are weakened." Asher actually looked worried for her.

He went to her side, dropping down on one knee, studying how pale she looked. Eliana was more than weakened. Keeping the gateway open was eating up all her reserves. Maintaining their conversation was rapidly depleting her. She needed Thalia back soon. Asher was unnerved looking at the strongest woman he had ever known who seemed a shell of her former self.

"What is happening to you?" He wanted to know.

She was interrupted from responding by the sound of someone approaching her door. Asher watched as Thalia entered the room. His dismay grew, as he took in the appearance of the woman. Thalia looked almost as bad as his wife. The energy in the room increased in strength at her entrance. He felt her add her power to bolster Eliana's.

"Can you please get Bet? We need to discuss things as a family." Eliana kept her focus on the mirror. She could not allow the passage to close.

Thalia lifted a chair to place it closer to Eliana. She placed her hand on her friend's arm as she sat. Together, they ignored Asher who stood over them. Whatever was going on with them, he was at a loss to understand.

Doing as she asked, Asher went in search of his daughter. He found her in the living room where his wife had indicated. Elron was not present when he entered the room. He asked Bet to accompany him back to her mother's room. When they returned, neither woman had moved. Their eyes were glued to the glass that fought them. The mirror was partially back to its reflective properties. Asher could see the edges were losing the portal's cohesion.

"Please stay, Thalia. You need to know these things as well. I cannot do this on my own." Eliana said when Thalia made to leave.

What she had to say affected all the races. She was sure that it was not an isolated incident. Somehow they were all losing their powers. Everyone needed to understand what was happening. Maybe together they could figure out why. Bet was distressed at her mother's weakened state. She could tell that something was dangerously wrong.

"I cannot see the past, present or future any longer. Time has been lost to me. As you can see, I am being drained of power. Thalia is experiencing the same effect. Alexa had none before she left. Bet, you have seen the same thing in Elron." Eliana explained to them.

"Why?" Was all Asher could think to ask.

"That I do not know. Something has been changed." Eliana said absentmindedly.

Asher paced the room, surprised to find he was feeling concerned for his wife. Unwilling to look into why that was so, he instead focused on understanding the problem. *What could have changed so profoundly to affect them this way?* Only a major shift in time would cause something like that. *Had they somehow changed the course of time?*

"Is this to do with Aidan being missing? Maybe his not being here is causing this." Asher extrapolated.

"Only if he has given up. I think that he has lost himself." Bet spoke up.

"If he has given up, then the Kaemorra will go missing forever. Without the Kaemorra, your link to the timelines will be gone. But, this does not explain the loss of power for Thalia." Asher was troubled over what it could mean.

Thalia's head snapped up at hearing her name. All this time, she had been concentrating on bolstering Eliana. She wanted her daughter back. If she was losing her powers, did that mean all witches and warlocks were losing theirs. She would have to reach out to others of her kind to hear if they too were overcome with that loss.

"Asher, we must prepare for the eventuality of failure. Our people, as well as Thalia's, will have to prepare for a life without magic." Eliana stressed.

Thalia was not ready to give up yet. Alexa had to return, they had to find Aidan. Seeing Thalia's resolve, Asher agreed with her. It was too soon to give up. They must trust that their children would set things right.

"Eliana, we will persevere. Have a little more faith. I will offer whatever strength I have to yours." Asher tried to boost her morale.

He saw the sudden tears form in his wife's eyes, the way her shoulders drooped upon hearing him. Bet had noticed too. She went to her mother, sitting down at her feet, resting her head on her lap. Asher wished he could offer more than words, but he still felt ambiguous towards her. He was still not ready to forgive and forget.

"How long before they come back?" He asked Thalia.

"They have another two hours. I don't know if we can keep it open longer than that." Her statement had them all terror stricken at the possible outcome.

Chapter 30

Alexa

Traveling through the dizzying effect of the portal had my head swimming. My limbs flayed around, as I was hurled around the emptiness of space. It seemed to take forever before the air cleared enough for me to see the end of the tunnel I was traversing through. Spinning out of control, I was being propelled at high speed towards a pinpoint in the distance. The end loomed before me as it grew in size.

A dark void in the distance was what I was being propelled towards. Reaching the end, I was pushed out by the force in the field. Ejected out into a darkened room, I landed heavily, sprawling across a hard surface.

Liam barely managed to get out of my way by rolling just as I exited. Rising to his feet, arranging his clothes, he held out his hand to help me up. I shook my head to clear it before attempting to rise. Taking his proffered hand, I stumbled to my feet. Dizziness had me swaying.

Liam held me in his arms to keep me from falling. Once he was certain I would be able to stand alone, he released me. Silencing me by placing a finger to his lips, I listened to the silence that permeated the room. The absolute absence of any noise was disquieting.

I feared we had arrived at the wrong time. There should have been a battle raging outside. The only light in our space was the glow being given off by the portal behind me. It eerily pulsed, fading in and out, illuminating our means of escape. How long it would remain open we did not know. We had to act quickly.

Our arrival point was a room no bigger than a large closet. It was a miracle I had not hit the opposite wall on my landing. The tight space kept me pressed up against Liam, who had an arm around my waist. A thick wooden door lay between us and the outside world.

The serene quietness was suddenly replaced by a cacophony of sounds. A rumbling had the room trembling beneath my feet. Sounds of people yelling, women screaming were suddenly heard from outside. Liam drew his sword, stepping to the door while keeping me behind him. With a last look to see that I was ready, he opened the door a sliver to see what we would be facing.

Outside our safe haven, men ran around, swords in hand, yelling instructions. Women were to be pushed to the inner rooms, guards were being told to go to the towers. Panic and disorder were everywhere. Sounds of running feet echoed in the hallway outside. We waited for an opportunity to venture out.

When it seemed like the wait would be long, suddenly the hallway cleared. Where did everyone go? One minute there was pandemonium, the next, silence fell around us. I could see Liam was as baffled by the sudden stillness as I was. He waited a moment longer, keeping me out of sight behind the door. Fascinated by what I had seen and heard, I had no time to be frightened. I had stepped into a world none from my time would ever see.

When he was sure the coast was clear, Liam grabbed my arm, pulling me out into the corridor. Gray stone walls ran along both sides of where I looked. We were in the circular tower of the fortification. Lit torches were hanging at intervals along the side walls. I had no idea where to go from there.

Liam carefully closed the door from where we had exited, trying not to alert anyone of our presence. It would not do to have someone find our portal. The corridors were deserted. Keeping me close to his side, Liam started going down the left passage.

I hoped he knew where he was going. I knew that at some point, the tower gave way to the main room, leading to the other buildings making up the soon-to-be castle. The English king would be arriving later that day. He would take possession and convert the fort into one of his castles.

Stealthily, we moved along, keeping close to the wall. The ground under our feet shook again as we made our way. Dust from the rock-faced walls clouded the hall in a haze. We arrived during the battle, just as I had wished. Whether it was sane was another story.

The incursion by the English was more brutal than I had envisioned. Cannon blasts were coming at an alarming pace. Making our way to the end of the hall, Liam stopped to peer down the adjoining corridor. Seeing it was empty, he guided me further into the castle. We had no clue where the book was being kept. How were we to find it while keeping safe?

The corridor we took led to the grand hall. As was the case with the corridor, the place lay empty. I was puzzled about where everyone could be. It was eerie how everyone seemed to be absent. I saw no soldiers, no inhabitants. Drawn from giving it anymore thought by another cannon volley, I tried to steady myself as the blast rocked the foundation under my feet.

I fell, landing on my knees heavily. Liam had barely kept his balance. He pulled me up, keeping an eye out for anyone coming upon us. My tunic was stained from the blood seeping from my scraped knees. I could feel a burning sensation from the open wounds. Nodding that I was fine, Liam once again led the way.

Keeping clear of the walls, Liam led me forward, his sword arm at the ready to defend us. I felt no presence of the book. Wherever it was, we needed to find it soon. Reaching the center of the main hall, Liam stopped, looking to me for any inspiration. I had none. He made a circle, walking around me, scanning for any indication of where we should go.

Where could everyone be? It was as if time had stood still. Only the sounds of battle outside the walls could be heard. As suddenly as these thoughts entered my mind, the sound of footsteps alerted us to someone coming closer. Liam took a defensive stance in front of me.

Both of us were startled at the appearance of a slight woman running into the room. From her expression, she seemed just as surprised to run into us. She stopped upon seeing us, her eyes shocked at finding us there. Saying something I did not understand, she spun around, escaping back down the hall she had come from. Liam let her go. There was nothing we could do except continue our search.

"Any ideas?" He whispered.

"None." I shook my head.

"If I remember correctly, there are two rooms through that corridor, and another one through where she went." Liam pointed out the two hallways opposite the one we had entered from.

"Let's try those first." I moved towards the ones opposite where the woman had gone.

Liam nodded and passed ahead of me. I followed close behind him, letting him take the lead. Peering down the hall, we were heartened to see no one about. I was still extremely unnerved that we had seen no guards within the castle. Were they all outside fighting?

Blasts of cannon fire could still be heard, each time rocking the ground beneath us. Their blasts seemed to have slowed. Were we in danger of being overtaken? Did it mean that soldiers had already breached the defensive lines? Had the castle been overrun? We needed to hurry. Liam kept his focus on continuing down the corridor. After looking into both rooms, we were no closer to finding what we came for. There was only one other room in this part of the castle.

With no other choice, we went down the hall the woman had taken. At the far end, a lone door stood closed. With each step closer to it, I felt a tingling sensation spread through me. Liam felt it too. He kept his sword in front of him, making sure I was out of the way. As we neared the door, it was suddenly pulled open from within. Liam pushed me away, ready for a fight. The woman we saw earlier, bowing slightly, pulled the door completely open and stepped aside to let us through.

Not trusting that it was not a trap, Liam kept his sword at the ready. I felt no threat from the woman. Stepping through the opening, I found myself in a vast room, lit by a few torches along the walls. In the dimness of the room, I noticed there was a man present at the other end. He waited, unmoving. Liam made sure that I was behind him, his watchful eyes on the two unknown individuals. We inched forward towards the center of the room. Behind us, the woman closed the door, and then walked around us to join the man.

"A bheil Gàidhlig agat." The man said. I glanced at Liam, and saw him nod slightly. I waited for Liam to tell me what it was the man said.

The man walked slowly towards us, holding his hands out to indicate he was not a threat. Dressed similarly to Liam, the man's tunic fell instead to his feet. His sleeves were made up of different colored patchwork materials. He stopped a few feet from us, studying Liam carefully.

His wrinkled face, with a heavy gray speckled beard, was devoid of emotion. The bluest eyes I had ever seen turned towards me. Tilting his head to the side, those blue orbs fastened on mine. Finally I saw his expression change to one of relief. Releasing me from his mesmerizing hold, I grabbed onto Liam's arm, as if searching for his protection.

"He asked if we speak Gaelic." Liam explained. "I can translate for you."

"No need." The woman spoke for the first time.

Her English was heavily accented, but easy to understand. I saw she was studying me in much the same way as the man. Slowly, she walked closer to us, stopping next to the man.

"Let us sit." She said.

There were no chairs in the room. I barely registered her words when I saw a table with four chairs materialize a few feet away. Sitting down, she waited for us to join her. I went to the table with Liam at my side. He was keeping as close to me as possible.

Making sure I was seated before taking the place next to me, he put his sword on the table in front of him. Smiling at the action, the other man sat down facing Liam. Without preamble, he raised both his hands over the table, as if tracing a circle with them. His action caused an object to gain substance on the tabletop. Where there had been nothing, an old book, yellowed with age, lay on it.

"You have come for this." The man spoke as we stared at it. His English seemed modern for the times.

"Who are you?" Liam wanted to know.

The two strangers exchanged a look, the woman answering for both.

"My name is Elethea and this is Conall. We have waited for your arrival. The book was placed in our protection when the events taking place outside were foretold. We could not risk the book being destroyed. Who we are is not important. What you must do is. We place it in your keeping. Return to when you have come from, make sure that it is used to restore the timeline." Her words jolted me from my staring at the book. They knew we were not from that time.

"I will guide you back. We must hurry. I have managed to forestall time, but I cannot keep it up. The way to your portal will be clear for the next few minutes. If we hurry we can make it before the castle is overrun. You cannot be here when the king arrives." Conall stood, walking to the door as he spoke.

Liam grabbed my elbow, pulling me up to stand next to him. He retook his sword, keeping it in his hand. Elethea picked up the book from the table and placed it in my hands. My curiosity over who they were, how they knew we were coming, would not be satisfied it seemed.

The urgency with which they were pushing us to leave was highlighted by the sounds of fighting coming closer. The sudden silence from the cannon blasts stopping meant that the defenses had fallen. It would not be long before the castle was stormed.

Holding the heavy volume against my chest, I let Liam lead me out to the corridor. We followed Conall down the hallway we had come from, surprised at how he knew where to take us. The door to the small room lay ahead, closed as we had left it.

In the distance, the calm gave way to screams and yells. The king's soldiers had entered the castle. The sound of clanging swords, men fighting was coming closer. We had little time to make our escape. Conall was opening the door for us. Elethea had her eyes closed. I saw the corridor shimmer as she covered our position under a shield.

"Go. Be safe. We are all relying on you." Conall pressed us to leave.

He stepped aside to let us enter. Liam motioned me to go first, and then stepped into the room behind me. I had a million questions and no time to ask them. Who were they really? I had a feeling that they were not from that time either. How did they know we were coming? Liam appeared to have the same questions, his face quizzical about what we had encountered.

"There is no time. I cannot continue to keep people out of our way. The castle is about to fall. We will meet again at the right time. Your questions will be answered then." Conall insisted.

He drew away, slamming the door on us. The open, cloudy,

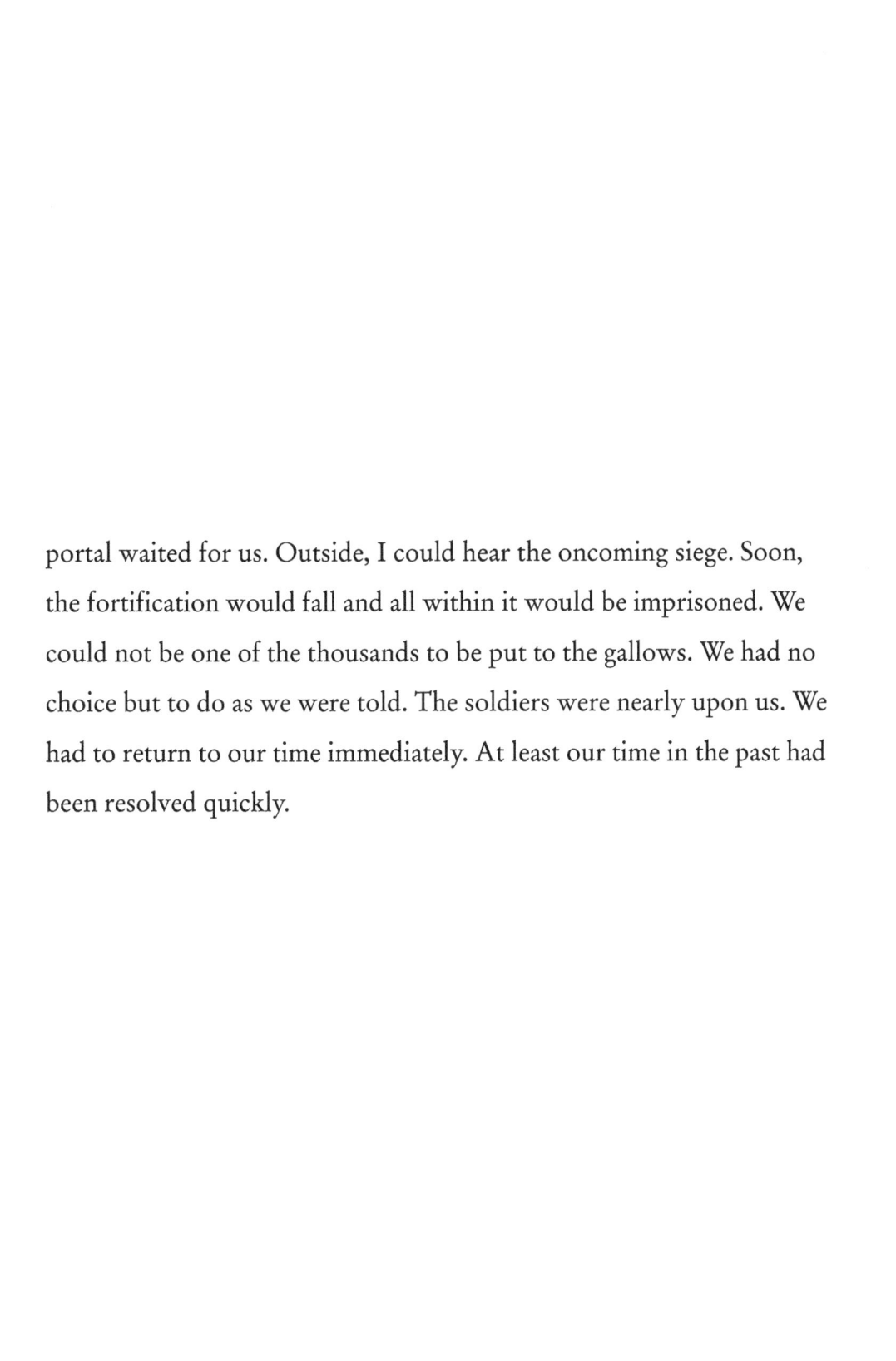

portal waited for us. Outside, I could hear the oncoming siege. Soon, the fortification would fall and all within it would be imprisoned. We could not be one of the thousands to be put to the gallows. We had no choice but to do as we were told. The soldiers were nearly upon us. We had to return to our time immediately. At least our time in the past had been resolved quickly.

Chapter 31

Alexa

Returning to the present was more harrowing than going into the past. The field fought us as we entered it. I immediately sensed the loss of power in the portal. Whipped about within it, I was separated from Liam. The white cloudy film that we had traversed previously was now like an electric storm.

Shutting my eyes from the dazzling display of cyan-colored bolts of lightning, I had no control over where I was being thrown. The snapping waves of light blinded me, making it impossible to keep my eyes open. I was blind to where I was being carried. My stomach rolled with the movement. All I could do was go along with wherever it was taking me. After what seemed like an eternity of nauseating pitching back and forth, I was tossed out of its turbulence.

Where I was, I could not tell. I was on my hands and knees trying my best not to vomit. Breathing deeply, I managed to somewhat settle my stomach. A vile taste remained in my mouth. The room was spinning around me. I focused my gaze on a spot on the floor, fighting to regain my equilibrium. A hand was softly rubbing my back.

Raising my head, I saw Liam's steady gaze regarding me with concern. His complexion was pasty, his skin as green as I felt. I let him help me up to my knees and gave no resistance when he took me in his arms. Kneeling, facing each other, his hand supported the back of my head while my cheek rested on his shoulder. My own hand was pressed over his heart, the beat of it increasing at our contact. I lifted my head to look at him. Pressed up intimately against him, his green eyes fastened on mine.

I watched, fascinated, as his head dipped, his lips coming closer to mine. Inch by inch, his eyes never leaving mine, Liam seemed to be waiting for a signal that I would rebuff him. I was frozen, mesmerized by the emerald irises that smoldered back at me. There was none of the black specks I usually noticed in Aidan's eyes. His were clear, shining in anticipation.

When finally he softly kissed me, the sweetness of it was intoxicating. He put no pressure on me, holding me gently, giving me a chance to break off the contact. My heart quickened, hammering in my chest, as waves of pleasure flooded me. I heard a soft moan escape my lips.

His arms wrapped fully around me, drawing me closer, as he felt my response. I melted against him, feeling every inch of his body where it touched mine. Soft light kisses continued their way to my cheek, my neck. I swayed against him, my limbs going numb from the intensity of what I was experiencing. If not for his arms, I would have crumbled to the floor.

I clung to him, both for support and in complete surrender. I returned his embrace, forgetting everything but the sweetness of his kisses. His mouth found mine again, exploring it leisurely, in no hurry. Liam brought one hand to the small of my back pressing me more firmly against him. His other hand came to rest on my ribs, just below my breast. He deepened the kiss, his tongue meeting mine as my toes curled.

"Glad to see you back." Bet's giggling cut into our moment.

Liam took his time responding to the interruption. He gave me a final gentle kiss on the lips, drawing back but keeping me within his arms. Blushing furiously, I avoided looking at Bet, or meeting Liam's eyes. My attempt to move away from him was impossible, as he kept me firmly in place. Liam would not budge.

I gave up fighting him. Still feeling unsettled from our trip back from the past, his arms were the only things keeping me from falling. I tried to focus on the here and now, realizing the object we had risked our lives to get had fallen out of my hands and was lying on the floor at my feet.

Noticing what I was looking at, Liam reached down and picked it up. With the book in one hand, his other hand took my elbow and easily pulled me to my feet. Relinquishing me, he put the heavy book in my hands. I still was unable to meet his eyes.

"So this is the legendary book? What does it say?" Bet wanted to know.

I was further embarrassed to see Eliana and my mom both showing their displeasure. They were seated steps from the mirror, haggard and pale. I had no excuse for what I had let happen. Wanting nothing more than to file the incident away to reflect on later, I traced my hand over the book's cover.

We had not had the chance to open it yet. Opening it carefully, I found within it words I could not understand. I was not surprised to see it was in Sidhe, nor that I was still unable to decipher it. Passing it to Liam, I waited for him to tell us what was written.

"Alexa." My mother rose from her chair, barely making it to me. She took me in a weak embrace.

As I held her, her strength left her. She crumbled to the floor, taking me with her. Sprawled on the floor, she tried to reassure me that she was fine by patting my arm. Her ashen face belied her reassuring gesture. In the reflection of her eyes, the portal's flashing lights drew my attention. I realized the passage to the past was still open.

Turning towards the mirror, I saw the increasing volatility of it was endangering the room. The sparks were leaving the interior and entering our time. As they traveled through the room, they hissed and whined before scorching wherever they landed.

Seeing the danger, Eliana let her concentrated energy drop completely. She looked spent, exhausted. Her glazed eyes folded back, as she lost consciousness. Collapsing from her chair, she lay sprawled on the floor near my mother. Bet's cry alerted Liam to his mother's situation. He flung the book on the bed, sliding on his knees to his mother.

"She is not herself." My mother whispered.

I could see that. While I helped my mom stand, Liam picked up his own mother. Cradling her in his arms, he placed her gently on the bed. I walked my mother to the window seat, opening the window completely to let fresh air in the room. The cool breeze seemed to partially revive her. Going to Liam, I stopped at the foot of the bed.

His mother was slowly coming back to awareness. Her eyes fluttered, struggling to open. Bet was arranging the pillows under her head. She perched on the side of the bed holding her mother's hand. Eliana slowly opened her eyes, their usual emerald brilliance dampened. Seeing us hovering around her, she made to sit up. She made it halfway before falling back on the bed.

"I will be fine. I just need some rest." She managed to say.

My mother came over to us. Leaning down, she touched Eliana's forehead. A crease formed on her brow. What she sensed had her frowning. Eliana gave an almost imperceptible shake of her head at my mother. Whatever my mom felt, Eliana wanted to keep it between them. Suspicion over what it might be was replaced by curiosity, as I watched Eliana reach out and pick up the forgotten book. She placed it on her legs, opening it up to read it.

"Do you know where the others are, Thalia? Please get them." Eliana asked my mother.

Leaving the room to assemble everyone, my mother moved sluggishly to do as Eliana requested. Her steps were measured, as if it took all her strength to manage them. At the door, she paused, her hand resting on the doorframe. I saw her take a deep breath before she continued out to the hall. Once she was out of the room, I returned my attention to the book in Eliana's hands.

The worry over my mom and Eliana's condition was temporarily brushed aside. We risked much to retrieve that book. Whether it would give us something to use was the question. I stood at the foot of the bed, eager to find out what the pages would tell us.

Liam left his mother's side to come over to me. His hand found mine, wrapping our fingers together. Squeezing them, he offered me courage and strength. Our moment earlier would need to be discussed, only I had no idea what to say about it. It had been wonderful and sweet. I did not want to give him false hope, even if his kisses made me forget about everything else for a time.

I was pulled away from my introspection as Rider entered the room with Asher. Surprised to find Liam's father there, the concern I glimpsed when his eyes landed on his wife gave me hope that he still cared about her. Eliana barely glanced at him. It was taking all her strength to stay alert. Asher hesitantly went to the head of the bed, standing next to her. He stood rigidly, his emotions now hidden behind an impenetrable wall.

My father on the other hand, had eyes only for me. His eyes teared up at seeing me safe. Blinking away the emotion, he simply nodded, smiling at me, as he came further into the room. Taking a place on the other side of Liam, he briefly hugged me.

At the door, the arrival of Rina and Elron was followed by my mother. They all gathered around Eliana's bed. Everyone was present and accounted for. I was impatient to hear what the book had to tell us. As Eliana lowered her head to start reading from it, Liam interrupted.

"Wait." Was all he said.

Startled, I turned to look at him, to see what made him stop his mother. He was concentrating on something unseen. His head was bent to the side, as if listening to someone. I recognized the sign from previously seeing other Sidhe do the same thing. Liam's face clouded at what he was being told. His lids lowered, focusing his attention entirely on the information he was receiving. I wondered if it was Aidan, at last, contacting us. Could he have escaped? My hopes were dashed at Liam's next words.

"Elsam is coming. We need to move."

My blood ran cold at his words. Fear of what Elsam and his followers could do held me frozen. Who could have been warning Liam? Everyone quickly reacted to his words. Asher was already helping Eliana rise from the bed. Bet joined Elron, standing by the door.

My mom and dad were approaching me. Liam was still in communication with someone. I remained rooted to my spot. Liam had more to tell us.

"It seems that Elsam followed Alexa's trip to Crete. He found nothing, which is obvious. Vanya says that he thinks Alexa already has the Kaemorra. He will be here within the hour. We need to get somewhere where he can't trace us." Liam further explained.

"Can she be trusted?" I wanted to know.

"She did help us escape." Bet answered.

I had reservations about Vanya's actions. Trust was not easy to give where she was concerned. While the others may give her the benefit of the doubt, I did not know the woman. Whether she was helping us or not, I still held back on believing her. She had turned against our side once.

Still, we needed to move. We could not risk that her information was false. I saw everyone was ready to leave, but we were wondering where to go. Liam had broken his link with Vanya and was waiting for me to decide.

Where to go, was another problem. The estate outside Verona should have been my first conclusion. For some reason, I was sure that it was not where we needed to be. Something inside me was guiding me to the one place I felt a connection with. My ancestor's home was where we would find shelter.

Whenever we were at Meredith's, it seemed like we were under protection. Her cottage in Scotland was where I had claimed my sword, where I met the immortal woman for the first time. Myrick tried to get to us there once, but he failed to fully materialize. Was it possible that Meredith had placed a spell on the place, not allowing anyone to harm us?

"We can go to Meredith's." I told everyone.

"Yes, we'll be safe there." Eliana, who had been watching me, agreed.

With a destination in mind, Asher immediately placed his hand on Eliana's arm. In a blink of an eye, they were gone. Why he still maintained the ability to transport and appeared unaffected by what was happening to the rest of us, was another question to ponder. It seemed my mother, Eliana and I were affected by whatever was happening. I knew that Elron had also lost whatever powers he had gained. Why the four of us were most affected was a mystery.

My attention was captured by the sight of my parents coming towards me. Liam waved them off. Seeing that I would have him to help get me out, they stopped. Rider held onto my mom, making sure he moved both of them to our new location. Left alone with Liam, I picked up the forgotten book, letting him touch my arm. Before I knew it, I was standing in front of Meredith's small cottage in Scotland.

Chapter 32

Elron

Elron saw Alexa and Liam appear not far from where he was having a heated discussion with Bet. It cut off their argument, as Bet turned her head to look at Alexa and her brother. Seeing them she seemed pleased to have reinforcements to back up her reasons for what she saw as the idiocy of Elron's idea. Elron knew Liam may side with his sister. What he meant to do would end any relationship Liam hoped to have with Alexa.

Liam may interfere when he knew Elron meant to bring Aidan back. Bet had other reasons for fighting him. They had only recently reunited, and her fear of something happening to him made her hesitant to see him in harm's way. Tapping her foot in irritation, her face glowering, she faced him again stubbornly. Elron still held Alexa's stare, whose expression showed clearly she was not pleased to see them fighting again.

Alexa would have entered into their disagreement if Liam had not cut her off. Holding her arm, Liam was staring intently at Elron, who simply shook his head at having to answer their questions. He ignored the two and returned his attention back to Bet. Outlining his strategy to her for the second time did not go over any better than the first had. Bet was not accepting the merit of his plan.

From the way she was staring at him, he knew he would have an uphill battle convincing her. Arms folded across her chest, she stood before him ready to do him physical harm. She would do anything to keep him from carrying out his intentions.

He understood her misgivings, but what he was thinking of doing might help them get a hint of where Aidan was being kept. Elron should have been there to stop Aidan leaving. He failed his friend. It was not only guilt that pushed him to look for anyway to find Aidan. They were quickly running out of time.

"Bet, I will be careful. Tory has agreed to join me. I feel it's the only way to figure out Aidan's location." Elron tried to explain to her again.

Bet was having none of it. She was vehemently shaking her head, refusing to follow his logic. Her anger was rapidly being replaced by panic. She held onto his arm, afraid to let him go. She remembered her captivity at the hands of those monsters.

Having Elron endanger himself, to be tortured as she had been, was more than she could bear. Troubled eyes held his, making him feel like a heel for putting her through that. If there was any other way, Elron would have abandoned his plans for her. He took her in his arms, holding her tightly against him.

"I promise to be back before you know it. Following Elsam may be our only chance to find Aidan." He felt her trembling, holding back tears.

Bet pulled out of his arms, visibly stamping down her emotions. He saw the exact moment she came to her foolhardy decision. This time it was his turn to shake his head at her. He could not allow it. There was no way she was coming with him. Seeing she was digging in her heels, Elron needed his own reinforcements to stop her from doing anything to jeopardize herself and their child.

His eyes found Liam, who was still trying to keep Alexa away. Bet noticed his attention focus on her brother, and narrowed her eyes when she saw what he meant to do. Calling out to them, he waved for Liam and Alexa to come meet them. Bet was incensed at his summoning them to interfere for his benefit.

"What is up with you two?" Alexa watched Bet, arms folded across her chest, staring daggers at Elron.

"This oaf wants to go back. He wants to follow Elsam to try to find Aidan." Bet huffed.

Alexa's eyes widened, hope filling her at Bet's pronouncement. At the same time, she understood Bet's reticence. *As much as she would like to get Aidan back, did she really want to place Elron in danger?* Alexa bit her lip to stop the words that would have angered Bet. She would give anything to have Aidan return to them.

Elron explained his strategy fully, believing they would accept his plan. Liam, surprisingly, agreed it was feasible. All he needed to do was lie in wait, watching as Elsam came and then follow him. Tory would be able to help shield them. His brother had a knack for appearing invisible when spying on others.

"I don't know, Elron. As much as I would like to find Aidan, do you think you can get away with it? Won't Elsam be able to sense your presence?" Alexa had hope for the first time. It was not without danger though.

Elron saw that Bet thought Alexa's remark meant she was agreeing with her. He was not sure where Alexa stood. He hoped she would be easily swayed, agreeing with him that it had to be done. *Do I have to convince both women?* He looked to Liam to aid him. Liam was lost in thought, probably looking for alternatives or thinking of all that could go wrong.

"Listen, I can take care of myself. I feel insulted that you think I can't handle this." Elron tried a different tactic.

Alexa raised an eyebrow at his feigned indignation. Even Bet seemed slightly amused at his attempt at levity. Taking advantage of the slight thaw in the women's attitude, he pushed his point further.

"Tory will blanket us. They won't know we are there."

Bet finally realized he would not be dissuaded from his scheme. Before accepting his decision and giving in, she wanted all the details. Elron went over his strategy for all of them again. Bet peppered him with questions, drilling him about what he would do if different situations arose. Going through the scenarios she threw at him, he was able to come up with ways to avoid capture, death and anything else she could think of.

"Fine, I'll come with you." She finally finished.

"No way! You are staying put for once. Do not make me tie you up." Elron threatened.

"As if you could!" Bet stepped away when he went to reach for her.

Elron begged Alexa with a look to try and convince Bet to stay. She must have something to say that would keep Bet there. Putting her in the middle of their argument was not fair, but Elron was past caring. He needed to convince Bet to stay, to keep their child safe.

"Bet, you have to think of your baby. Elron is right, you can't go off with him. You were already subjected to enough pain the last time you were captured. I trust that he will come back, that he will keep out of trouble. If he doesn't he will have both you and me to contend with." Alexa pressed her point.

Bet's hands went to her belly. A frown formed on her lips, remembering all she had gone through. Realizing she would be putting her baby in harm's way again, Elron saw the fight leave her. Giving Alexa a grateful glance, he took the step separating him from Bet, gathering her in his arms.

"Babe, I need to know you are safe. Please do not do anything foolish. Promise me." He pleaded with his lips close to her ear.

Bet lifted her head so she could look at him. He saw she was resigned to his leaving. She nodded slightly in agreement, but Elron needed to hear the words. He gave her a long look, waiting for her to speak.

"I promise." She finally said.

"I'll make sure she doesn't take off again." Liam spoke, giving his sister a pointed stare.

Bet rolled her eyes at him. Elron was glad they would be looking after her, but he knew Bet well. She would stay if she wanted to stay. He hoped this time she would keep her promise, that he was not misplacing his trust in her. Giving her a long lingering kiss, he stepped away to contact Tory. They had to arrange where they should meet. He reached out to find him, communicating with him silently. His brother's response had him shaking his head.

"Tory is already at the inn, hiding near the tree line. No one has shown up yet. I must go." He went back to Bet and placed a kiss on her forehead. They lingered, gazing into each other's eyes. Bet nodded and took a step back from him.

"Be safe. If I don't hear from you every hour, I will come find you." She asserted.

Elron smiled at her threat. He went to Liam, placing his hand on his shoulder. Liam tilted his head, as they conversed silently for a few moments. Whatever they spoke of, it was over in seconds. Elron walked away from them, fading from their sight gradually and then he was gone.

Chapter 33

Alexa

The weather was remarkably pleasant. Spring temperatures had arrived early this far north in Scotland. The sun beating down warmed the skin and the breeze held promise of southern air. I had spent the last few hours listening to Bet's constant rumblings on being forced to stay while Elron was off putting himself in danger. Her voice droned on behind me, incoherently, while I lost myself to my own thoughts. Every now and then, her words registered, bringing me momentarily back to her.

"I should have gone with him." Bet was gloomily staring out the window of the cottage.

It was the same phrase she had been repeating intermittently. Having nothing to say as a response to her statement, since it was not a question, I let her continue venting. Meredith's home was still the same as when we had left it. The divisions in the interior were as I had adjusted them on our first venture to the property. The main living space, made up a living room area and kitchen, led to a hallway housing the four bedrooms. I was sharing a bedroom with my parents while Bet shared with hers. Liam and Rina each had one to themselves.

I had sent Liam off, less than an hour before, to the small town closest to us for food. Rider and my mom escaped Bet's agitation by going with him on the errand. Conjuring food or anything else was impossible for me. My mother was equally unable to use her power for the simplest tasks. Why we were experiencing this loss was confounding us all. I knew it had to do with Aidan. Whatever he was going through was affecting everyone.

Nightmares haunted me at night. I saw his bruised, broken body lying lifelessly whenever I closed my eyes. Liam could sense what I was going through. It was one of the reasons I asked him to go out. There was nothing he could do to ease my mind. Bet's voice broke into my misery again, turning my attention to other matters.

Eliana and Asher were out walking the grounds. I was pleased they were at least speaking to each other. From the doorway, I watched them round the corner and continue their stroll to the other side of the house. The queen was weak, barely able to maintain the appearance of normalcy.

Asher was supporting her, as they meandered along the cliff. Her ashen face, along with her frail limbs, was showing the strain she was under. Bundled up under a heavy woolen blanket draped across her shoulders, her striking size seemed to have diminished. She leaned into her husband, using his body to stay upright. They were just as concerned as I was over their missing son.

"How could he trust Tory to keep them safe?" Bet continued her fretting.

Ignoring what I imagined as her muttering to herself, my gaze was drawn to Rina, sitting on a rock not far from the well where I had received my sword. She had her face tilted towards the sun. Smiling at the warmth it gave, she was dressed in a simple sleeveless sheath. How she was able to stay out there with no coat or shawl was remarkable. Her thin dress, leaving little to the imagination, must have offered no protection.

From the way her lips were moving, I knew she was trying to communicate with her mother. She was receiving no response to her calls. We were on our own to figure out how to fix things. I examined the area around the well, remembering Aidan's surprise at Elsam's sword offering itself to me. Even that object was now changing. Lying on my bed, the sword was becoming tarnished, losing its brilliance. Everything and everyone were being affected by whatever was draining our magical energy.

"Are you listening to me?" Bet had turned to face me.

Adjusting my focus to her, I turned my head to see she was peeved at my lack of response. I had let her vent, thinking that eventually she would calm down. Maybe that was the wrong way to handle her. More upset than before, she saw my lack of reply as me agreeing with Elron. I left the doorway and went to the table. Pulling a chair up to sit down, I patted the one next to me for her.

"Sorry, Bet." I was truly sorry to see her upset. "Elron will be fine. You need to take care of yourself. Upsetting yourself will only distress the baby. Try to calm down. Liam should be back soon. You need to eat and rest." My words slightly mollified her.

Pouting, she left the window to come join me. She took the chair I had indicated, dropping her head on the table. Resting her forehead on it, she closed her eyes, letting a heavy sigh escape her lips. She had promised to stay, to not take off after Elron. I felt this time she meant to keep her word. Elron kept his promise to keep in touch. He had communicated with her twice since leaving. The link they spoke through was weak, but it was better than nothing.

Before I could offer her further reassurance, Liam walked in, followed by my parents. They were carrying huge bags full of food and other necessities. Putting the bags on the table, my mom went to the hearth. She gathered kindling from the stack of wood next to it and began starting a fire. No one spoke as they went about their business. Their glances stole once in a while to Bet, wondering how long before she would start complaining again.

We were all getting cabin fever. Pulling pots from the rack over the fireplace, my mom got ready to prepare supper. We would have to cook our own food until we figured out how to reclaim our powers. Rider was emptying out the bags, arranging items on the table according to whether they needed to be cooked or not. I felt no hunger, no need for anything.

"Alexa, walk with me." Liam held out his hand.

Wary about leaving Bet alone, I hesitated to get up. She had sat up when the others entered the room, watching quietly what each was doing. Her eyes were drawn to the food, her hunger obvious. She settled on an apple, picking it up and taking a bite.

"Go, I'll eat and then go rest." She told me with her mouth full.

"I'll make sure she does. I won't leave her side." My mom promised me from where she was putting a pot on the fire.

Knowing she would be in good hands, I grasped Liam's hand and let him lead me outside. I was curious what he wanted to discuss. We still had not addressed the earlier kiss. I was still uncertain what it meant or what he expected from me. Not looking forward to rehashing my confusion, I was surprised when he pulled me towards Rina.

"It's total chaos, Liam. They are all up in arms over what is happening." She said as we neared.

Had she been able to reach her mother? I was eager to hear news of Meredith. Would she see me soon? I stood in front of Rina waiting to hear more. What she said next was unnerving.

"The gods cannot reach agreement. Each has their own agenda, as usual. My mother says that Cronus is keeping Meredith prisoner. He will not allow her to contact us. There is fear among some of them that Alexa will destroy the timeline further. I haven't been able to find out why or how she would do this." Rina was speaking to Liam.

I swore. Liam's shock at my outburst was obvious by his raised eyebrow. It was something I hardly ever did, but I was beyond frustrated. I had been thrust into this situation, pointed towards a goal, with no guidance on how I was to achieve what they all expected of me.

"Tell your mother that if I don't see Meredith, I will make sure to cause them nothing but grief. I will make sure that every last one of their fears comes true." I spoke harshly.

Rina looked scared at my outburst, fearing that somehow the gods were listening in on our conversation. I did not give a rat's ass if they were or not. I was angry and annoyed by the lack of cooperation I was getting. Thunder sounded off in the distance, causing Rina to jump. Her frightened eyes searched the sky for impending disaster.

"You don't understand who you are dealing with, Alexa. These beings are omnipotent. They have existed since the beginning of time. Their idea of time is measured in millenniums. Our lifetime is nothing but a second to them. At one time or another, each has been at war with at least one of the others. They take pleasure in our suffering, seeing it as some kind of test on our belief in them. Do not anger them. It will only make things harder for us." Rina's voice was hushed as she warned me.

I was past caring. Staring at the sky, I wished they would come for me. I would give them something to think about. Pivoting on my heels, I left Rina and Liam, walking back to the house. Whatever they did, it could not be worse than the situation I found myself in.

I stormed into the house, going directly to my room. Avoiding my parent's stares, I slammed the door shut, going to my bed. I flung myself down, landing face down on the mattress. I barely exhaled a breath before a soft knock on the door sounded, stopping me from screaming my rage.

"Alexa, is everything all right?" My mom asked through the door.

"Nothing is all right." I yelled back.

She slowly opened the door, peering in to see me stretched out on the bed. Seeing my vexation, she came in, and closed the door behind her. Concerned over why I was angry, she lay down beside me. I turned to my side so that I faced her. She regarded me intently, trying to figure out what was wrong.

At her prodding, I told her what Rina had been up to and that we were not going to be getting any help. Once started, I let everything out, my feelings for Liam, Aidan, the way I was scared of doing the wrong thing. She listened to my incoherent ramblings, her eyes tearing up at my obvious confusion.

"I know this is hard on everyone, sweetie, but I think it is worse for you. You cannot avoid what is causing your distress. Alexa, you need to tell Liam that you do not feel the same about him. You know it is Aidan you belong with. What you are feeling is the effect of the distance between you. It will only get worse as time goes on. You know in your heart I am speaking the truth. Liam is not for you. Your attraction to him has always been about your stubbornness to accept that sometimes things are out of our control. Just because Aidan was joined with you by some prophesy, does not mean he was not meant to be yours. You have to find him. Only then can we all regain our strength. The longer he is missing, the worse our situation will become." The earnestness with which she spoke was hard on me.

How could I break Liam's heart like that? He had stood by me, giving me strength and courage through all we had gone through. I believed mom when she said we were all affected by Aidan's absence. It was the reason we were all drained. Was I ready to accept Aidan for all that we were destined to be?

"If you don't tell him now, it will destroy him later. Just think on it, Alexa." My mom rose from the bed.

Having said her peace, she pulled me up, pushing me towards the door. From my bureau, she picked up the book I had clearly forgotten about. Placing it in my hands, she opened the door, asking me to follow her.

Chapter 34

Asher

Asher had been focused more on the view than his wife's presence. Walking alongside her, he could think of nothing to say to engage her in conversation. In the past, they would have had much to discuss. Their interests were always aligned. Now, he had no idea what to say to her. With his arm hooked through hers, he supported her as she took small steps near the cliff.

If he did not guide her, she would have weaved dangerously close to the edge. He stole a glance down the steep slope, seeing the shore was completely submerged beneath waves that crashed the rocky coast. The sea below was agitated from the gusts of wind that blew from the west. The sun had dipped to the horizon, taking its warmth with it. His light jacket was affording him little protection. He turned away from the cruel wind, deciding it was time to go indoors.

Eliana gave no notice, as he guided her towards the stone walkway back to the house. They had just reached the path when she stumbled and fell, collapsing face first on the hard surface. Landing heavily, she made no sound to indicate she was even aware she had fallen. Asher knelt next to his wife, concerned when she did not attempt to rise. Her cheek was pressed against the stone with her visible eye staring glassily into the distance. Her sheen face was pale from the exertion of the walk.

Castigating himself for not paying attention to her fragile state, he cursed silently. He should have sensed she was close to passing out. *What is the matter with me? Am I so self-involved that I could not see past my own slights? Has she given up completely?*

He took her hand, feeling her pulse race as she fought to catch her breath. They were very close to the house, the door a mere two steps away. She had not been able to reach it. His jaw clenching, fighting the recriminating emotions welling up inside him, he put all his energy into helping his wife.

"Let me carry you." Asher offered.

Eliana's emerald green eyes were half closed, shrunken in her face. She had no strength left to speak. Her eyes lowered, her head barely moved to acquiesce to Asher's offer. Lifting her gently into his arms, he carried her inside to the bedroom allotted to them. In the main room, Bet rose from her seat to come with them. Her movement was halted by Asher, who waved her off. Her mother needed to rest, not have people hovering over her.

Inside their bedroom, he settled her on the bed, making sure to place the pillows under her head so she was comfortable. Grateful that no one had followed them, Asher placed a chair next to Eliana's bed. He did not want to speak to anyone. Sitting down, he watched her lie there unmoving. His worry over his wife was awkward for him. He knew he should still be angry with her, but fear of losing her was overriding that emotion.

"You can go, Asher. I need only rest." She whispered, with her eyes closed.

Does she think so little of me that she believes I would abandon her in this state? He could not leave her like that. Maybe once everything was settled, they could revisit what they would do. For now, he would offer his support.

"It's Aidan, isn't it? He is the cause of this." Asher was certain his son's captivity, being kept from them, was creating the issues they were facing.

Eliana did not respond. Her eyes remained closed and she seemed to be asleep. Asher moved to pull the comforter up to cover her. When she felt the cloth brush her skin, her eyes snapped open. She regarded him, his face so close to hers. Her steely gaze held him prisoner. *How long has it been since we were this close?* Asher was taken aback to discover she still could move him. His body had an instant reaction to her proximity. He drew away, sitting back once he had covered her. A small smile twitched on her lips.

"Do not fear, Asher. I cannot pounce on you." Her eyes held amusement.

Allowing a grin, he looked at her, seeing some of the woman he had fallen in love with. *Will we ever be able to put back what she destroyed? If she had to do it over again, would she still take the same course?* He had never understood how her mind worked. Trust between them was fractured. It would take a lot for him to place his faith in her again.

"Yes, to answer your question. Aidan is the cause of this." Eliana watched her husband, expecting him to leave now that he had his explanation.

Asher leaned back in his chair, stretching his legs out. He assumed a comfortable position for what he wanted to discuss with her. It was past the time to get some answers. His wife, suspicious of why he remained, shifted uncomfortably on the bed. He was inwardly pleased to see her unsure of his intentions.

"Tell me about your son." He asked her.

Her sudden intake of breath was the only indication that he had surprised her. She knew exactly which son he was referring to. Tearing her eyes from his, her fingers trembled as she started arranging the comforter around her. *Will she answer me honestly, or try deception?* Asher would not put anything past her. Eliana's fear was palpable. Keeping her face downcast, she hesitated before answering him. Once she did, her trembling voice betrayed how difficult it was to relive the past.

"As you are aware, Elsam and I were involved for some time

before his incarceration. I was unaware of what he had been up to. A month after I had sentenced him, I found myself with child. With no husband, I made excuses for being absent from my duties. Vanya was a godsend to me. She handled things efficiently while I was indisposed. When I started to show, I made up an excuse, a need to go out of our land on pressing business. Vanya stayed behind to run things. When the boy was born, I returned secretly, handing him over to Vanya to raise. Vanya named him Solas. She kept him away from court and I never saw him again." She stopped, looking to see how Asher was reacting.

She saw exactly what he was thinking from his incredulous expression. Asher was skeptical at what she had admitted. *How could she have kept herself away from her child?* He knew her to be distant with his children, but she always cared enough to guide them through life. *Is it possible to cut the cord between mother and child? Had she never wondered how he was?*

"It wasn't easy, Asher. It was something that needed to be done. I knew Elsam would be free one day. I couldn't risk him knowing of Solas's existence. Elsam was always ambitious. Could you imagine what he would have done with that information? I was waiting for you, for our life together." Her voice begged him to understand.

Asher had never met Elsam. He knew of who he was only from their history, but not who he had been to his wife. His ambitions to rise above his station were legendary. He could just imagine what Elsam would have done with the information. Forcing her to acknowledge their son, he would have risen to the throne. Asher and Eliana would have been kept apart, their children never coming to be. Understanding her reasoning made up for some of the lies she had told. Forgiveness was another matter. He was not ready to go that far yet.

"And me. Statue. Any reason for why you kept me there?" His voice came out harsher than he had intended. He saw her flinch, looking past him to the window.

"I kept you there for your safety." Was all she said.

Safe? What about being kept frozen, feeling the slippage of time was for my safety? What does she mean? Asher did not comprehend how she thought he had been safe. Only the mermaids' company had kept him sane. Hundreds of years went by, his children grew, missing out on their lives.

"I did not know who to trust, Asher. Knowing your impostor was spying for Elsam, I could not let him know I was aware he wasn't you. God only knew what they would have done to you. I at least knew where you were. Believe me, that man and I never shared a bed. I moved him out of our bedroom on the pretext that I was tired of his company. I had spies following his every move. It was the only time I did not confide in Vanya. I must have sensed something in her to keep me from spilling the secret. I never gave up on us. Looking for a safe way to release you was all I could think of." Her voice sounded hoarse from emotion.

Asher held back going to her. Something still made it impossible to forget the purgatory she had left him in. Her eyes implored him for understanding. Tears welled and then ran down her cheeks. Turning her face away to hide her pain, Asher felt like a heel. Rising from his chair, he made to go to her, but was interrupted by Thalia. Seeing she had walked in on a private moment, her hand covered her mouth while her eyes clouded with contrition.

"What is it, Thalia?" Asher tried to put her at ease.

"Are you up to joining us? We need Eliana." Thalia retreated from the room once she had received his nod.

Chapter 35

Alexa

With my chin resting in my hand, my elbow on the table supporting its weight, I drummed my fingers on the surface, waiting expectantly for everyone to gather. The time it was taking had my stomach tied in knots. I did not know what time it was, but could almost hear the seconds of a clock ticking away. On the table, the brown-colored cover of the book was waiting to be opened. I had not taken my eyes off of it once since plopping down into my chair.

A gold-colored emblem, emblazoned on it, held my rapt attention. It was familiar, yet I could not place where I had seen it before. Was it a serpent or a dragon's head? The outline was chipped, faded from age. Two blood red, reptilian eyes stared back at me. What were they trying to tell me? The image seemed to slither and slide, mesmerizing me with its motion. Could anyone else see it? Hypnotized by its movement, I jumped when Liam grabbed my hand, stilling its incessant rapping.

I refused to glance his way. The questions I would find in his eyes, I wished to avoid for the moment. His touch momentarily took my attention away from the object that had held me transfixed. When I focused back on the book, I found the emblem still, unmoving. Had I imagined it?

I barely noticed Liam stretching out my fingers, massaging them gently and placing my hand palm down on the tabletop. Letting go of me, I could feel his stare, trying to draw me to look his way. My fingers itched to start drumming again. How much longer would it take for our parents to get there? Massaging my temples, I pushed down the impatience of having to wait.

Whatever was written in the book, I hoped it would bring me closer to Aidan. Elron had not found him yet. Next to me, Bet was, for the time being, calm and relaxed. True to his word, Elron communicated with her hourly. She explained to me that it was getting increasingly more difficult to reach each other, but that just knowing he was safe was enough for now. I was relieved that she had remained, not giving into her impulse to go after him. How long that would last, if they lost contact, I could not hazard a guess. Bet was impossible to predict.

Whatever was going through her mind, she kept well hidden. Only the crease on her forehead was any indication of how hard she was concentrating on keeping the line of communication between her and Elron open. It was coming up to the hour for him to reach her. Her mounting agitation had her eyes darting back and forth as she waited. I prepared myself to physically restrain her if Elron did not check in. Watching her twitch in her chair, debating whether to sit or stand, I knew all too well how volatile she could be.

Finally, our parents arrived. Coming into the room, Asher carried Eliana in his arms. Her loss of strength was progressing, showing no signs of abating. Putting her on a chair, Asher wrapped a blanket around her, only seating himself when she brushed off his fussing. Her complexion was pasty, her gaze unfocused. She looked shrunken under the heavy blanket. My parents had followed them into the room.

Coming over to where I sat, Rider stopped, standing silently near me, next to my mother. His gaze landed on me, troubled by what he must have seen. I gave him a tentative smile to reassure him. With everyone present, Liam reached to pull the book to him.

From the corner of my eye, I watched him pull back the cover to the first page so that he could start reading. What I saw was a replica of the emblem from the cover, followed by words that made no sense. The language it was written in was nothing but scribbles to me. My mind could not process them nor convert them to the English language anymore.

As he silently read, my mother's warning played in my mind. She was standing behind me, out of sight, with Rider next to her. Her hands rested on the top rail of my chair. I could not see them, but I felt their tense presence. I had yet to decide what to do about her advice. Thinking on it had already given me a headache. Liam knew I was avoiding him. He was perceptive enough to figure out I needed space.

All I knew was that her words increased my resolve to find Aidan. What to do about Liam was another matter. My feelings for him were still ambivalent. My thumb traced my bottom lip, recalling the sweetness of his kiss. Being in his arms, I had felt safe and cherished. I was not sure that it was stubbornness over being forced to be with Aidan that pulled me to Liam. Was it attraction or dependence? Did I lean on him only because of some misguided need to choose my own destiny?

"It doesn't say where to find it. More riddles to decipher." Liam broke into my thoughts.

He was staring at me, searching my face to know what I was thinking. It was not the time to get into it. Until I could figure out my true feelings, it would do neither of us any good to pretend that his brother did not factor into what I ultimately decided. Still, he could tell that something was bothering me. Avoiding his stare, I looked at the book, hoping he would return his attention to the opened manuscript.

His gaze stayed on me for a few more seconds before he returned to his reading. My mother placed her hand on my shoulder, trying to settle my growing panic. I wanted to flee to my room and give in to the tears that were threatening. In the uncomfortable silence that filled the room, Liam returned his attention to the yellowed pages in front of him.

"Can you just read it to me, please?" I asked.

Liam cleared his throat before he spoke. The tension he was feeling was obvious by the way he held himself. Shoulders hunched, hands clenched, he concentrated his attention on the written passage before him. My mom was right. I had to put things right before I hurt him further.

"I'll read it to you. Just give me a minute to translate it properly." Liam continued scanning the page.

While he read, I glanced towards the open door. Outside, I could see Rina pacing, agitated at what was being communicated to her. Her lips were moving, her face scrunched angrily, while staring up at the sky. She had not given up on soliciting help.

Between her and her mother, I was hoping they could convince Rhea to let us see Meredith. I knew it was a long shot, but I was leaning on the side of cautious optimism. My anger at the goddess's inaction had subsided. Instead, impatience at their vacillating had grown.

"Okay, here goes. Most of what is written is only history, but these words seem to be what we are looking for." Liam started to recite from the book.

The goddess awaits the chosen at Asserbo. The castle will guide the way. Only with the crystal can entry be gained. Awaken the army to battle evil, and then choose the path of redemption.

"What is Asserbo? What does it mean?" The word had no meaning for me.

"Asserbo is a place in Denmark. There is a ruined castle there. It was built originally as a monastery for monks. It was much later that it was used as a castle." Eliana explained.

From my earlier vision, I knew what I had to do, which path to take. It was the only way to save everyone. I had foreseen the events in my vision, back when I actually was able to have visions. None of the others knew what I was planning. I had to keep that to myself. If they found out, they would try to talk me out of it.

The dangers of putting what I had seen into action were unknown. I only knew that it was what I was meant to do. Turning my attention back to the matter at hand, I found Eliana studying me, a slight smile on her lips. She knew and understood my need to keep it a secret.

"This army, is it Freya's? The book back at the estate had a picture of me with them." I asked her directly.

She thought for a moment before responding. I was struck by how much more lively she seemed. Her complexion was more rosy, the bags under her eyes gone. Seeing her, more or less, back to her ethereal state, I wondered what it meant. There was a glint in her eye, as our eyes met.

Out of nowhere, I felt a current of energy make its way up my spine. It tingled its way through my arms and down my fingers. The elevated energy caused a spark where my fingers touched the table. Lifting my hands, I stared at them. Before I could mention what I was experiencing, Eliana rose. She folded her blanket, draping it over the back of her chair. Leaving the table, she leisurely walked back and forth while speaking.

"Asserbo was an ancient worship site for Freya. The monastery was built upon its remains. You must get the Kaemorra and go there. We will need Freya's army to defeat Elsam. Alexa, you already know what must be done. Once you have completed your choice, I will make sure to set things on their proper course." She walked towards the door, her eyes going to Rina.

Her statement that I knew what to do caused the others to stare at me. I shook my head at them. No, I was not ready to tell them. They would just have to trust me. The book had outlined our course. We knew where to go, but the Kaemorra's location was still a mystery. My thoughts stopped, my body stilled.

Frozen, I focused on the sensation building in me. I felt another delicious, energizing tingle run up my spine that had my fingers twitching. A rejuvenating feeling cascaded through me. I was suddenly more aware of everything around me, more centered. The air surrounding me was charged with electricity. My mom moved to go stand beside Eliana at the door. They were both fascinated with what was happening outside. I was unable to go to see what held their interest.

Feeling the power increase inside me, I was kept from any action by the electricity that snapped around me. Small bursts of energy escaped my hands. Bet had managed to screech her chair away from me, avoiding the sparks that bounced off of me. As suddenly as the pulses grew, they steadied themselves.

From within the cracking bolts that surrounded me, my eyes followed Rider's stride to meet up with the two women in the doorway. Whatever was happening, I welcomed the growing power in me. Did this mean that Aidan was close? What had changed to bring back our abilities? The power inside me expanded, settling itself. Gaining control over the sparking energy, I pulled it inside me.

"Elron says he has followed Elsam to Greenwich. Elsam is in his tower. Aidan must be there, hidden under a shield." Bet spoke. "He is returning to us with Tory. He says he too has felt a change in his abilities."

Liam was focused on me, watching quietly as I reacted to the news of Aidan. Denying that the news made my heart race was impossible. I would go after him, find him and bring him back. Steeling myself against the arguments that would ensue over going after Aidan, I fought to master control of the energy around me. I was able to dampen its strength enough to allow me to stand. I needed to see what was happening outside, why I had my power back. A few steps towards the door had me colliding with Liam's chest, as he blocked me.

"Stop. No way. You can't go acting like Bet. We need to think things through and plan." Liam had placed himself between me and the door, while Bet showed annoyance at being singled out.

I was preparing to fight my way out when I saw my mom race outside. Liam half turned to see what caused her quick exit. His mother was frozen, stunned in the doorway. Trying to get around him, I managed to make it to the door before I felt his hands grip my arms from behind.

Twisting me towards him, he wrapped one arm around my waist while keeping his other hand on my forearm, where its grip was already bruising my skin. He hauled me against him, keeping me pinned, unable to escape. With my feet off the ground, I struggled to regain my footing. His jaw clenched while he held me. He was royally pissed at my rushing off into danger.

"Put me down." I yelled at him.

Liam's response was to pull me closer to him, giving no sign of relinquishing me. Bet wisely kept out of his way. It was impossible to fight him. His strength was more than I could handle. My arms were pinned to my side, giving me no chance to zap him.

"I will put you down if you promise to stay by my side. Do not think of running off without me." Liam's voice was laced with anger.

"Fine, put me down." I responded to him, incensed at his actions.

Slowly, he released me, but kept hold of my arm. I glared at him to let go.

"For all that is holy, is that who I think it is?" My mother's exclamation was tinged with surprise.

Needing to see what she was seeing, I sent a jolt of electricity at Liam, giving me the opportunity to escape from his hold. His face registered surprise at my shocking him. Before he could recover, I bolted outside.

Chapter 36

Alexa

I made it outside and had just stepped onto the path leading to where my mom ran off to, when I was forcefully held back. Having recovered much more quickly than I had anticipated from my zapping him, Liam again stopped me from going any further. His arms wrapped around me from behind, keeping my arms and hands prisoners.

My feet dangled, inches above the ground, from being held pressed up against him. I was beyond angered at his manhandling me. A pulse worked itself through me trying to break loose. Leaving my fingertips, it had nowhere to go except the ground next to his feet. I squirmed to find a foothold. Liam only held me tighter. Suddenly, my whole body shook. That feeling was something new.

An electric current was gradually encompassing my whole body. It spread from the top of my head, down to my toes. Covered in a bluish-tinted glow, I felt a jolt leave me and enter Liam. His whole body jerked from the unexpected shock. The effect forced him to release me, as the current charged through him.

Where one moment I was held forcibly up against him, the next I was free. Liam was thrown and found himself lying prone on the ground. Without waiting to see if I had seriously hurt him, I made my escape and tore down the path.

In the distance, my mother was standing next to Rina by the water well. They were both gaping at a being who sat on the ledge of the infamous well. Surrounded by a glaring light, it was impossible to make out who it was. My feet slowed while I haltingly stepped forward towards them.

"Greetings child." A voice I recognized spoke.

Hearing that voice, my steps quickened, afraid she would disappear on me. I reached my mother's side in seconds. In front of us, Meredith was calmly seated on the ledge of the well, her body enveloped by a blinding light. If not for her voice, it would have been difficult to make her out.

Shielding my eyes with my hand, I was at a loss for words. I had been awaiting her arrival, but now that she was in front of me, I had no idea what to say to her. Seeing I was blinded by the light surrounding her, she muted the glow, allowing me the chance to view her clearly. It was amazing, and maybe a little bit weird, to look upon a face so like my own. What do you say to an immortal?

"Sit with me." She patted the ledge of the well next to her.

Uncertain of her intentions, I kept my distance and sat down on the patch of grass next to her feet instead. Rina had already dropped down on her knees, awed to be in Meredith's presence. I was not as impressed by the woman. She had, so far, brought nothing but grief to my life. The only reason I needed her was to tell me what I had to do and how to save Aidan.

Why did she set this ridiculous prophesy in motion? What had I done to be dragged into this? While all these thoughts ran through my mind, Meredith was regarding me with interest. I stared back at her, while the rest of our party kept their distance. Only Liam came closer, dropping down next to me. Meredith considered him under hooded lashes. Intrigued by him, she appraised him openly. Liam returned her stare, unwilling to be intimidated by her. She chuckled softly at his boldness.

"Why were you allowed to come?" I pulled her attention back to me.

She smiled, in a way that can be best described as sultry. She exuded sexuality in a way I never could. Her dress was in the style of the ancient Greeks. White, flowing, it was cinched just below her breasts, a deep v-shaped neckline exposed an ample cleavage. Her uncovered arms were tanned, defined by toned muscles. With a face of perfect proportions, eyes a clear sapphire blue, she was beyond beautiful. She was perfection. Being this close to her, I saw marked differences between us. I could never be that alluring.

"My mother has sided with your quest. She will allow me to help, but within limits. I am to tell you how to locate the Kaemorra, but nothing more. You know what must be done." Her voice was melodic, hypnotic.

A multitude of questions ran through my mind. Why did she set this in motion? Why was I pushed into this situation? Looking at her, I found her staring at the sky. Would she leave before giving me answers? Cocking her head to the side, she was listening to a voice from above. Nodding, she fixed me with her stare, speaking softly.

"I have lived so long, Alexa, that it was an affront to be so easily captured by someone beneath me. That the Sidhe queen, Eliana, allowed one of her subjects to harm me angered me immensely. I wanted to punish her and all her kind. It seemed fitting that she pay with the ultimate sacrifice. I set in motion a plan that would save her people by losing her child. It seemed a fitting punishment at the time. Only later did I calm down enough to see the error of my ways. I had to change the course I laid out. Placing it all on your shoulders was also wrong. I see that now." Her confession held no remorse.

Admitting she had done this out of childlike anger should have at least been said with contrition. I sensed no emotion from her. Her attention was diverted to Eliana, who had walked closer to us.

The two were both responsible for the choices they had made. I could not blame one without also finding the other at fault. The time for recriminations was long past, however. We all had to work together now.

"I found myself unable to decide how to fix what I had done. It was too late to change the course of the Kaemorra disappearing. Knowing that it would have to be during your lifetime, I made sure to have my child start the lineage with you. All your ancestors before your birth were protected, but only you would inherit my full powers." She continued.

What was she talking about? Is this all the powers she had? I would have thought she would be stronger than I was. Her soft laugh at having heard my thoughts broke off suddenly. Her attention was diverted by something or someone. Sighing, she half-closed her eyes as if concentrating.

For a moment, I thought I saw irritation flit across her features. I must have imagined it because when she gazed back at me, her face appeared devoid of emotion. Only her blue eyes sparkled, as she continued speaking. I was impatient to hear news of Aidan, the Kaemorra and where to go from there.

"In time. Let me continue. I also needed to make certain that the queen's son did not perish. I was assailed with guilt over trying to cause someone's death. My own mother took me to task over the matter. Alexa, I was further aghast to discover that her son was your soulmate. The stars aligned themselves to find you the perfect mate, only I was to be the catalyst for you losing him. The only way to correct my mistake was to have the joining commence before your meeting. I have caused much suffering." She was looking at Liam as she spoke.

Liam went rigid next to me, stricken at her words. Her words confirmed what he must have known. Even without her saying anything, he must have known the truth of it. I would have chosen

Aidan over him in the end. Who could fight the stars and destiny? Was Meredith really and truly upset at what she put in motion? She gave no sign that she understood the turmoil she had put us through. Why did she have the joining start? I still needed to understand how it was to help us.

"Your joining caused a ripple in time. The future is not clear-cut any longer. You have options before you now. Returning the Kaemorra to the queen is but one way to go. You have already foreseen what you must do. Do not deviate from that course no matter what the danger. Know that in the end you will find a way back."

Her words had my mother silently staring at me, suspicious of what I meant to do. I was saved from having to answer her questions by Meredith, who rose from her seat and held out her hand for me to take it.

I stared at the hand of that being. She gave me a reassuring smile, as she took a step towards me. Whatever she needed of me, I had no choice but to go along with it. Placing my hand in hers, she helped me to stand. Liam got up, ready to follow wherever she led me. As the others watched, she guided me to a clear, open space in the field we were in. She let go of my hand and stepped away from me.

As soon as she had retreated a distance away, a ring of fire erupted, encircling me within its flames. Through the veil of flames, I saw Liam attempt to breach the wall. The flames were too tall, too powerful to permit him access. The scorching heat it emitted made it impossible to approach. I was a prisoner in the center of it. Liam turned his fury on Meredith, who shrugged her shoulders at his glare.

I had no way to escape the rising flames that had burst from the ground. Facing me from the other side of the inferno, Meredith spread her arms, her head tilting towards the sky. The sound of the roaring fire blocked out the words she spoke. The incredible heat had sweat blurring my vision, my breath choked. Dizzy from the lack of air, I fell to my knees. My eyes moved heavenward, looking away from the inferno before me.

From up above, I watched a beam of light slowly descend to where I struggled for breath. On reaching me, it surrounded me, blinding me with its force. I felt it gather its power, felt an electric discharge slam into me. The force of it was unbearable.

A scream of agony tore from me, as wave upon wave of electricity ran through me. My backed arched, my body convulsing from the onslaught. Collapsing completely onto the ground, I shook uncontrollably. The unrelenting fury of the assault seemed never-ending. How long it went on was lost to me. I was close to losing consciousness.

Outside the fire ring, I could barely make out those watching. I could barely hear anything but my own screams. Their yells for Meredith to stop were nothing but background noise. Collapsing onto my side, Liam's face came into view from beyond the firewall.

Unable to touch me, he merely lay on the ground facing me. Whenever he tried reaching through the flames, the crackling energy jerked his hand away. The fear on his face must have mirrored my own. The emotion was quickly replaced by crippling pain, as another bolt struck me. When I thought I could not take anymore, a final blast hit me. It hit me with such force, I blessedly lost consciousness.

"Alexa, sweetie, can you hear me?" Mom's voice brought me back to awareness. I dazedly tried to focus on her.

I moaned, feeling like a freight train had run over me. Moving was excruciating. Every muscle in my body ached. I could only lie there, trying my best to recover. Spent electricity was still coursing through me. Once in a while, I would jerk from a sudden pulse of power.

I blinked my eyes to clear my focus. The sensation of my mom stroking my hair was intensified. I could feel each strand of hair react to the motion. With my cheek resting on the damp grass under me, I could see each drop of dew that clung to the blades. My mom was hunched over me, feeling my pulse. Each breath I took sounded amplified in my ears.

I had to get up. Meredith had to explain what she did to me. Trying to sit up, I found all my strength had deserted me. My arms were numb. They lay unresponsive, useless to me. My legs were in a similar state. Glancing around for Meredith, so she could explain herself, I saw Liam struggling to free himself from a force field. His hands were pushing against the impenetrable wall, unable to break through. I saw no evidence of the flames that had kept him from me. Liam was yelling, furious with Meredith.

"Let him go." I managed to form the words through listless lips.

Meredith, who was standing over my mother, held her hand out towards Liam, fixing her gaze on me. She dropped her hands, releasing him instantly. Liam, once freed, barreled over to me, falling to his knees. I was gradually getting back the mobility of my limbs. Liam helped lift me so that I was sitting up. Positioning himself behind me, he let me brace my back against his chest. Wherever our bodies touched, I received a tingling sensation. His every breath flowed through me.

"It will take a few minutes. You can already feel the added power." Meredith spoke calmly.

She was right. What I had felt before was nothing to what I was sensing now. I felt apart from the world around me, like I was on a different plane. People's auras were flickering, the whole area was giving off prisms of light. But it was the sounds that had me flinching. Heartbeats melded together creating drumrolls in my ears.

"It will mute itself out. You will have greater control as well. It will be instinctual to you. Now before I leave, there is one more thing I have to tell you." Meredith waited for me to focus on her.

"The Kaemorra was taken from where I had placed it. I cannot go into who took it or why, only know that they have been dealt with.

Now, you need to go to the Gods' temple. There, you Alexa, must enter alone. No one else from here can go in with you. At exactly noon, follow the sun's light to find the clue to the location of where it has been hidden. You must hurry. Elsam is close to figuring it out. You cannot allow him to retrieve it." She warned.

Where was this temple? Seeing my confusion she answered me.

"The Parthenon, of course. Go to Rome. I hope to see you again. If not, Gods be with you." Meredith explained.

"Wait." I managed to get out. I still had many questions in need of answers.

Answers were not going to be given. Meredith gave me a brief smile before turning her attention to the sky. Lifting her hands towards the heavens, she was enveloped in a shimmering light. I watched, transfixed, as she morphed, creating a blinding light that rose up into the air. When it hovered over us, it seemed to blaze brighter. It left us, climbing higher and higher, before exploding and casting its rays outward.

Chapter 37

Alexa

It was in this state that Elron and Tory found us. Their appearance came seconds after Meredith had departed. I was still recovering on the ground, Liam supporting me, and everyone was speechless. Bet immediately ran to Elron, jumping into his waiting arms. A smile warmed my lips at seeing how happy they were. Those same lips drooped upon feeling my heart skip a beat. Aidan's blood, flowing through me, waned in intensity. In my mind, an image of him formed.

He was bloodied and tormented. It was the look in his eyes that shook me. Glazed and unfocused, they lacked any spark. Liam brought me out of the vision by caressing my cheek. I fought down the panic of what I had glimpsed. I shook my head to clear it. Elron was watching me over Bet's shoulder, as he continued to hold her. He moved Bet to his side, his hand still around her waist and started over to us.

Tory on the other hand, looked unsure what to do with himself. He knew something was going on, but had no clue what. Able to finally move, I stood up unsteadily. Liam gave me no opportunity to distance myself from him. He followed me up, his arm wrapped around my waist to support me. I made the mistake of glancing at his face. His mournful expression gave away his total dejection. Everything Meredith had told us hurt him in ways I could only imagine.

"What is it?" Elron wanted to know, looking to me for answers.

I had none. Pulling away from Liam, I left it to the others to explain. I made my way to the edge of the cliff, gazing out at the waves rolling in from the sea. To say I felt invigorated would not do justice to what was going on inside of me. Meredith was right. Power unlike anything I had ever experienced was coursing through my body. It was like a snake coiled within me, ready to strike. I wanted to test it, to hurl it at someone, preferably at the gods themselves for putting us through this.

"Aidan needs to be rescued." Elron came over to join me.

His voice was hushed, so that only I could hear it. He waited for me to respond, keeping behind me, out of sight. Somewhere out there, Aidan was lost and hurt. Yes, I would find him. I had a distinct perception of him, knew exactly where he was. I could feel him again.

Silently rejoicing at the knowledge that our link was still there, I clamped down on the emotion. Even though I could sense him, what I felt from him filled me with dread. He was lost in nothingness. His mind was consumed in a black void.

Only the knowledge that I had to get to Rome kept me there. Otherwise I would have gone directly to him. Without answering Elron, I walked back to the others with him following me. We had to get to the Parthenon, get the clue, and finish this once and for all.

"We leave in half an hour. Get ready. It will be noon in Rome in about an hour." I walked away, leaving them to get prepared. Issuing orders was new to me. I was surprised how everyone jumped to do as I said.

Elron followed me indoors. I could tell he wanted to know what I meant to do about Aidan. I was not ready yet to involve him in my plans. I kept my own counsel, worried that in revealing my intention, he would attempt to stop me. There was only one way to save Aidan.

Once I had the clue, I would send Elron and Liam to retrieve the Kaemorra. I was going to find Aidan. Keeping my plan to myself, knowing I would get arguments from all of them, I mentally prepared for what lay ahead.

"If you go, when you go, I will support you. Only you can get through to him." Elron surprised me.

I stopped mid-step, taken aback that he saw what I was planning. Was I that obvious? He gently shook his head, stopping me from speaking. He had noticed Bet walking towards us. She knew something was up, but Elron quickly stepped to her, cutting her off from nearing me. He placed his arm across her shoulder and walked off with her. Knowing he would keep my secret, keep the others away, I entered the cabin, going straight to my room.

Inside, my sword was again glistening where it lay on the bed. It beckoned me to it. The return of its sheen was but another effect of our getting our powers back. I grabbed the sheath that Aidan had given me and draped it over my shoulders.

Picking up the sword, an echoing sigh seemed to spring from it. I slashed it through the air, watching the words inscribed on it glow brighter. They appeared to leave the blade and hover over it. The sword was mine. It had picked me. I felt tied to it in ways I could not explain. Feeling its response to my touch was like being accepted, deserving of its loyalty. My hand stilled its motion, staring at the magnificence of it.

Carefully, I inserted it into the holster. It hung comfortably down my back. Next I went to the bureau. On it lay my blade with the infused healing stone. It was already sheathed in an ankle holster. I took it, sliding it into my boot and tying the straps around my calf and ankle. The next thing I grabbed was my jeweled box. I had no need of it to find Aidan. His presence in the far distance was a beacon. I only took the box for sentimental reasons. My parents had, after all, gifted it to me for my birthday.

Needing something to wear to cover the sword that draped down my back, I used my new powers to call for a long leather coat. Seeing the item materialize, the memory of seeing Aidan in a similar one came to mind. He had looked daring and captivating in his. A slight smile formed on my lips at the memory. Soon, I would be with him.

Hurrying, I put on the soft leather coat and left my room to join the others. Rider and my mom were the only ones missing. The main room was overcrowded, as everyone milled about. Seeing me enter the room, Tory disengaged himself from his conversation with Rina. He came to me, hugging me enthusiastically. Lifting me off the ground, the force of his arms around me made me catch my breath. I was happy to see he was back to his infectiously affectionate self.

Letting me go, he was forced to step back by his brother. Elron stepped between us, asking to speak to me alone. I gave Tory's arm a squeeze, smiling as I left his side. Following Elron, we stepped outside for privacy. I could feel Liam's eyes burn holes in the back of my head, suspicious of what we were discussing. Once we were alone, out of sight of the others, Elron took something from his pocket and offered it to me.

"Here, you can give him this when you see him." He placed the vial of blood I had given him in my hand.

His hand wrapped around mine, hiding the vial within my palm. His eyes were glued to someone behind me. I did not need Elron to tell me who it was. His countenance made it clear that Liam stood in the doorway. Slowly, keeping my face neutral, I turned to face him.

Liam was staring at my hand that was still held by Elron. The vial might as well have been out in the open. Liam knew what I held. Elron let go of my hand, bowed his head slightly and stepped back. I kept my palm closed while sliding the glass vial into my pocket. Liam was now studying my face. Penetrating emerald eyes held mine. In them I could see a mixture of pain, acceptance and distrust. He knew I was up to something.

"Alexa, we're all ready." Rider interrupted us.

"Get everyone please, Dad. I'll wait over there." I pointed in front of me, out in the open space of the property.

I walked over to the clearing, feeling their eyes on my back. I needed a second to compose myself. Leaving it to Elron to diffuse the situation, I waited with a heavy heart for them to meet up with me. I could do nothing to ease Liam's hurt. That I had contributed to it made me culpable. I should have known better. Listening to their footfalls, as they made their way to me, I could identify each one of them.

Their individual signatures were like images in my mind. Liam was shuffling, disheartened, behind the others. Even with my back turned, I could see the rest of my friends and family leaving the cabin. One by one they came to stand next to me.

Once they had all gathered around me, without a word, I visualized a park I knew on the hills above Rome. They had no warning as I moved us, taking everyone with me, as I jumped to our new location. Their shock was evident on their faces, knowing I moved everyone at once. I would not need them to help me jump around the world. I was now able to travel on my own.

Looking at my watch, the time read eleven fifteen. We had forty-five minutes to get to the Parthenon. I took off immediately, leaving them to follow me. I had no wish to hear their comments. I was focused on our goal. The park was on the street above the Trinita dei Monti church. The Scalini Spagna, or Spanish Steps, as they were commonly referred to, was just in front of it. I hurried through the park, making my way to the street adjoining it. Behind me, the others kept up with my long strides. Out on the street I turned left, continuing towards my destination.

The Trinita dei Monti church appeared on the hilltop, its double steeples distinctive in design. A large obelisk faced it from across the street. From there we went down the Spanish Steps, walking past the Piazza di Spagna, and taking the street leading to via della Maddalena. It took all of fourteen minutes to reach the Parthenon.

The temple was overcrowded with tourists who were milling about at that time of day. Our group assembled across the Piazza della Rotonda, which fronted the old temple to the gods. The circular structure, with a front portico lined with Corinthian columns, was imposing. A rectangular vestibule linked the entrance to the interior. I had only seen pictures of the round rotunda inside.

With no idea on how or where our clue was to be found, I prepared to walk through the doors as the hour approached. I had to go in alone. Meredith had told us that only I could enter. What to expect once I was inside had not been disclosed. Steeling myself, I took two steps towards the church, only to be held back by Rider. His hand gently grasped my arm.

"Alexa, be careful. We don't know who or what could be waiting inside." He warned me.

"I know, Dad. I'll watch out for any dangers, but I can't feel any." I reassured him.

Leaving his side, I ascended the remaining steps to the front opening. Inside, more tourists milled about. They were all immersed in enjoying the statues and reading the information signs. Entering, I placed myself to the right of the doorway. The marble floor, with its rich red circle in the center and yellowish-brown squares surrounding it, stretched across the room.

Massive and imposing, the room I found myself in was illuminated from above. Centered on the ceiling that rose from the circular walls, the dome above me had a perfect round opening letting in the sun's rays. The light being cast was centered on the circular mosaic design on the floor.

Continuing further into the space, I advanced towards the middle of the room, stopping once I was beneath the dome opening. Above me, through the opening, the sun was fast nearing its summit. I glanced at my watch, seeing that there were less than thirty seconds before the time read noon.

Around me, people went about their business, ignoring me, as I waited for something to happen. Only whispered conversations between the people reached my ears. Their hushed tones echoed throughout the room. My ears picked up their random remarks regarding the beauty of the old church.

As I scanned the room, I was surprised to find the motions of those around me slowing. Their movements seemed stilted. I was drawn away from wondering what it meant by a noise above me. Looking up, the dome's opening appeared to grow in size. Suddenly, a beam of reddish-hued light descended from the opening above.

People around me seemed to freeze, their movements ceasing, as the aura descended towards me. Standing under the dome, the light coming down appeared to dim, creating a shadow over me. Gazing into the reddish hue, I saw an image of a man start to form. His face covered the opening, blocking out any remaining light from above me.

Gliding down towards me, his presence filled the room. His body coalesced as he neared me, taking on the form of someone I vaguely recalled. When he was a mere foot away from me, his feet touched down, facing me as I watched him studying me back. He looked so much like Jasper, the leader of the witches and warlocks, I wondered if they were related. There were a few marked differences, but the two could have been twins. He started speaking, giving me no chance to question him.

"I have much to say so listen carefully. You do not have much time. The Kaemorra is in Freya's temple. On the island of Zealand, outside the coastal town of Helsingor, her temple has been lost to time. Your friends will be able to find it by following the coastline. It lies to the south of Lake Kobberdam. With a drop of your blood, the Kaemorra will show itself. They must safeguard it until you are ready to complete your mission. You have your own path to follow. Find Aidan, rescue him. Only with him can you finish this once and for all. I will plant the vision of where your friends need to go in your mind. You already know where Aidan is being held. Hurry before it is too late. Elsam is close to finding the Kaemorra. Although he needs your blood to possess it, it is possible he may lie in wait for you and force it from you. He has amassed a formidable force of shadows and Daimons. He must not be allowed to gain possession of it. He will use it to open his homeland only for his followers. From the seat of power he will wreak havoc on earth, unleashing both shadows and Daimons on this land."

I had not been able to get in a word since he started talking. In my mind, a vision of a deep forested area grew. I would send the others there. More than ever, I knew I had to leave them to go get Aidan.

"There is no time for questions. Go. We will meet again if things go as planned." He said before I could voice my questions to him.

Without fanfare, he simply vanished before my eyes. The red aura that had surrounded him faded, the people around me started to move. The image that he planted in my head pushed to the forefront of my mind. How was I to maneuver it so that I was free to go rescue Aidan?

Preparing for the arguments I would be facing, I held little hope of convincing them. There had to be another way. Jostled by a tourist who walked into me, the time came for me to leave the temple. Excusing himself, the tourist returned to admiring the dome above him. I stilled my mind, finding the signatures of those who had come with me. Closing my eyes, I pictured everyone back at our estate.

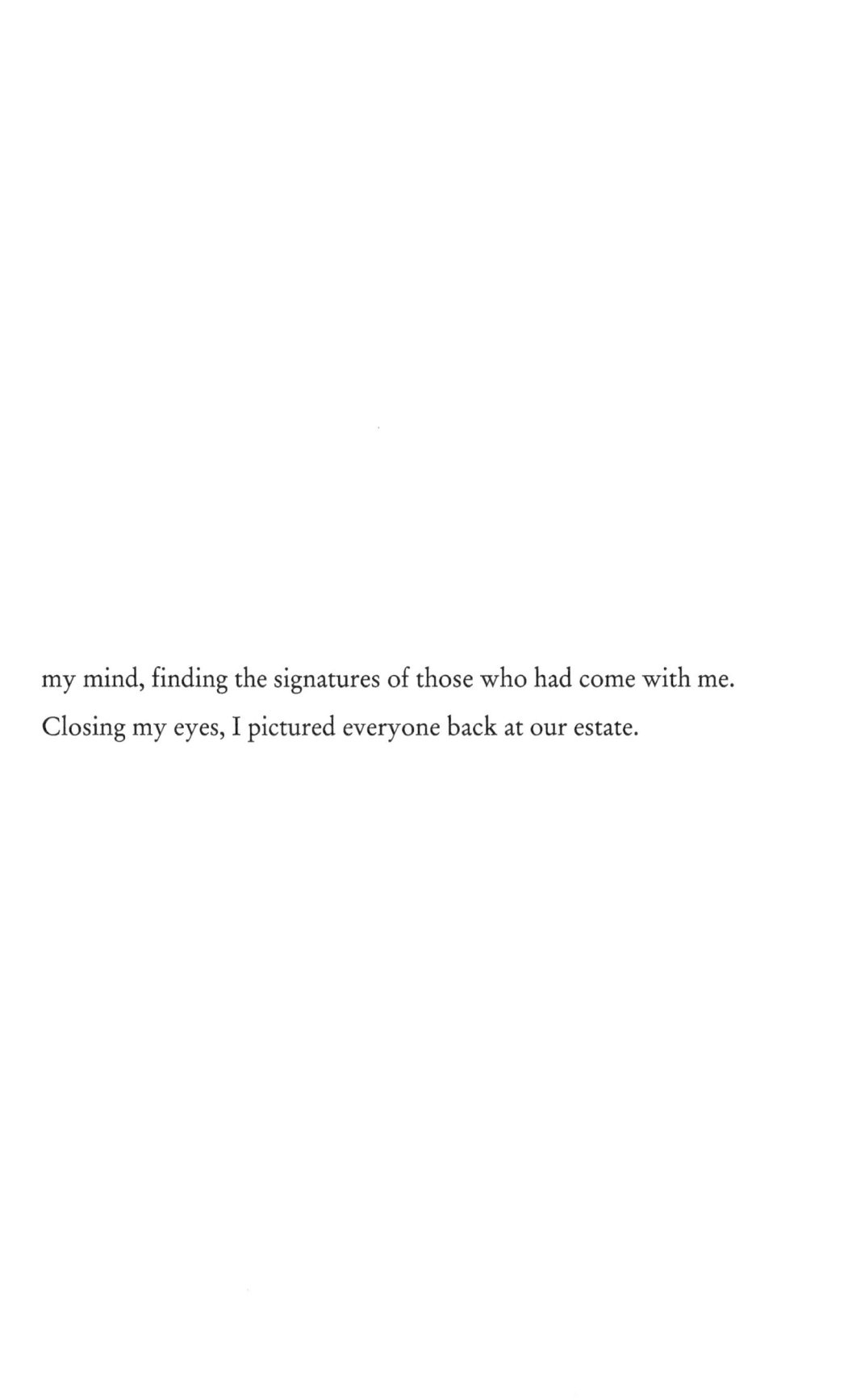

Chapter 38

Alexa

The arguing was still going on inside. No one noticed me leaving, quietly, to seek solace outside. Their rising voices collided, as their emotions took hold. Mostly, they were frightened for me and what I intended to do. I had transported us back to the estate outside Verona earlier in the day. I placed us all in the main room, which welcomed us in a mix of its living room and buffet setting.

Hunger drove me to the table. The savory aromas of cooked meats and assorted vegetables were eclipsed by the heavenly aroma of cinnamon, burnt sugar and rich chocolate. Scarfing down one sweet confection after another, I finished with a generous helping of strawberry shortcake.

I took my plate back to the couch, sliding my legs under me as I sat. The silence as we all ate gave me time to assess the safety of the property. My senses told me that we would be safe there again. Elsam, for some reason, never came to find us there.

Seeing they were all finished eating, I placed my plate on the coffee table. Only after filling them in on what they needed to do, and what I meant to do, did they all start speaking at the same time. They bombarded me with their belief of the dangers, the idiocy of my plan.

Everyone jumped in with their own ideas of how to proceed. Only Elron stood by my side. Liam had gone quiet, carefully watching me, as I listened to the growing disagreements. Once his attention was diverted, I escaped, leaving them all to continue without me.

Walking down to the beach, the full moon lit my way. I was standing where Aidan usually stood, facing the lake, alone in the twilight. Blocking out all the sounds around me, I focused on Aidan's essence, feeling his loss of fight. Guilt of what I had done to him ate away at me. I had to find him, had to make things right between us. Our link was still there, but was growing weaker. It was as if he were slowly cutting his ties with me.

"You will have to leave without them knowing." Elron's voice cut into my thoughts.

He had stepped next to me, soundlessly, his appearance surprising me. I must have been too preoccupied to notice his arrival. I knew he was right. The others would not let me go alone. I would have to leave without them knowing.

"I will go during the night. Hopefully everyone will take time to sleep. Take my blood, Elron. Use it to retrieve the Kaemorra." I slipped the vial out of my pocket, wanting him to use it to find the crystal.

He closed his hand around mine, the vial still gripped within my fingers. Staring at where our hands joined, he seemed unsure of what he wanted to say. Raising his head, his eyes met mine.

"Bring back my friend, Alexa." For the first time, I felt Elron open himself up so I could feel his emotions.

What I felt was a deep love for his friend, his companion and student. He had known Aidan most of his life. He had been tasked to train him, to teach him as a boy. Their friendship had grown beyond teacher and student. Elron considered Aidan a brother.

"I will bring him back, Elron. You have my promise on that." I squeezed his hand with tears blinding me.

I would do everything I could to bring Aidan back where he belonged. Relinquishing my fingers, he took the vial from me, placing it in his own pocket. Back in his reserved state, he backed away from me. I sensed Bet coming to where we were. We watched her as she came to meet us. She could tell we had been discussing Aidan.

"I won't tell you what to do. I have mixed feelings about it. On the one hand I want you to find my brother, but on the other, I want you to be safe." She spoke, as she reached us.

"It is the only way. I know what I must do." I responded.

Telling them good night, I left them together to return inside. In the living room, only my mom and Rider were still discussing what I meant to do. Seeing me, they stopped speaking, staring at me beseechingly to rethink my course. They must have understood there was no changing my mind. Rider pulled my mom into his arms, as she wept quietly.

"I'll be back before you know it. Go find the crystal. Elsam must not be allowed to reach its location first." I tried to sound confident.

I only had one other person to see before I left. He was the only one who would try the most to stop me. I found Liam in his room, lying on his bed, staring at the ceiling. He did not acknowledge me as I entered the room and sat down on the bed near his feet. I thought of what I could say to ease any pain I was causing him.

"It is dangerous and foolhardy. I cannot allow you to go." He spoke first.

His calm delivery belied the emotions raging within him. I could feel his fear, anger and hurt. Lowering my eyes, I stared at a spot on the bedcovers. I had much to say and little time to ease into it. It was never my intention to hurt Liam. If I were guilty of pushing Aidan away, I was equally guilty of using Liam.

"I have handled everything badly. From the start, I have fought against what Aidan and I were supposed to be. I wanted my own choices. Being linked, joined to your brother, without any choice brought out the worst of my stubbornness. If not for him, I would want nothing but to be with you, Liam. But, I know now that I belong with him. I can't escape the fact that his being gone has ripped a hole in me. I will not be able to live with myself if I don't help him. I have to let him know that what he saw that night was not what he assumed. I have to reach him somehow." I avoided looking at Liam, as I told him what lay in my heart.

Movement from the bed brought my eyes up. He lifted off his pillow and took my hands. A small frown marred his lips. His eyes bored into mine, trying to see what I may be hiding from him. I held myself rigid, hiding my thoughts from him.

"As much as I love you, Alexa, I have known in my soul that we were not meant to be. I will find a way to live with how I feel, but know that I will always be here for you. My brother is a lucky man to have you. You cannot help what or who is in your heart. Still, I will not allow you to place yourself in danger because you feel responsible." His stubbornness almost made me smile. Only the way he was looking at me stopped me.

Seeing he was completely serious, I took my hands from his and rose from the bed. I had to make sure he was unaware of my intentions. If he knew I planned to leave as soon as I left his side, he would not let me go. Turning towards the door, I avoided looking at him, as I came up with a story.

"We will discuss it more in the morning. I think everyone needs to sleep on it." I told him, walking to the door.

"Alexa." My name coming from his lips stopped me. I really did not want to turn to face him, but knew that if I did not, he would know something was up. At the doorway, I steeled myself to look back at him.

"You wouldn't be lying to me, would you?" He searched my face for any subterfuge.

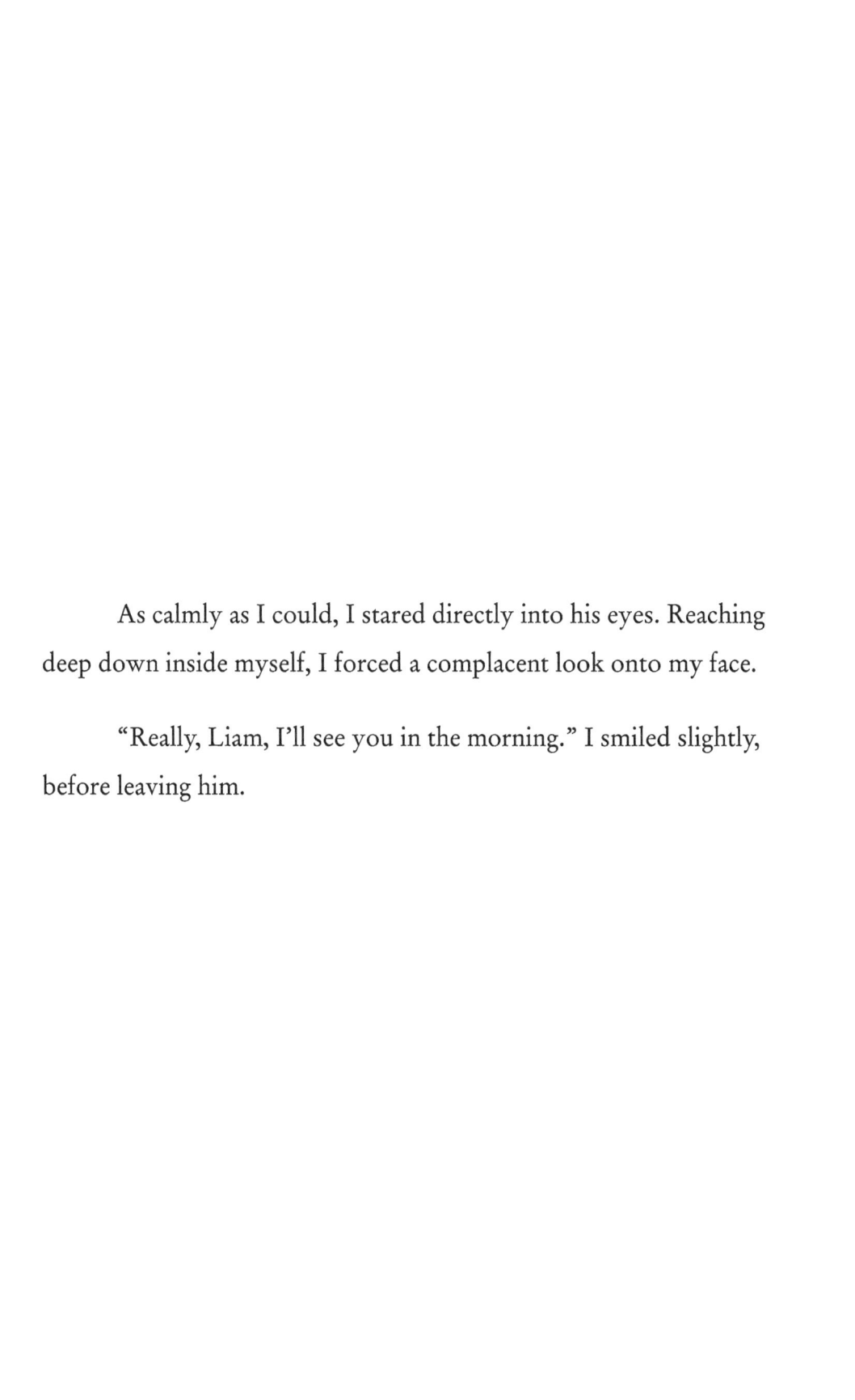

As calmly as I could, I stared directly into his eyes. Reaching deep down inside myself, I forced a complacent look onto my face.

"Really, Liam, I'll see you in the morning." I smiled slightly, before leaving him.

Chapter 39

Liam

Liam knew the moment his eyes opened the next morning that Alexa was gone. The ease with which she had lied to him made him furious that he had fallen for it. Worry quickly replaced the anger he felt. She was alone facing a danger she could not possibly be aware of.

Jumping out of bed, he dressed in the clothes that he had dumped on the floor the night before. Picking up the strewn garments, he swore under his breath at being deceived. He ran his hands through his hair, not caring how unkempt he looked. He had to find the others and plan on rescuing her.

In the bathroom, he splashed cold water on his face. His reflection gave him no comfort. He looked as he felt. No amount of grooming would make him seem any less irate. His eyes flashed with irritation at her actions. She was no better than his sister.

Pushing away from the sink, he entered his room to grab his sword. He would find her and forcefully keep her by his side. Downstairs, the only person in the room was Elron. He sat, as if waiting for him. Liam knew from looking at him that Elron was aware Alexa was gone. He had known all along what she meant to do. Before he could say anything, Elron spoke first.

"We have our own mission to accomplish. Do not let her determination be in vain. We must find the Kaemorra so that when she returns we can finally end this. She will be back, Liam. Have faith in her."

Liam paced, anger and acceptance fighting for dominance in him. A part of him knew what Elron said was the truth. The part of him that loved Alexa, though, was unable to let go of the fear that she had placed herself in harm's way. He had no idea where she had gone. Finding her would be near impossible. Having the choice of whether to accompany her or not taken from him was not sitting well with him. She should have let him go with her.

"Having you there would not have helped Aidan." Elron spoke to his thoughts.

Liam knew Elron was right. This all started because of his attraction to Alexa. He should have kept himself in check. His brother would not be in that position if he had kept Alexa at bay. It did not make his worry lessen. Alexa was still somewhere out there, alone, facing who knew what. Pacing was doing little to calm him. He flopped down on one of the sofas, staring daggers at Elron for his complicity. Itching to do something, he stood and began his pacing again.

Liam paused his steps as Rider and Thalia entered the room. Seeing his agitated state, they immediately knew what the cause was. Thalia gasped, as realization of what had occurred dawned on her. She glanced at Rider to see if he was aware. His look told her that he had already guessed that his daughter was gone.

"When?" Was all she could manage to get out.

"Sometime before dawn." Elron answered her.

Liam grasped what Elron admitted and faced his friend. *So he knew all along, and still let her go alone. Why did he keep it from me?* But he knew why. If he had known, he would have tried to stop her. Elron facilitated her escape.

"You bastard! How could you let her go like that?" Liam cruelly addressed Elron.

His anger was beyond his control. He would have struck out at Elron if Bet had not walked into the room and held onto him. Pushing her away, he watched as Bet lost her balance, falling on the floor. Elron ran to her, lifting her carefully, making sure she was not hurt. After he was sure she was not, he stepped up to Liam, grabbing him by the shoulders. He fought back the urge to punch Liam for striking out at Bet.

"You are not the only one worried about her, not the only one who cares. It had to be done. We need your brother back, Liam." Elron gave him a shake.

Clenching his fists at his sides, Liam tried to control his churning emotions. Elron was right again. *Thalia and Rider must be just as scared of Alexa being out there alone.* He struggled to regain control. His fear for her was like a burning ember inside him. He did not know if he could extinguish it. Clearing his mind, Liam tried to focus on the here and now. He breathed in deeply before letting the air out. Bet was watching him from the sidelines, next to Thalia.

"Sorry, Bet." He told his sister, contritely.

"I'm fine, Liam. Just focus on what we need to do." His sister joined Elron.

Thalia walked further into the room, collapsing onto the sofa. Her face was pale, stricken at her daughter's actions. Rider went to her, sitting down and trying to comfort her. With his arm across her shoulders, he gathered her to his side, murmuring softly to her.

Liam could not rid himself of the foreboding. He had a premonition of disaster. In the doorway, his mother appeared, finding him still held by Elron. Her eyes showed empathy with what he was going through. Behind her, his father recognized the emotions his son was experiencing. Together, they continued into the room, both having nothing to say to ease the situation.

Rina and Tory walked in together, as if knowing something had riled everyone. Eliana showed concern for her son, seeing him agitated, being handled by Elron. When she started to go to him, Asher kept her back by taking her hand. Her eyes sought his for an explanation.

"The only thing we can do now is go to Denmark, find the Kaemorra and keep it safe." Asher squeezed her hand.

Liam broke away from Elron's grasp not knowing what to do. He walked around the room like a caged animal. Action was what he needed, something to do. He would go crazy imagining Alexa in all sorts of deadly situations. Trusting that she knew what she was doing was difficult.

"Fine." He forced himself to sit on one of the armchairs. "What do we do?"

Asher, Elron and Rider discussed their options. Liam half listened, as they went over the locale and what they might face. Tory had come to sit near Liam. His face showed concern for what Liam was going through. Rina still stood by the doorway eyeing him warily. His mother was fighting the urge to go to her son, to offer advice. Liam almost laughed at the notion of his mother being afraid of anything.

Feeling all eyes on him, Liam had had enough. *Do they really think I will lose it again?* He rose from his seat, feeling their gaze follow his movement. Eliana opened her mouth to speak, but Liam cut her off.

"You can all stop trying to handle me. We have a place to get to. Let's get going." He said, walking out of the room to prepare.

Chapter 40

Alexa

With my eyes closed, I had an image in my mind of the room they had placed me in. Carrying me into the cell, I had been unceremoniously dumped on a hard surface. Stifling the moan from the rough handling, I waited for the sound of the door closing before opening my eyes. I sat up on the cold, hard stone bench as soon as I felt their signatures diminish. Feigning unconsciousness while fighting the urge to harm them had taken all my willpower. I could not risk them becoming aware that I had full use of my powers.

The point of my being captured was to find Aidan and escape. It took every ounce of self-control I possessed not to burn everything in sight. I needed to get my bearings, learn as much as I could before I got us both out of there. Walking purposely into their trap was the easy part. I needed to listen to what was being discussed in the chamber above me. My ears picked up on everything that was being said. Elsam was crowing at my capture, how easily he had subdued me. Myrick on the other hand was more cautious, suspicious of my being so easily detained.

"The girl is nothing. She cannot stop my plans." Elsam boasted.

There was more than one of his cohorts who doubted his

statement. Fear of speaking out against him kept them silent in his presence. A growing split in his ranks was evident in the way they held off voicing their opinions. Every thought was transmitted to me. Concentrating on the ongoing conversation, I felt Vanya when she entered the room above me, followed by her son, Solas. I puzzled at his hesitancy to go near his father. Both mother and son stood by the entrance, listening to his gloating.

"Sire, you must let me have her. I must know what powers she is gifted with." Myrick interrupted Elsam.

Elsam was irked with Myrick. Whatever had drawn them together, they now had little use for each other. Myrick's only interest lay in me. His need to understand me was almost maniacal. I was sure the man had lost any sanity long ago. His thoughts were crazed. He had no idea how close Elsam was to destroying him.

"I will hand her over to you as soon as I have the Kaemorra. She is of little use to me afterwards." Elsam responded with a sneer. His contempt of the man was painful. I saw his mind form ways to torture and kill the warlock. The vivid, excruciating images made my stomach heave.

I hoped my friends and family had already retrieved the Kaemorra. They should have arrived at the site by mid-morning. One of the reasons I wanted Elsam to find and capture me was to keep him preoccupied. Any delay I caused him meant more time for the crystal to be in our hands.

Aidan was close, somewhere within the fortress I found myself in. Myrick did a great job of shielding the place, but with my new level of abilities, I could feel Aidan nearby. I had to get to him soon. Listening to Elsam drone on was giving me a headache. A slight disturbance in my senses had me looking for the cause. Vanya's mind reached mine, warning me that I was being monitored. Her warning made me curious. She had helped Bet and my parents when they were held. Which side was she on? Could I trust her? Taking heed, I pulled back, closing the link to the room above.

I got up from what was my bed to stretch my legs. My cell was a nine by six foot space of stone. The only way out was the heavy wooden door that had been barred from the outside. Using my powers to unlock it and escape would be easy, but I did not want to alert anyone that I had their use.

I would have to bide my time a bit longer. Until I was reunited with Aidan, I had no reason to leave. My purpose for being there was to get to him. Only then would I take us both out of there. The protection over the tower was not as complete as Myrick imagined. There were plenty of holes to maneuver through.

From outside, the soft steps of someone making their way to me, made their presence known. I had just sat down again when the door creaked on its hinges. The wooden door was opened slowly to allow Vanya to enter. Peering behind her, she made sure the coast was clear before studying me silently. She looked nothing like the woman I had previously met. Her whole appearance spoke of the hell she had been living in. Why was she still there? She had ample chances to cut her ties to Elsam. She was free to come and go.

"Listen to me. I don't have much time. They will notice me gone. You will be brought up to be shown to the others. Do not let them see how powerful you are. I will try to do as much as I can to get you out of here." She started speaking quickly.

"I have to get Aidan out. I will not leave without him." I cut off whatever else she was going to say.

"Aidan is in another cell on the floor below us. I haven't been allowed to see him. Elsam is distrustful of me. He is only keeping me around because of Solas. It may be impossible to get him out." She finished.

She had no idea what I could do. Only my will not to kill them all right away kept them alive. I saw her turn to look behind her. As suddenly as she had appeared, she shut the door, closing me back in. Feeling her slink back down further into the corridors, she faded into the background. Whoever was coming, they did not feel the need to silence their steps. The heavy sound of their feet hitting the stone floor echoed in the cavern outside.

The door swung open again, allowing Myrick to take Vanya's place. His hideous scarred face sneered at me. I watched him coolly as he came closer to me. He was trying to cast some spell over me to be compliant. Hiding a smile, I went along with it, looking meek. Grabbing my arm, he pulled me from the room. He dragged me through the corridor that led to the stairs. I let him pull me forward, climbing the jagged steps up. In the grand foyer of the main floor, guards stood on each side of the entrance where Elsam awaited me.

My first thought upon laying eyes on him was that he would have been good looking if not for his viciously curved smile. He was extremely tall, well-built and possessed an ease with his frame. Beside him stood his son, Aidan's half-brother. Solas was regarding me with interest. He had a perplexed expression on his face, probably wondering what all the fuss was about. Seeing my small frame, he must be wondering why everyone was apprehensive of me. Pushed from behind, I stumbled as I was guided to stand before Elsam.

He stepped down from his throne, making a circle around me. His laugh as he studied me gave me a moment of fear. Clamping down on it, I steeled myself to face him. Coming back to stand in front of me, I met his stare, showing I was not afraid of him. His eyes turned a dark green at my not blinking.

Fury replaced his sneer. With the back of his hand, he hit my face, causing me to fall back. My hand came up to my cheek that burned from his slap. Through the tears that sprung, I saw Solas look as if he would come to me, help me somehow. Only the return of Vanya, who held him back, stopped him from interfering. I saw his jaw clench, his eyes fill with hatred for the man who had injured me. Rising back to my feet, I came to stand inches from Elsam, my eyes only reaching his broad chest. I wanted so badly to hurt him, but only the need to get to Aidan held me back.

"Make sure to draw her blood. I have need of it. Take her away. She bores me." Elsam walked away, sitting back on his chair.

Feigning disinterest in me, he let Myrick take me away. All the while, I could feel his eyes boring into my back. He was afraid of me. The fact gave me courage. Myrick wasted no time in getting me back to my cell. Throwing me in, I landed hard on my knees. Blood oozed out from the scrapes I received from his manhandling me. He waited for me to get up from the floor before speaking. Malice covered my vision, as I stared at him. My fingers twitched to retaliate.

"I don't know how strong you are, if you are faking. It won't matter come morning. I have a friend coming who will be able to handle you. You will be coming with me whether Elsam wants it or not. By tomorrow night you will be back in the States in my possession. For now, a guard will draw your blood as Elsam directed." His words caused me trepidation. Were my plans falling apart? What could he possibly mean?

Chapter 41

Elron

Elron had found the spot near noon. Leaving everyone else back at the estate, he had traveled only with Liam to Lake Kobberdam. There, on the southernmost tip of the lake, nestled in the dark forest, the first clue appeared to him. The moss and grass that covered the land seemed to glow at his feet. A strange, eerie silence covered the land.

Under his feet, each step he took made the glow surge to show him the way. It illuminated a path through the forest, around the trunks of the trees, towards the southeast. Following the lit path, Elron called out to Liam to join him. Together they marched through the forest coming out onto an open field. They could see the shimmering light leading out towards the center.

The field in front of them was overgrown grasslands. Still, they could make out an area that lay flat, devoid of plant life in the middle of it. The ground looked like it had been burned at some point. Nothing grew within the circular space. The light led them to an area, where it created a circle around the diameter, to mark the spot. Liam took a step into the open area of the field. Once his foot landed in the clearing, the ground trembled underneath him. In the center, a disturbance in the land had the area shifting, opening up, as something rose from beneath it.

Before their eyes a towering sculpture was rising towards the sky. The ground continued its rumblings while Elron studied the area for any threats. He carefully surveyed the ground around the base of the growing structure. He could see no reason not to proceed. Still, he held back. His hand grabbed Liam's arm to stop him. They should be careful. Seeing no danger did not mean there was none. The land gave a final groan before everything went silent.

From that distance, Elron saw the sculpture had stopped its climb, having completely risen from its burial place. His mind could not believe what he was seeing. Liam, standing next to him, was in as much awe as he was. Falling to his knees, Elron gave a silent prayer of guidance to the figure before him. Liam simply bowed his head, acknowledging the deity.

The perfect representation of Freya, the Norse goddess, faced them from the middle of the field. Even from the distance, her eyes were regarding the two men, seeming to have been expecting them. The path continued to glow before them, leading to her. Throwing caution to the wind, Liam was the first to reach her, running across the field, eager to find what they were there for. Elron, at a slower pace, made his way more carefully. Reaching Liam, they both stared at the stone figure of Freya.

At the base, a dish made of emerald crystals, glittered under the sun. Following his instincts, Elron removed the vial holding Alexa's blood from his pocket. His fingers removed the stopper, certain of what he was to do. Leaning down, he placed several drops of her blood on the dish. Liam watched his actions without a word. While Elron closed the vial and returned it to his pocket, Liam leaned down to read an inscription.

"It says, Resting Place. What do you think that means?" Liam asked his friend.

"Maybe it's where someone important is buried." Elron had no idea when it came to gods and goddesses. It could mean anything.

Liam shrugged and looked at the drops of blood resting on the small plate. *Now what? How long did they have to wait?* It was not long before they got a response. The sculpture seemed to animate as they stood before it. Freya took a more human appearance. The gray stone was replaced by a more luminous white marble.

Around the base, the lit grass glowed brighter. The light rose up to cover her in an iridescent brilliance. Elron shielded his eyes from the glare. He saw objects appear within her hands. As suddenly as the light built, it disappeared. Stunned, he stared at what she held. In one hand she held a paper, fading and brittle. In her other, the glint of a red ruby crystal was positioned in her palm. The Kaemorra waited to be picked up.

"Take the crystal, Liam. I'll handle the paper." Elron nudged his friend, who seemed frozen.

Liam roused himself, grabbing the Kaemorra quickly from the

goddess's fingers, afraid it would magically disappear. Holding the famed gem in his hands, he felt its weight and studied its lines. Shaped like a diamond, it glinted and glowed. Unable to stop looking at it, he was poked by Elron, who now held the paper. Liam put the crystal away, storing it in his jacket pocket.

"What does it say?" He asked Elron.

"It is in a language I do not understand." Elron held it out to him.

Liam carefully took the paper, seeing exactly what Elron meant. He could not read it either. He was interrupted from further study of it by a growing rumbling sound. The ground beneath his feet trembled, making him jump back a safe distance from the base of the statue. Stumbling away, they both put as much space as they could between themselves and the statue of Freya.

As the shaking continued, they watched as she dropped slowly back into the earth where she had come from. In seconds, the land lay undisturbed, as if nothing had occurred. Elron looked around, seeing nothing to raise any alarms. The glowing path had also vanished.

"Let's take it back with us. Maybe mother will know what it is." Liam held the slip of paper gingerly. He could not risk folding it. Keeping it in his grasp, he made sure to keep it as still as possible.

Nodding at his suggestion, Elron readied to return to the others. Making sure to let Liam go first, he let him dematerialize before following. At once, they were both back on the estate, arriving one right after the other in the main room. The room lay empty and bare. Only the massive table filled the space near them. All the other furniture was missing. Liam called out to his parents, while Elron mentally found and asked Bet to get everyone together.

With each step Elron took around the room, it took his needs into consideration and slowly transformed into its living room setting. It kept the over-sized table available to them. Liam went to it, seeing a hardcover book that would keep the fragile scrap of paper he still held flat on its surface. Its yellowing color stood out against the stark white backdrop of the book. They would need to find some cellophane to encase it in. Otherwise they risked it being destroyed.

"Liam, you're back. Tell me you found it!" Eliana rushed into the room, anxious to find out their news.

Liam removed the Kaemorra from his pocket, walked up to his mother and presented it to her. Eliana's hand shook as she reached for it. For so long, the crystal had been lost to her. Already she was feeling some of its power making contact with her. Her hand wrapped around the smooth edges of the gem. She blinked back tears at having it back in her possession.

For the first time, she sensed hope that they would prevail. Asher made his way to his wife, seeing the brilliance she held in her hand. He too was affected by its presence. Their eyes met in understanding. They were one step closer to reaching the end.

"Well done, both of you!" Asher remarked.

One by one, everyone came in to gather around the Kaemorra. Now that they had it in their midst, Liam was wondering where they could put it to keep it safe. He thought about possible locations, but all were open to Elsam finding it.

"Where can we keep it hidden until we need it?" He asked the people in the room.

Their blank stares told him they had no ideas either. Maybe they could come up with a plan to have it guarded all the time. It was an impossible task. Too much could go wrong. Eliana was about to speak when Elron beat her to it.

"I think I know where we can put it." Elron spoke into the hush that had followed Liam's question.

Chapter 42

Liam

Liam walked the gardens in Deis-dé oblivious to the peaceful surroundings. It had been less than an hour since their arrival. Elron's idea to hide the Kaemorra in this protected land had been brilliant. Elsam and his followers could not enter it without one of their group. It had been enchanted, long ago, to accept only those true to the Sidhe race. Elsam's black heart would refuse him entry.

Liam left them to place the Kaemorra in the vault beneath the house. He saw no need to accompany them. His mind was preoccupied with Alexa. Her ongoing absence was eating away at him. Not knowing if she was captured, if she was hurt, was enough to drive him to distraction. Placing herself in danger was lunacy.

Hearing footsteps behind him, he stopped his meandering, turning to face who was approaching. Bet was slowly making her way to him. His sister could not hide her own worry for Alexa or for Aidan. Liam, for the first time, started to feel his own culpability in his brother's situation. He had tried to stay away from Alexa. *Damn it, I did my best.* Aidan had not understood how difficult it had been. Hurting her, lying to her, pushing her to Aidan nearly killed him.

The image of her face when he had belittled her feelings was still ever-present in his mind. The scene from the library played on repeat as well. Her hurt at his cruel words still caused him immense regret. He wondered how Aidan could not see how she had felt. Why he did not sense her emotions was something Liam had yet to figure out. Aidan could read her thoughts, but not what was in her heart.

"They have called a meeting. We need you in the living room." Bet informed him when she reached him.

Bet could sense he was upset. She went to touch him, but Liam pulled away. He did not need pity or sympathy. What he needed was to find Alexa and Aidan. This meeting better be about that. If not he would go out on his own to locate them.

"Liam, it will work out. I can see how torn you are." Bet tried to offer whatever comfort she could.

"I did this. Bet, I did this. His being gone, her taking off after him is my fault. If only I had stayed away. I should have left when things got complicated." Liam admitted.

His every action had been wrong. He could not blame being possessed by the shadow alone. He should have known better. Pain ripped through him. Remembering the loss of his own mate, he knew exactly what Aidan was going through. *How could he forget about her?* His mate had been taken from him centuries before. She had simply ceased to exist. Liam had no answers to how or why. He only knew she was gone by their link being broken.

Only if she were dead would that have been possible. *How long did I grieve?* Centuries. His heart had never fully recovered. Alexa had filled a part of it. She had re-awakened his propensity to love. *How did I let things get so out of control?*

His sister silently shook her head at him. Her expression was painful for Liam to see. She did pity him. Eyes the same color as his, regarded him with sorrow. Liam could not take being consoled over his actions. He went to leave, to return to the house. Bet stepped in front of him, blocking his escape.

"Listen to me you idiot. You are not alone in the blame. There is much to go around. Aidan should have known better. Our brother is not blameless in this. He chose to leave instead of confronting what was going on. Come back inside. We have plans to make." She hooked her arm through his, pulling him through the garden.

Liam said nothing on the way back. Aidan and Rina were the only ones he had spoken to about his mate. His family knew nothing about what he had endured. His absence all those years hid the reason. They all thought he was out patrolling and guarding against any threat to their race. They had no clue that he had lost his mate.

Now was not the time to get into it. He let Bet guide him to the patio doors and push him inside. In the great room, everyone was already gathered. Alexa's mother and father were speaking quietly by the ornate fireplace. His parents were seated on one of the sofas. Tory and Rina were standing to their right. Elron came to Bet, took her hand

and guided her to a seat of her own.

"The Kaemorra is safely hidden. We must make plans to extricate Alexa and Aidan from Elsam's tower." Elron began.

Liam was all for that. Itching to get started, he was ready to transport. Seeing his agitation, Elron's next words caused Liam to narrow his eyes.

"We can't go off half-cocked. Myrick has placed spells over the area. We cannot be certain where they are. Last time I was near the tower, I had no sense of anyone. It will be difficult to determine if they are there or being held elsewhere. We have to be smart about this."

Liam walked over to a chair near his parents and sat down heavily. Elron was right, again. The man was making too much sense for his liking. *When did he become the sage one?* He would listen to what Elron had to say for now. Getting captured themselves would be disastrous.

"We need a small group. I think Liam and I should go in. We can scout the area for any signs of them." Elron continued.

"I will come as well." Rider insisted.

Of course Rider would want to go find his daughter. From Thalia's expression, there was nothing that would hold her back either. Liam could see she would follow them. Having her there may prove beneficial. Magic may be needed if they hoped to free the captives.

"No, Bet you are not coming!" Elron responded to Bet's reaction to his plan.

Narrowed eyes met his, stubbornness filling them at Elron's pronouncement. Liam would not want to be Elron after the meeting. Bet would put up a fight.

"We will leave within the hour. It is almost dusk on earth. It should be dark by the time we get there." Elron stood to get ready.

Liam watched as Bet followed Elron out of the room and up the stairs. Her voice could be heard from above, as she fought to be included. Whatever Elron told her was lost as they entered their room. Liam rose from his seat, going to Rider and Thalia. Rider was trying to talk sense into Thalia. She in turn was not to be swayed.

"She may be useful, Rider. We may need her powers." Liam addressed Rider.

"I can't talk her out of it anyway. We'll meet you outside as soon as we are ready." Rider pulled his wife along, as he walked out of the room.

Liam watched them go with a pang of envy. *Will I ever have what they do?* The years they spent apart to keep Alexa safe had not diminished the love they felt for each other. Respect and understanding were at the core of their feelings. Liam wanted that. He lost his mate a long time ago and had not thought to look for that kind of companionship again. He doubted he would ever find someone to replace her. She had been everything to him. Alexa had awakened something in him that he had thought was dead.

"You will find true happiness again, Liam. Do not despair. There is someone out there made for you. Keep yourself open to the possibility." His mother whispered to him.

She had sensed his emotions. Standing to his left, her hand rested on his shoulder. Believing in her words was difficult for him. He was still smarting from Alexa choosing Aidan. His heart would need a lot of healing before he opened up to that kind of hurt again.

"Mother, for now, I can only focus on finding them and finishing this once and for all. Love is not in the cards for me." Liam gently smiled at her, not wanting his words to sound like a rebuke.

His mother simply gave him a knowing smile. There was something in her eyes that made him want to believe. *Had she gotten a glimpse into his future?* He did not want to know. It was better to live out his days without getting his heart broken again. Leaving her side, he went to get ready.

In his room, he took his sword, a small blade and his jacket. Glancing around, he found nothing else that he needed. He walked back downstairs, finding the others waiting for him. Elron opened the door, stepping outside while they all followed. Rider put his hand on Thalia's arm to pull her through the void, to their destination. Elron nodded to Liam to go next.

The calmness of the night, as they stepped out onto the banks of the Thames River, greeted them. Greenwich was asleep. Only a few lights illuminated windows along the coast. Crickets could be heard around them. Elron waved with his hand for them to follow. They had some ground to cover to reach where they needed to go.

Arriving there, a good distance from Elsam's tower, masked their presence in case anyone was monitoring them. Rider knew exactly where they were headed. His steps were sure, as he led the way. Thalia, familiar with the locale, kept pace with him. Liam saw an imperceptible shiver run through her. *Was she remembering their captivity?* This time, no one was getting captured.

After an hour of trudging through endless forest, Elron held his hand up for all to stop. Liam could see the outline of the tower rising above the trees in front of him. They were close. Rider called their attention to a place they could huddle and discuss their next step. Behind the immense cedars, they gathered round together.

"I feel nothing." Elron whispered.

Thalia concentrated on finding a trace of Alexa. Shaking her head, she let them know she could not find her either. They had nothing to go on. *How will we ever find them?* Liam could tell that Elron was running through possibilities and that no solutions were coming to him. Aside from storming the tower, taking the chance that they might succeed in having the advantage, there was not much they could do. It would be folly to try.

Rider reached out to Liam, touching him lightly on the arm. With his other hand, he held a finger to his lips asking them to be quiet. *Had he heard something?* Liam strained to hear through the night's noises. A soft footfall somewhere in front of them drew his attention. Whoever was out there, they were trying to be quiet.

"Anyone out here?" Someone whispered.

Elron quietly drew his sword, readying for an attack. The sound of continuing steps fell closer to them. A shadow drew closer. When the person was almost upon them, Elron silently jumped out from behind the rock. He grabbed the person and pulled them behind their hiding spot.

Chapter 43

Liam

"Solas. What are you doing here?" Elron asked the hooded man.

Liam stared at his half-brother, seeing him in person for the first time. He saw a striking resemblance to Aidan, but his build was more like Liam's. Lying on the ground beside Elron, Liam could see Solas was about the same height as he was. His hood had partially fallen away, giving him access to Solas's face.

Even in the darkness, Liam could see his eyes matched his own. There the similarities ended. Solas had Aidan's nose and cheekbone structure. He found Solas regarding him with the same curiosity. The man was going over Liam's own features, matching and disregarding any similarities. His shrewd eyes were hooded beneath his black eyelashes.

"I've been searching for you since this morning. I was surprised you let her come alone." Solas's voice was deep, with a raspy timber.

Elron let him go. Solas sat down behind the boulder, pulling his hood completely off. His jet-black hair gleamed under the moon's light. It was cropped short, almost shaved atop his head. It made his chiseled face stark and angled. Keeping his face towards Elron, he ignored Liam, addressing Elron directly. Peeved, Liam drew closer to them. He insinuated himself between them. Solas gave him a heated look before speaking to Elron.

"She's been put in the lower levels. Myrick has added extra protections around her. He brought in an ancient this afternoon. There is no way to get her out through the tower." He let them know.

Liam was skeptical of his words. *Why should we trust him? This man was raised by Vanya. We should take everything he says with a grain of salt.* He watched Elron absorb Solas's words. Solas tilted his head at Liam, giving him another blistering look. Liam grinned at his half-brother. It would take more than a look to make him quake. Solas ignored him and went back to conversing with Elron. Once there was a break in their conversation, they all waited for Elron to come to a decision. Liam had little patience left, but could think of nothing to do.

"How can we get her and Aidan out?" Elron asked Solas.

Solas seemed to be thinking. He cocked his head to the side, as if listening for something. Peering in the direction he had come from, something seemed to take his attention. In the distance, Liam heard another set of footfalls coming towards them. Instantly on guard, his sword still in his hand, he readied to strike whoever it was.

"It's my mother. She's alone." Solas told them.

Liam sat back down, next to his half-brother, waiting for Vanya to reach them. He was not willing to trust anything Solas said. He was ready to fight. Rider was of the same opinion. He pulled Thalia behind him, keeping her pressed against the hedges.

"Solas. Have you found them?" Her voice could be heard from around the rock.

Solas gave a soft birdcall, drawing her attention to where he was. The men were on alert for any subterfuge. Vanya stepped around the boulder, sitting down beside her son. Liam took the opportunity to watch the woman who had betrayed his family. She looked thinner, pale and nervous. Her eyes would not meet his.

"We don't have much time. I was only able to slip out for a few minutes. Solas you must go back. He has noticed your absence." She spoke to her son.

Solas took off without a word, running quietly back towards the tower. Vanya rose to follow him with her eyes, as he raced off. Her nervousness was contagious. Liam was assaulted by a bad feeling. *Will Solas betray our position?*

"Vanya. What can you tell us?" Elron got her attention.

"Myrick will be taking Alexa back to the States with him in the morning. Elsam has agreed to give her to him for his experiments." Vanya spoke hurriedly.

Experiments? Liam was instantly fearful of what that meant. Myrick was an insane individual. He shuddered to think what types of experiments he would subject Alexa to. Thalia gasped at Vanya's words.

Rider was holding her, as she shook with rage.

"Can we get her out?" Elron wanted to know.

"Not from the tower. Your only chance is to get her while they are transporting her. The boat will be moored on the banks behind us. Myrick will have her brought there at dawn. He is not taking any chances with her. She is strong, Elron. She has been able to hide it from Myrick for now. What I felt from her is remarkable. You cannot let him get away with her." Vanya filled them in.

Liam would get her back. He would fight heaven and earth to save her. He had no doubt that Elron and Rider would do the same. The plan seemed too easy, too orchestrated. He was unsure of its validity. But with no other option, they had no choice but to accept what Vanya was telling them.

"What about Aidan?" Thalia asked.

Vanya's face changed. Liam watched as sorrow filled her features. *Is my brother gone? Is it possible that Aidan had ceased to exist without me feeling it?*

"He is in the deepest dungeons. I've only seen him twice. He is lost. He sits there staring off into space, giving no indication of whether he knows where he is. The guards have been unable to get him to eat or drink. I wish I could help with him, but he is too guarded." Vanya's voice trembled with emotion as she spoke.

Liam was filled with anguish at hearing his brother's state. Remorse at thinking Aidan kept away on purpose filled him. His brother had lost the will to live. He lost his world in thinking Alexa was with him. *How did this happen? How could I have allowed it to get to this point?*

"We will find a way. Do not lose hope, Liam." Thalia sensed his thoughts.

"I have to go back. I can't be gone too long. Elsam has become paranoid. He sees traitors everywhere." Vanya readied to leave.

Liam took hold of her arm before she could depart. Vanya impatiently waited for what he wanted to say. Liam could see she was anxious to return. The fear in her was palpable. *Why go back?* Liam did not understand why she would put herself and her son in danger.

"Why Vanya? You could leave. Take Solas and go." Liam spoke his question.

Vanya let a small laugh escape her. She shook her head at Liam.

"There is no escape from this madness. I have to do all I can to stop him. I will make sure Solas is safe, but I will not let Elsam win. He has lied and stolen everything from me. I will have my revenge Liam for all he has done. He will not use my son to further his goals. Solas has made me see that I have been wrong about many things. He is my saving grace. Watch out for him if something happens to me. He is your brother. His loyalty is to you and your family." A tear slipped free. She brushed it away, leaving them in a heavy silence.

Liam was left feeling a deep sadness for Vanya. In the end, he hoped she would survive. Her death would be a steep price to pay for all she had done. He was sure his mother would have the same feeling on the matter. Knowing where Alexa would be, he felt a pressing need to act. They had to be ready come morning.

"We should scout the area near the bank." Elron suggested.

Chapter 44

Liam

They had spent the remainder of the night watching and listening for any signs of their being discovered. So far they only heard a few guards making rounds around the base of the tower. The bank of the river near the mooring had not been patrolled. A boat arrived shortly before dawn.

The thirty-five-foot yacht swayed in the water, idling empty. Its two seamen left it to enter the tower. Liam watched them, as they tied the boat, made preparations and left it empty. He wondered if he should board it, hide beneath deck. Elron had advised against it.

"It shouldn't be long now. Vanya said they would take her at dawn. Be ready." Elron told them.

Hidden above the shoreline, near the trees, they waited for any sign of movement. Thalia took to praying to the goddess for her daughter's safe return. Her lips silently moved as she stared at the boat. Rider was lying on his stomach, stretched out alongside Elron. The men had hardly spoken since the break of dawn. Their eyes were focused on the shore, where they waited for a glimpse of Alexa being moved.

Liam was alone in the same position a few feet from them. He was losing patience, waiting for something to happen. The slightest sound had him ready to jump up and fight. Waiting was excruciating. Behind him, from the tower, only silence reached him. *How much longer will it be?*

Elron inched his way over to Liam, crawling on his stomach to avoid detection. Tall grass billowed around him as he crept closer. Liam waited for him, hoping he had some insight on the reason for the delay. The sun was already rising in the east. Daylight had started to filter through the clouds that hung overhead. Myrick should have appeared by now.

"It shouldn't be much longer." Elron mouthed when he reached Liam.

The quiet was broken by sudden voices coming from the tower. The door at the base of the tower had been opened, exposing two men and who Liam hoped was Alexa. In a long hooded robe, the person he assumed was Alexa had their hands manacled. Liam could not be certain it was her. Her features were hidden.

"Now my dear Alexa, we have a long ways to go." Myrick spoke, pushing her from behind.

Alexa caught herself, her footing slipping on the wet stone path. She refused to answer Myrick. Instead, she marched steadily towards the pier. Myrick laughed behind her, a crazed laugh, causing the hair on Liam's arms to rise.

"There, there, dear. No need to be silent. We have much to

discuss, you and I." Myrick mocked.

Elron held onto Liam, who was ready to launch himself at Myrick. Timing was everything. They had to wait until Alexa reached the pier. Thalia had set a trap, a spell to render Myrick immobile while they rescued her daughter. Rider had already moved closer to the shore. Elron and Liam held their positions.

"Nothing to say I see. Oh well, I am sure I can get you to talk while we travel." Myrick's comments were nauseating Liam.

If he could have rammed his hand down the man's throat and removed his tongue, Liam would have happily done so. He counted to ten. Then he counted again. Alexa was almost at the pier, just a few steps more. As she passed under the spell, he saw her back straighten, warning Myrick of something up ahead. The man quickly sidestepped the spell, jumping down the pier onto the sand. His laugh echoed across the landscape.

"Get her inside. Quickly!" He yelled at the guards.

Thalia blasted Myrick with a spell. He was pushed back, into the waves. He continued laughing, showing how far gone into insanity he had drifted. Thalia sent another shockwave at him. He managed to evade her attack. Grabbing onto the rope spanning the outer hull of the boat, he pulled himself into it. The sound of the engine rumbled to life. They had no time left.

Liam raced to the pier too late to haul himself aboard. He

watched helplessly as the distance grew. Trying to transport aboard it was impossible. The boat was protected. *How could we have screwed up so badly?* Alexa was gone. They had no idea where he was taking her or what he would do to her.

Rider reached Liam just before Elron. Rider was cursing the fates for his daughter's predicament. Thalia was standing where she had been, watching with terror in her eyes as her daughter was taken from her. Liam added his own curses to Rider's.

As the boat raced further away, becoming nothing but a speck, an explosion rocked it. Liam saw pieces of splintered wood from the hull fly into the air. Speechless, he watched as flames overpowered the shell of the boat, leaving nothing in its wake. Liam stared uncomprehending at what his eyes had registered.

His knees buckled, as realization grew. His legs collapsed under him. The pain of his body weight coming down, his knees connecting with the sharp rocks under him, did not enter his shocked mind. From deep within him a harsh guttural sound escaped him. *She is gone. She is gone.*

The words replayed in his mind. His eyes misted, his body shook, unable to take his eyes away from the inferno in the distance. A voice was yelling her name repeatedly. It took him a full minute before he recognized it was his own screams he was hearing. He whimpered a final, Alexa, before falling silent. *Alexa is gone.*

About the Author

Nia Markos was born in Montreal, Canada and is of Greek heritage.

After thirty years working in the financial sector, she has turned her passion of reading into a new career in writing.

Released in the Crystal Series

Elements

Venture

Harmony

CPSIA information can be obtained
at www.ICGtesting.com
Printed in the USA
BVHW040259030221
599228BV00009B/614